S0-BBH-362

PART ONE

METAMORPHOSIS

THE
GOLDEN
TRIANGLE

THE GOLDEN TRIANGLE

FRANKLIN M. PROUD

St. Martin's Press   New York

To Susan

First published in America by St. Martin's Press 1977
Copyright © 1976 by Franklin M. Proud
All rights reserved. For information, write.
St. Martin's Press, Inc., 175 Fifth Ave., New York, N.Y. 10010.
Manufactured in the United States of America
Library of Congress Catalog Card Number: 77-24120

Library of Congress Cataloging in Publication Data

Proud, Franklin M   1920-
   The golden triangle.

   I. Title.
PZ4.P96Go   1977   [PR6066.R625]   813'.5'4   77-24120
ISBN 0-312-33785-X

CHAPTER ONE

The Penthouse suite and executive offices of a Philippine corporation, Santa Rosa Lumber & Plywood Company, occupy the 24th and 25th floors of the Garcia Building in downtown Manila. The 14th floor of the same building houses the Philippine-American Research & Development Corporation. The two concerns engage in totally different lines of endeavour. There should be no connection between them.

Unbeknownst to the former corporation, and known by only a very few of the latter, there was one connecting link – Samuel Gerard Harper.

Sam Harper was Executive Vice-President of Santa Rosa. His residence was the corporate executive suite. He was 38, handsome, had prematurely gray hair and was a bachelor. He was not socially inclined and entertained rarely but was nonetheless a familiar figure in Manila and most of the major cities in Southeast Asia.

Harper was also Sector Chief, Southeast Asia, for the United States Central Intelligence Agency, which operated behind the façade of the Philippine-American Research & Development Corporation. He had been with the CIA for 17 years; with the management of Santa Rosa for 14 years. To both jobs he brought dedication, efficiency and an undisputed talent for organization and administration. He was highly regarded by both employers.

Harper had been Agency Sector Chief for five years, since just after the completion of that Garcia Building. His area of operational control was Southeast Asia, excluding South and North Viet-Nam, Cambodia and a large portion of Laos, but including several provinces of Southwest China. The division of command in Laos was not to Harper's liking.

What enabled Harper to exercise his dual control, without any knowledge on the part of the private corporation and but scant knowledge within the Agency ranks, was a windowless room on the 25th floor which did not appear in the architectural plans of the Garcia Building. Access to this room was through a shower stall in Harper's bathroom, or by a side panel in the private elevator to the penthouse. The room was fitted out as a compact office. It was fed with a continuous stream of intelligence through telephone recorders, closed-circuit television and a pneumatic tube from the 14th floor. It contained a scrambler telephone, decoding teleprinter and a number of other security devices. It was the nerve-centre of the Agency's regional operations.

Late of an evening in mid-January 1968, Harper sat in this sanctum scanning a print-out from the decoding machine. He stood up and walked over to a bank of combination-locked filing cabinets. Locating the two dossiers he wanted, he placed them side by side on his desk.

Before opening the folders, he glanced at a wall map which extended from ceiling to floor. His gaze centered on Chiang Mai, in North Thailand, then swung down to dwell briefly on a point near Lok Ninh on the border of Cambodia and South Viet-Nam.

He turned his attention to the folders. One bore the label 'Judson Quentin Winters'. The second, and thicker, dossier was titled 'Joseph Asquith Stanford, Major, U.S. Special Forces'. Harper knew the contents of both files intimately. He opened them and absently rifled through Stanford's file.

Stanford had been selected for the Chiang Mai operation some time ago. He should have arrived in Manila for the necessary preparations in October, yet here it was January. The curt explanation Harper had received was that Stanford could not be spared from operational duties. Harper appreciated that the delay was no fault of Morrison in Saigon, but of Lewis Cantrell, who exercised broad powers of authority in clandestine operations. Stanford was without doubt blameless, yet Harper harboured an unreasoning resentment against the unknown major. Sam Harper was not accustomed to being thwarted.

Harper had sent a strongly worded protest to Langley. It appeared to have had the desired result. The decoded message indicated the pick-up point and the date of rendezvous was 22nd January. The aircraft would have to be at the plantation airstrip at dawn on three consecutive days, from the 21st to the 24th.

Harper picked up the scrambler telephone and issued or-

8

ders to initiate the required action. Replacing the phone on its cradle he returned to the files.

He attached the decoded message to the top of Winters' file. Removing the metal fastener from Stanford's dossier, he fed its contents and the folder into a paper shredder. He gained a measure of grim satisfaction from this act of obliteration.

Now, unless something happened to Stanford within the next few days, the long-delayed operation in Chiang Mai – the operation codenamed 'Fanfare' – would be set in motion.

CHAPTER TWO

He arrived at the rendezvous point before dawn. In the gray half-light, he wearily stripped off his sodden bush clothing. Painstakingly, he removed the bloated leeches he'd accumulated wading upstream. Slowly, he dressed again in the mud-encrusted trousers and bush jacket. He sat down and with his back against a tree trunk, to await daylight. He ached with fatigue.

The sky lightened and slowly changed through gray-green to pink. When the rim of sun began to inch above the rubber trees, he stood up. Through the tangled foliage, he watched the long-slanting rays of morning sun churn the thin ground mist which clung to the coarse grass of the airstrip. Halfway down the short field, a faded wind-sock hung limply in the still air. The only sound was of birds chirping in a bamboo thicket on his left. He glanced with annoyance at his watch.

Before he sighted the aircraft, he heard the muffled throb of its engine. He stiffened and carefully scanned the rubber trees on the far side of the airstrip. Nothing stirred.

The Cessna came in low over the tree tops. It touched down and bounced along the uneven turf. At the far end of the strip, it turned and taxied back. When it reached a position almost opposite his place of concealment, the plane swung about to face down the field. As the engine idled,

9

shards of morning sunlight bounced off the slowly turning propellor blades.

He waited a full minute before parting the bushes and stepping into the knee-deep grass edging the airstrip. He swung a gaze to left and right along the fringe of jungle. There was no sign of any movement. Satisfied, Stanford strode purposefully towards the waiting aircraft. At his approach, the cabin door swung open to reveal the pilot with a carbine levelled menacingly at Stanford.

In the Cessna, the pilot watched the approaching figure warily. He hadn't been given any description of the passenger he was expecting. The man nearing the plane was blond-headed, hatless, and with no distinguishing marks of rank or unit on his faded olive-drab bush clothing. He should be the pick-up. He certainly wasn't Vietnamese. On the other hand, he could be an army deserter or, worse still, a Frenchman or other foreigner in league with the Viet Cong. The pilot was taking no chances.

When Stanford came to within ten feet of the plane, he stopped. Raising his voice to be heard above the splutter of idling engine, he called out to the pilot, 'Got a light?'

'Yeah,' came the cautious reply, 'what're you smoking?'

'Luckies.'

The pilot grinned and swung the muzzle of his carbine to one side. 'Okay, Mac. Hop aboard and let's get this kite the hell out of here.'

Stanford climbed in and settled himself in the seat beside the pilot. As Stanford fastened the seat belt, the pilot leaned over and closed and latched the cabin door. Brakes on, the pilot eased forward on the throttle. The light aircraft trembled and strained against the brakes as the engine pitch rose to a shrill whine. Releasing the brakes, the pilot gave the plane full throttle. The Cessna leaped forward and bounced down the grass strip gaining speed. They lifted off and banked into a steep climbing turn as they skimmed over the rubber trees. At 7,000 feet, the pilot steadied onto a north-westerly heading and adjusted his trim for level flight. Turning to Stanford, he grinned broadly and said, 'No VC reception committee.'

'You wanted some action?'

'Hell, no. Waited twenty minutes for you yesterday morning. Thought the locals might have got the message.' Nodding in the direction of the rear seat, he added, 'That suitcase is for you.'

Glancing behind himself, Stanford saw a battered valise on the seat. Reaching back, he pulled it over the back of his seat onto his lap. He hesitated a moment before unsnapping the clasps and lifting the lid.

The suitcase was neatly packed. He examined the contents. It contained sport shirts, slacks, socks, underwear, handkerchiefs, a brown suede belt, a pair of scuffed loafers, a plaid sports jacket, a leather case of toilet articles and a silk dressing gown in a violent shade of mauve. None of the articles were new. Resting on top of the dressing gown were a leather wallet and an American passport. Extracting the wallet and passport, he closed the case.

For several minutes, he sat staring fixedly at the passport. Then with a shrug, he flipped open the cover. Staring up at him was the face of a young man with wavy blond hair and a full moustache. Without conscious direction, Stanford's hand rubbed his close-cropped head then down his bristled cheeks to pull thoughtfully at his upper lip.

He turned his attention to the identification. Name: Judson Quentin Winters. Date of Birth: March 16, 1932. Place of Birth: Mount Judea, Arkansas. Height: 5 feet 10½ inches. Hair: Blond. Eyes: Blue. Complexion: Fair.

So this was to be his new identity. The height and descriptive colouring were fairly close. He'd missed the weight and checked back to find it to be 165 pounds. That was also close enough. He didn't think he resembled the photograph. Still, passport photographs are notoriously misleading. With long hair and a moustache, he could well look somewhat similar. It was the date of birth which amused him. Stanford was ten years Winters' senior.

He inspected the wallet. A plastic fold-out contained a naval discharge, social security card and a number of credit cards; all bearing the name and signature of J. Q. Winters. In a pocket of the wallet, he discovered some soiled receipts and several blurred photos of Winters and a very attractive Filipina. He admired Winters' taste in women. Inside the wallet, were two hundred dollars in American currency.

Replacing the wallet and passport, he closed the suitcase and slid it forward onto the floor at his feet. Unfastening his seat belt, he started to disrobe. As he unbuttoned his jacket, his thoughts dwelt on his newly acquired identity. He assumed there was, or had been, a real life Winters. The name intrigued him. What contractions or combinations of Christian names would Winters have used? J. Quentin? Pretentious and unlikely. Judson Q? No, too formal. Probably a simple contraction such as Quent, or Jud. He decided that the latter sounded reasonable. So Jud Winters, he was to be.

When stripped down to his skivvies, he turned his attention to the terrain over which they were flying. Beneath the plane, was a canopy of dense jungle. To the north, stretched a darker green tract of rubber plantation. Ahead, the jungle thinned to give way to a grassy plain where clusters of straw-roofed dwellings and checkerboard paddy fields clung to the banks of serpentine streams which emptied into a broad brown expanse of river. It would be the Mekong, which meant they were already in Cambodia.

Stanford attracted the pilot's attention by tapping him on the shoulder. Pointing ahead to the river, Stanford made a diving motion with his palm. The pilot nodded and put the Cessna into a shallow dive.

When they reached the river, the pilot side-slipped and turned the aircraft to send it skimming over the placid surface in mid-stream. Stanford slid back the door window. The slip stream whipped the bundled bush clothing from his grasp. He followed these with his jungle boots and web belt to which were attached his Colt 45 and sheath knife. He made a thumbs up gesture to the pilot.

On the climbing turn, Stanford looked back to note that the heavy articles had been swallowed by the turgid waters. The clothing still floated on the surface.

Donning clothing from the suitcase, Stanford's thoughts were troubled. The shedding of his bush clothing and weapons had forcibly brought home the irrevocable nature of his changing status. Over the past few days, the Long Hoa operation had allowed little time for him to dwell on the implications of his new assignment. Having had less than five hours sleep in the last two-and-a-half days, he was too tired to give it much thought now. In the past, with the OSS and on detached duties from the Special Forces, he had often assumed cover identities. But they had always been short-term to achieve limited objectives. This switch was of a different nature. He felt curiously remote and beset by vague misgivings.

They were over the green-mantled peaks of the Cardamon Range. 'Where're we heading?' Stanford questioned.

'Thailand ... U-Tapao Airbase. That's where I drop you, Mac.'

Stanford nodded acknowledgment. Leaning back in the seat, he closed his eyes. Within minutes, he dropped into fatigue-drugged sleep.

He was jolted from sleep as the light aircraft touched down on the long runway. His mouth tasted sour and his ears ached from the descent. Holding his nostrils between thumb and forefinger, he blew hard to clear his ears. He glared at the pilot. Oblivious to his passenger's discomfort, the pilot taxied the Cessna towards a parking apron.

A black Ford station wagon stood at the edge of the concrete apron. The pilot swung the plane in a half-circle alongside the automobile and cut the engine. 'Okay, Mac. End of the line,' the pilot said affably.

Stanford alighted stiffly and reached back into the Cessna to retrieve the worn valise. A young man left the side of the Ford and walked briskly towards Stanford.

Coming up to Stanford, the young man smiled warmly and extended his hand. 'Mister Winters,' said the man. It was more statement than question.

Stanford hesitated. It was disconcerting to hear the name spoken aloud. 'Yes,' he acknowledged, shaking hands, 'Jud Winters.'

'Name's Dan. Dan Garrity. I've been sent to accompany you.' Motioning towards the waiting Ford, he added, 'We'd better get going.'

'Where?'

'We've got an Air Force VIP jet standing by to take us directly to Clark Field.' Garrity's smile broadened. 'Under the circumstances, we felt we might dispense with the Thai immigration formalities.'

Stanford slept most of the way to the Philippines. When they disembarked at Clark Field, he still felt stiff, but more rested.

Garrity ushered Stanford into the rear of a waiting sedan. 'Cigarette?' asked Garrity, shaking one from the pack.

'Thanks.'

Offering his lighter, Garrity said casually, 'I was observing you while you slept during the flight. The resemblance is remarkable. Let your brush cut grow out, sprout a moustache, and with a few minor alterations you could be Jud Winters' twin brother.'

Stanford had assumed there was a living prototype, but this abrupt confirmation caught him off balance. It was a moment before he queried, 'You know Winters?'

'I knew him. He's dead.'

'How? When did it happen?'

'A few months ago ... September. He was shark fishing off Cebu. Must have fallen from the boat. The other man in the boat threw Winters a line, but before Jud could reach it the sharks got him.'

'Was Winters an Agency man?'

'Not exactly. Before my time, he'd done some work for us running military hardware to the Celebes. After that, he undertook a few minor activities on our behalf. But he was considered too irresponsible, too unreliable to play on the first line team.'

There was a good deal more he wanted to know about the late Jud Winters, but Stanford decided to drop the subject for the moment. Stretching out his legs, he let himself relax into the seat. He mulled the few facts he'd already gleaned. It seemed something more than coincidence that he so closely resembled the dead man. Winters had met his death in September, the same month Stanford had been advised of the assignment. It was possible that his selection had been on the basis of the marked likeness. He resolved to examine that aspect in detail later.

Reflectively, he puffed on his cigarette as his thoughts veered into another channel. Who mourned the late Jud Winters? Did Winters have a wife and children? What in hell was he getting into with this impersonation? Ruefully, he admitted that it was a little late to be considering these questions. For better or worse, he *was* Jud Winters and had been from the moment he'd boarded the Cessna. And at that moment, for all practical purposes, Joe Stanford had ceased to exist.

By now, the unit would have reported him missing from the Long Hoa operation. He would be listed MIA. Later, he would be posted as 'presumed dead'. In Viet-Nam, only the CIA Chief of Mission, Morrison, and Joe's immediate superior, Lewis Cantrell, would know of Stanford's continuing presence in the land of the living. In Langley, Virginia, the transition to Winters would be a matter of record in a dossier and tucked away in a computer memory drum. Here, in the Philippines, someone would know his true identity, but probably wouldn't care one way or the other.

He butted his cigarette. Turning to Garrity, he asked 'Where are we going?'

'A secluded little shack in Makati, which will be both home and classroom for the next few weeks. I think you'll find it adequate.'

CHAPTER THREE

There could be little doubt about the seclusion of the residence. The grounds extended over an area of some five hectares, with almost half a mile of asphalted driveway leading from the wrought-iron entrance gates to the main house. A steel wire meshed fence, topped with strands of barbed wire, enclosed the entire estate. Filipino guards, armed with automatic weapons and accompanied by vicious Alsatians patrolled the grounds and outer perimeter. Often during his sojourn within the confines of the property, Stanford felt like a prisoner.

But 'little shack' it was not. The main house was a rambling tile-roofed structure of Spanish style. A spacious inner courtyard boasted a well-tended garden, flagged terrace and ornamental fountain. Close to the main dwelling, a series of outbuildings housed the guards and servants.

On the morning of his first full day as Jud Winters, Stanford was wide awake when dawn lightened the curtained windows. He hadn't been able to adjust to the unaccustomed luxury of linen sheets and a soft mattress and had slept fitfully.

He stepped from the bedroom onto a tiled galley facing

15

the courtyard. He had expected to be the only one stirring at this hour and was surprised to see Dan Garrity and another man seated at a table on the terrace. They were being served coffee. Both men glanced up at his approach. Smiling, Garrity rose to his feet.

'Jud,' Garrity said pleasantly, 'let me introduce you to Doctor Duarte. Doctor, this is Jud Winters, the man we've been discussing.'

The thin dark man had also risen. During the introduction, he had been studying Stanford's face. Now, he flashed a quick smile and extended his hand.

Stanford acknowledged the introduction. When they were all seated, Garrity said mildly, 'The doctor is here to take care of those minor alterations I mentioned yesterday.'

Despite the doctor's assurance that the facial surgery called for nothing other than local anaesthesia and that it was quite all right for him to eat, Stanford had little appetite.

Following breakfast, the three men proceeded to the surgery, a room opening off the gallery. A white-gowned Filipina nurse stood by an autoclave from which rose a thin wisp of steam. From an illuminated panel, an X-ray of a skull grinned at them. Blown-up photographs of Winters' face attached to clip-boards, were ranged along a shelf. Instruments were neatly laid out on a towel-topped table beside a surgical table. Stanford realized that these preparations must have been carried out while he slept. Garrity wasn't wasting any time.

It was a week before the angry red and purple discoloration around his eyes faded to a sickly yellow. The throbbing ache of his jaw and lower lip gradually subsided, but his face was still sore and tender. Doctor Duarte, who visited daily for the first week, seemed well satisfied with the progress. Stanford was advised that the bandages shielding his nose could be removed on the coming weekend, but it would be several months before all traces of swelling would disappear.

In spite of his discomfort, the annoyance of slurred speech and a gargoylish appearance, Stanford was given no respite. His instruction started on the morning following the cosmetic surgery. His initial task was to become thoroughly conversant with the life, habits and character of the deceased Winters. For this purpose, Garrity provided a dossier which seemed remarkably complete.

Judson Winters was born in the pine-shrouded hills of Arkansas, near the small town of Mount Judea. His mother, Elizabeth Winters, née Quentin, had died in the process of introducing Jud into the world. She left a husband and a daughter three years older than Jud. An aunt had come to live with the family and take care of the children. It was during the depression years and life in the district was far from easy. Jud's father worked as foreman of a highway section gang and was, considering the era and local standards, comparatively well off.

When Jud was four, Winters senior became involved with the sixteen-year-old daughter of a local druggist. Scant minutes ahead of a confrontation with the irate rifle-toting pharmacist, Winters struck out for California, taking with him his teenage paramour and young Jud. Jud's sister, Joanna, remained behind with the aunt.

They settled in Salinas, where Winters found employment as a truck driver. He married the young girl, who a few months later produced a daughter. Jud had acquired a stepmother and a half-sister, although the former was to maintain her status for only a short space of time.

Before Jud was seven, his young step-mother tired of her marital duties. She deserted the family, taking her clothes, the family savings and the new Chevy. She left behind Jud's half-sister, Betty-Anne.

The reduced Winters family moved to Vallejo. A young housekeeper was employed to look after the children. Within less than a year, she was the new Mrs. Winters.

Jud attended elementary school in Vallejo. If he didn't establish an enviable scholastic record, he came close to hitting an all-time high for truancy.

Through loans and extended credit, Jud's father managed to swing the purchase of two trucks. He set up a company and went into contract haulage. By the time Jud reached high school age, the fleet had been expanded to eight trucks. Business was flourishing in a war-expanded economy. The Winters' family's financial difficulties were resolved. They moved to Richmond.

Jud's high school record in Richmond was little better

17

than that of elementary school in Vallejo. He also had several brushes with the local police on charges of petty theft and brawling. For stealing a car, he was placed on probation. These increasing troubles with the local authorities were a large contributing factor to his father's decision to move across the bay to San Francisco.

Completing his final year of high school in the Bay City, Jud's attitudes suddenly changed. The catalyst in this reaction was a female classmate named Christina Jannsen. It was her influence which must have decided him to continue his education, an endeavour for which he'd displayed little enthusiasm in preceding years. Jud enrolled at the University of California.

For the next two-and-a-half years, Jud and Tina were practically inseparable. Then, unaccountably from the dossier record, the young couple broke up.

Jud quit university in mid-semester. As a reservist, he made application for active duty in the navy. He was accepted in the rank of Lieutenant jg and sent to join a destroyer flotilla based in Sasebo, Japan. The tin can to which he was assigned was engaged in coastal patrol and bombardment of the Korean mainland.

There was nothing remarkable about Jud's naval duty. His efficiency reports indicated an officer of average ability, with a tendency to resent authority. He was twice reprimanded for excessive drinking, but otherwise completed his tour of wartime service without incident. At the conclusion of the Korean War, Jud took his separation in Japan and moved to Tokyo.

In late 1952, Jud's father was killed in a highway accident. Controlling interest in the company, Winters' Hauling & Storage, had gone to Jud's current step-mother. Jud, Joanna, and his half-sister, Betty-Anne, were bequeathed minor shareholdings in the trucking company and lump-sum settlements from life insurance policies.

For two years, Jud lived in Tokyo off the proceeds of his inheritance. He moved into an apartment with a night club dancer named Akiko. He spent money with lavish disregard. When his funds were nearing exhaustion, he abandoned, or was abandoned by Akiko. He arranged to sell out his interest in the California company and left for the Philippines.

In Manila, Jud met up with some of his ex-service buddies.

He was persuaded to invest his modest capital into a shipping company which had bought and fitted out two World War II-vintage PT boats, converting them into coastal cargo craft. For his cash contribution, Jud was given command of one of these vessels.

It was during his brief stint as master of this vessel, which Jud had christened, *Christina II*, that he came to the attenton of the Agency. The CIA were involved in the clandestine supply of arms to the anti-Sukarno insurgents. *Christina II* was privately chartered to run small arms and ammunition from a point in the Sulu Archipelago to certain obscure beaches in the vicinity of the Celebes harbor of Manado. As return cargo, Jud carried bagged nutmeg and other high-value spices, which somehow found their way into the market without the troublesome formalities of the Philippine customs service. These ventures were profitable. Had they continued without interruption, Jud should have ended up a wealthy man at an early age. Fate, in the guise of an Indonesian Air Force fighter-bomber, intervened.

Jud was ashore when the event occured. From a palm-shaded beach he watched in horror. *Christina II* was anchored well off shore in a shallow bay. The military aircraft made two passes straffing and bombing the hapless craft. A few feet of superstructure, which protruded above the surface at low water, was all that remained of his investment.

It took Jud almost a month to find his way back to Manila. He found that the shipping company had been liquidated in his absence. Reluctantly, his partners turned over Jud's share of the profits. He had enough to invest in a night club just off Roxas Boulevard.

For the next eight years things went well for Jud. His share of the return from club profits and the back-room casino was more than adequate, even after stiff pay-offs, to permit Jud to live in some style. He seemed to have been drinking heavily during this period. He was frequently missing from his usual haunts for days, even weeks, at a stretch. Sharing his good fortune was a mistress, a young Filipina movie actress, Isabel Carlotta Aquina. But once again, fate stepped in to shatter the idyllic pattern of his life.

In 1965, political pressures were brought to bear on Jud and his partners. There was also a question of taxes on undisclosed gambling earnings. Jud found it expedient to leave the country.

The next 14 months were spent in Viet-Nam, where Jud busied himself selling mutual funds to the rapidly swelling number of American GIs. There was a brief CID report in the dossier linking Jud with black market currency transactions through an accomplice in Hong Kong.

By late 1966, Jud's problems with the Philippine authorities were amicably resolved. He returned to Manila, but to find a few changes. The night club had been seized for tax arrears. His mistress had married a wealthy Filipino. Jud found himself at a loose end. It was during this period that he had been occasionally employed by the Agency. His assignments had been to report on the background and activities of former partners and associates.

Early in 1967, Jud had raised capital to purchase a small beach club in Talisai. Subsequent documentation indicated the club to be on the verge of bankruptcy.

The penultimate document was a terse report of Jud's fatal accident. It was dated 17 September, 1967, and signed by somebody named R. G. Cranston.

The final item on the file was a cryptic machine print-out advising that replacement parts were ready for delivery at the previously designated LNAL location and must be picked up between January 21st and 24th.

Stanford concluded that the message referred to himself. To be termed 'replacement parts' was hardly flattering. LNAL must indicate the plantation airstrip.

CHAPTER FOUR

Although the villa was equipped to handle many more guests, Stanford and Garrity seemed to be the only ones in residence. In fact, during the entire first week of his indoctrination, Doctor Duarte was the only other non-Philippine Stanford had seen on the premises.

It was Sunday morning. The doctor had just left after removing the protective bandages. The swelling was reduced, but his nose was still tender. The discolouration

20

around his eyes lent his face an unhealthy aspect. And to add to Stanford's discomfort and irritability, his growing moustache was an itchy annoyance.

They were reclining on beach chairs in the courtyard. Stanford shifted his position to regard his companion. 'Dan,' he said, 'I've a few questions.'

'Fire when ready. But I don't guarantee answers.'

The response annoyed Stanford. 'Godammit,' he snapped, 'don't be flip. I want some straight answers.'

Garrity swung his legs over the edge of the chair and sat up facing Stanford. 'Sorry,' Garrity said, his face serious, 'Wasn't meaning to be flippant. I'll do the best I can, but in some areas I don't have all the facts.'

'How long am I supposed to be confined in this maximum security prison?'

'Until we're satisfied you can pass for Winters. I don't mean just a physical resemblance. When you leave here, you'll *be* Winters.'

'How long do you expect that to take?'

'The end of February. May be longer.'

'Kee-rist. Another month. What then? Chiang Mai?'

'Hell no. It'll take another month for you to learn something about the tropical hardwood business. For that, you'll go to Mindanao to the Santa Rosa logging camps and the mills in Zamboanga. After Mindanao, you go to Talisai to wind up Winters' business affairs. You might say that Talisai will be the acid test. Sort of a passing out exercise.'

Stanford's thoughts went back to the material he'd been studying. It was comprehensive, as far as it went. But was it adequate for a confrontation with Winters' beach club staff? He didn't think so. 'I'll need a more comprehensive briefing on the club and its business.'

'You'll get it. The dossier you've just gone through was pretty general. Starting tomorrow, I'll feed you the detailed stuff. I don't think the month will drag. We haven't even started on the profiles of the various Chiang Mai personalities ... your fellow spooks, and the other side's teams. Tomorrow, you also start taking Thai lessons.'

'It seems pretty elaborate,' Stanford said dubiously.

'Yes, I suppose it does. It isn't though. The manufacture of a deep cover can take years ... even decades. What you're getting is a crash course. And it had better be damned good. Your life will depend on it.'

'Look, Dan,' he said in a conciliatory tone, 'I appreciate that playing nursemaid is a pain in the ass. I'm no stranger to cover identities and am fully aware of their vital importance. The only thing that puzzles me is why Chiang Mai rates all this. I was led to understand that it's a relatively quiet area. I'll agree that coordinating an intelligence network reguires cover. Damned good cover at that. But the preparations we're undertaking now smack more of a highly clandestine mission.'

Garrity looked uncomfortable. 'I'll have to concede you the point. And this is one of the areas I was talking about. I know something about the Chiang Mai operation, but not all of it. I do know that it's taking on a good deal of significance. That background, you'll get from the Chief.'

'The Chief?'

'You'll meet him. Week after next, I think. He'll fill you in on the Santa Rosa aspect as well as the 'black operation' aspects. Incidentally, you should be highly flattered. There aren't more than six people in Southeast Asia who know his identity. I'm fortunate enough to be one of those trusted few. You'll be number seven.'

Garrity was as good as his word. On Monday morning, he unloaded on Stanford a mountain of files dealing with foreign espionage agents, Thai and Burmese officials, tribal leaders, Laotian operations, Southwestern China background – and Judson Q. Winters.

Although he didn't neglect the other background material, Stanford concentrated on Winters.

The supplementary documentation was voluminous, covering a period from Jud's childhood up to and including late 1967. Included were school and probation officer's reports, service documents, credit reports and in-depth interviews with relatives, friends and associates. There were also photocopies of the beach club accounts, dunning letters from creditors, personal correspondence and a thick album of photographs.

The relationship between Jud and his second step-mother was one of hostility. He had never accepted her authority. She had been unable to discipline him or evoke any emo-

22

tional response other than sullen resentment. She considered Jud a rebellious good-for-nothing. From the time he'd joined the navy, his only contact with his step-mother had been a formal exchange of correspondence when he was divesting his corporate shareholdings.

The only member of the family with which Jud had maintained any sort of relationship was his half-sister, Betty-Anne. She was married to an economist employed by the Stanford Research Institute, had a six-year-old son named Judson, and lived in Huntington Beach, California. Jud's contact was confined to a desultory correspondence and an exchange of cards at Christmas. He had never seen his namesake.

Christina Jannsen had been traced. She was married to a doctor who practised in up-state New York. Childless, she had adopted a girl and a boy. In confidence, she had disclosed the reason for her abrupt severance of her relationship with Jud during their junior year at college. She had become pregnant. At Jud's insistence, she had undergone an abortion in her fourth month. The operation had been badly botched by a San Mateo quack and had resulted in her inability to bear children. Her love for Jud had soured into bitter resentment. While her earlier harsh judgment had softened over the years, since Jud's departure neither had made any attempt to communicate.

From the accounts of both Betty-Anne, and Christina, some insight into Jud's attitude towards his parents emerged. He idealized the dead mother he had never known. In part, he blamed himself for her death. But by far a larger measure of guilt for his mother's death, Jud reserved for his father. Jud had both hated and feared the senior Winters.

Interviews with Jud's former mistresses were revealing. Both women indicated that Jud could be gay and charming, but was given to periods of deep depression and excessive drinking. Neither Akiko nor Isabel felt that Jud had loved them very deeply. Akiko added that while Jud often played around with some of her hostess friends, he had been violently jealous when he discovered her continuing devotion to an old admirer.

A review of the club accounts left no doubt of pending insolvency. For the months immediately prior to Jud's death it looked as though he was his own best customer, and practically his only one at that. He had let the business slide. On several occasions, he'd gone off on extended drunks. The fact that the staff had been stealing him blind was only thinly disguised in the bookkeeper's figures.

From the time of Jud's death, the monthly payrolls and current commitments had been met from Agency funds. Money orders had been sent from Manila to Talisai, ostensibly from Winters who was on a monumental drunk. An accountant, representing himself as having been sent by Winters, had gone to Talisai to check the books. He had returned with the photocopies contained in the supplementary material.

The composite picture was of a confused and rebellious man, resentful of authority and suspicious of emotional involvement. If Jud had not been already an alcoholic, he soon would have been one. Still, insecure and emotionally immature though he was, Jud had displayed a marked talent for landing on his feet. Stanford found the picture oddly appealing. He recognized that the true basis for empathy lay in the fact that Jud, like himself, was a loner.

As his time in Makati stretched into weeks, Stanford found himself identifying more and more with the dead man. True, he was making a conscious effort in that direction, and there were other contributing factors. Garrity adressed him by nothing but 'Jud'. As the discoloration slowly faded from his face, and his hair and moustache took on substance, he started to take pride in his new appearance. Still, when the day of subconscious transferrence arrived, it came as a surprise.

He had been in the habit of making a sincere effort to adopt the point of view he felt Winters would take. He would ask himself the question: 'How would Jud look at this?' Then one day, his question was 'How would *I* see it?' And in its usage, the first person singular pronoun had referred to Jud. It was by no means a complete transference of identity, but he found he could now think as Jud Winters. It was a bewildering dichotomy, but in a sense he actually *was* Jud Winters. From that day, he called himself, and thought of himself, as Jud, but a Jud guided by the sobering influence of Joe Stanford.

Dan Garrity had watched the slow metamorphosis with profound satisfaction.

24

CHAPTER FIVE

Garrity's particular field of concern was Mainland China and the overseas Chinese population throughout Southeast Asia. He admitted that his knowledge concerning the Thailand operations was sketchy. He knew something of the long tenure of office of Jud's predecessor, and disclosed the fact that the former Chiang Mai Area Coordinator had been killed in an ambush by Meo bandits the previous August.

'Good Christ!' Jud exclaimed. 'Is everybody connected with this operation a corpse? Does that mean I have to go in there and start building another network from the ground up?'

'Not at all. But I'll have to confess that I'm not *au courant* with the situation. That's one of the things the Chief wants to discuss with you personally.'

'I have the uncomfortable feeling, Dan, that I'm opening a can of worms. Who was my predecessor?'

'Lindstrom. Lars Lindstrom.' Garrity dug through a pile of files and brought forth a thick folder. 'His history's all in here. You'll find the more current Chiang Mai reports somewhere in that stack on the bookcase.'

Jud sighed. 'Okay,' he said, 'leave me to my homework.'

Lars Lindstrom had a lengthy and interesting history. He was a Swedish national who had lived in North Burma prior to the Second World War. During the war, throughout most of the Japanese occupation of Burma, he stayed on in Lashio. His sentiments were violently anti-Axis. The record showed that he had been most helpful to Wingate, Merrill and Stillwell during the Burma campaign.

In 1944, things had become too hot for Lindstrom. He made his way down through Shan States to Northern Thailand. In 1945, he purchased an interest in a local ceramics factory and settled down in Chiang Mai. It appeared, however, that he still maintained strong contacts in Burma and with the Kuomintang in Chungking and Kunming.

Following the war, when the CIA was established under the Truman Administration, Lindstrom had been recruited into the Agency.

25

A few years later, when the Chinese Nationalist Third Army fled from Yunnan Province into Burma, one jump ahead of Mao Tse-tung's pursuing forces, Lindstrom's wartime connections proved invaluable. At that time, the Karen tribesmen were in revolt against the Burmese government. Once again, Lindstrom's contacts served the Agency well.

In Northern Thailand, the Agency became deeply involved with the Kuomintang 93rd Division. The Chinese unit was funded and supplied through a dummy trading corporation in Bangkok called Sea Supply. It was a high-priority project. Lindstrom enjoyed the confidence of Wild Bill Donovan, then the American Ambassador to Thailand, and had established close personal contact with General Li Mi, who commanded the so-called Yunnan Anti-Communist and National Salvation Army. From the dossier, it was amply evident that at that time Lindstrom had considerable prestige and wielded strong influence.

Then the picture started to change. It became obvious that the Kuomintang guerillas were far more interested in grabbing a slice of the illicit opium traffic than they were in harassing the Communist usurpers in Yunnan. Continuing subsidy of the Kuomintang was becoming an embarrassment to the U.S. Administration. Sea Supply fell into disrepute and was quietly folded, but support continued indirectly through Taiwan.

If Lindstrom had not outgrown his usefulness entirely, it was obvious that his influence was considerably diminished.

In 1955, there was correspondence in the file indicating that Lindstrom's retirement was under discussion. The focus of attention had by then shifted to the growing American involvement with the Diem regime in South Viet-Nam. The Burma-Thailand region was downgraded to a watching and listening post. Arguments were presented which favoured Lindstrom's retention on the grounds that in a downgraded context his many connections were still of value. These recommendations prevailed. Lindstrom stayed on in Chiang Mai as Area Coordinator. He was then 50 years of age.

In 1961, there was an upsurge of interest in Thailand as a support base for the Viet-Nam and Laotian involvement. But none of this directly affected Lindstrom. Laos had already been removed from his area of jurisdiction, and no airbases were being considered in North Thailand. Again, there was talk of retirement, and again it was considered that he filled a harmless post in an area of stagnation. He stayed on.

Late in 1964, a peculiar note crept into the reports. It appeared that a number of Lindstrom's situation appraisals stirred interest. There were a number of pencilled notations in the margins of several sheets.

From 1964 onwards a process of slow erosion had taken place. As agents were assigned from Lindstrom's control to other areas, they were not replaced. One by one, other agents were arbitrarily switched from Lindstrom to other controls. Over a period of three years, Lindstrom's network dwindled to a skeletal structure.

The last document on Lindstrom's file was the report of an investigation into the circumstances surrounding his death. There had been no witnesses. Much of the report seemed based on hearsay or pure conjecture. The bullet-riddled bodies of Lindstrom and his Thai drivers were the only solid and inescapable facts presented.

At the bottom of the final report, was a notation scrawled in red ink – 'Reactivate Soonest.'

From what Garrity had said, Jud had had the impression that it was Lindstrom's sudden death which had caused the agents to be switched to other control channels. This wasn't borne out by the facts. With, or without, his knowledge, Lindstrom had been deliberately denuded of operational authority long before his death. Why? The man was well into his sixties and could have been retired. Jud found it puzzling.

He examined the Chiang Mai report files for the preceding four year period with a critical eye. The answer was there. When he discovered the evidence, he frowned and swore softly.

Jud divided the known foreign agents' files into three categories; 'Russian', 'Chinese', and 'others'. Into the latter category, he bulked the French, German, British, Italian and Japanese agents. He started with this latter group of files. Although he didn't consider these 'friendly nation' agents too significant, he nonetheless made himself familiar with their backgrounds, faces, physical characteristics, mannerisms and *modus operandi*. Where known, he cross-referenced the agent's contacts, sub-agents and position in the espionage structures of his particular organization.

The Chinese stack of files was surprisingly small. Jud concluded that the Cultural Revolution must have seriously disrupted the overall command structure. A sizeable number of known agents had either been recalled, or simply disappeared. Jud questioned Dan Garrity on the subject.

What Garrity had to say was hardly comforting. He pointed out that the hard-core espionage structure was probably pretty much intact and active. Overseas Chinese communities throughout Southeast Asia afforded both Mainland China and Taiwan with frightening potential for the gathering and dissemination of information. Little success had ever been met in attempts to infiltrate these tightly-knit communities. After all, Garrity had said with a shrug, the Chinese practically invented the spy business.

Jud singled out one file for special attention. This was the dossier of Wong Liu Chan, owner and operator of the Golden Dragon Restaurant in Chiang Mai, and reputed to be the kingpin in the Northern Thailand and Northeast Burma region. The information contained in the folder was disappointingly limited.

The files dealing with the USSR operatives were more extensive and complete as to structure and detail. It was almost two weeks before he reached the last and most voluminous dossier in this group. He had purposely saved this for his special attention.

Jud flipped open the cover. The genial countenance smiling up at him from the identification photograph was of a chubby balding man of middle years. The caption beneath the photo read: 'Heinrich (Hank) Keppler.'

Heinrich Keppler was born in Zurich in 1913. His mother was Swiss; his father German. Following his early schooling in Switzerland, his secondary education commenced in Kiev and was completed in Moscow. Although Keppler still retained Swiss citizenship, he had been a member of the Communist Party since 1933.

In Moscow, in 1943, Keppler was recruited into the CHEKA and underwent two years of intensive and specialized training. In 1940, he was sent back to Zurich to join a Party cell. When the Nazi war machine surged out of

Austria to race eastward across the steppes, Keppler was already well established in an espionage function. For the duration of the war, he was to remain in Switzerland, rendering invaluable service to his Russian masters.

Keppler appeared in Chiang Mai in 1946 at the age of 33. He was amply endowed with funds and set himself up in the antique export business. The business flourished from the outset, but was of secondary importance. His primary function was to establish a network devoted to espionage and counter-espionage. From all accounts, he was equally successful in this undertaking.

In November of 1952, Keppler married the daughter of a highly-placed Thai official, the Vice-Governor of Chiang Mai province. In time, the union produced three children; two boys and a girl. Already well established in the community even before his marriage, Keppler's social position was assured by his nuptial alliance. He was one of the best-known and most well-liked of the local foreign community. He was a gregarious man of considerable personal charm.

Keppler's cover activity in the antique business afforded him an excellent opportunity to travel widely, not only in Southeast Asia, but to Europe as well, a schedule ideally suited to someone engaged in clandestine activities.

The latter portion of the dossier indicated that Keppler's region had remained comparatively quiet for over a decade. Keppler had not been idle though. During the lull, he had extended his business interests and commercial activity. He was reputed to be a very wealthy man.

There were area divisions within the KGB organization which did not parallel those of the CIA. The file conceded that Keppler, as Resident Agent in Chiang Mai, was not the top regional authority. Yet it was not known to whom, or to what location, Keppler reported. It was considered unlikely to be Rangoon. Either the Soviet Embassy in Vientiane, or Bangkok, was suggested as the likely control. For some years, he was known to have been under the command of the embassy in Phnom Penh, but an administrative reshuffle appeared to have dropped Keppler. For some reason, the Agency operatives had not been able to trace Keppler's current chain of command.

It would not pay, Jud thought, to underestimate this man. His local popularity and personal charm tended to mask

29

Keppler's Teutonic tenacity. Jud could not afford to be deluded on that score. All the evidence pointed to Keppler as an able, clever and extremely dangerous opponent.

Jud visited the villa's library. To his satisfaction, he found that there was a wide range of books on Oriental antiquities. This subject, he now added to his continuing studies in the Thai language, codes, ciphers, photography and microphotography.

Garrity, Jud decided, had not stretched the truth when he'd said that the month would not drag. It almost seemed to Jud that there weren't enough hours in the day. Almost every file he studied opened up another line of research.

CHAPTER SIX

Jud was pouring himself a cognac when he heard the muffled thumping of a helicopter. He went to the window, in time to witness the ungainly bird settling gently onto the lawn.

A few minutes later, Garrity ushered a conservatively dressed man into the library. So this was the Chief. Jud eyed the man with undisguised curiosity.

'Jud,' Garrity said, 'may I introduce Sam Harper.'

Jud's first impression had been wrong. The silvery-haired man couldn't have been much older than Garrity. The hair was misleading.

Harper studied Jud's face a few moments. 'An astonishing likeness,' he said, his voice betraying satisfaction. 'If I didn't know better, I'd swear I was meeting the original. Excellent. Dan here tells me you've made splendid progress, but that you feel there have been a few gaps in the briefing.'

'A few,' Jud said. 'Drink?'

'Yes, scotch and water, please.'

Jud turned a guestioning glance to Garrity. 'Dan?'

'No thanks,' Garrity answered. 'I'll leave you two to your questions and answers.'

The ice tinkled in Harper's glass as he seated himself in one of the easy chairs. 'Where,' he said affably, 'would you like to begin?'

'Santa Rosa Lumber & Plywood Company,' Jud answered promptly. 'Is it a dummy corporation? Garrity mentioned

30

logging operations and mills, but he wasn't too clear on the details.'

'No, we're by no means a front structure. It's a legitimate and long established company with extensive holdings and impressive sales. I have the honour of being Vice-President, I can assure you, I earn my salary. So will you.

'How am I to fit into the picture in Chiang Mai?'

'Our Northern Thailand office was established in Chiang Mai four years ago. It has had absolutely nothing to do with Agency activities. Its function is tropical hardwoods buying – principally teak logs for veneer plywood. One thing I must make clear. Once you're on your own, you will have to perform adequately, better than adequately, as a buyer or I will not be able to justify your retention by the company.

'We ran ads for the opening in Chiang Mai in all the local papers, and major newspapers throughout the area, in October. Your application as Winters is on file as of October 28th. A confidential report on your interview for the position is in company files, dated 6th November. As most companies do, we took our sweet time reviewing the applications. You were advised by letter last week that you were the successful applicant. Magnanimously, we gave you two weeks to settle your affairs before reporting to Zamboanga. You were sent an airline ticket and a small cash advance.'

'You will be in Mindanao for the better part of a month. Three weeks in the rain forest camps, and a week in the plywood mill. When you leave there, you will proceed directly to Cebu.'

'To wind up my affairs. How long is that supposed to take?'

'Considering the shape things are in there,' Harper said drily, 'I would think you could wrap it all up in an hour. I suggest you just turn over the keys to your Filipino manager and walk away from the disaster. You're due at the Santa Rosa office in Manila by the end of the first week in April.' Harper reached into his pocket and brought forth a ring of keys. 'These,' he said, handing the keys to Jud, 'are the beach club keys. You'll need them.'

'Who,' Jud questioned, 'is R. G. Cranston?'

Harper looked at Jud quizzically. 'One of our agents. Why?'

'He wrote the report dealing with Winters' fatal accident. How many people know of that sad event?'

'Four. Cranston, Dan Garrity, myself . . . and now you.'

The answer surprised Jud. He thought that at least Langley would have been informed. His astonishment must have shown on his face. Harper amplified his last statement.

'Cranston signed the report, but I wrote it. It wasn't Cranston who was present on the scene, but myself. Under no circumstances could I afford to be linked with the event. When Winters fell from the boat, he was gone in a matter of seconds. There was nothing left to identify and therefore no point in advising the local officials and advertising my presence. When I returned the boat to the rental people, I told them Winters had gone ashore at Talisai. I had the club advised by messenger that Winters had decided to go up to Manila. Later, I arranged for a cancelled air ticket to verify his trip. Cranston happens to bear a superficial resemblance to me and could have passed himself off as me if the necessity ever arose. That's why his signature is on the report.

'Under normal circumstances, Winters' file would have been closed and the Agency advised. They would have been had it not been for a singular coincidence.

'Your file was on my desk. I was in the process of devising a foolproof identity for you in Chiang Mai. Winters' file was also on the desk. I noted the similarity in height, weight and colouring. Then I realized it would not be too difficult to convert you into a replica of Winters. I temporarily shelved Winters' dossier. If this masquerade works out as I now believe it will, we've had an unbelievable break.

'Now, I intend to remove the report from the file and destroy it. Apart from we four, the world will believe that Jud Winters is very much alive, has straightened himself out, and found steady employment.'

It was a plausible story. A helluva coincidence, but stranger things had happened. Yet Jud could not escape the nagging suspicion that the story was too plausible. 'Then I wasn't selected for this assignment on the basis of a resemblance to Winters?'

A look of annoyance flashed across Harper's face. 'Certainly not. You were hand-picked for your experience with northern hill tribes, familiarity with the general area, and a marked facility for foreign tongues. Winters' death is purest

32

coincidence, but it provided a cover identity we couldn't have hoped for. There are even more advantages than you imagine.'

I'll bet, Jud thought. He was far from satisfied, but decided to let the matter rest for the moment. There were other questions to be satisfied and the hour was growing late. He changed the subject. 'When did you discover that Lindstrom was working both sides of the street?'

Harper was visibly shaken. He recovered rapidly. 'A little over four years ago. How did you determine that? It's not reported in Linstrom's dossier.'

'It should be, shouldn't it?' Jud asked softly.

'It's on record in Langley,' Harper answered with asperity. 'I asked you how *you* discovered it.'

Jud said evenly, 'It's there in Lindstrom's file, and the Chiang Mai report files, for anyone with an ounce of brains to see. The first indication I got was the advance advice on the Sputnik launch. The Russians kept that pretty quiet before the launch in case it failed. For Lindstrom to have gleaned that gem from any of his existing sources is beyond incredibility. Ergo, it was leaked. Probably by friend Keppler to demonstrate good faith.' Jud laughed. 'At that time, Lindstrom's reports seemed to have been a source of hilarity and mirth. I'd be willing to bet that nobody paid the slightest attention to his coup on Sputnik.'

Harper was watching Jud narrowly. 'As far as I can determine,' he said flatly, 'the report wasn't taken seriously enough to relay to Langley. Nonetheless, one questionable piece of information shouldn't signify that Lindstrom was a double agent.'

'No,' Jud agreed, 'it shouldn't. But from the time of that report other unmistakable little tit-bits appear on a more or less regular basis. They don't seem to have been noticed until '64. Then Lindstrom was slowly leeched of his trusted minions. I take it that the decision was not to rap his knuckles for being a naughty spy, but to give him a few spurious nuggets as feed-back.'

The muscles along Harper's jaw tightened. 'A known double agent can be useful,' he said stiffly. 'I didn't take the helm until late 1963. It was some months before I moved through all the back files and Chiang Mai was not our most active region. I didn't discover Lindstrom's duplicity until mid–'64. Then I took appropriate action. I considered removing him from his post, but it wasn't a region of vital importance.'

Harper's remarks were curiously revealing. *Duplicity* was an odd word to employ, especially for one engaged in espionage.

'Would you say,' Jud said mildly, 'that a rumour that the Agency was dickering with Shan leaders was vitally important?'

Harper's brows contracted. 'Lindstrom should not have had that information. I thought he had been adequately defused, but it is next to impossible to cut a man off from sources of intelligence when he has had better than thirty years to build up regional contacts.'

'He reported that early in August, didn't he?'

'Yes,' Harper snapped.

'Was it true?'

'Partially. It's all part of a larger issue.'

'Could he have confided this intelligence to Keppler?'

'He could have. I don't know. Unfortunately, he was ambushed and killed before he could be questioned.'

'Yes. Most unfortunate.' Jud knew with instinctive certainty that Lindstrom had been liquidated on Harper's recommendation. Permanently *de-fused*, to use Harper's expression. Jud had been about to ask for confirmation of his suspicion. He thought better of it and decided he'd already pushed too hard. He backed off. 'Would it make much difference if Keppler knew of the approach to the Shan?'

'I don't think so. Rumours of that nature are constantly being circulated.'

'But that one had some substance. And it might have led to speculation on the larger issue you mentioned.'

'It might have. It might yet. It will be one of the problems which you will face in your assignment.'

'Which brings me,' Jud said easily, 'to my most important question. What is my assignment?'

The stiffness went from Harper's shoulders and his features relaxed into more amiable lines. 'What were you told by Morrison and Cantrell?' he asked.

'Hadn't a chance to see Morrison prior to my departure. Cantrell told me very little. I was advised that I'd be taking over in Chiang Mai as area coordinator of the networks in

34

Southwestern China, some portions of Northern Laos, Northern Thailand and Burma. Nothing more. It wasn't suggested that my predecessor had been killed; that the networks had been compromised and virtually disbanded, nor that I would be assuming the identity of a dead man.'

Harper smiled faintly. 'Cantrell knew little more than he disclosed. Morrison could have told you Lindstrom was dead. Neither of them had any knowledge of Winters.' He settled himself more comfortably in his chair. 'Up to now, references to Chiang Mai would lead you to believe it to be a stagnant backwater. It is. But it won't be for long.

'There is evidence of increasing Chinese interest in Eastern Burma and Northern Laos. The continuing Kuomintang presence in the north of Thailand and the Shan States could well pose a growing problem. I suspect that the narcotics traffic throughout the area will become an increasingly thorny issue. All those factors are going to make life hectic for you.

'But there is a larger aspect which will concern you. For some time now, we have been in contact with some of the deposed and exiled leaders of Burma. Due to the chaotic economic conditions in Burma, there is a growing opposition to Ne Win's left-leaning neutralist policies. In consequence, there is an increasing sympathy with the exiled group. Insurgency now smoulders just short of the flash point. If we can make common cause of ethnic aspirations, and lend support, a potent force will have been created. If Ne Win isn't deposed, at least he will be forced into a position of compromise. At worse, we will have created an effective pro-Western buffer which will prove an obstacle to Chinese infiltration and influence. Whichever way it goes, it will prove something of an embarrassment to the Soviet influence within Burma.

'To date, the efforts to weld the Burmese and minority factions into a cohesive force have not met with spectacular success. In my opinion, part of the problem lies in the fact that our contacts have been through Bangkok where we have conflicting departmental views. My proposal is that the direction of this effort be transferred to Chiang Mai, which is a more logical geographical location. Funding for the project will continue through Bangkok, but under the direction of Chiang Mai. That, the direction of our proposed support of the insurgency, will be your major task.

'Concerning the compromise of your networks, you are mistaken. While it is true that agents were slowly removed from Lindstrom's control, the network didn't wither and die. Any agent who could have been compromised by Lindstrom has been assigned to other postings or staff duties. You will find that the structure has been maintained with the addition of new and excellent men. They will be transferred to your control as soon as you are established.'

'Didn't Lindstrom ever suspect he was being short-circuited?' Jud asked.

Harper hesitated. 'I don't believe he did. He had built up such a widespread base of minor informants that he probably felt we were merely effecting an economy of American personnel. On the other hand, I think that Keppler may have suspected what we were doing.'

His hesitancy gone, Harper continued in a didactic manner. 'In order to counter any lurking suspicions, we didn't disband the structure entirely. On Lindstrom's death, we placed a man in the area as an ostensible replacement. His code name is 'Mabel'. He is, in fact, the American Vice-Consul – or one of them, since there are two in Chiang Mai. His name is Carver. He believes himself to be the Agency man in residence. The remnants of Lindstrom's truncated networks report through Carver. And so will you.' At Jud's look of consternation, Harper smiled. 'You will in theory, but not in practice.

'This is one of the advantages we have achieved by your becoming Winters. As soon as you arrive in Chiang Mai, a stranger and an American stranger at that, our opposition colleagues will immediately start checking your background. It will be quickly discovered that you have undertaken some minor chores for the Agency here in the Philippines. But even a cursory glance at your record will reveal that we wouldn't be likely to entrust you with anything other than the role of paid informer. So, that's what you'll be. From time to time, you will drop by and chat with Carver. Keppler and the like will quickly dismiss you as harmless. It goes without saying that you must do everything possible to foster that impression.'

Harper reached into the slim brief case he'd brought with him. 'Here,' he said, handing Jud a manila envelope, 'you

36

will find a complete list of the agents who will report through you, together with their code names, locations and cover identities.'

The chopper blades whirred and the bird lifted off. Seated beside the pilot, Harper took a deep breath and exhaled slowly to regain his composure. The evening had not gone as he'd planned. He was irritated, annoyed and apprehensive.

Stanford had managed to place him on the defensive. Harper knew that for a good portion of the evening he'd been skillfully grilled. He wasn't used to such treatment. He was not given to snap judgments, but felt a deep resentment and dislike for Stanford. He should have been forewarned by some of the pungent comments in Cantrell's documentation.

During the interrogation concerning Lindstrom, Harper had been sure Stanford was going to ask whether or not the death had been an Agency-inspired execution. Harper had been prepared to answer coldly that it had been. He wondered why Stanford had veered away from the question.

A good many people had reviewed Linstrom's dossier. But in no case, other than himself, had any reviewer grasped the significance of the Sputnik report. Stanford hadn't missed it, and had gone on to draw the correct conclusions of the subsequent action. Harper recognized he was dealing with a much shrewder man than he'd anticipated. He foresaw trouble in the months ahead.

CHAPTER SEVEN

In the four days since his arrival in Hong Kong, Heinrich Keppler had acquired three items of T'ang dynasty pottery. He had every reason to be pleased. He was miserable.

The cause of his despondency was threefold. Normally, he planned his business trip to Hong Kong between mid-October and the last week in December to take full advantage of the superb autumn weather, but here it was the last week in March and the weather was oppressively muggy. He had already planned his European trip, and should have been in

37

Paris by today. And last, but by no means least, this un-scheduled Hong Kong visit was in response to a brusque summons.

It was 9 : 30 Sunday morning. Low clouds hovered over the harbour. The Peak was shrouded in mist. Leaning against the railing at Queen's Pier, waiting for the arrival of his host's cabin cruiser, Keppler was uncomfortably hot – and the day had hardly started.

He gazed moodily down at the oily water lapping at the concrete piling. He wished the craft would arrive. Better yet, he wished the damned cruise was over and it was Tuesday morning. Tuesday, he was booked on the Air France flight to Paris.

A mental picture of Heide, reclining voluptuously nude on mauve sheets, in her apartment on the Avenue Foch, flashed into his mind. With that thought, Keppler's mood improved slightly.

Wiping a film of perspiration from his brow and the crown of his bald head, he lifted his eyes to absently scan the busy harbour. A cream and green ferryboat churned the water as it slid out from the finger of the Star Ferry wharf. Then he noticed a white-hulled cabin cruiser making for Queen's Pier. As the distance narrowed, he could make out the name on the bow – *Krishna III*. The momentary lifting of his spirits by thoughts of Paris and Heide, evaporated.

The trim craft slid smoothly alongside the landing steps. The Indian owner, with the other guests who had embarked earlier at the Royal Hong Kong Yacht Club, was seated be-neath the stern canopy. Recognizing Heinrich, his host flashed a smile and waved. Picking up his flight bag, Keppler trotted down the steps, waited until the deck rose to his level, then cautiously stepped aboard. Picking his way aft to join the rest of the yachting party, Keppler adjusted his features to project an affability he was far from feeling.

As the day progressed, Keppler's disposition improved. By the time they cleared the inner harbour, a light breeze served to relieve the oppressive humidity. As they left the narrow channel and turned into the gentle swell surging between The Brothers and the mainland, the sun broke through the overcast. A white-jacketed Chinese steward served drinks. Keppler relaxed, accepted a tall gin and tonic and entered into the general conversation. Mindful of his

38

appointment later that evening, he resolved to drink sparingly.

The *Krishna III* nosed into a small cove, surrounded on three sides by steeply rising hills, and dropped anchor. There was no habitation and the only indication of human presence was a footpath which followed a winding course along the face of the slopes.

Until late afternoon, *Krishna III* was the only craft to occupy the bay. Then, close to 6 : oo p.m., a gleaming white ketch slipped quietly into the cove. Her mizzen and foresail already dropped her mainsail slid smoothly down the aluminium mast as her anchor chain rattled in the hawse. Swinging slowly to her hook, the ketch lay about fifty metres off the *Krishna III.*

Keppler had been anticipating the arrival, but as the afternoon had lengthened he had entertained the hope she would not appear. He was ensconced in the one corner of the afterdeck settee, reading a paperback. He put down the novel and picked up a pair of binoculars. Focusing on the ketch's bow, he read the polished brass letters on a mahogony plaque – *Sagittarius.*

The blackness was broken only by the *Krisna III's* dimmed lights reflected from the water, and the single twinkling anchor light of the ketch. On board the cabin cruiser, the crew and most of the guests had turned in for the night.

On the foredeck, Keppler lay beneath a blanket on an air mattress. Glancing at the luminous dial of his watch, he noted it was close to midnight. He got up and doffed his shirt. Clad only in swimming trunks, he padded over to the boarding ladder and lowered his bulk into the cool water. With a slow stroke, he struck out in the direction of the ketch, his progress betrayed only by a thin wake of phosphorescence.

Passing beneath the ketch's transom, he located the boarding ladder and started to pull himself from the water. He paused part way up to regain his breath.

Wraith-like, a girl appeared above him on the ketch's deck. She assisted Keppler over the side. She escorted Keppler through a hatch into the wheelhouse. Although the only illumination came from the dim light of the binnacle, heavy curtains were drawn across the side scuttles. The girl handed

Keppler a large towel and a terry-cloth bathrobe. He dried himself vigorously and gratefully donned the robe against the chill of the interior air-conditioning.

Sliding open a hatch, the girl preceded Keppler down three steps into a well-appointed saloon. In the light of a deckhead dome light, Keppler perceived the stolid figure of Shepilov.

Shepilov was a gray man. His hair and bushy eyebrows were iron-gray. There was a grayish pallor to his broad Slavic features. Even his rumpled suit was a sombre shade of gray.

Seated on a leather settee behind the saloon table, Shepilov made no effort to rise or greet Keppler. Not until Keppler was seated, did Shepilov acknowledge the presence. 'Drink?' queried Shepilov in a grating voice. He spoke in Russian.

Keppler eyed the bottle of vodka on the table with distaste. In Russian, he answered, 'Thank you, but cognac if you don't mind.'

With a glance from his heavy-lidded eyes, Shepilov signalled the girl. Keppler watched her movements at the compact bar as she poured a generous drink into a brandy snifter. When she had placed both the glass and bottle of cognac before Keppler, she mounted the steps to the wheelhouse. With a soft click, the hatch slid closed behind her.

'We will not waste time, Comrade Keppler,' rasped Shepilov. 'We are far from satisfied with your latest reports.'

Despite the coolness of the cabin, Keppler's palms were uncomfortably moist. 'Why?' he asked.

'Facts. We need facts. We cannot act on assumptions.'

Keppler considered his reply. It was true that he'd arrived at conclusions based more on instinct rather than solid proof, but he had not anticipated this reaction. He stalled. 'I take it you refer to my report concerning American intervention in Burma?'

'Yes.'

Weighing his words carefully, Heinrich spoke in defence of his reported deductions. 'For over two years, I have considered that Lindstrom's cooperation with me was known to the CIA. He had not proven of much value as an informant. His knowledge of the American build-up in Laos and Thailand was limited and sometimes misleading. I felt that some of his facts were deliberately distorted; not by Lindstrom, but by his superiors. It is not CIA policy to leave a man in an area for over twenty years. Also, he was well past sixty and . . .'

'You have been quite some time in that area yourself, Herr Keppler,' Shepilov interjected.

The implication and the intentional usage of German, were not lost on Heinrich, but he continued evenly, 'From an agent closely connected with the exiled Burmese group, I learned that overtures of support were being advanced from an unknown quarter. I believe Lindstrom may have had some knowledge of the matter.'

'You based your reports on this belief?'

'Partially. Lindstrom intimated to me that he had information concerning a CIA approach to some of the dissident Shan Leaders. He was to give me more detailed information. Before he could, he was killed.

'As far as I know, Lindstrom didn't have an enemy anywhere in the territory. He could have been killed by bandits, as the story went. Or Lindstrom could have been eliminated by his own group. I checked and double checked. No Meo tribesmen had been operating in that area. No known gang of bandits had been frequenting the immediate vicinity. But not too far from the scene, two American anthropologists had been making a study of Yao village culture. Coincidentally, they departed the day after Lindstrom's death. I have no *proof*, but from everything I have been able to determine I am convinced he was killed by the CIA.

'The question was, why? And the only answer which satisfies me is that the CIA are planning some operation to which Lindstrom's continuing presence would be an embarrassment, if not an actual threat. Either they intend to expand their operations in Northern Thailand, or they have a renewed interest in Burma. I favour the latter.'

'You could be right, Comrade. If so, it is vital we know for certain. Your conclusions are based on supposition. What we *must* have are facts,' Shepilov stated flatly.

Shepilov poured a shot of vodka into his small glass. Raising the glass, he downed its contents in a single gulp. Replacing the glass on the table, he regarded Keppler for several moments. Finally, Shepilov leaned forward and locked his stubby fingers together. 'I will tell you,' he said, 'just why we attach so much importance to the Burmese situation.

'Our problems with the Chinese are far from resolved. Any pressures exerted on China's southern and western flanks, which cause her to siphon troop divisions away from her northern frontier, should be welcomed by us. In line with that reasoning, you would think we would not object to the Americans stirring the pot in Burma. You would be wrong.

'Within the next four to five years, public sentiment and political considerations in the United States will result in her disengagement from Viet-Nam. Without strong provocation, they would not rush into another misadventure of that nature. The withdrawal of American troops, and the inability of the British to maintain strong forces east of Suez, will create a power vacuum in the sub-continent. We intend to exploit the situation to the fullest. Our sphere of interest and influence in the Mediterranean and the Middle East will be extended to embrace India, Pakistan and much of Southeast Asia.

The key to this, Comrade Keppler, is supremacy of the seas. Within the next decade, we will be the world's dominant naval power. In fact, as our Commander in Chief, Admiral Gorshkov, has stated, we have already achieved that status. All that remains is for us to secure world-girdling bases for our naval operations.'

'The American navy,' Keppler observed drily, 'might dispute Admiral Gorshkov's claim.'

A suggestion of a smile touched Shepilov's face. 'The Americans,' he stated, 'suggest we are defficient in aircraft carriers. Ever since their debacle at Pearl Harbour, they have been morbidly occupied with the importance of carrier operations. We have some experience with such preoccupations. It has taken us three generations to live down the humiliation of our naval disaster at Port Arthur. In an era of missile warfare, we believe the American naval concept to be outmoded. It is the submarine upon which the balance of naval power hinges. In that realm, our preeminence is without peer.

'This year, we will begin operating units of the fleet in the Indian Ocean. In order to expand these operations, we must acquire new naval bases. This we will do, first in the Arabian Sea, next in the Bay of Bengal, Singapore and Indonesia, and finally, in the South China Sea. If the Americans had used their heads, they would have progressed the war in Viet-Nam as all-out military conquest. In so doing, they

42

could have denied us the South China Sea for longer than we care to think. Now, with strengthening ties in North Viet-Nam we can count on a secure base in the Baie d'Along. Eventually, we hope to develop what is potentially the finest naval base in Asia : Cam Ranh Bay.'

'Won't the Japanese challenge such expansion?' Keppler questioned.

Shepilov unclenched his fingers and spread his palms flat on the table. 'They are pursuing an aggresive policy of economic expansion. Ultimately, we must come into conflict with their aspirations. However, like all island nations, they are vulnerable. With vastly superior sea power, we can simply choke them off from oil and raw materials.'

Shepilov poured himself another shot of vodka. 'Perhaps,' he continued, when he had swallowed the fiery liquor, 'you can now appreciate our concern with Burma. Whether the bases we acquire in the Bay of Bengal are in East Pakistan, India, the Andaman Islands, or Burma itself is immaterial. What is of paramount importance is to ensure that no other major power, particularly the United States, threatens our littoral and maritime supremacy.

'The neutralist socialist state now existing in Burma is admirably suited to our purpose. We must, and will, take prompt action to counter anything which threatens to disturb that status quo. Is that clearly understood, Comrade Keppler?'

Yes, Keppler understood perfectly. The Slavs were on the swarm, and he, Heinrich Franz Keppler, descendant of the Ostrogoths, was caught squarely in the middle of this restless dream of empire. To Shepilov, Keppler said simply, 'I understand.'

'Good. We must have detailed information concerning any American aspirations in Burma. You may call on me for anyone or anything you need to assist you in the task.' Shepilov leaned back in the settee, indicating the discussion was closed.

Keppler drained his brandy glass and rose. As he started up the ladder to the wheelhouse, he was arrested by Shepilov's parting comment :

'We would be most distressed to see you deprived of the material benefits from your Chiang Mai activities, Comrade Keppler.'

He handed the bathrobe to the girl, and eased himself down the ladder into the water. His mind was sorely troubled.

CHAPTER EIGHT

The inter-island flight from Mindanao landed at Cebu City's airport early in the afternoon. Jud engaged the services of a taxi and set out directly for Talisai beach resort.

The taxi crunched to a stop in a gravelled parking area behind the club. Retrieving his suitcase from the front seat, Jud paid the driver. As the taxi backed out of the empty parking lot, Jud stood surveying the low building.

The structure was even more dilapidated than he'd anticipated. Under the overhang of a palm-thatched roof, the bamboo walls were dull gray, mottled cancerously with peeling patches of lustreless varnish. Beside the kitchen's rear entrance, stood an overflowing garbage pail and a stack of empty San Miguel beer crates. Flies buzzed lazily around this refuse. The unraked gravel of the parking lot was littered with scraps of paper and sun-browned sections of broken palm fronds. It was a depressing spectacle. He wondered how Winters had ever expected to attract customers.

Thunder rumbled menacingly. Several large raindrops, advance guards of an approaching squall, slapped onto the roof thatch and pock-marked the dusty gravel. With an apprehensive glance at the darkening sky, he picked up the suitcase. Searching in his pocket, he located the key ring Harper had given him. He strode towards the flagged walk at the side of the building.

The tropical downpour struck in full force as Jud reached the archway in a vine-covered trellis. He ducked inside the entrance, where a faded stretch of overhead awning afforded some protection. Rain drummed on the canvas canopy and cascaded in streams through rips and worn patches. Warily skirting these leaks, he picked his way through weathered rattan chairs and tables towards the roof-protected bar.

Nobody was in attendance behind the bar. Perching himself on one of the rush-seated stools, Jud lowered his suitcase. 'Carlos!' he yelled.

The noise of someone stirring came from the far end of the bar. A tousled mop of black hair, followed by a brown sleep-clouded face rose slowly from the other side of the bar top. The eyes widened in recognition. The expression of mild annoyance at this intrusion into his siesta was dispelled by a widening grin. 'Hey, Boss, where you come from?' Carlos queried.

Winters' accommodation was spartan. The room was small and sparsely furnished. At one end of the room, stood an armoire, its hanging space and shelves housing Winters' limited wardrobe. At the other end, a frayed curtain screened off the toilet, shower and washbowl. In between the extremities were a table and straight-backed chair, serving as a desk; a chest of drawers, crowding against the desk; a large rattan easy chair with faded cigarette-burned cushions; and a narrow cot, at the foot of which sat a large metal trunk. The flaking walls boasted two framed photographic studies of nautical scenes and an outdated calendar.

Carlos had, at Jud's request, produced a stack of bills, receipts and the smudged account books. Seating himself at the table-desk, Jud addressed himself to a study of the current financial picture.

The recorded purchases of liquor and beer tallied with reasonable accuracy with the bar sales. The sales were discouragingly low. It was probable that Carlos did not record a good many of the purchases and simply pocketed the cash returns from this undisclosed bar stock.

Carlos Rivera's wife, Consuelo, supervised food purchasing and the kitchen. In this department, there was a singular discrepancy between purchases and restaurant sales. The excess amounts of foodstuffs bought were sufficient to feed not only the Riveras, their relatives and friends, but a large percentage of the local inhabitants as well. Wryly, Jud noted the inordinately high and recurring incidence of repairs to the kitchen and bar refrigerators. Without doubt, claims of staggering spoilage would be advanced to account for the operational losses.

Now that he'd actually viewed the premises there were some recorded purchases which he found curious. He hadn't paid much attention to these in Makati. He checked back over the accounts for the entire year of operation, to find that such items appeared with consistent regularity. These were paint, paint brushes, mops, brooms, awning canvas, table cloths, napkins and back-bar accessories. The club showed little or no evidence of the usage of these items. In addition, the replacement purchases of dishes and glass-ware suggested that the club was frequently visited by destructive typhoons.

It saddened him that Winters had been systematically swindled. That he was being driven into bankruptcy by his thieving staff was an all too obvious conclusion. Yet, some-how, he felt this didn't fit with Winter's character. He had come to identify closely with Winters and it didn't make sense that a man who had been able to survive in a dog-eat-dog environment of hustlers and fast-buck operators could degenerate so rapidly. From the evidence, however, it look-ed as though Winters had been too sunk in dejection and alcoholism to appreciate his position, or care. And when Jud had seen Winters' quarters, he had been struck by an-other contradiction. In the past, Winters had always dis-played a talent for living well with a marked preference for luxurious surroundings and the company of attractive women. The austerity of the Talisai accommodation didn't fit that pattern. The entire set-up had about it an air of impermanence.

In addition to its lock, the trunk at the foot of the bed was fitted with a hasp and padlock. Locating the correct keys on the ring, Jud unlocked the trunk and lifted the sturdy lid. The trunk was only partially filled. On top, the neatly folded suits were filmed with mildew and gave off a musty odor. He allowed the trunk to air for several min-utes before investigating beyond the first layer.

At the bottom of the trunk, amongst shoes, books and a camera case, was a locked metal box. Jud brought this from the trunk, and sorted once more through the keys until he found the one which opened the box.

The contents of the metal box were a revelation which was to completely alter Jud's thinking and clear up a num-ber of the contradictions which had been puzzling him. The uppermost layer of personal papers – Winters' certifi-cate of naval discharge, his record of courses from the Uni-

46

versity of California, Philippine Coastal Master's papers, legal documents pertaining to his various business enterprises and a photostat copy of his birth certificate – were of little interest. It was what lay beneath which provided a shock.

He examined a number of share certificates with interest. One of these was for 1,000 shares of Winters' Hauling & Storage Company, Incorporated. It was a surprise to find that Winters had not divested himself of all his holdings. Next, was an insurance policy for 20,000 dollars showing Betty-Anne Beekers as the beneficiary. Then came several title deeds to property in California. In a tarnish-blackened silver frame was a photograph of a laughing-eyed girl wearing her blonde hair in a page-boy cut. It bore the inscription : 'Forever Yours – Tina'. Then, at the bottom of the box, Jud came upon a sealed envelope which was to provide the biggest surprise of all.

Inside the envelope were 4,000 American dollars in $100 bills. There were also two bank books. One was for a peso account in the First National City Bank in Manila. It showed a number of withdrawals, leaving a credit balance of 8,000 pesos. The second was for a Canadian dollar savings account in a Vancouver branch of the Bank of Montreal. This account was in the name of John Quentin. The signature on a deposit slip tucked in the book was unmistakably in Winters' handwriting. The last entry recorded in the book was a $9,000 deposit the previous May. The credit balance of the account made Jud purse his lips in a silent whistle. It was 47,000 dollars.

Winters had been a long way, a very long way, from being bankrupt. The evidence of the share certificates, property deeds and bank balances put Winters net worth in excess of 100,000 dollars. The implications were startling.

The Canadian account, which would provide Winters with an undisclosed position of liquidity, was under an assumed name. The conclusion Jud reached was that Winters had been making preparations to leave the Philippines. The floundering beach club was nothing more than an elaborate deception designed to give the impression Winters had lost his savings and was destitute. It was a well conceived and cleverly executed fraud which had taken some time to construct. It would also require the connivance of Carlos and his wife. The plan had probably been to sell the club at a substantial paper loss to Carlos or some other nominee. Later, refurbished and showing profit, the club could be resold at a good figure, with Carlos given a share for his participation in the fraudulent scheme. There were two other likelihoods which suggested themselves. The club was probably doing a better business than that reflected in the accounting; and Jud Winters had not been nearly the excessive drinker he'd pretended.

He gathered up the share certificates, property deeds and the envelope, and transferred them to his own suitcase. Tomorrow, when he'd had a chance to thoroughly air the clothing, he'd repack the trunk and arrange for its shipment to Chiang Mai.

As he washed the grime from his hands at the washbowl, he grinned at his reflection in the brownly-mottled mirror. 'Jud, baby,' he said aloud, 'you're an uncommonly crafty sonuvabitch.'

'Carlos,' Jud questioned, 'did the man I sent from Manila to audit the books ask to check the storeroom?'

Carlos looked surprised. 'No, Boss.'

'Good.' Deciding to satisfy his curiosity, he added, 'Think I'll give it a check-out myself.'

'Sure thing, Boss. I get the key from Mamacita.'

The storage space was windowless. While Winters' living quarters were provided with nothing but a table fan, the storeroom was air-conditioned. Carlos switched on the overhead lighting.

It was pretty much what he'd expected to find. Cases of liquor, liqueurs and tinned foodstuff were stacked along one wall. Shelves were loaded with cartons of glasses, crockery and cutlery. There were piles of new tablecloths and napkins. There was a long mirror and glass shelving, undoubtedly intended for a re-modelling of the back-bar. Tin after tin of sealed paint and varnish, along with cleaning equipment and paint brushes lined a bottom shelf. There were rolls of copper-wire screening and a large bolt of green and white striped awning canvas. Everything was here which would be required to bring the beach club into first class condition.

He motioned for Carlos to switch off the light. As Carlos

48

locked the door from the outside, Jud said, 'Okay, make arrangements for the sale of the club.'

Carlos turned to Jud with a broad smile. 'Okay, Boss. When you sign papers?'

'Tomorrow morning. Have to catch the Manila flight in the afternoon. Have the papers ready before noon.'

The club was constructed in the shape of a letter U on three sides of a central tiled terrace. One arm consisted of the trellis with its extension of awning. A shorter arm was formed by the right-angled building wing containing the storeroom, staff quarters, Winters' room and terminating in changing rooms for the club customers. At the open end of the U, the terrace faced onto the beach. Here, raised to the level of the terrace, a concrete swimming pool provided bathing facilities. The shark-infested coastal waters made such pools standard equipment for all the beach clubs which dotted the shoreline. At both ends of the pool, short flights of stone steps led down to the strip of sandy palm-shaded beach.

He sat on the bottom step watching the huge red ball of sun sinking towards the western horizon. His bare feet absently traced patterns in the warm sand. He tossed the key ring into the air and watched it reflect the evening sunlight as it descended to land with a soft clink in the sand at his feet.

It had struck him while he was examining the storeroom. From the nature of the contents of the locked metal box within the trunk, Winters would not have entrusted his keys to anyone. They would have been hidden in a safe place, or kept on Winters' person. Then how had Harper obtained them?

His thoughts went back to the report of the fatal accident. Winters had met Harper in Cebu City, where they had then rented a small boat to ensure privacy for their discussions. Jud assumed that Winters had not gone to Cebu prepared for an outing in a fishing boat. That meant that he was in the boat fully clothed. Presumably, these keys were in his pocket at the time of the accident.

The conclusion he reached was chilling in its implication. Winters must have been killed in the boat. Harper must have gone through the corpse's clothing to remove anything

49

which could possibly identify the body should the sharks leave anything identifiable. The body had then been pushed over the side to the waiting sharks.

That was how Harper came to have possession of the keys. But why in the name of heaven would Harper hang onto them? He should have just thrown them overboard. Unless he needed the keys. Unless he planned to pass off an imposter for which the keys could provide substantiating identification. Harper had not returned to Talisai. He had no knowledge of the contents of the trunk or its metal box. Obviously, neither had the investigator who had been sent to the beach club some weeks ago.

What motive could Harper possibly have had for killing Winters? This is where Jud reached a startling conclusion. True, Stanford had not been notified by Cantrell of the nature of the Chiang Mai assignment until late December, but it had been hinted at as early as September when Stanford had been recalled from the Phan Loc operation. In fact, he must have been selected for the assignment as much as a month earlier than that. And there, was Harper's motive. The killing of Winters had been a coldly premeditated murder to provide a cover identity for Stanford. Because of nothing more than a striking physical resemblance to a Special Forces major he'd never heard of, Winters had been callously sentenced to death.

There was, of course, no proof of any of this. There had been no witnesses. Jud was basing his reconstruction of a hypothetical crime on wholly circumstantial evidence. But it all dovetailed neatly. Another aspect of the accident which had puzzled him was now logically explained. For Harper, as Sector Chief, to make personal contact with a minor agent, was a flagrant breach of Agency procedure. But a mission such as this, without any official sanction, could hardly be entrusted to an underling. Having passed sentence, Harper would have no choice but to undertake the execution personally.

It added a frightening dimension to the impression he'd formed of Harper following the Makati meeting. He granted that Harper was a dedicated and gifted organizer, planner and administrator, but to detract from this image, he considered Harper as a perfectionist, totally devoid of a sense of humour. Coupled with almost unlimited authority, such

50

a combination could produce a dangerous man. Just how dangerous, Jud was beginning to appreciate.

What if Jud was to voice his suspicion? It would be his word against Harper's. By now, Harper would have removed and destroyed the report of the accident. As far as the world was concerned, it was Major Joe Stanford who was missing and presumed dead. Judson Winters was very much alive. At this moment, he was sitting on the steps of a Talisai beach club, watching another godammed glorious tropical sunset.

PART TWO

THE MUMMERS

CHAPTER ONE

At the Manila head office of Santa Rosa, Jud picked up his passport, an airline ticket to Bangkok and a cash advance against salary and expenses.

Jud stayed only three days in Bangkok, just long enough to complete his non-immigrant formalities and attend to some shopping for clothing, photographic equipment and a number of items he thought might be difficult to obtain in the northern city. On Thursday morning, he cabled the Chiang Mai office that he would be arriving by train the following morning.

At 10:15 a.m., the Northern Express slid smoothly to a stop at the Chiang Mai terminal.

Jud stepped onto the platform. In a sharp contrast to the air-conditioned comfort of the sleeping coach, the heat of the day struck him like a blast from an open furnace. He had been advised that Chiang Mai could be even hotter than Bangkok during the summer season. If today was any criterion, he was prepared to believe it. Still, at an altitude of 1,000 feet, Chiang Mai escaped most of the enervating humidity of the delta.

The station platform was scrupulously clean. Fluted concrete pots containing ornamental shrubs and flowering plants were placed at intervals along the walkway. To the left of the rear entrance to the main building, was a carefully-tended formal garden. The cumulative effect was to encourage a favourable first impression of Chiang Mai.

As Jud entered the airy building, a brown-skinned man dressed casually in white detached himself from a group of Thais. Coming up to Jud, the man smiled and extended his hand. 'You must be Winters,' the man said amiably and, without waiting for confirmation, added. 'I'm Rudolfo. Lucky thing your cable reached me yesterday. Wasn't expecting you until next week and had planned on running up to Chiang Dao this morning.'

Jud shook Rudolfo's hand. 'Sorry if I disrupted your schedule.'

Rudolfo laughed. 'A few days, or a couple of weeks ...
up here, it makes little difference. Have you any luggage?'

Jud pointed out the porter who stood patiently to one
side with Jud's brief case and overnight bag.

'That all?' queried Rudolfo.

'Plus another suitcase and a couple of boxes in the bag-
gage car.'

'Give me your checks. I'll have the driver pick them up
later.'

Waving to the porter to follow, Rudolfo guided Jud to
the parking area in front of the station where a cream Toyota Crown stood waiting. Rudolfo introduced the grinning
driver as Boonsok.

As they drove a short distance along a wide flame-tree
shaded boulevard, Rudolfo outlined the programme he'd arranged.

'I've booked you into the Railway Hotel temporarily,'
Rudolfo explained. 'Mr. Harper wrote instructing me to find
you a villa. He specified a minimum of three bedrooms.
Since I gather you're a bachelor, they must be planning a
company guest house.'

Jud smiled. 'Something along those lines. They want to
move the present office into the new villa. There was a
mention of some of the directors coming up here for big
game hunting.'

Rudolfo snorted derisively. 'The only game they're likely
to track is the two-legged variety. Colonel Garcia was here
last year. The trophy he took back was a dose of clap. But
you'll have plenty of time to prepare for their arrival. None
of them would be caught dead up here this time of year,
or during the rainy season. They shouldn't bother you until November. I've a couple of likely looking houses lined
up. We can take a look at them tomorrow. This afternoon,
I'll pick you up at 4:30 and show you the town. Tomorrow,
we'll check out the villas, then I'll take you along to meet
the people at the Forestry Department and a few other
useful citizens of our village. No rush though. Nothing
moves very fast in this heat.'

'What about your trip to Chiang Dao?'

'No hurry. We'll go there next week. You'll enjoy the
teak forest country. Much cooler than here.'

Jud's first few weeks in Chiang Mai were hectic, leaving him little time to devote to his primary task of setting in motion the area intelligence operation.

He found he had much to learn. In Manila, and in Mindanao, no mention had been made of Thai hardwoods other than teak. Now, he learned that Santa Rosa, in addition to its own plywood requirements, acted as a buying agent for a number of Korean and Japanese mills. There was a steady demand for cheaper timber and peel logs such as yang, pradoo, dang, teng, rung and the redish-yellow makar. Rudolfo placed his emphasis on teak, but did not neglect the bewildering array of lesser species. Jud learned the growing areas and how to differentiate between the grades of logs for each of the esoteric woods.

From Harper, Jud had gathered that teak buying was highly competitive and had formed the erroneous impression this was a matter of price bidding. This was not the case. All teak purchasing was through the Thai government monopoly, the Forest Industry Organization, at a fixed price. The price was high; too high in Rudolfo's estimation, but with every indication that demand and diminishing supply due to poaching and overcutting would drive the price even higher. Where the experience entered the picture was to ensure that Santa Rosa was allocated an edequate portion of the dwindling supply. And in this arena, Rudolfo performed with the flair and élan of a high-wire artist. Although Rudolfo assured Jud it was all a matter of practice, Jud was beset by grave doubts. Becoming Jud Winters, wizard timber-buyer, to say nothing of Jud Winters, master-spy, looked like a pretty complicated act.

In essence, the secret of successful buying demanded skill, guile, diplomacy and the judicious application of bribes and favours. Jud quickly recognized that Rudolfo was a master at the art. It was a neat trick to strike a balance whereby first class teak logs were made readily available, yet keep the kickbacks within reasonable limits. Jud watched and learned.

It was essential that Rudolfo show Jud as much of the forest region as possible. Even had they had more time, Rudolfo explained, it would still have been a rushed job. By mid-June, the rains would make travel difficult; by July, next to impossible. During the season of heavy rains, logging operations virtually ceased. As Rudolfo laughingly pointed out, even elephants have their limitations.

For the up-country junkets, they left the air-conditioned Toyota in Chiang Mai and travelled instead by the company-owned Land Rover, which could negotiate the unsurfaced roads and rough tracks leading to their more remote destinations. As they skimmed along on the surfaced highways, or bounced and jolted into the mountains, Rudolfo imparted a steady stream of information. He gave penetrating character sketches of the officials and people connected with the forest industry they were to meet at the next destination, or elaborated on those at the preceeding point of call. His conversation was liberally spiced with anecdotes and historical background. Often, he would stop the driver to draw Jud's attention to some interesting feature of the terrain. It was obvious that Rudolfo had become deeply attached to this part of the country. It was equally apparent that his feelings were reciprocated. Wherever they went, Rudolfo was welcomed with warmth and genuine affection. Jud hoped fervently that this same welcome would be extended to him when he was left to do the job alone.

Jud questioned Rudolfo concerning terrorist activities. Rudolfo conceded that there was unrest, but was undecided what could be attributed to Communist directed subversion, general dissatisfaction and demonstration against government imposed restrictions, ethnic rivalries, or simple banditry. He conceded it to be a combination of all four, with armed brigands the chief culprits. In his first year, he stated, he'd been stopped several times in the more remote regions. Since then, he'd been unmolested. He attributed this to the fact that his occupation was of no political significance to any local guerrilla forces and that it was known by now that he carried very little money. By now, through whatever strange but efficient bush telegraph which operated in the region, Jud's presence would be known. The immunity enjoyed by Rudolfo should extend to Jud. Nevertheless, Rudolfo cautioned, it was best not to tempt fate by travelling the roads by night and, at all times but *especially* following the February poppy harvest, he should keep well clear of the opium caravan routes where the trigger-happy Kuomintang guards were in the habit of shooting first and asking questions later.

It was not until he was almost due to leave on his mid-May transfer to Manila that Rudolfo disclosed two additional sources of teak. A highly illegal but nonetheless brisk trade flourished in smuggled Burmese logs. Jud was introduced to a colonel of the Thai Border Patrol Police who, for a modest fee, could make these logs available. The second avenue of supply was more complicated. Teak logs from both Burma and Thailand were smuggled across the Mekong into Laos, where they were rough-sawn and sold back into Thailand as processed Laotian timber. Rudolfo told Jud how and where such teak could be procured, but warned that neither the quality nor the supply could be relied upon. It was, at best, an emergency source which Rudolfo had utilized only in times of dire shortages.

This Laotian source interested Jud. He questioned Rudolfo at more length and found that while there was good quality teak in Laos, the Laotian forest industry wasn't developed sufficiently to be reliable.

'Is it cheaper than Thai teak?' Jud asked.

'A damn sight cheaper.'

'Why couldn't it be bought in Laos and shipped to Bankok as duty-free transit cargo?'

'In theory, it could be,' Rudolfo conceded. 'Thought about doing it last year when the local price went up. But there are a few drawbacks. You would have to ship by the Thai Express Transport Organization. I figured that one way or another, they'd manage to make it a costly operation. To protect their own pricing, they'd undoubtedly make it too expensive to warrant the risk. Then, I just couldn't figure out how to get quality control in Laos. I decided to leave it alone and I'd advise you to do the same.'

Jud nodded in agreement and dropped the subject. Soon, very soon, he'd be making contact with the agent by the code name 'Wood', Jean-Paul LeFarge in Vientiane. If some sort of legitimate teak trade could be worked out between them, it could simplify and facilitate matters as a plausible business relationship.

CHAPTER TWO

The villa Jud selected was situated at the far end of the westward extension of Rajdamnern Road. It was a large house in extensive grounds on the slope at the base of Doi Suthep. To the north, the property adjoined the university lands. The villa itself was built on sharply rising ground which became, at the rear, the steep face of the mountain. It was an ideally secluded location.

During the limited time his travels with Rudolfo allowed him in Chiang Mai, Jud progressed the renovation. He engaged the services of a contractor and firm of decorators.

The back of the house was almost flush with the sharp rise. The front rose to a height of two storey's on tall supports. This space allowed free circulation of air beneath the front section of the villa and formed a convenient carport. With the contractor, Jud laid out plans to utilize one third of this space to better advantage. The front portion would be constructed as the company office, to the rear of which, cutting directly into the earth and rock, would be a photographic lab.

To Rudolfo's amusement, Jud constantly carried his Nikon camera on their field trips. Shooting roll after roll of film, Jud had established himself as an avid shutterbug.

It was a week after his arrival in Chiang Mai before Jud found time to pay respects to J. Anthony Carver at the American Consulate. Jud found it a disturbing experience.

Carver had been advised to expect Winters, whom he obviously considered a lowly paid-informer and an object for contempt. It was equally evident that Carver considered himself a cut above the average mortal. The Vice-Consul received Jud with patronizing condescension.

Carver's interest quickened slightly when he learned Winters would be called up to make frequent up-country trips in conjunction with his employment as a hardwoods buyer. Carver advised Winters to keep on the alert and render reports concerning Communist activities in the remote areas.

Jud agreed to keep his eyes open and report anything of interest he might encounter.

It was almost certain that Carver's office was bugged. Jud found it alarming that Carver exercised no security precautions. In Jud's estimation, Carver was an idiot, a pompous ass and a man to be avoided a much as possible.

It was several days after his meeting with Carver before Jud had an opportunity to call on Perkins.

The USIS Information Centre was located in a large converted residence, its wooden facing painted a reddish-brown. Jud drove through the wide gates and parked to the right of the building.

The girl at the library and reading room information desk directed Jud to the far end of the spacious ground floor, to where a doorway revealed a narrow balustraded staircase leading to the upper floor. Jud mounted the stairs, pausing at the landing to gaze out the window. He paid scant attention to the view of lawn, road and walled wat across the street. His thoughts were on the meeting about to take place. Perkins would be a key figure in the operation. He would be the only Thailand-based agent to know that Winters was the Area Coordinator. The success or failure of the resuscitated network and the Burmese project would hinge largely on how effectively Perkins functioned as Jud's communications link. Jud prayed fervently that he wasn't about to encounter another Carver.

The card in the slot beside the door read: 'C. R. Perkins'. Jud stood in the doorway, observing the young man who sat behind a desk littered with papers, files and stacks of books.

Absorbed in scanning the contents of a thick folder, Perkins was unaware of the presence of a visitor. His brow was furrowed in concentration. Glasses perched on his freckle-dusted pug nose. He ran his fingers in a combing gesture through tousled brown hair, then idly scratched the back of his neck.

Jud's heart sank. He guessed Perkins to be in his early twenties, twenty-five at the outside. Jud had expected an older, more experienced, man for the assignment.

'Mister Perkins?' Jud spoke from the doorway.

The young man started. Sunlight glinted off his glasses as he looked up. 'Yes?' he questioned.

'My name's Winters.' There was no reaction. There shouldn't have been any. Perkins should know only the code name, 'Pitt'.

Perkins smiled and rose. 'Come in Mr. Winters. What can I do for you?'

'Just a social call,' Jud said easily. 'Ed Gledow, in Manila, asked me to drop by and say hello.' Now, he waited for a reaction. 'Gledow' was the identifying codeword.

Perkins hesitated for only a fraction of a second. His smile didn't alter. 'Ed Gledow,' he said. 'Didn't know he was in the Philippines. Haven't seen him since New York . . . must be all of two years. How is he?'

Jud felt a little easier. The kid hadn't blown his cool. He'd just met his boss for the first time and he'd handled it like a pro. Smiling slightly in approval, Jud said, 'Ed's getting by. He's doing pretty well in the import, export game.'

Perkins reached down to close the folder and push it to the side of his desk. 'It's about quitting time,' he said. 'How about joining me for a drink and bringing me up to date.' With an impish grin, he added, 'Fancy old Eddie getting tinto import, export. Thought he was all set in the advertising biz.'

Perkins chatted easily as they passed through the downstairs reading room, but lapsed into silence once he was in the Toyota. It was Jud who broke the silence.

'Is your office bugged?' Jud questioned.

'I don't think so. No reason it should be. But it doesn't pay to take chances.'

Jud nodded agreement. 'By the way,' he said, 'the first name's Jud . . . short for Judson. You'd better start calling me Jud.'

'Okay. Mine's Chris.'

Perkins had been observing Jud quizzically. Noting the scrutiny, Jud smiled thinly. 'Am I what you anticipated?' he asked.

'I don't know. I've been sitting here on ice for four months . . . waiting for 'Gledow'. Was beginning to think the game had been called off on account of rain. Did have a sort of mental picture, but you don't fit it. You're younger than I expected.'

Jud could have made the same comment. He let it pass. 'Where were you briefed?' he asked.

'Virginia.'

'How much background were you given?'

'Very little. All I know is that they consider this an important operation. I'm to follow your instructions and orders implicitly and without question. Also, I'm to protect your cover identity, whatever it is, with my life.'

'I doubt if that will prove necessary,' Jud said drily. 'You know all the key agents by location and code name?'

'Yes, but none of their actual identities. Except you ... from about fifteen minutes ago.'

'You will know only two more, the agents with whom you will have personal contact. One of them is the man you know as 'Garth'. He's the Reverend Doctor Charles Cox, of the Mission to Christ's Karen Mission School in Mae Sariang. Within a few days, you will receive a letter from the good doctor requesting assistance with his English classes. Commencing next week you will become closely involved through your AUA Language Program, with Cox's praiseworthy endeavor. You will visit Mae Sariang on a weekly basis. From time to time, I'll give you verbal messages for Cox. Neither of your contacts know who I am, nor will they. Their direction will come through you from Pitt.''

'Who's my other contact?'

' "Emily" ' in Bangkok.' Jud noted a quickening of Perkins' interest. He felt almost sorry to have to disabuse the young man. 'How often do you get to Bangkok?'

'About once a month. Sometimes twice. Depends on whether or not the director wants to visit the bright lights.'

'We'll work out something a little less dependent on whim. When do you expect to make the next visit?'

'End of the month.'

'That's when you meet the man called "Emily". He's the owner and proprietor of a bar-restaurant called the Windjammer. It's located on Sukhumvit Road, near the Rex Hotel. It's going to become one of your favorite haunts on your excursions to the big city.'

They turned through the stone gateposts onto the freshly gravelled driveway leading to the villa. The sun was already well below the crest of the mountain and the house and grounds were in shadow. The gardener was still working, thinning a clump of shrubs, but the workmen had departed for the day.

Jud conducted Perkins on a brief tour of the empty villa. In the partially completed study, Jud apologized for the clutter of tools and wood shavings. Pointing to the bookshelves, he said, 'There is the excuse for our association over the next few months.'

'Don't quite follow you,' Perkins said with a puzzled frown.

'Begrudgingly, you're going to help me fill up those shelves with books ordered through you and borrowed from your library. Since I'm a lazy bastard, you'll not only bring me the books you lend me, but pick them up when I'm finished with them. Many of the reports I receive and send will be through you. They will be on microfilm. I'll show you how they'll be inserted in the books.'

Perkins nodded his understanding, but made no comment.

Jud continued. 'Do you play chess?'

'A little. Not well.'

'Your modesty becomes you. You're about to become an enthusiast. Supplying me with books from the USIS library isn't calculated to spark much of a friendship. In fact, you'll grumble and let it be known that I'm one cheap sonuvabitch with a lot of crust to ask such favours. Chess will be the catalyst which converts your reluctant cooperation into a more enduring relationship. It will account for your frequent visits to the villa. Later, as our budding friendship ripens, you will also develop an interest in photography. I'll tell you more about that aspect before your next trip to Bangkok.

As they descended the front steps to the carport, Perkins said, 'I've been holding onto a couple of parcels for you. They're in the office safe. When do you want them?'

'That'll be code books and a supply of high-speed fine-grained film for microphotography. I'll let you know when I need them. You should also receive a couple of heavy crates within a few days. Have you someplace secure to store them?'

'Should be okay in the publication storeroom if they're well sealed and don't stay there too long. Anything else?'

'Get in the car. On the drive back into town I'll give you

a couple of verbal messages I want encoded and sent out by diplomatic pouch. And I want a special communication forwarded to Wood in Vientiane. It must be sent by the quickest routing possible. His activities often make it difficult to locate him. You will advise him to be present at the Concorde Restaurant between 1:00 and 2:00 p.m. on Saturday, June 8th. He will be contacted by someone using the identifying code word '*cafard*'. Got that?'

'Yes, sir, if you'll tell me how to spell the name of the restaurant and that code word.'

Jud spelled both words. He was gaining confidence in Perkins. The young man had a faculty for grasping things quickly. 'And drop that "sir" crap,' Jud added.

'Sorry. Afraid it's automatic. I address my superiors and elders that way as a matter of courtesy. At my age, that's almost everybody.'

CHAPTER THREE

By the spring of 1952, Heinrich Keppler had been a resident of Chiang Mai for six years. Happily, he had discovered in himself a natural flair for the antique business which provided his cover. From the outset, his dealings had met with success and profit.

In order to establish himself more firmly in the small community, Heinrich decided a suitable marriage would be advantageous. After due deliberation, he settled on Sasima, the eldest daughter of the Vice-Governor of Chiang Mai province, as the object of his affection. Through mutual Thai friends, he arranged a meeting with the girl. Sasima displayed interest, which grew to infatuation, in response to Heinrich's ardent court.

A stumbling block was encountered in the opposition of Sasima's family to the match. Being of high station and distantly related to the Thai royal family, Sasima's parents considered her marriage to a *farang* as being out of the question.

Heinrich was not discouraged, being of the firm conviction that persistence could overcome most, if not all, obstacles. He was proved correct. A combination of Sasima's importunings, and growing evidence of Keppler's improving financial status, gradually eroded parental resistance. In November, at a ceremony in the bride's home, Heinrich and Sasima were joined as man and wife.

Although his suit had not been inspired by romantic considerations, Heinrich was fond of Sasima. If she failed to arouse his deeper passions, Heinrich still had every reason to be well pleased. In time, as she presented him in turn with two sons, Franz and Kurt, and a daughter, little Sasima, Heinrich's affection grew stronger. He considered himself a good husband and father. At home, he was attentive and indulgent. His infidelities were conducted with discretion and far enough removed from the local scene to preclude detection and censure. There are, he often thought, some decided advantages to a solid grounding in clandestine activities.

From the middle 50's, when the political focus shifted from his immediate area of operations, Heinrich's espionage function made few demands on his time. His intelligence-gathering organization functioned smoothly and with a minimum of supervision. He was able to evolve a pattern of extended business trips which took him to Europe in the spring and the major cities of Southeast Asia each fall. He was subject to recall at a moment's notice, but for well over a decade no such emergency had arisen. He had been lulled into complacent acceptance of his well-ordered routine.

On this trip, in the spring of 1968, there was a marked difference. It was no consolation to Heinrich to appreciate that the problem was of his own making. He mentally kicked himself for having recorded his suspicions concerning American interest in Burma.

Shepilov had been about as subtle as a typhoon. Heinrich had been jolted by the unpleasant reminder that the comfortable existence he had so painstakingly built in Chiang Mai could be terminated abruptly and irrevocably at the whim of his masters.

The trip began badly and became progressively worse. Heinrich's delayed Paris arrival made it necessary for him to reschedule a number of appointments. The solace and sexual satisfaction provided by his mistress, Heide, failed

66

to soothe his jangled nerves. They quarrelled and Heide refused to accompany Heinrich on the rest of his trip unless his temper improved.

All through the trip, Heinrich had half-expected to be recalled to Thailand. That he had received no such summons, had not allayed his gnawing concern. In Barcelona, he reached a decision. He cabled cancellations of his remaining appointments in Madrid and London and booked an Iberia flight to Rome and an Alitalia flight to Bangkok. Feeling a belated guilt concerning Heide, he got through to her by telephone. Explaining that he'd received a cable advising him of illness in the family, he apologized, assured Heide that he loved her and that he would forward a cheque from his Swiss account. Heide expressed cool sympathy.

On the long flight from Rome, Heinrich had ample time to reflect on his actions of the past weeks. With candour, he admitted to grevious errors of judgment. At the root of his troubles was the simple fact that he'd overreacted to Shepilov's implied threat. Fear that his position in Chiang Mai might be in jeopardy had caused Heinrich to magnify petty annoyances out of all proportion. As a consequence, his usual business acumen had deserted him. In the months to come, some fence mending amongst his business associates would be required. He did not relish the thought. Even less appealing, was the fact that he would arrive back in Chiang Mai well ahead of schedule, with several weeks of blisteringly hot weather in store. The conclusion he'd reached in the bar of the Ritz Hotel in Barcelona had overridden his distaste for the heat. As he'd seen it, the only solution was to return to Chiang Mai and devote his energies to proving, or disproving, the suppositions which had placed him in this dilemma in the first place.

Normally, as each business trip neared completion, Heinrich found himself looking forward to rejoining his family with mounting pleasure. This homecoming was an exception. The Alitalia flight was late in its Bangkok arrival. Heinrich missed his Chiang Mai connection and had to spend several hours in the domestic flight departure lounge. The realization that his business trip had been something less than successful did little to ease his irritation. And he was beset by the knowledge that he could look forward to being afflicted with the rash and prickly heat which always bothered him in this season.

Heinrich's dark mood persisted for a week following his return from Europe. Gradually, he returned to an approximation of his ebullient self. There were, however, several things which disturbed him and it was most irksome to recognize that he needn't have cut short his trip.

His sub-agents, with contacts in such fertile producers of information as the American Embassy, the Joint U.S. Military Advisory Group, and from within the Burmese clique itself, reported that while the original overtures had offered substantial assistance in financing and arms, there had been no follow-up action. While the financial character of the offer indicated CIA involvement, the delay in following through presented contradictory evidence. More than two decades of exposure to CIA methods of operation had convinced Heinrich that one of its cardinal faults was impatience. He was surprised and concerned that there had been no developments over the past weeks.

He turned his attention to reports concerning newly arrived foreigners in Chiang Mai. Apart from transient tourists, the influx was remarkably light. There were only three.

A Japanese businessman, Mr. Senzo Nakura, had arrived on April 11th. He was staying with Japanese friends. The report was slim. Nakura represented a large Tokyo industrial conglomerate. So far, the interest he'd displayed had been in raw materials; fluorspar, tobacco and hardwoods. On the surface, innocuous inquiries, but Heinrich knew better than to dismiss Nokura lightly.

Despite Shepilov's disclaimer, Heinrich knew the Russians were very much alarmed by the creeping Japanese economic infiltration of the sub-continent. Japan had the industrial capacity to sustain a modern war, was slowly consolidating access to natural resources on a worldwide scale and, like Russia, probably had never abandoned dreams of empire. Shepilov had dismissed this threat as easily contained by naval power, yet Heinrich was aware of the deep underlying Slavic fear that one day the industrial might of Japan could become wedded to the manpower resources of China. The humiliation of the crushing Russian defeat at the hands of the Japanese at the turn of the century was still a galling reminder of Japanese capabilities. Heinrich was very much alive to the weight placed on reports of Japanese activities by his superiors.

An American, Judson Q. Winters, had arrived in Chiang Mai on April 19th. His employment was with Santa Rosa Lumber & Plywood Company, where he was taking over as local manager.

Some years previously, Heinrich had investigated Santa Rosa and their local buyer, Rudolfo Carbella. There were American interests involved with the Manila-based company, but essentially it was a Philippine owned and operated concern. Heinrich had concluded both it and its representatives were nothing more than what they purported to be.

There were, however, two items of significance in the report on Winters. His occupation presented him with an opportunity to travel widely throughout the area. To Heinrich's mind, such mobility alone warranted caution. Then, Winters had called on Carver. Heinrich knew that Carver was Lindstrom's successor, however the fact that agents had diminished during the latter part of Lindstrom's tenure, and had not been expanded since Carver's takeover, led Heinrich to believe that a secondary intelligence channel existed. So, while Winters' visit could have been nothing more than a courtesy call on the consulate, as a precautionary measure, Heinrich would request a background check.

The most recently arrived foreigner was also an American, Lieutenant Colonel Clinton D. Bridgeman, U.S. Army. He was taking up staff duties with the Radio Research Field Unit. The 7th RRU was but one of thousands of electronic listening posts girdling the globe, monitoring friend and foe alike, to feed continuous data back to the computers of National Security Agency headquarters at Fort Meade, Maryland. In at least one area of NSA'S operations, Keppler was under no illusions concerning the effectiveness. NSA's skills at breaking codes and ciphers had drastically limited the flow of radio communications by and between Heinrich and his organization. Return to the horse-and-buggy era of espionage, the complicated and time consuming 'dead drop' and personal courier, had imposed annoyances Heinrich would sooner forget.

In the normal course of events, any officer or enlisted man joining one of the NSA units in the area, received

Heinrich's particular attention. In Bridgeman's case, there were even more compelling reasons for special consideration. A lengthy coded message outlining his military background had preceded Bridgeman's arrival.

Bridgeman was forty years of age. He graduated from West Point in 1948. Following service in Korea, he had gone to post-graduate studies in mathematics and physics. In 1956, he held a staff job with USIB – United States Intelligence Board – in Washington. From 1958 to 1964, Bridgeman served as military attache in Saigon, Algiers and Ankara. In 1964, he was assigned for a three year stint of staff duties with the newly-formed Defence Intelligence Agency. He went from the Pentagon to Fort Meade, presumably in preparation for this Thailand posting.

Bridgeman's entire career, with the possible exception of Korea, had been devoted to military intelligence. On the face of it, to be seconded from DIA to NSA, was unusual. NSA set its peculiar electronic wizardry apart from the mundane functions of the other intelligence agencies. Bridgeman's postgraduate studies could have a bearing, or, and to Heinrich a more likely answer, a *black operation* was in process of being launched. In such a case, inter-agency rivalries could be set aside and the lieutenant colonel could even be cooperating with the CIA.

As Heinrich reasoned, the appearance of an officer of Lieutenant Colonel Bridgeman's qualification, at this time, and in this place, could hardly be coincidence.

CHAPTER FOUR

Jud was lunching in the Concorde Restaurant in Vientiane. As he toyed with his salad and cold lobster, he kept his eyes on the noontime customers. A number of Frenchmen were assembled at the bar, noisily engaged in a game of dice. At the tables clustered around the dance floor, American, French and Lao patrons enjoyed their mid-day repast. Nowhere could he locate LeFarge. As Master Sergeant Charles Dubois, LeFarge, was well known to Jud. He wondered if, like himself, Dubois had undergone a facial transformation to assume his present role. Or it might be that LeFarge had not received the message.

Promptly at 1:00 pm, a group of three Frenchmen entered the bar-restaurant. After exchanging ribald pleasantries with the dice players, they proceeded to a reserved table. From the deference of the head waiter, it was apparent the three were regular and respected customers.

Apart from the absence of uniform, LeFarge was unchanged from the master sergeant who had served as Stanford's second-in-command nine months earlier. Jud wondered if Cantrell had arranged LeFarge's presence in Laos, knowing that Stanford was destined to be Area Coordinator. If so, Jud owed Cantrell a debt of gratitude.

Jud watched the trio. It was LeFarge who ordered for the three and approved the wine. LeFarge dominated the animated conversation. From the attitudes of LeFarge's companions, from their ready laughter and nods of assent, Jud deduced that LeFarge held a position of authority.

At 1:25, Jud placed his napkin on the checked tablecloth and motioned for his bill. Counting out kip to pay the bill, Jud added a generous tip. Pushing back his chair, he rose unhurriedly to his feet. It was time to make his play.

As LeFarge was in the act of raising his filled wine glass, Jud passed the table. Seemingly by accident, he jostled the extended elbow. The contents of the glass cascaded onto LeFarge.

'*Merde!*' exclaimed LeFarge. Tilting back in his chair, he looked in dismay at the wine dripping from the matted black hair on his chest and the widening red stain on his open-necked shirt.

'Excuse me,' Jud said mildly.

'*Salaud*,' growled LeFarge.

Jud eased his foot to a position against the rear leg of LeFarge's chair. 'What did you say?' he questioned politely.

LeFarge glared up at him without recognition. '*Salaud. Salaud Americain*,' he snarled.

With a swift motion of his foot, Jud swept the chair from beneath the precariously-balanced Frenchman. LeFarge crashed to the floor. Throughout the restaurant, conversation ceased abruptly.

Jud was all to well aware of the agility of the stocky

71

Frenchman. As though shot upwards from a catapult, Le-Farge bounded to his feet. Quick as he was, Jud could not avoid the roundhouse punch which grazed his right cheek stingingly.

'*Cafard Tonkinois,*' Jud snapped angrily.

For a fraction of a second, LeFarge hesitated. In that instant, Jud caught the Frenchman full in the mouth with a short left cross. Stunned by the blow, LeFarge lurched backwards into an adjoining table. The two Lao, who had been quietly enjoying their lunch, now looked down in consternation at LeFarge, who lay sprawled in the wreckage of food and cutlery which a moment earlier had been their meal.

Jud heard the scraping of chairs and the *snick* of a switchblade. From the corner of his eye, Jud saw the flash of the blade as the man behind him lunged. Swaying sideways, Jud pivoted. The lethal thrust passed close enough to slash Jud's shirt. Grasping the man's wrist, Jud jerked him forward to deliver a knee in the crotch. As his opponent doubled in agony, Jud brought his raised foot down so that the full weight of his heel smashed onto the man's instep. As Jud released his grip, the knife clattered onto the table and the man sank to the floor to lie groaning and clutching his groin.

Across the table, the second man was pulling a revolver from the pocket of his tight trousers. Measuring the distance, Jud grasped the edge of the table. He tensed . . .

'*Assez Jacques!*' rasped LeFarge from the debris of the broken table.

The man named Jacques hesitated in confusion. Jud relaxed his grip on the table. LeFarge rose to his feet. He explored the inside of his mouth with his tongue, grimaced, and spat a broken tooth onto the floor. He spoke in rapid French. 'We want no trouble here, Jacques. I should not have lost my temper with this clumsy fool.'

The group of dice-playing Frenchmen had abandoned their game and started to surge threateningly forward. Le-Farge halted them with a motion of his hand. Several Americans had started to rise from their tables, but subsided when they saw the Frenchmen stop. A hum of conversation started up again.

Rubbing a trickle of blood from the corner of his mouth

with his thumb, LeFarge gave a lop-sided grin and addressed Jud in English, 'You have a punch like the kick of an Algerian camel, *Monsieur*, but you must be crazy to start a fight against such odds.'

Michel, the taller of the two restaurant proprietors, had come from behind the bar to stand hovering at the edge of the brief fight. Sensing the danger was past, he moved forward. Gesturing excitedly, he complained of the damage. With an obscene jerk of his finger, LeFarge silenced the owner's tirade. 'Charge it to my account,' LeFarge said curtly. Mollified, but muttering angrily, Michel withdrew.

The man on the floor had struggled to a sitting position. LeFarge glanced at him, saying to Jacques, 'Help Yves. We'd better get out of here before *les flics* arrive.' Turning to Jud, LeFarge spoke once more in English. 'The management isn't happy with us, my impetuous friend. I suggest we remove ourselves to someplace where you can repay the drink you wasted on my shirt.' LeFarge laughed at his own witticism. The tension which still pervaded the bar, eased.

Outside the restaurant, LeFarge ushered Jud into a parked Citroën. Getting in behind the wheel, LeFarge slammed the door. As he eased the car into the street, LeFarge said, 'You believe in pretty rough introductions, *Monsieur* Pitt. You're lucky you didn't hit me any harder, or I might not have been able to stop Jacques. He's an excellent shot.'

Jud chuckled. 'The name,' he said, 'is Jud. Jud Winters ... I didn't expect you to react so violently to a little spilled wine.'

Le Farge shrugged. 'I have a quick temper, and around here you will find many places where Americans are not too popular. You took a big chance starting a fight.'

'Oh, I don't think so Charles. You and I have handled tougher citizens in the past.'

LeFarge started. Frowning, he looked closely at Jud. His eyebrows arching, LeFarge gave a low whistle. '*Mon Dieu*, Joe!... I thought your voice seemed familiar. But with that hair and moustache, it's impossible to recognize you. And they've done something to your face. Made you better looking. In fact, *mon Commandant*, a *beau garçon*.'

Smiling, Jud said, 'Sorry I can't say the same for you. You're the same ugly bastard you always were, in spite of a change of name.'

73

LeFarge laughed, then winced and tenderly explored his mouth and lip with an exploring finger. 'Even the name is unchanged,' he said. 'In Corsica, I was christened Jean-Paul Etienne Ciavaldini. When my father died and my mother moved to Lille, she must have found the name too troublesome. She reverted to her maiden name – LeFarge.'

'So Dubois was only a *nom de geurre*?'

'Yes, exactly. I'm happy to be back with my true name . . . and with my old associates of the *Union Corse*. Now, I'm a *capo*. It isn't so much a cover identity as it is for real.'

'Convenient,' Jud said drily.

'Very. Picking a fight with a Corsican *capo* can get you killed very, very dead.'

'Didn't expect your pals to be of quite such murderous intent, but I'd have promoted the scrap anyway. With a guy like you, it's about the only way to begin a friendship.'

'We're supposed to become asshole buddies?'

'That we are, and, I hope, business associates as well.'

LeFarge looked questioningly at Jud. 'What do you want to do now, or are we just going to drive around and gab?'

'No. Now, we hit five or six of your favourite bars, where our unlikely, but growing friendship will become a topic for local gossip. In the process, we'll get bombed out of our skulls.'

'A pleasure,' LeFarge said, beaming. He turned left from Rue Chanthakoumma onto Rue San Sen Thai. 'We can start here at the Tropicana,' he said. 'You buying?'

'What else . . . I'm an American, aren't I?'

From the Tropicana, they touched base at the Constellation, Bar Mekong, the Settha Palace and finally, Lulu's. It was a progressively convincing performance.

Sunlight streaming through a curtained window woke Jud. He sat up, and winced. His breath was sour and reeked of stale liquor fumes.

Vaguely, he remembered that he had consented to accompany his good old buddy Jean-Paul home. He had a fuzzy recollection of LeFarge driving a weaving course through deserted streets, and that somewhere along the line they'd hit a gatepost.

Jud surveyed the room. His clothes were heaped on a chair. At the end of the room, an opened door gave access

74

to a bathroom. He got out of bed gingerly and headed in that direction.

He found LeFarge sitting in a chair in the living room. The Frenchman was clad only in shorts. In front of him, on a low coffee table, was a bottle of cognac. The maid entered and placed two cups and a pot of coffee on the table. Jean-Paul poured two steaming mugs of black coffee, topping them up with cognac. 'If you feel as bad as I do, you can use one of Dr. LeFarges handy home remedies.'

'What in hell did we drink in lieu of booze?' Jud asked as he sank into a chair opposite LeFarge. 'My mouth tastes like the trailing edge of a careless Indian's dhoti.'

'Maybe bourbon and cognac aren't the best mixers. Toward the end of the evening, you were insisting on cognac with a bourbon chaser. Man, we really drank up a storm.' After a sip of the scalding coffee, Jean-Paul added, 'Since you were picking up the tab for our little party, I presume that extends to a smashed headlight and a crumpled fender.'

'The hell it does.'

'That's what I was afraid of. Cheap sonuvabitch. Remind me to go by pedi-cab the next time you feel like hitting the town.' Jean-Paul said with a grimace.

Jud grinned. 'Much damage? Seem to remember you clipped the gate coming in.'

'It won't cost much to fix the gate.'

Jud gazed around the room. 'Pad wired?' he asked.

'No. But grab your cup and we'll go out on the terrace,' Jean-Paul said, picking up his mug, the cognac bottle and the coffee pot.

When they were seated at a glass-topped table beneath a vine-covered trellis, Jean-Paul said, 'There's a time for fun, and a time for work. I suppose this is the latter.'

'Uh huh.'

'When do you want me to switch over and start pushing the paper work your way?'

'Soon. Maybe next week. I'll let you know.'

'And now?'

'Now, I'd like a rundown on a few things.

'Have there been any recent area developments you would consider significant?'

Jean-Paul deliberated before answering. 'There are three

75

things which might be of interest.' Again, he paused to consider.

'The Chinese Army Engineers have started construction of another road in Northern Laos. The others all run through Phong Saly province to various points in North Viet-Nam. This one starts on the Yunnan province border at Meng-Lan and is surveyed almost due south to Muong-Sai. Its a double-surfaced all-weather road capable of handling heavy traffic. Under the terms of the agreement signed by Phoumi Nosavan in Peking, in 1962, the road's quite legal. The only puzzling thing is, what the hell's the purpose?

'Muong-Sai is a nothing place and can't possibly be the intended terminus. As I see it, there are three possibilities. It can be purely a face-saving device in answer to American highway construction in Viet-Nam and Thailand. It can be a bid to annex territory in Northern Laos. Or, extended further south and west, it might indicate an intention to step-up support to Commie insurgents in both Laos and Northeastern Thailand. My bet would be the latter. Anyway, I'll keep you posted as the roadbuilding goes ahead.

'The next thing is that, within the last three weeks, the People's Army have moved two new divisions into the Paoshan and Want'ing areas, close to the Burmese border. Could mean nothing more than routine shifts of deployment. I'll keep you advised on troop movements.'

As Jean-Paul lapsed into silence, Jud prompted, 'That's two. What's the third item?'

'Oh, sorry. Yeah, well the other thing is that I've received a report that Colonel Tsuji **has** shown up in Kunming.'

Jud took it that Tsuji must be Japanese. He'd heard the name someplace; but couldn't connect it with an event. He frowned.

Jean-Paul noticed Jud's bewilderment. He grinned. 'Gather that Tsuji wasn't mentioned in your briefing. Not surprising. He dropped out of sight about six years ago.'

'Who is he, and what makes his presence in Kunming noteworthy?'

'Colonel Masanobu Tsuji. During World War II, he was Chief of Staff to General Yamashita's 25th Imperial Army in the Malaya, Singapore invasion.

'In 1939, Tsuji was appointed to the Headquarters Staff of the Japanese Expeditionary Forces in China. In Nanking, he became actively involved with the Tao Renmei Undo – the East Asian Federation Movement. Basically, the concept of the movement is that Asians should never fight Asians. For Tsuji, who is violently anti-Caucasian and fanatically pro-Oriental, the movement suited him beautifully.

'After the war, Tsuji figured he might get caught up in the war crime trials. Instead of returning to Japan, he went to ground in Southeast Asia. For three years, he wandered around disguised as a Buddhist monk. For all I know, he *was* an ordained monk. Anyway, when the heat was off, he returned to Japan. He became a Councillor in the National Diet. He also got his ass back into the Tao Renmei Undo, and became quite a wheel in the movement. Only now they'd changed the concept a little and instead of an Asian federation they were just pumping for close cultural and economic cooperation.

'The interesting thing is that back in '62 he was here in Vientiane with a Japanese mission. One day he disappeared. He was supposed to have been seen in monk's robes walking north from Vientiane. When he didn't reappear, most people figured he'd gone into seclusion in some remote vat, or become a hermit monk. Nothing more was heard for almost four years, then he was reported to have re-established contact with his old Chinese buddies in Nanking. Don't know if the disappearing act was his own idea, or if the movement planted him back in China. It doesn't matter much one way or the other. He's and old man in his late sixties by now ... and his brand of Asian cooperation is a little hard to sell at this point in Chinese history.'

'Don't sell him short,' Jud said. 'In the course of history, some pretty durable movements have been founded by a few dedicated fanatics. Keep a watching brief on his activities.' Jud poured himself some more coffee and laced it with cognac. With his next question, he deftly switched the conversation into a new area. 'What do you know about the forest industry in Laos? To be more specific the teak log business?'

Jean-Paul's face registered curiosity. 'Not much. A bit out of my line. Why?'

'Can you get me some prime teak logs ... about 200 metric tons?'

'If it's here, I can get it. I may not know teak, but with

77

organization we've got I could get you the crown jewels on twenty-four hours notice. Where and when do you want the teak?'

'About a month to six weeks. Here in Vientiane,' Jud answered. He smiled. 'You haven't asked why?'

'Mine not to question why.'

'You're a credit to the best traditions of the Agency, *mon cher* Jean-Paul.'

'Balls.'

'Disregarding your uncouth comment, I'll tell you why I felt it necessary to acquire this granddaddy of all hangovers. Our alcoholic friendship is about to blossom into a business deal. You provide teak and yang logs on a continuing basis. This gives me a valid excuse to come here frequently, and for you to visit me in Chiang Mai.

'There's a good reason for this. It isn't intended to replace your present channels of communication, merely to supplement them. Normal reports will continue to be sent through here and Long Cheng, but I want those reports to stick to bald facts. Interpretations and conclusions, I want from you as personal evaluations. And there's another reason. One of my main jobs is coordinating an operation which includes hill tribesmen, notably Mon, Karen, Kachin, Chin and Shan . . . although, strictly speaking the Shan aren't hill tribes. Already I foresee problems Washington hasn't dreamed of. I value your knowledge and experience with hill tribesmen highly. I want you to work closely with me as a check against any miscalculations at my end. Does it sound reasonable?'

Jean-Paul took a moment to answer. 'So they've got you dabbling in hill tribe revolt. It can be a dangerous game. Is there anything specific you want me to check out?'

'Yes. Through regional sub-agents, I have a pretty fair check on the Mon and Karen, but not too much on the others. I want you to run cross-checks on the ethnic leaders. I want an appreciation of their real hopes and ambitions, and whether or not they'd be willing to cooperate with outside groups such as Burmese insurgents. Would the ethnic minorites accept Burmese leadership? Could you get such information?'

Jean-Paul was smiling. 'So that's it. The name of the game is 'Screw Ne Win'. I'll say one thing for the Agency's idea on buggery ... they're ambitious. Yes, I can help. My contacts with the Mon are nil; with the Karen, confined to the northern tribes. But through my, ah, business, I'm in solid with Lashio and Tachilek. That covers the Shan. And with the Kachin, Chin and Wa, my connections are equally good. You didn't mention the Wa. Are they part of the plan?'

'Not at the moment, but they could be. Better sound them out as well.'

'Okay. I'll get you the answers, although it might take a little time. You may not like what you hear.'

Jud frowned. 'I don't have to like it. I just want to be sure it's not horseshit.'

For a few minutes, the two men sat wrapped in their respective thoughts. It was Jean-Paul who broke the silence. 'You know, I hate to say it, but I'm relieved. When you mentioned "business" yesterday, I had the horrible feeling you might want to get into the drug running game. I couldn't have helped you there. It's a closed shop.'

'How goes it with your nefarious cover activities?'

'Flourishing. You might even say, booming. You probably hear a pile of crap about the narcotics business. Laos is really just peanuts compared with the Shan States and the Kachin and Wa production. About 80 to 90 percent of the raw opium, morphine base and the Number Three grade heroin is for local Asian consumption. The Chinese have a lock on that business. We negotiate for the balance. But that's plenty.'

'Are the mainland Chinese suppliers?'

'Maybe a little, through the Wa and Kachin. But the Chinese aren't growing for export, if that's what you mean. They're scared of it. They remember what opium did to them 150 years ago. When you have a population of close to 800 million, most of whom are living under pretty depressing conditions, you have one helluva potential market for opium. The Chinese are afraid to get into the growing in case it gets out of hand. They *could* change this policy, but I doubt it.'

'What's the Agency's involvement?'

'There's been a flock of bullshit about that too. They're up to their ass in the business, but only indirectly. To finance Vang Pao's Meo mercenaries, the Agency buys up the hill tribe's cash crop of opium ... and destroys what doesn't

79

go for legitimate medicinal usage. The only problem is that not all the crop is declared. And there are growing areas which the Agency may suspect, but doesn't admit to the knowledge. And, apart from paying mercenaries salaries, they drop rice to the isolated hill tribesmen. So, in a sense, the Agency is subsidizing the growing end of the business.

'As for direct involvement, a few Air American and Continental fliers succumb to a fast buck and knowingly run the stuff. But most of them either don't know they're carrying it, or close their eyes to it. It's pretty damned hard to check the cargo kickers and the passengers they pick up and drop at remote locations.'

'So you're just living off the crumbs from the Chinese table?'

'Yeah. About 100 tons a year. That's enough to feed quite a few habits in Europe and the States.'

'And create a few users.' Jud said caustically.

'I presume so, but that's not my end of the business. Here we're strictly middlemen, expediting agents. You won't like to hear this, but I often find the American attitude amusing.'

'Yeah, it's a scream.'

'Considering that a century ago Yankee traders were busting their asses to cut in on the British opium trade to China, now that the traffic's reversed, it's almost poetic justice.

'The other day, an Air American chopper pilot was sobbing on my shoulder. He has two teenagers in Los Angeles. His 16 year-old son is mainlining H. His 14 year-old daughter is on pot, speed and acid. He thinks that if she isn't already on horse, she soon will be. And guess what his job is?'

'I can hardly wait to hear.'

'He delivers rice and ferries passengers to remote mountain villages up around Ban Houei Sai. That's territory controlled by Vang Pao's father-in-law and one of the biggest opium producing regions in the country. The pilot knows it. He also know's that there are several heroin refining plants in operation up that way. He *must* know he's often carrying the junk as undeclared cargo. What he doesn't know, is that the crafty little bastards up that way have figured a brand new angle. They de-gut the corpses of war dead and sew in ten to fifteen kilos of Number 4 Heroin in plastic bags. If the bodies were a bit bigger, they could stuff in a payload twice that size. Anyway, one of the pilot's duties is to deliver the bodies to designated locations for ultimate burial. On every such trip, he's packing quite a payload. You don't find that funny?'

A wave of nausea swept over Jud. 'Hilarious,' he said.

CHAPTER FIVE

On his return from Vientiane, Jud was surpjrised to find that the contractor and the decorator had finished in a dead heat. The villa was ready for occupancy. Jud hired a maid and a cook, and moved into the villa on June 11th.

The decorators had done a good job. Against the off-white walls of the sitting room, contrasting with the white marble facing of a wide fireplace, the drapes, upholstery and carpet harmonized in a color scheme of cool blues and greens. At one end of the room, a built-in bar had been constructed. Leading off the bar at right angles, an archway gave access to the study.

One wall of the study was bookshelves from ceiling to floor. Opposite this, broad windows gave a view of the tree covered-slope, lawn and garden. The far wall was of hand-rubbed teak panelling around a brick fireplace. On the mantelpiece, Jud placed two silver-framed photographs; the one of Tina he'd taken from the trunk in Talisai, and a shot of a younger Jud Winters, standing on the deck of *Christina II*.

The study was furnished with a teak writing desk, three comfortable wing chairs and a pedestal-mounted chess table he'd had built by a cabinet maker in a side street off Wualai Road.

Jud added certain additional refinements to the villa over the next two weeks. These modifications, he undertook by himself, working at night after the servants had retired.

In the photo lab, he installed the developing and enlarging equipment purchased in Bangkok. Then, at the rear of a wall-mounted cabinet at the far end of the windowless lab, Jud cut through the cement and brickwork into the rock and earth beyond.

Three of the four crates which had been delivered through Perkins, contained a wall safe, a metal pan with a plastic compartment and a drop chute, and a releasing device which connected to a locking plate. A long slot had been cut into the top of the safe. Jud fitted the pan atop the safe, with the drop chute in the slot. He fitted these into the gaping hole, then carefully led connecting wires to the locking plate at one side of the safe. After he had filled the metal pan and plastic container, he cemented the assembled safe and security device into place. Next, Jud altered the back of the cupboard so that one half of the back, when released from a locking catch, slid aside to reveal the face of the wall safe and the lock plate at its side. In the safe, he deposited his code books, supply of microphotography film, and those microfilmed or decoded reports not yet destroyed in the acid bath beneath the developing sinks. He also placed in the safe the envelope of money and the bank book for the Vancouver account of John Quentin.

When he had cleaned up any evidence of his work, and remounted the wall cabinet, Jud moved the Santa Rosa office from its downtown location to the room off the photo lab. He arranged with the postal telegraph office to have the company telex shifted to the new location.

He had one task outstanding. Purposely, he had had the cabinet maker leave space at the rear of the drawer in the inlaid chess table. He now installed the device in the remaining box which Perkins had received. This was a small battery-operated ultra-sonic transmitter which, when activated by a pressure switch, became a jamming heterodyner on any electronic listening installation within a 20 foot radius of the chess table's position. As yet, Jud was confident the house was not bugged, but the day might not be far distant when it would be.

It was Heinrich Keppler's custom to entertain at a party in celebration of his return from his annual spring and autumn business trips abroad. On Saturday, June 15th, Mr. and Mrs. Heinrich F. Keppler hosted a reception at their residence.

Keppler circulated among the chatting knots of Thai

and foreign guests with practised ease, adroitly shifting couples and individuals to achieve maximum common interests and a minimum of friction. With barely imperceptible nods, both Heinrich and Sasima directed the white-coated servants to the tasks of passing hors d'oeuvres and refilling glasses. As was to be expected, Keppler devoted a good deal of his time ensuring that the three newcomers to the city were made to feel at their ease.

Although Senzo Nakura intrigued Heinrich, he found it next to impossible to conduct any meaningful conversational exchange with the Japanese. For one thing, Nakura agreed with everything Heinrich said. This unqualified assent was accompanied by a fixed toothy smile, and sibilant intakes of breath. Nakura looked like a caricature of a Japanese actor in a low budget Italian movie of the American War in the Pacific. He resolved to have as little personal contact with Nakura as the confines of the small town would permit. Any observations would have to be conducted by Heinrich's local operatives.

Extricating Bridgeman from a group including Wong Liu Chan, Heinrich conducted the army officer to a knot of people surrounding another Chinese, this one resplendent in a military dress uniform. Deftly moving Bridgeman into the centre of the group, he introduced the American to General Ling Po.

Heinrich was baffled. He had observed Bridgeman closely. The lieutenant colonel affected a manner of hearty good fellowship. He smiled, chuckled and laughed readily at the tritest of sallies. Presented with the slightest opening, Brigeman jumped in to dominate the conversation. While his stories were amusing, they were of little point or substance. His too-ready compliments verged on the fullsome. He seasoned his speech with a liberal sprinkling of expressions and his jargon common with contemporary American youth. Bridgeman's performance reminded Heinrich of college sophomores Keppler had encountered during a business trip to the States two years earlier. The illusion was heightened by Bridgeman's unlined boyish countenance and a brush cut which all but concealed a sprinkling of gray hair.

The Joe College approach didn't strike Heinrich as suited to intelligence gathering. Bridgeman could scarcely gain much from a conversation where just about the only voice was his own. The uncomfortable thought struck Heinrich that his own methods might be outmoded and that Bridgeman's technique might represent the *dernier cri* with the '*in*' crowd of espionage. Heinrich hoped not. It looked like an exhausting and unrewarding procedure. He concluded that Bridgeman was either a buffoon suffering from over-exposure to military attaché duties, or an uncommonly clever and consummate actor.

From a purely professional standpoint, Keppler considered Judson Winters the least interesting new arrival in Chiang Mai. He watched Winters as the reception progressed, but not with the clinical depth he was reserving for Bridgeman and Nakura. Heinrich noted that Winters fitted easily into each group, but took little conversational initiative.

During a lull in Heinrich's circulating amongst the guests, he noticed Winters standing by himself, idly examining a Chinese porcelain. Detaching himself from a Thai colonel and a talkative Rhodesian tobacco buyer, Heinrich threaded his way through the crowd toward Winters. Pausing well short of Winters, and at an angle where his attention would not be noticed, Heinrich observed Winters closely. The man's detached scrutiny of the object d'art, the set of his shoulders, the balance of his body and the lean hard fitness of the man, imparted to Heinrich a fleeting impression of the latent lethal force of a cocked crossbow.

Reaching Winters' elbow, Keppler remarked, 'Are you interested in Chinese porcelains, Mr. Winters?'

Smiling, Jud turned to face Keppler. 'Afraid I know very little about them.' Nodding toward the blue and white floral and leaf patterned jar, he added, 'But it's certainly a lovely piece of art.'

Keppler was pleased. The wine jar was one of his most prized possessions. 'Yes,' he answered, letting his gaze rest fondly on the porcelain. 'It's very early Ming dynasty. Hung Wu, which puts it somewhere in the late 14th century. The silverwork around the rim was added later by some Turkoman craftsman. When I acquired it in Beirut, I was assured that it came from the collection of Suleiman the Magnificent. Perhaps it actually did. At any rate, I prefer to believe it did so.'

84

'I presume it's valuable.'

'Priceless would be a better word. It really shouldn't be here. Belongs in a museum, but I'm too selfish to part with it.'

Jud chuckled. 'I wouldn't know Early Ming from Middle Macy. I just knew it appealed to me. Since I've recently been involved in the furnishing and decorating of my house, I suppose I'm a bit more sensitive to such things. You must forgive my ignorance, Mr. Keppler.'

Heinrich beamed. 'Hank,' he corrected. 'All my friends call me Hank.' Jud inferred from this that he'd just been voted into the club. Heinrich continued. 'Yes, someone told me that you'd leased the Viraphong house. Lovely location. Your wife joining you soon?'

'Call me Jud,' Jud said, in response to Keppler's informality. 'As for a wife, I'm not married. Not even engaged. When I get a bit more settled in, I may seek to rectify the oversight. The girls in Chiang Mai are truly lovely.'

'Yes,' Heinrich agreed readily, 'they really are. You should give serious consideration to female companionship. Our little town can get pretty dull during the rainy season which is about to descend upon us. Know quite a few young ladies and, if you like, I can arrange a number of introductions.'

Jud grinned. 'I'd appreciate any assistance you could give me. Been here almost two months and all I seem to have met are business associates. Up to now, my work has been pretty demanding. Understand it slacks off during the rains and, frankly, I'm looking forward to the slow-down. Maybe then, I can devote a little time to my hobby of photography, and the other delightful pursuits you suggest.' Jud gestured to an inlaid chess table close to the fireplace. 'I've also taken up chess recently. As soon as I can get the villa in a bit more presentable shape, I'd very much like to have you drop over and give me a few pointers on the game.'

'I'd be more than delighted. Afraid I'm just an amateur, but I enjoy the game,' Keppler accepted with enthusiasm. While the status of amateur might be technically correct, Heinrich was a skilled player. Chess was one of his favourite diversions and there were few enough opponents in Chiang Mai to offer him much of a challenge.

After an exchange of a few more pleasantries, Heinrich

excused himself and bustled off to attend to his duties as host.

Some fifteen minutes later, tiring of the banal exchanges, Jud sought out his host and hostess to take his leave.

Heinrich watched Jud's retreating back. His initial assessment of Winters was favourable, but tinged with a strange presentiment. In Heinrich's estimation, Winters was both an adventurer and a loner. From his experience, Keppler had found that such people had a magnetic attraction for trouble. He had the feeling that Winters' appearance in Chiang Mai heralded some as yet undefined problems. He shrugged.

Heinrich's gaze swung to rest on the Ming wine jar. An uncomfortable thought struck him. There were four things in this life best calculated to arouse Heinrich's enthusiasm; his children, a beautiful woman, works of antiquity and chess. Within a very short space of time from their initial meeting, Winters had managed to touch on three of the four subjects of appeal. An odd coincidence.

Heinrich decided he must cultivate Winters more closely. He also resolved to amplify his original request for background data on the man.

Three days after the Keppler reception, a parcel was delivered to Jud's office. On removing the wrapping and opening the box, Jud discovered a tissue-cocooned vase of blue and white Chinese porcelain. The period markings of the base had been covered with a sticker which read: 'Middle Macy'. Jud removed the sticker. From the character markings, Jud recognized the vase to be late Ming, of the T'ien Ch'i period. It was a handsome gift indeed.

CHAPTER SIX

The rainy season, the time of planting and growing the rice crop, passed. With the slackening of the rains, the ripened grain was harvested. By November the days were hot and clear, the evenings cool.

For Jud, it had been a period of preparing the soil, planting and waiting for his crops to mature. But by November

86

he was a long way from harvesting the fruits of his labour. Soberly, he reviewed the results of his six month sojourn in Chiang Mai.

In a purely mechanical sense, Jud had no complaints. The changeover of agents and sub-agents to his control had gone smoothly. By various secure means a steady flow of information moved through the intelligence networks to the Chiang Mai focal point.

For his summary evaluations to the Sector Chief, Jud had evolved an effective avenue of communication. He reduced his reports to microdots which he inserted in photographic study blow-ups. On a regular basis, Perkins hand-carried photographic studies to Bangkok for display in the USIS Library on Patpong Road. Those containing the microdots were code identified and did not go on display until the microdots had been removed and forwarded to Manila.

In the area of promoting a Burmese insurgency movement with any semblance of unity, Jud had achieved very little in the way of tangible results.

In Eastern Burma, the Shan, and to a lesser extent the Kachin and Chin tribesman, were prospering from the illicit trade in opium and smuggled forest products. In cooperation with Kuomintang mercenaries, the Shan fielded a small but effective army which not only conveyed the opium caravans but maintained an uneasy balance between Ne Win's government forces and those of the encroaching Communist Chinese. In effect, these tribesmen had achieved something like a *de facto* political and economic autonomy and would not be inclined to cooperate with the Burmese insurgents without substantial concessions and inducements, neither of which were within the present means of the insurgency movement.

Of the hill tribes, only the Karen were in sufficient numbers to make a significant contribution. Yet, while they appeared sympathetic to the cause, they were suspicious, lacked clear-cut objectives and were wrangling between their various sub-regional factions.

Within the mélange of ethnic minorities, only the Mon seemed willing to lend their full support to the movement.

The leader of the Burmese expatriates within Thailand was Dr. Nyi. His leadership was weak and the movement

87

was rife internal bickering. Jud's approach to Dr. Nyi was circumspect and cautious.

In setting up a channel to fund the movement, Jud had utilized Thai banking facilities to funnel currency from an Agency account in Switzerland. To date, he had allowed only a trickle of funding through this channel, reasoning that anything more would be wasted effort until he had sound evidence that the Burmese group could resolve its internecine difficulties.

With the supply of arms and ammunition, Jud exercised control through his tight fiscal policy. Weapons were not supplied directly but through a Thai Army source on a clandestine basis. The system was designed to look like a rip-off of American military aid to Thailand – which it was in fact as well as fiction. To oversee this phase of the operation, Jud had selected two highly qualified agents. A Turkish soldier of fortune named Bakir acted as middleman in the arms supply. Edward Hughes, an ex-officer of the British Malay Police Force, was advising the insurgents on the setting up and operation of clandestine training bases. Through reports from these agents Jud received an accurate accounting.

In the light of his experience and information to date, welding the faction-ridden insurgency movement into any sort of a cohesive and effective force looked like a pretty hopeless task. The restraints Jud was imposing were not designed to hamper the operation but to make it as difficult as possible to trace, and next to impossible to prove, American involvement.

To this point, Jud's methods had received Harper's approval and presumably that of higher authority as well. Of late, however, Harper's directives had become increasingly insistent that the operation be accelerated.

Jud appreciated that Harper must be under a considerable amount of pressure to speed-up the action. The CIA was by no means the only American agency involved in the project. Jud was well aware that the Defence Intelligence Agency, through its various service branches, had established and was maintaining contact with the Burmese insurgents and a number of the tribal leaders. In one way or another, State Department, USOM and Drug Enforcement Agency officials were also getting into the act. That reports from these agencies conflicted with Jud's was becoming increasingly obvious.

A DIA report to Washington, which had been brought to Jud's attention through Harper, had indicated that, if adequately supported financially, Dr. Nyi asserted he could field two divisions. To Jud's sure knowledge, at this time, even with unlimited funding at his disposal, Nyi couldn't have mustered a battalion. Which reported opinions were given the most weight would depend on which agency commanded the most clout. Langley was obviously under pressure from the Pentagon. If official opinion swung in favor of the military assessment, it wouldn't be the first time that the Pentagon had swayed the Administration against the advice of the Agency.

Another sore point with Jud was Lieutenant Colonel Bridgeman's activities in the region. Ostensibly, Bridgeman was in charge of the project to establish a sophisticated electronic listening post on Thailand's highest peak, Doi Inthanon. But Bridgeman had devoted a good deal of time to contacting Karen leaders and had become very friendly with General Ling Po. Jud suspected Bridgeman's influence to lie behind rumours of additional military aid to the Chinese General's 93rd Kuomintang Division. Jud was strongly opposed to any such Agency involvement in what would amount to covert support of the illicit opium traffic.

As Jud saw it, and had stressed in his reports, the crux of the Burmese insurgency question was leadership. If strong leadership emerged, an effective instrument with its various ethnic components presenting a united front might be possible. The trouble was that Jud could perceive no one remotely resembling a forceful leader anywhere within the present ranks of the insurgents.

U Thong, the deposed ex-leader of the Burmese political exiles, presented a possible solution. As a spiritual leader he commanded the respect of all factions. The problem was that U Thong was languishing in Rangoon under house arrest. If he could be spirited out of Burma and induced to lead the faltering insurrection, the movement might have some chance of success.

Jud devised an operation plan to achieve this aim. In order to conceal the fact that it was an American conceived and executed project, the plan called for the participation of British Intelligence units. Jud forwarded his proposal through Harper.

In his role as hardwoods buyer, Jud was experiencing almost as many frustrations as he was with the Burmese insurgency. He was beset by two major problems, one of which was on his own making.

Jud was notified in late July that LeFarge had accumulated the required tonnage of teak logs. Jud flew to Bangkok to obtain Thai transit authorization and to book shipping space to Manila. The Thai officials agreed to truck the logs from Nong Khai to Bangkok's Klong Toey docks by the Express Transport Organization. They demanded a guarantee bond and an additional deposit equal to the full import duty. Jud completed the financial arrangements through Santa Rosa's bank, then flew to Vientiane to arrange through LeFarge for weight checks and quality inspection, and the shipment of the logs across the Mekong to Nong Khai.

No obstacles were encountered in moving the logs to Thailand and obtaining customs clearance. Trucks provided by ETO started the loading. Each truck was to carry a load of ten metric tons. Before returning to Chiang Mai, Jud supervised the loading of the first three trucks and was satisfied the procedure presented no problems.

In the final stage of the transit, the last of the twenty trucks checked at the police-controlled weighing station near Bangkok was declared three tons overweight. Authority to enter the government-controlled dock area was withheld.

Jud flew to Bangkok to clarify the misunderstanding. Officials were polite, apologetic, but adamant in their refusal to accept the shipment at the docks. The check point weight certificates for the first 19 trucks showed no shortages. Either one or two trucks had been short-loaded and the last vehicle purposely overloaded, or the certificates had been falsified. Either way it indicated collusion between the police and ETO.

Jud was left no alternative but to rent storage space outside the enclosed Klong Toey dock area until his dispute could be settled. Cargo space on the Manila-bound vessel had to be cancelled, the ship already having been delayed a day awaiting loading of the logs.

It took Jud two months, several trips to Bangkok and the

payment of substantial bribes and a token fine before he received clearance to ship the logs.

The Santa Rosa head office was not amused. The bribes, fine, demurrage, storage fees and double handling charges brought the cost of the Laotian teak to well in excess of what they would have paid for Thai logs. Moreover, the quality of the Laotian logs was substandard. And, to add insult to injury, it was to be another four months before the guarantee bond and customs deposit were released.

Rudolfo Carbella's fears had proved well-founded. That should have been the end of Jud's experiment. It wasn't.

In September, and again in October, Jud proceeded with limited shipments of yang logs from Laos. These shipments were on a basis of payment against delivery alongside at Klong Toey. LeFarge arranged for close supervision both at Vientiane and Nong Khai. Without demur, Jud paid modest bribes from Agency funds.

The second cloud on Jud's commercial horizon came from the Land of the Rising Sun, in the form of Senzo Nakura.

Nakura proved to be the advance man for a team of negotiators from the Mitsusaki group, who arrived in August to enter into negotiations with the Thai government. The Tokyo-based conglomerate offered the establishment of two Thai-Japanese joint venture operations. One was to be a pulpwood plant to be located close to the extensive pine forest region in northern Chiang Mai province. The second proposal was to be set up a veneer and plywood factory at Chiang Dao.

Using the leverage of these still unconcluded negotiations, Nakura was attempting to secure long-term commitments on hardwood logs principally teak. He was quietly offering premium payments in the form of bribes to key officials.

Jud advised the Manila office of these developments. He received instructions to match the Japanese kick-back offers to a specified level. It looked as though a stiffly competitive situation was in the process of development.

It was hardly, Jud concluded glumly, the best time to be embarking on his cover career.

In spite of Harper's recommendation to the contrary, Jud's proposal concerning U Thong was approved by the CIA's Deputy Director of Plans with only a few modifications. Harper was advised accordingly, which did little to improve his resentment of Winters.

It wasn't that Harper disagreed in principle with Winters' methods or recommended courses of action, but there were larger considerations. Harper was under pressure to produce results. While Harper agreed with and supported Winters' situation evaluations, the operation appeared stalled. Somehow, Harper would have to force Winters into speeding up the entire process. This, Harper now appreciated, was going to be no easy task.

Winters had proven to be far more astute and effective than Harper had anticipated. By now it was patently obvious that Winters was capable of independant action and would stubbornly resist anything he considered as compromise. Harper wished fervently that he had not vested fiscal control in Winters, nor granted the Chiang Mai Area Coordinator such wide discretionary powers.

Harper was faced with several courses of action. None were to his liking.

Jud received the coded message from Harper on December 12th. It directed him to increase cash disbursements and expedite arms supply to the Burmese group immediately.

Jud's face was grim as he reread the decoded message.

He telexed the Santa Rosa head office advising that he was coming to Manila to discuss future shipments of Laos teak. Without waiting for a reply to his telex message, he went directly to the Chiang Mai airport and caught the afternoon flight to Bangkok.

CHAPTER SEVEN

The atmosphere in the Santa Rosa boardroom was strained. The Chairman of the Board, Colonel Francisco Jose-Maria Garcia Martinez, sat at the head of the polished mahogany table. On the chairman's right, sat Sam Harper, his features betraying no emotion. The four other Filipinos and one American, ranged around the board table were not known to Jud. Their faces reflected varying degrees of hostility.

Colonel Garcia leaned forward, locking his fingers together on the table. His hoarse voice betrayed annoyance as he addressed Jud. 'Despite the substantial loss we sustained on the first Laotian shipment, you now propose we approve an even larger consignment of teak from that source. What makes you confident the next one would be any better?'

'The first shipment was in the nature of a test run,' Jud said easily. 'As my report to Mr. Harper indicated, I fully expected obstacles and a probable loss. I must admit that...'

Colonel Garcia cut in. 'We are aware of your reports, but the loss was higher, considerably higher, than your estimates. I'll be frank with you Winters. Had it not been for the persuasiveness of Mr. Harper, you would have been dismissed.'

'That would have been a mistake, Colonel,' Jud said evenly. There was a quickening of interest around the table. Few people had the temerity to dispute Garcia. As though he had not heard Winters correctly, the colonel's eyebrows raised. He said nothing. Jud continued. 'As I was about to say, I admit that the costs ran a good deal higher than I expected, but until we'd tried the trial run I had no way of judging where, how or how badly they'd hit us. I regret that the initial shipment had to be large enough to make it attractive bait for the Thais, which increased the loss. A smaller shipment, or even several shipments, might have gone through unmolested before they made their move. But now I know how to protect future shipments. We should not suffer any loss on the next consignment.'

'What about quality?' Garcia growled.

'Unfortunately,' Jud answered, 'I let some inferior logs go through on the first shipment to make up the full tonnage I now have a man in Vientiane to check weights, cull out everything but 1st Class logs and supervise the handling both in Vientiane and Nong Khai. He looked after the two yang log shipments. We encountered no difficulties.'

'No,' grated Garcia, 'but that's yang. The Thais would have little interest in blocking yang logs. However, Winters, our primary concern is teak.' The colonel hunched forward even further, his eyes fixed intently on Jud. 'What the board and I want to know, is why you feel it so essential that we broaden our present methods of procurement?'

Jud placed one hand, palm down, on the table. 'Colonel,

gentlemen,' he said seriously, 'the reason I came to advance this proposal personally, instead of submitting it as a written request, was to stress the seriousness of the situation. You are all aware that the Mitsusaki interests are making a strong bid in the teak market. I am convinced that other Japanese groups will follow. The 1st Class teak logs will become harder to obtain and the price will rise accordingly. I feel that we should make every effort without delay to get in on the ground floor with alternative sources of supply. Laos is one, and a good one. It presents problems, but it's virtually untapped and, as yet, not attractive to the Japanese.'

Jud knew from the expressions on the board members' faces that his argument had impressed them. He sat back in his chair and let his hand drop into his lap.

'It might interest you to know, Winters, that we have started negotiations with the Thai government for a joint plywood plant,' Garcia stated.

Jud had not known this. 'Good,' he said. 'But bear in mind, Colonel, that the Japs have a six month edge on you. I hope you're in a position to match or better their long-range credit terms.'

Neither Jud nor Garcia missed the quick exchange of glances which went around the table. The colonel leaned back in his chair. For a moment, he drummed on the table with his stubby fingers. Clearing his throat, Garcia stilled the murmur of voices. Looking at each man of the board in turn, Garcia received a nod of assent. Turning to Jud, the colonel grated, 'You have the board's approval to proceed.'

As the men rose to leave, Garcia's voice cut through the noise of conversation and the scraping of chairs. 'Mr. Winters.' Jud turned to face the colonel. There was a semblance of a smile on Garcia's face, as he said, 'May I wish you the compliments of the coming festive season.'

'Thank you,' Jud said, smiling.

Jud had scarcely entered his room in the Manila Hotel when the telephone rang. Picking it up, he said, 'Winters.'

'Mr. Winters, this is Mr. Harper's secretary. Mr. Harper wishes to know if you could join him for dinner this evening?'

'I think it could be arranged.'

94

'Fine. Mr. Harper will have a car at the hotel for you at 7 : 30.'

The maitre d'hotel at the Frangipani Room escorted Jud to the rear of the dining room, where Harper was waiting at a table in an alcove.

When the maitre d'hotel left them, the smile of welcome, which had suffused Harper's face, faded. 'You didn't come here to discuss teak, but for the duration of the dinner we will confine ourselves to Santa Rosa's affairs.'

'Sounds reasonable,' said Jud, as he studied the menu.

'Your Laotian teak shipment put me in a most difficult position.'

'So I gathered. I wouldn't worry about it. You'll come out of it smelling like a rose. If you felt so strongly about it, why didn't you cast a dissenting vote at this afternoon's board meeting?'

'With Garcia and the rest of the board in favour, I had little option. I'll have to admit, you put on quite a performance this afternoon. Garcia's a tough old bastard. Not many people would have the guts to face him down the way you did. It impressed him, as well as the rest of the board members. It didn't impress me. You and I were the only ones there who knew you couldn't lose; that if necessary you could utilize other funds to offset any possible loss.'

Jud chuckled. 'I would have done that on the initial shipment. I wasn't handing Garcia a pile of crap. I may not know much about the hardwood business, but I can sure as hell recognize a squeeze play when I see one. The Japanese are going to have Santa Rosa pushed out of the teak business unless Garcia and his board take prompt action. Thanks to LeFarge, I may have been able to give them a shove in the right direction. But you're right. I'll come out a hero, even if I have to dip into *La Compañia's* till to make up the difference.'

Harper frowned. He didn't like Winters' casual usage of the nickname by which the Agency was known in Central America. He might have voiced an objection, but at that moment a white-jacketed waiter appeared to take their order.

When the waiter departed, Harper said, 'If I'd known what you were attempting with the Laotian shipments, I'd

95

have stopped you. I don't see any reason for you to establish such a close liaison with LeFarge.'

. 'I do,' Jud said shortly.

They lasped into silence. For the rest of the meal, their conversation was sparse and limited to company affairs.

At the conclusion of the meal, Harper said, 'I'll buy you a nightcap at a little place I know not too far from here. Then I'll drive you back to the hotel. I imagine you're tired from this morning's flight and will want to rest up before your return tomorrow morning.'

Jud had said nothing about going back to Bangkok tomorrow. He smiled faintly.

Harper was driving a gray Ford Mustang. He weaved into the traffic on Roxas Boulevard, before resuming the conversation. 'You object to my last directive,' he said abruptly.

'I do. Most emphatically.'

Harper drove at a steady pace. His features were rigidly set. 'I consider,' he stated flatly, 'that your coming to Manila without authorization is insubordination. Moreover, my orders require neither justification nor amplification. However, since you're here, I will clarify certain matters. I am in agreement with most of your proposals concerning the Burmese group, but it may have escaped your attention that the service intelligence agencies wield considerable power on the hill. Their assessments, specifically those of DIA are running counter to ours. In some areas, we must compromise.'

'Such as?'

'If we don't increase the supply of arms beyond the dribble you are permitting, the issue will be taken out of our hands and the armament supplied more directly. The Pentagon, as you well know, favours a more direct approach to the insurgents. Then there is the matter of military advisers to instruct in the use of the weapons and modern tactics.'

'Shit. That's all we need. A bunch of brush-cut GIs masquerading as youth counsellors and sports directors to advertise our involvement. What in hell can our kids teach the hill tribesmen about tactics in their own terrain. If any instruction in the more sophisticated weapons is required. Bakir has my authority to call on a limited number of Thai

Special Forces instructors. As for increasing the arms supply at this stage, it could have highly undesirable results, if not wreck the operation irretrievably. The major portion of the funds supplied for arms purchased would disappear into Swiss bank accounts; excess arms would be sold to Communist insurgents in the south, and arming our boys before they have adequate leadership could produce a half-assed revolt which would resolve little or nothing and be an embarrassment to us. All that's been in my reports. Why in hell do we have to rehash it?'

'Your reports have been most explicit. But there is now heavy pressure for action and results.'

Jud sighed heavily. 'When and if Bakir, or our contact in the insurgency group, convince me that sufficient mercenaries can be recruited, I'll open wide the flood gates. Until then, . . .'

Harper drove in silence for almost a full minute. Finally, he said coldly, 'I could remove the financial control from your hands. Frankly, I've been tempted to do so. But that would mean you would no longer control the operation, and I *do* agree with you in principle. Had you not come here as you did, you would have received a message today advising you that your proposals concerning U Thong have been approved. I opposed on the grounds that, since the Philby affair, I'm reluctant to place that much trust in MI-6. But it has been approved at the highest level. If he is agreeable, you will have U Thong on the scene by the end of February.

'I'll modify my last directive to this extent. You may limit the cash flow between now and March, but it must then be substantially increased. After U Thong is established as a political refugee in Thailand and has assumed direction of the insurgency, you will comply with his financial demands.

'I'll have the question of military advisers held in abeyance, but there are two things I want clearly understood.' Harper's voice took on a metallic quality. 'Under no circumstances will you come to Manila again without prior authority. And, U Thong, or no U Thong, this operation will not be aborted. Block me, and I'll see to it that you're destroyed.'

Harper swung the Mustang in a U-turn and headed in the direction of the Manila Hotel.

Jud sat in the downstairs bar of the Manila hotel. As he nursed a bourbon and water, his thoughts were far from cheerful. He may have won his point, but it was at best a Pyrrhic victory. What lay ahead was anybody's guess, but of two things he was sure. One was that if U Thong bombed out, Jud knew he wouldn't play the game out by Harper's rules. The second unpleasant item was that Harper's had been no idle threat. It was patently obvious that Harper would not back off.

Jud sighed. So much now depended on a moon-faced little man in Rangoon who, at this moment had no idea what role destiny, assisted by MI-6 and the CIA, was shaping for him. Jud hoped the little man would prove equal to the part.

CHAPTER EIGHT

The Rincome Hotel opened in January, 1969. Rapidly, it became a popular hostelry with tourists and a point of rendezvous for many of the locals.

On an afternoon in late February, Heinrich Keppler stood at the top of the marble stairs leading from the lobby up to the cocktail lounge. He was expecting the arrival of Jud Winters. The plan was to have a couple of drinks in the Peacock Room before driving out to Jud's house for an early dinner, followed by one or two games of chess.

In the months since their meeting, chess had become something of a ritual with Jud and Heinrich. Jud, contrary to his disclaimer, had been a better than average player. Over the months, playing at least once a week with Chris Perkins and two or three times a month with Heinrich, Jud had improved rapidly. Heinrich enjoyed the games and was hard put now to win, or even to draw.

As Winters came through the glass doors and strode across the lobby, Heinrich frowned. Winters had been much on his mind of late, and Heinrich knew he must take some form of positive action. It distressed him.

As Jud mounted the steps towards Heinrich, he heard a startled gasp and a woman's voice say questioningly, 'Juddy?'

Jud froze. Forcing a smile, he turned and faced towards the lounge.

She was sitting in one of the green-upholstered chairs. Her blue eyes were wide with surprise. The blonde hair was shoulder length, instead of the page-boy cut of the photograph on his study mantelpiece, but there was no mistaking that it was the Christina from Jud Winters' youth. At her side, watching Jud curiously, stood a girl in her early teens, clad in a bathrobe several sizes too large for her slender frame.

Jud felt as though the step upon which he stood had suddenly become a rapidly descending elevator. Jesus Christ, he thought, what a time for this to happen, With Keppler witnessing the scene, Jud had no choice. He couldn't pass it off as a case of mistaken identity. He would have to brazen it out and hope and pray for the best. The astonishment on his face was by no means feigned. When he answered the woman, there was a catch in his voice. 'My God, Tina!' he exclaimed.

She made no response. With a nervous gesture, her fingers brushed her cheek. Her lips trembled in a smile. She looked not only startled, but frightened.

Half-turning towards Keppler, Jud said, 'Excuse me, Hank ... an old friend ... I ...'

'Certainly.'

Jud descended to the lobby then mounted the carpeted steps to the lounge. As he approached Tina, he watched her face closely for any sign of dawning awareness of his imposture. What a helluva twit, he thought. Of all the people in the world, this is the last one I wanted to bump into.

Her face reflected hesitant anticipation, but no sign of wavering doubt concerning his identity. The surgical transformation must be even more effective than he'd thought. Of course, an eighteen year span since their parting should have changed Jud somewhat anyway. What he most feared

99

was that his voice and speech mannerisms would betray the masquerade. And when two people had been as close as Jud and Tina had once been, surely her intuition, if nothing else, would sense a difference. His mind was blank. He'd have to take his lead from Tina. Her first remark wasn't helpful.

As though not trusting her legs, she didn't rise from the chair. When he stood before her, she reached up her hand. 'Hello Juddy,' she said, a slight quaver in her voice.

He grasped her hand and noticed it was still trembling. He attempted a smile of reassurance. 'Hello Tina.' Christ he thought, how banal can we get.

Tina recovered some of her composure. With a guilty start, she remembered they weren't alone. Looking at the girl beside her, Tina said, 'This is my daughter, Nicola. Nicky, I'd like you to meet an old friend of Mummy's ... Mr. Winters.'

'Hi,' the girl said, smiling at Jud.

From his briefing, he knew that Tina had married a Doctor William Atcheson and that the couple had adopted two children. But there had been nothing to indicate that Winters had ever known of this. He would have to play it that way. Before acknowledging the introduction, Jud shot Tina a questioning look. She smiled faintly in response.

'Mom,' Nicola said, with a touch of impatience.

'Alright, Nicky. But no more than an hour. When Craig gets back, we're having an early dinner.'

'Okay, Mom.'

The western wall of the lounge was glass, giving an unrestricted view of the garden, with chairs and tables clustered around a kidney-shaped swimming pool. Nicola swung around and ran lightly on bare feet towards the glass door at the far end of the lounge. At the door, she paused briefly to flash a smile. 'See you, Mr. Winters.'

Jud became aware of the fact that Keppler had joined them. Smiling apologetically, Jud said, 'Sorry Hank.'

'Not at all,' Heinrich said, beaming. 'Isn't this the lovely young lady of the photograph in your study?'

'That's right. Tina, I'd like to introduce a friend of mine, Heinrich Keppler. Hank, this is Christina ...' He paused in obvious confusion and looked imploringly at Tina.

Tina had risen. She laughed. 'You must forgive us, Mr. Keppler. We've been out of touch for quite some time and I haven't told Jud my married name. Christina Atcheson.' She held out her hand.

'A pleasure, my dear. I hope your stay in Chiang Mai will be long enough to afford me the pleasure of inviting you and your family to dinner.'

'Thank you, Mr. Keppler, but I'm afraid that won't be possible. We're with a tour group which leaves tomorrow morning.'

At this disclosure, Jud felt a surge of relief, yet his face registered disappointment. Turning to Keppler, Jud said, 'Hank, I wonder if you'd be so kind as . . .'

'Of course, Jud. I'll take a rain check. You two must have a million things to discuss. If you'll excuse me, Mrs. Atcheson.'

Jud watched the departing figure of Keppler with a mixture of relief and foreboding. While he didn't want Keppler exposed to Tina, Jud didn't relish the thought of being alone with her himself.

Through the glass, Jud watched Nicola dive gracefully into the pool. Tina followed his gaze. 'No, Jud,' she said, 'It isn't a miracle of medical science. Nicky's an adopted child.'

'It shook me,' Jud said. 'She looks very much like you.'

'Post-natal selection.'

Craig, he assumed, must be the other adopted child, but as yet Tina hadn't confirmed the fact. He tried an oblique approach. 'You expect your husband?'

For a moment, Tina looked puzzled, then her face cleared. 'Oh, you mean Craig. He's my adopted son. My husband's name's Bill. He's a doctor, an obstetrician. He couldn't get away from his practice in Plattsburg. The weather was so ghastly this winter that Bill thought the children and I should get away for a month or so. He booked us on this tour of the Orient.'

They lapsed into silence for a moment. They both started to speak at the same instant, and broke off in confusion. Jud took the initiative. 'Look,' he said, 'why don't you and the children have dinner at my place. The cook was expecting one guest anyway. I'll just telephone her to prepare for two more.'

'I'd love to, but you needn't phone the cook. The kids can eat here. They're quite capable of looking after themselves.' She noted his fleeting look of consternation. Resting her hand lightly on the sleeve of his jacket, she smiled and added, 'What's the matter? Are you afraid to be alone with me?'

He smiled wryly. 'Yes. Tina. I think maybe I am.' It was a truthful answer.

Tina went up to her room to get a sweater and then out to the pool to tell Nicola of the plans for dinner. Jud wondered bleakly what malevolent little Asiatic deity had contrived this improbable meeting.

As he drove the short distance to the villa, she sat studying him. 'You've changed, Juddy,' she observed.

'Twenty years is bound to make some difference,' he countered lamely.

'Eighteen,' she corrected. 'No, I didn't mean that. We weren't much older than Craig and Nicky then. What I meant was that when I last saw you, you were a teenager. Now you're a man. It's strange, as though I'm meeting you for the first time.'

He smiled. 'You're still as beautiful as you ever were, Tina. You haven't changed much.' It was true. She didn't seem to have aged much from the photo likeness in his study. He knew that in another two months she'd be thirty-seven. She looked no more than in her late twenties.

Tina brushed the soft hair from the side of her face and gave a pleased laugh. She sobered. 'I used to wonder what it would be like if we met. Thought of all the clever things I'd say. Funny, I can't think of any of them now. Did you ever think of how it would be?'

'I have,' he answered laconically. He had considered the possibility so remote that he'd dismissed it. He wished now that he'd given it a bit more thought.

As they turned through the gates, Tina said, in agitation, 'My God. I didn't think to ask. Am I about to meet a Mrs. Winters?'

He looked at her with genuine amusement. 'No,' he answered lightly, 'Not even a mistress, or an adoring native wench.'

'I'm sorry,' she said contritely. 'That was pretty stupid of me. Have you been married?'

'No. Confirmed bachelor, I guess. Nothing against women. It's just that I'm not very good husband material.' As he made the statement, he realized it applied equally to Winters and himself.

When they entered the house, the first thing Tina wanted to see was the photograph to which Keppler had made reference. Jud led her directly to the study. She examined the portrait critically.

'Gosh,' she said, 'I look so damned young.' Making a moue of dismissal, she turned her attention to the photo of Winters standing in the forecastle of the converted PT boat. *Christino II* was clearly discernible on the bow. Turning from the photo, she said, 'Presuming she's named after me, I'm flattered.'

He grinned. The Freudian symbolism in Winters' choice of name had amused him, and he was sure hadn't escaped Tina. 'She was a beautiful craft. Sleek, fast, handled well in stormy weather and answered obediently to my every command. Unfortunately, fickle lady that she was, one day she got bombed and left me stranded.'

At her look of perplexity, Jud laughed. 'Tell you about it after dinner. Right now, I suggest a martini.'

While Jud stirred a jug of martinis, Tina browsed around the sitting room. She paused in front of one of his photographic studies, with the scrawled 'J.Q.W.' in the bottom right hand corner. It was a shot taken at dawn from a vantage point overlooking a mountain village. In the background, the slope dropped away steeply into curling morning mists. The distant mountain peaks were hazy in the early light. He had used a filter and developed the shot with a sepia tone. The effect was dramatic.

'Olive or twist?' Jud queried.

'Twist, thanks,' she said, coming over to the bar to perch on a stool in front of Jud. She rested her chin on her hand and regarded him thoughtfully. 'I didn't realize you were so talented,' she said. He added a twist of peel to each glass, and handed her one. 'The photographs. Some of them aren't bad. Good enough to supplement my meagre income as a timber buyer. I've some down in the lab I'll show you after dinner. If there's one that appeals to you, you can have it as a memento of a strange and wonderful meeting.'

She laughed. 'You'd better not initial it, I'll have enough

trouble explaining our meeting to Bill as it is. He'll probably think I tracked you down somehow anyway.'

'Did you?'

'Of course not. Betty-Anne and I occasionally wrote to each other some years back. I knew that you left the navy and stayed in Japan. She told me you'd gone on to the Philippines. But I haven't heard from her for ages. Suppose I thought you were still there. We are due to go through Manila on the return leg of this trip, and I will admit I did think of trying to find out what had become of you. But, my God, to find you in a remote place like Chiang Mai. It's almost beyond belief.'

She looked again at the pictures and photographs on the walls. 'The photo studies *are* good,' she said, returning to her earlier comment. 'It came as a surprise to find you'd improved so much. God, do you remember all those shots you took in Tahoe? I thought. . . .' Her words trailed off as she noted Jud's face cloud in a frown.

'Tina,' he said, choosing his words carefully. 'I'd rather not go back over those days. It could be painful for both of us. I have never forgotten a moment that we shared, but I don't want to relive them now.' His voice became gentle, as he added, 'I want to know everything that's happened to you since you left, but I don't want to reawaken old and sad memories. Can you understand what I mean, Tina?'

Her eyes became misty. 'Yes, Jud. I think I understand.'

Inwardly, he congratulated himself. He hadn't the vaguest idea what might have happened in Tahoe.

During dinner, with occasional prompting from Jud, Tina gave an abbreviated account of her life over the past 18 years.

She told him how depressed she'd been after peritonitis had necesitated the hysterectomy. Her father had sent her east to a modelling school in New York. Even when she'd completed the course and signed with an agency, she'd hated the big city and was homesick for San Francisco. She and another girl from the agency rented a small apartment on West 87th. She hadn't gone out much that first year.

Then she met Bill Atcheson. He was 29, taking post-graduate studies in obstetrics in New York University Hospital. She was attracted to the serious young doctor. They started to date steadily.

Tina smiled across the table at Jud. 'Bill's good looking, but I don't think you'd call him dashing or handsome. Now, his hair is thinning and totally gray. He doesn't get enough exercise, and has a paunch. Of course, he was better looking when we met and I was impressed by his maturity. What attracted me to him was that he was so different from you. He was serious and attentive, and never moody the way you used to be. He had his future planned and didn't want to set the world on fire the way you did. On our fourth date, he asked me to marry him and I accepted. We had to wait until he finished at the hospital and accepted a place in the Plattsburg clinic. We were married in San Francisco. Mom and Dad were delighted and gave us a new Buick as a wedding present and we drove east.'

Jud had listened intently. He wondered what she would say if she knew the man sitting opposite her was even older than her Bill. True, his hair wasn't graying yet, and certainly wasn't thinking either, but he found himself sympathizing with Atcheson. And, in Tina's account, Jud thought he detected a note of defensiveness. He sipped thoughtfully from his wine glass. 'Do you love him?' He asked quietly. it was a dangerous question, but Jud somehow felt it was important to know the answer.

The look on Tina's face was hard to define. 'What is love?' Is it that crazy teenage thing we shared? Yes, I love Bill. It doesn't reach the wilds peaks of excitement we shared, but it doesn't have those valleys of despair either. When Bill came into my life, I was bitter and frightened. He gave me understanding, stability and a sense of security. I think that's the most important thing in a woman's life, Jud . . . security.'

Tina sipped her wine. 'You know,' she continued, 'It's a funny thing. I hated you at that time. Blamed you for ruining my life. It was Bill who defended you. I'd told him all about you and the abortion. He said you weren't to be blamed too much. He pointed out that with the family background from which you came, it wasn't unreasonable for you to panic at the thought of fatherhood and marriage. He even implied I could have been partly to blame. I hadn't thought of it in that light. When I did, I found I didn't hate you as much as I thought. I tried to see it through your eyes and found I didn't blame you quite as much. That's when I first wrote to Betty-Anne.'

They had coffee and liqueurs in the study, where the servants had lit a log fire against the coolness of the February evening. Now, it was Jud's turn.

He touched lightly on the highlights of Winter's life as he knew them, from the days in Sasebo, to Tokyo, following the war, and then the Philippines. He dwelt on the partnership in the shipping venture, and his days as master of a speedy gun-runner. The part of the story concerning the Indonesian bombing of the *Christina II*, he invested with pathos and humor. Where his knowledge of events was sketchy, he invented, embellishing his tale with humorous anecdotes. Tina seemed enthralled. He was quite pleased with his imaginative account.

He concluded with the later years as owner operator of a night club and gambling casino, his enforced exile in Viet-Nam, and his return, only to become involved in the disastrous beach club venture. The Talisai misadventure, he explained, led directly to his present employment with Santa Rosa.

'Do you ever think of coming home?' Tina asked.

'Home?' he answered questioningly. 'I've been away too long. I don't think I'd be able to fit back into Stateside living and I sure as hell don't know who'd offer me any kind of a job.' He hesitated, then added, 'Maybe someday, if I can accumulate enough bread, I'll think seriously of going back.' He was speaking for himself, not reflecting Winters' views. Winters had certainly put together enough savings and property and had been on the verge of going someplace, if not Stateside, at the time of his death.

He stood up. With a poker, he stirred the fire and placed two fresh logs on the coals. From behind him, her voice questioned softly, 'Are you happy, Jud?'

'Yeah, sure,' he answered gruffly, then turning he smiled and said, 'I'll get you another drink.'

At the bar, he poured Tina another Drambuie and measured out a large dollop of cognac for himself. Her last question had annoyed him, although he didn't know exactly why. After all, he mused, what in hell is happiness? Related to Winters, it was absurd. A corpse is beyond emotion. In his own case, happiness was a condition which had little meaning. It never occurred to him to ask himself such a question.

When he returned with the replenished glasses, she was sitting hunched forward, her elbows on her knees and face in her cupped palms, gazing intently into the leaping flames. She spoke in a barely audible voice. 'I don't know why I lied.'

'About what?' He was mystified.

'My marriage. I don't know why I pretended. It hasn't been good, even from the beginning.' She paused and sighed heavily. 'It isn't Bill's fault, it's mine. We made love before we were married and he just didn't turn me on. Bill knew it. He said it was natural and that I was still recovering from the shock of the hysterectomy. I believed him, because I wanted to. He said that with time we would adjust to each other. I believed that too. But it wasn't true. I never have. I've always felt terribly guilty about it. I respect Bill, and I guess in a way I do love him, but there's just something missing. You know I'm not sexually cold, Jud. I've tried. I've tried so hard. It's hurt Bill, but I can't fake it, or at least not well enough to fool him.

'Bill thought adopting the children would help. In a way, it has. We both love the kids and it made us a family. But it damn well hasn't made me any more responsive to Bill.'

She was silent for a moment. She leaned back in the chair and continued with a voice which trembled with emotion. 'I thought of divorce, for Bill's sake. He wouldn't hear of it. He said he loved me and it wouldn't be fair to the children. Maybe he's right. I don't know.

'For the past six years, we've had separate rooms. For the past three, he's been having an affair with an Italian nurse at the clinic. He thinks I don't know. Christ, half the town knows. I don't blame him. In fact, it's almost a relief and makes me feel a little less guilty.'

Not once had she looked at Jud. He felt an odd sense of guilt as though he was usurping a privilege not rightfully his. He would have liked to say something to stop the flood of confession, yet he wanted to hear her out. He was not a compassionate man, but he felt a deep sympathy for this tortured woman.

She turned her head and looked up into his face. Her eyes were bright with unshed tears. 'Oh, Juddy,' she said imploringly, 'make love to me.'

He was still holding the two glasses. He placed them on the chess table. Wordlessly, he held out his hand to Tina.

CHAPTER NINE

Their first love-making that night was far from satisfactory. Tina had been overly tense. To Jud's astonishment, he had reacted with the quick passion of youth and had been unable to stem the pulsing tide. It had been over almost before it had begun.

For some time they lay in each other's arms, their bodies touching lightly. They talked of inconsequential things, then slowly, almost timidly, their hands moved in caressing exploration. Gradually, the banked fires of their passions were rekindled.

In their second coupling, there was nothing of the timidity of the first. Tina met his hard deep thrusts with arching back and lunging pelvis. She reached her first orgasm quickly, with a startled gasp. Her moans grew louder as she reached a second climax. His stabbing plunges continued and increased in tempo. They reached a crescendo simultaneously in an explosive convulsion, mouthing half-articulated obscenities and clutching each other fiercely.

His head was thrust down beside hers, his lips brushing the side of her throat. As his strangled gasping subsided, he breathed deeply of the scent of her hair and the musky odor of their passion. Her fingers gently stroked the back of his neck.

In a small voice, she said wonderingly. 'I think that's the way it's supposed to be.'

He kissed her bruised lips and the tip of her nose. 'But seldom is,' he added.

He pulled the blanket up to cover their sweat-drenched bodies. They lay intimately together. Her fingers traced the line of his shoulder and her hand slid under his arm and around him to pull him close.

'Where did you get that?' she asked, as her fingers stroked the long diagonal scar along the small of his back.

'The scar. Nothing romantic. Stray chunk of shrapnel grazed me in Korea,' he lied.

Holding him close, she murmured sympathetically.

One arm across his chest and her leg pressed to his, she

fell into a contented sleep. Her head lay on the pillow close beside his, her breath softly fanning his cheek. He gazed at her face, soft in sleep, her lips slightly parted in a faint smile. Gently, he brushed a tendril of hair from her forehead.

The tensions of the past months had ebbed from him. He felt drowsy and languid. He knew perfectly well that making love to this woman had been both foolhardy and stupid, yet he didn't regret it. He closed his eyes. He reflected rather sadly that a dead man would get the credit for an act of love that had been pretty wonderful. His last thought before sleep claimed him was that for letting go of a girl like this, Jud Winters deserved to end up as shark bait.

Tina shook him gently. His transition from sound sleep to alert wakefulness was so rapid that it startled her. He sat up. Rubbing the stubble of his night's growth of beard, he glanced at the bedside clock. The time was 5:30. Tina, he noted, was fully dressed.

'Sorry to wake you, darling, but I must get back to the hotel before the kids get up,' she said, smiling down at Jud.

'Should have thought of that myself,' he said, swinging his legs over the edge of the bed.

As they drove towards the hotel, Tina snuggled close to him, her hand resting lightly on his thigh. Suddenly, she asked, 'Are you in some kind of trouble?'

'Not that I know of. What makes you ask?' Her question surprised him.

'A little over a year ago, two men came to the house and questioned me about you. More recently, last September, another man appeared, asking much the same questions. They were very inquisitive. I couldn't tell them very much.'

'Didn't they say who they were?'

'The first two said they were making some kind of a credit check. The other man showed me some sort of identification and told me he was from Internal Revenue. But the questions were so detailed and personal, I wondered about it. Thought you might be in some kind of tax trouble.'

He laughed. 'After that beach club bust, I should have a tax write-off for life. Don't worry about it. They were probably just what they said they were. We live in an age of bureaucratic snooping.'

He pulled up short of the Rincome entrance and cut his lights. 'What time's your flight?'

'Ten o'clock this morning, but we're supposed to leave the hotel at nine.'

'I'll pick you up and drive you to the airport.'

She hesitated. 'I'd rather you didn't, darling. I'd love to see you, but I honestly think that the kids will guess what's happened. They probably will anyway ... at least Nicky. But if they saw us together, I couldn't hide my feelings and they'd know for sure. Do I sound silly?'

'No. I hadn't thought of that angle. Afraid I'm the one who's stupid.'

She leaned over and kissed him. 'The hell you are. You're wonderful.'

He escorted her to the hallway leading to her room. She stopped him short of the door. Fumbling in her purse, she found a pen and a small notebook. She scribbled on a page, tore it from the book and shoved it into the breast pocket of his jacket. 'That's my address,' she said. 'Will you write me?'

'Yes,' he said, knowing full well that he wouldn't. He suspected she knew it as well. Then, frowning, he added, 'But you must remember, Tina, we can never go back and relive the past. The Jud Winters you knew has been dead a long time.'

She favored Jud with an oddly penetrating look. The ghost of a smile touched her lips and eyes. 'I know,' she said softly. She moved close to him, pulled his head down and kissed him hungrily. Then she was gone.

He stood in the hallway, bewildered, until the muffled click of her closing door snapped him back to reality.

As he drove the short distance back to the villa, his thoughts were oddly mixed.

He had been a damned fool to make love to Tina. It wasn't just the idiotic chance he'd taken of being discovered to be an imposter. But Christ, it wasn't just that. His villa was bugged with listening devices. It had been since his first up-country trip following the rainy season, when technicians had come, claiming to be from the telephone company.

He'd discovered most of the hidden microphones, but had left them where they were. The bedroom was no exception.

Mentally, he reviewed the evening's conversational exchange. There had been nothing of an incriminating nature said in the sitting or dining rooms. The study, with its scrambling device, was safe. What about the bedroom scene? Slowly, he grinned. Anyone who reviewed that soundtrack would get an earful. As far as he could recall, there had been nothing said between them that could be suspicious. On the contrary. An imposter would hardly have risked the acid test of copulation. He had, but it looked as though he'd lucked out.

He puzzled over Tina's cryptic parting remark. Could she have guessed he wasn't Winters? Then it struck him that not once, from the moment they'd started to make love, had she again called him either 'Jud', or 'Juddy'. His eyebrows raised in disbelief. He was almost positive she *did* know, but was keeping the knowledge to herself. She had accepted his reference to Winters being dead at its face value. Christ, he thought, if I live to be a hundred, I'll never understand women.

He thought of the two investigations she'd mentioned. The first would be the Agency investigators compiling Winters' dossier. But who did the second questioner work for? Someone was displaying an avid interest in Winters. The bugging of his house didn't bother him nearly as much as this new wrinkle. Long ago, Keppler would have discovered from a background check that Jud Winters had worked as an Agency informer in the Philippines. The bugging was a logical consequence. In addition, his former driver, Boonsok, suddenly become too sick to work and had been replaced by a man whom Jud had discovered to be one of Keppler's informers. Jud suspected that his cook and maid were also some of Keppler's people. All that, he could appreciate as normal precaution on Keppler's part. But an indepth background check on Winters was something else. He could think of no reason why Keppler should go beyond a routine check. Maybe, with the KGB, such thoroughness was standard practice. He sure as hell hoped so, but he'd better be damned careful.

CHAPTER TEN

He poured himself a generous cognac. In the study, the fire had subsided into dully-glowing embers. He dropped another log into the hot remnants of its predecessors. Seating himself, he cradled the brandy snifter in his palms. Moodily, he watched thin wisps of smoke struggling to attain the status of licking flames.

His emotionally-charged meeting with Tina had disturbed him in more ways than one.

First of all, he mused, there was the question of identity, or to be more accurate, false identity. That was the crux of the matter. To be sure, his role demanded that he must *be* Winters. For a year now, he'd learned to think, talk and act as he felt Winters would. He'd altered his drinking habits to conform to the image. He'd cultivated a fair cross section of the town's young bar hostesses to maintain Winters' reputation as a stud. But until last night, he hadn't appreciated how deeply he'd submerged himself in the masquerade.

With Tina, he'd experienced a peculiar disorientation. He had listened to her story with an unaccustomed degree of sympathy. Unaccountably, he had felt pangs of remorse for actions which had been entirely Winters'. He was so subconsciously identified with Winters that when he had voiced his own sentiments on the subjects of marriage and returning to the States, it had been with a sense of guilty betrayal of Winters. If Tina's fleeting presence had done nothing else, it had served to bring his hybrid personality into focus.

Perhaps, he thought, there was some subliminal process in progress, creating an entirely new personality. If it stirred feelings of compassion and tenderness; emotions he'd long thought atrophied in himself, then maybe it wasn't such a bad idea. In fact, since neither Winters nor himself were what he would term attractive characters, any change would be an improvement.

He was not given to introspection. Until a year ago, his calling had been as an expert in the gentle art of assassination. Such a trade rarely invites the preoccupation of self-analysis. But Tina, with her questions, had called up long-buried recollections.

Abetted by the hypnotic effect of the flickering flames, he allowed his memory free rein. Like the rescreening of an old documentary film, some parts blurred and erratic, others vividly clear, the highlights of his life unreeled through the projector of his mind.

When he was less than a year old, his parents were killed in an automobile accident. His grandparents raised him on their Idaho farm. His childhood had been prey to all the small triumphs and tragedies of boyhood and he didn't consider there was anything remarkable about the early years.

He supposed that life had started when he entered the University of Washington, in Seattle. That wasn't strictly true. Life had really started when he'd dropped out of college in the middle of his sophomore year. He and his roommate, Mike O'Donnell, had gone to Vancouver to join the Royal Canadian Air Force.

In Prince Edward Island, he washed out of flight training. He became a bombardier in the RCAF.

When America entered the war, he was already a veteran of many bombing missions over the continent. He was transferred to the Airborne Infantry as a corporal.

In 1944, he was assigned to the Office of Strategic Services. He was parachuted into Northern Italy to join an OSS team working with a partisan group. The OSS team was commanded by Captain Lewis Cantrell.

He fully appreciated that this had been the crucial factor in shaping his life. There had been other points of decision, times when he could have turned away from what was to become a way of life, but it was when he joined with Cantrell's team on the shores of Lake Como that his feet had started down the long road leading to the present.

On Cantrell's orders, he'd undertaken his first act of assassination. He had killed before that assassination, in line of combat duty, and had killed many times since the Lake Como incident; so many times that he had long ago lost count and could not remember many of his targets without an effort of concentration. But that first of his planned executions stood apart in his memory.

In the years which followed Lake Como, he became an acknowledged expert at the killing game. His weapon of preference was a knife, but he was equally proficient with gun, garrote, or the knife-edge of his bare palm. His services had never lacked demand.

In 1945, he was promoted to second lieutenant. Cantrell, now a major, had requested his services in an OSS mission to assist a resistance force in Northern Indo-China, headed by a revolutionary who went by the alias of Ho Chi Minh.

He stayed in Indo-China with the OSS operation, then as a lieutenant attached in a liaison capacity to the French Expeditionary Forces until 1952. He was then sent to join a Special Forces Group operating behind enemy lines with the United Nations Partisan Infantry, Korea – UNPIK.

1953 was the year that Stanford found himself back in the Western Hemisphere for the first time in thirteen years. His grandmother had died while he was still in high school; his grandfather, while he'd been with the OSS in Italy. There had been nothing to attract him to the States and he'd spent his infrequent leaves in Europe. But even now that he was back on North America, he was still a long way from the United States. His posting was to Momotombito, a volcanic island in Nicaragua's Lake Managua. He was to assist an American known as Colonel Rutherford in the training of guerrillas recruited to support a CIA sponsored coup to overthrow the Guatemalan government of President Jacobo Arbenz Guzman.

His attachment in a training role was short-lived. A number of key Communist figures in Guatamala and some troublesome Communist operatives in Honduras, El Salvador and Nicaragua had been marked for elimination. With the cover identity of an insurance adjuster, Stanford shuttled between these countries. One by one, the targets marked for death met with fatal accidents.

Tina's commenting upon his scar had brought back vivid memories of one incident. It had been in El Salvador that his luck had very nearly deserted him. He relived the moment.

In a chilling rain, he waited patiently in an alley close to a *cantina* on the outskirts of San Salvador. His intended victim finally emerged from the bar, to saunter unconcernedly past the mouth of the alley. Stanford stepped lightly up behind him, looped the wire around his neck and dragged the man into the blackness of the alleyway.

Stanford was stooping over, disengaging the piano-wire garrote, when a slight sound alerted him to danger. As he lunged sideways, Stanford saw the faint gleam of a machete and the looming shadow of its wielder. The slashing blow would have decapitated him, but as he rolled clear it only sheared across his lower back. His switch-blade in his hand, he rose in a crouch. The momentum of the machete swing had carried his oponent forward. Already off-balance, Stanford's would-be executioner lurched and slipped on the rain-slicked stones of the alley. Stanford caught him with a karate chop to the neck and before the man could recover the knife was plunged to its hilt in his kidneys. With a strangled sigh, the man collapsed across the corpse of his dead colleague.

Dizzy and light-headed from the exertion and loss of blood from his wound, Stanford managed to make it a few blocks and collapse into a taxi. But before leaving the alley, he'd had the presence of mind to slip the garrote into the nerveless fingers of the topmost body.

As the driver careened through the slippery streets, to deposit his *gringo* fare, as directed, at the nearest hospital, Stanford lost consciousness.

When he came to, he was in a hospital bed. He was advised that though he had lost a lot of blood, the wound was not serious. The flap of flesh had been sutured back in place, but the doctor informed Stanford that the scar would remain with him for life. The doctor had not been wrong.

He rarely thought about the incident. The scar was where he could not see it and his back only stiffened slightly in cold damp weather. Until Tina's exploratory caress, that close brush with death had slipped almost completely from his mind.

His thoughts skipped over the next few years, touching only on the locations of his activities.

In September, 1954, Captain Asquith Stanford joined the training staff of the 77th Special Forces Group (Airborne) at Fort Bragg, North Carolina. When the Hungarian revolt erupted in 1956, he applied for European assignment. His request was accepted with alacrity.

As Dick Charters, a foreign correspondent accredited to

the Washington Sun, Stanford arrived in Vienna. He arranged refugee escapes, engaged in intelligence work and, once again, his talents for dispensing quick and quiet death were called on. With Vienna as his base of operations, he travelled widely throughout Europe for the next three years.

Then, much to his disgust, he was again employed in instructional duties, this time with the 10th Special Forces Group at Bad Tölz, Germany. It was an assignment of short duration. By May, 1960, he was whisked back to Central America, to a coffee plantation called Helvetia, high on the Guatemalan Pacific slopes. Once again, he was training a force of guerrilla revolutionaries. This time, Cubans.

Stanford was not involved in the actual Bay of Pigs debacle. By then, he was attached to a 5th Special Forces 'A' Team on his first tour of duty in Viet-Nam. He returned to Fort Bragg in 1963, as a major.

By late 1966, he was back in Viet-Nam. He was still attached to 5th Special Forces, but was working directly for 'The Brig', the nickname by which Cantrell was now known. Stanford commanded a counter-terrorist unit for most of that period. It had been from an operation of his former unit, an abduction of a National Liberation Front official from the village of Long Hoa, that Stanford had disappeared to wade upstream into the night. At dawn, on the morning of January 22nd, 1968, with his rendezvous at the plantation airstrip, this latest phase had commenced.

Nine days after his clandestine departure, on January 31st, 1968, the Tet Offensive erupted in Viet-Nam. It made Stanford's efforts, all the killing, if not meaningless, at best an exercise in futility. But by then, Stanford was Jud Winters.

Jud stared moodily into the glowing coals. The review of his variegated career had gained him nothing. What, if anything, had he achieved over those years?

Romantically – zilch. There had been women in his life, many of them, but most of his romances had been fleeting in character. The way his life had shaped, it could hardly be otherwise.

Professionally? He had gleaned a good deal of knowledge concerning guerrilla tactics, intelligence gathering, the principles of interrogation and psychological warfare, weapons and unarmed combat. He had risen to the dizzy heights of major. And he had reached the conclusion that messing about with the politics and economics of banana republics was almost as futile as stirring a similar ooze in the Orient. About the only thing he could consider a positive accomplishment was the fact that a natural facility in languages had given him fluency in French, Italian, German and Spanish. If he remained in Chiang Mai much longer, he could add Thai to the list.

Financially? Here he had no complaints. Much of his employment had been in isolated locations where he couldn't have spent money even had he wanted to. His romantic episodes had cost little. Over the years, the major portion of his salary and allowances had gone directly into a Swiss account, as had the proceeds from the sale of his grandfather's farm. He had made a few wise investments. At the moment, his net worth was in excess of 150,000 dollars, most of that in cold hard cash in Switzerland. He could, he recognized, cut-out at any time – if they'd let him.

He often wondered what would have happened if, in 1945, when the OSS was disbanded, he'd opted for State Department instead of Army Intelligence. At the time, he'd had the option. He'd had no particular liking for the army, but he appreciated that he wasn't a team player and had a distaste for administrative work. Cantrell, on the other hand, had gone to State, then through the Central Intelligence Group to CIA when it was formed in 1947. Cantrell had risen to the equivalent rank of brigadier general. A bit better than major. Still, Stanford doubted if his employment would have been much different even if he had gone State and then joined the fledgling Agency. In effect, he had spent a good deal of his career seconded to Agency activities anyway. Advancement for a solitary operator like himself would have been slow in any event. And here he was solidly entrenched in a purely Agency function, whether he liked it or not.

The only advantage he could see to having been with the Agency from its inception was that today he would be senior to that sonuvabitch, Sam Harper.

A band of sunlight slanted through a gap in the study drapes. It splashed across the desk, an empty brandy glass and the gray ashes of the grate.

Jud woke with a start. He sat up. His neck was stiff from the awkward position in the high-backed chair.

Jud rose, yawned and stretched. As he idly scratched his chest and stomach, he thought about the day which lay ahead. Today, if everything went according to plan, U-Thong should arrive in Bangkok. This evening, Chris was coming for dinner. And, along with the routine chores the day might bring, Jud had to make preparations for to-morrow's trip up-country to Phrao.

He yawned again. 'Tis a busy life we timber-buying spies lead, he thought wryly, as he slouched from the room, rubbing the back of his neck.

CHAPTER ELEVEN

Heinrich Keppler was not a happy man.

He sat in a reclining chair on the screened porch, his feet and pudgy legs resting on an ottoman. He was wearing only shorts, the waistband unbuttoned to ease the pressure on his lunch-distended paunch. He was miserably hot in the late May heat, despite the fact that the stand-mounted fan was turned to its highest speed and blowing directly on his chest and shoulders. Absently, he scratched the heat rash at his waist. His unhappiness, however, stemmed not only from this discomfort.

As he had many times over the past months, he reviewed the developing situation which was transforming his idyllic paradise into a minor hell.

Following his summons to Hong Kong by Shepilov, little of any significance happened for almost six months. Shepilov considered that the approach to the Burmese expatriates was nothing more than a probing tactic. Although he didn't report it, Heinrich did not agree. An uneasy feeling per-sisted that this was but the lull before the storm.

In October, he embarked on his usual Southeast Asian selling and buying trip. On his return in early December, it was to find his fears confirmed.

The reports had been slow in reaching Heinrich. Dr. Nyi

had been in receipt of limited funding for almost three months.

If Heinrich had been puzzled before, he was now more confused than ever. The Burmese insurgents had indeed been bargaining with the Americans. Dr. Nyi had repeatedly asked for small arms and financial assistance. Working on the theory that funding and equipment always follows closely on the heels of the introduction of American military advisers, Nyi had entered a plea for advisory personnel. What Heinrich found surprising was that Dr. Nyi's importuning met a deaf ear. Yet financing was being provided, if only in dribbling increments.

It was early January when the first chill winds, harbingers of Keppler's gathering storm, made themselves felt. The deposed Burmese leader, U Thong, had been released from house arrest in Rangoon and had travelled to London under a doctor's care. The excuse given out was that U Thong required medical attention not available in Rangoon. There was evidence, however, that U Thong's ill health was more fiction than fact. There were indications that the London trip had been quietly engineered by MI-6. Then, once in England, U-Thong had simply vanished. The significance of the disappearance was not lost on either Heinrich, or his superiors. The international machinery of the KGB swung into frantic action. To no avail.

To Heinrich's distress, the enigma of U-Thong was resolved in late February. The rotund little Burmese stepped off a TWA flight at Bangkok's Don Muang International Airport. The following day, it was announced in the press that U Thong had been granted political asylum in Thailand. A few days later, Heinrich learned that U Thong had made contact with the Burmese insurgents. And, even more alarming, financial support for the rebels commenced to appear in substantial amounts from an undisclosed source. The winds of Heinrich's storm had reached gale force and showed no signs of abating.

Heinrich cancelled his European business trip. In March, he met with Shepilov in Singapore. Two other men, both total strangers to Heinrich, were present during the three days of sober discussions. On the second day, the group was joined by the regional directors from Rangoon and Bangkok.

A number of courses of action were debated. One of the

strangers, a man named Grubnev, suggested that U Thong be liquidated. It was Shepilov who vetoed this, contending that it was better to have a live leader, of as yet unknown potential, than create a dead martyr. Although the solid proof of American backing was still not available, and despite the obvious participation of British Intelligence, it was now conceded that U Thong's backing had to be American. The very volume of the financial support precluded any other source. It was finally decided that the immediate approach should be to adopt a 'wait and see' attitude. Increased economic aid would be employed to bolster the Ne Win government. Keppler and the other regional agents were to utilize every means to exploit differences and personal ambitions within the factionally-split insurgents and every effort was to be made to determine the extent and direction of American planning.

Events moved rapidly. U Thong's presence was bringing a hitherto impossible cohesion to the ranks of the insurgents. Such was his personal prestige, that a number of the ethnic leaders were now seriously considering joining forces with the Burmese insurrectionists. Although no arms were being supplied directly, a steady flow of American small arms and automatic weapons were being procured by clandestine purchases from the Thai army. A Turkish soldier of fortune, Abdul Bakir, and an English ex-police officer named Hughes were giving training advice. Ample funds to pay for the weapons, the foreign experts, recruitment and training were available through Bangkok banking facilities. These funds, Heinrich learned, were replenished through drafts drawn against a Swiss banking house.

Grudgingly, Heinrich admitted that the operation displayed a highly professional touch. He would not have credited that the CIA could exercise such caution and restraint. It might be suspected, even acknowledged, but at no point could American involvement be proven. Such stratagems were uncharacteristic of American ventures into power politics. It could herald a new sophistication in American policy, but this Heinrich doubted. By nature, Americans are a brash outgoing impatient breed. The more likely explanation was that regional control of this particular enterprise was vested in an individual of caution and with an appreciation of Oriental subtlety. Such a man would be a dangerous adversary.

There were other clouds on Heinrich's horizon. In mid-May, he was assigned an assistant. The man's name was Ted Graves. He was an American, of Hungarian extraction. He was a personable young man of 32. His cover for the assignment was an appointment as assistant professor of archaeology at Ching Mai University. Between Grave's academic interests and Keppler's dealings in antiques, there was sufficient similarity to make their association believable.

Whatever Heinrich's faults, a lack of acuity was not amongst them. He appreciated that Shepilov's selection of Graves was no accident. His youth would serve as an ever-present reminder of Heinrich's age and lengthy tenure in Chiang Mai. Without doubt, this was calculated to act as a spur to Heinrich. And it was not unlikely that Graves was being groomed as an eventual replacement for Keppler.

Heinrich was not averse to retirement – providing he could remain in Chiang Mai, following an orderly supercession. He refused to dwell on the possible alternatives. A good deal, he appreciated, would depend on his handling of the present situation.

Although Graves could not have arrived other than fully briefed, Heinrich reviewed the developments in the light of his own interpretation. Graves was blessed with a sharp analytical mind. In essence, the two men agreed on the probable direction of events and the methods best calculated to thwart the intent. To Graves, Heinrich set the task of exploring every possible avenue to promote dissention within the ranks of the insurgents. For himself, Heinrich reserved the formidable job of determining the American aims.

It was to this noteworthy pursuit, that Heinrich was devoting this blisteringly hot May afternoon.

With a heavy sigh, he brought his gaze from his sunlight flooded garden to a stack of files which sat on a rattan table at his side.

Heinrich had started with certain basic assumptions and by inductive reasoning had narrowed his search down to more or less acceptable limits. The direction of the insurgency operation emanated from Washington, but it had to be coordinated from within Thailand. The questions were, where in Thailand and who was doing the coordinating?

For an operation of this nature, there were necessary prerequisites. One of these was communication. Adequate facilities existed at the major Thai cities and at all the American airbases. For reasons of security and conflict with military interests, Heinrich eliminated the bases. That still left a goodly number of urban locations. Diplomatic pouch, while not essential, would be a most helpful adjunct. Heinrich considered those locations which supported American activities – Bangkok, Songkhla, Udon Thani and Chiang Mai. There was also a USIS Branch Post at Khon Kaen. Of all these, Heinrich considered all but Bangkok and Chiang Mai as too remote and too far from the scene of activity to be worthy of consideration. Bangkok would present conflicts between military and embassy interests. If he were choosing a geographical location, it would be as close to the Shan States and the bulk of the Karen as possible compatible with areas suitable for clandestine training. Which brought him right to his own backyard; Chiang Mai, or its near vicinity. This was no revelation to Heinrich. He'd reached this conclusion more than a year earlier.

Which left him only : 'Who?'

Over the past weeks, Heinrich had reviewed the dossiers he maintained on all *farangs* in the region. There were over four hundred Americans alone, and the man he was looking for need not necessarily be an American. By a process of careful selection, eliminating many for one good reason or another, Heinrich had winnowed the dossiers down to forty which he considered as possible suspects. He was now engaged in bringing that number down to a more manageable level; to those individuals he was singling out for further action. So far, he had only five in this category. They were a Rhodesian, an Australian and three Americans – Lieutenant Colonel Bridgeman, Anthony Carver and Judson Q. Winters.

Winters' file lay on the top of the folders Heinrich had placed to one side. It was by far the thickest of the files. And it was on this particular folder that Heinrich was looking glumly at the moment.

Heinrich had singled Jud out for special attention many

months earlier. Although the measures Heinrich had adopted had failed to confirm his suspicions, they had done little to allay them. In fact, in February, Heinrich had decided to supplement his already tight surveillance of Winters with more direct action. Then a totally unexpected twist had caused him to revise his thinking. That had been the appearance of Winters' old sweetheart in Chiang Mai. But that had been three months ago. The situation had changed. Reluctantly, Heinrich had been forced to the conclusion that he had been thrown off the track. He had reverted to his earlier thinking. Once more, Jud had become a prime, if not *the* prime, candidate. Heinrich intended to put his original plan into action with a minimum of delay and, as an added precaution, have those people in the community with whom Jud had become friendly closely watched.

CHAPTER TWELVE

In late May, Jud received instructions to report on the availability of pine trees for peel-logs. It was early June before he got around to complying with the directive.

Forestry officials advised Jud that the high-altitude slopes of 7,000-foot Doi Luang Chiang Dao were heavily forested with two-needle mountain pine. He mapped out an itinerrary to include an investigation of the area.

Following his normal round of visits to teak forestry stations in the first week of June, he cut back into the mountains north of Taeng River. Beyond the initial ridges, above the 3,000 foot level, he found virgin pine forest. Many butts of the venerable conifers were well over a metre in diameter. But obscuring rain and heavy mist made it impossible to judge the extent of the timber stand. Had he suspected that the rains this early in the month would be so heavy, Jud would have postponed his survey. He would have to return to the region when the rainy season drew to a close.

The Land Rover laboured to the crest of a ridge. As it started the descent from the 3,000-foot ridge-line, it emerged at last from the clouds which had reduced visibility to a scant few yards.

Jud's driver, Noppadol, breathed a sigh of relief as he braked the vehicle and skidded to a stop in the coarse grass at the edge of the logging road. The high country frightened him. He was firmly convinced that a host of evil spirits lurked in the gloom of the rain forests and the eerie, silent, clutching mist which so often pervaded high altitudes. True, they were still some 2,000 feet above the floor of the valley, but now that he could see the muddy track winding down into the bamboo thickets he felt much easier.

The ridge they had just crested marked the end of the tortuous mountain driving. Of the remaining 20 kilometers between this point and the highway, the better part of the descent was a relatively easy gradient. He would no longer require the four-wheel drive he'd been using for the past few hours.

As Noppadol shifted the lever forward to disengage the four-wheel drive, Jud shrugged out of his plastic raincoat. His movement dislodged the Winchester .375 Magnum resting against his right knee. Instead of stowing the rifle in the clip-brackets above the windscreen, he slid it behind him into the metal cab, the barrel resting against the spare tire clamped to the back of the seat and the butt wedged against the metal box which contained the first-aid kit, photographic equipment and spare ammunition.

The Land Rover jolted back into the ruts of the narrow road. Jud reached forward and pushed open the air vent beneath the wind-shield. Relaxing against the backrest, he idly viewed the surrounding scenery. Above them, lowering clouds pressed down threateningly. The peaks of the encircling mountains were hidden in the gray mass. Behind them, the ridge was now obscured as wispy tentacles from the cloud base licked at the tree tops and groped down the slopes. It had stopped raining, but the respite promised to be short lived.

They were proceeding through a tunnel of foliage, leaves and branches scraping the sides of the vehicle, when thunder growled menacingly and rain drummed on the canvas top of the Land Rover. In the shadowed depths of the forest, the gloom intensified. Noppadol geared down to second, switched on the windshield wiper and flicked on the headlights. Jud shut the air vent. Above the whine of the engine, the steady swishing of the wiper mingled with the sounds of the wet shrubbery slapping against the sides of the car.

Jud glanced at the Thai driver. Noppadol's features were set in an expression of strained concentration. Jud smiled. He well appreciated the superstitious Thai's fear of the high country and denser forests.

As they continued the descent, the forest gradually thinned to scrub-jungle. Although thunder continued to rumble, the rain slackened. Visibility improved as the storm-induced twilight lessened. Noppadol shifted back to third, switched off the headlights, and drove with more assurance over the rain-filled ruts.

They heard the stream well before they could see it. Dropping into a defile where giant *mai huak* bamboo arched above them, they skidded around a sharp bend and slid to a stop with the front wheels on moss-blackened gravel scant inches from the rushing water.

Noppadol surveyed the broiling, brown stream dubiously. He glanced questioningly at Jud.

When they had crossed this creek that morning, the water had been lapping at the hub-caps. Swollen from the rain, it now looked almost a foot deeper. They could well get stuck in mid-stream, but the alternative, to wait for the level to subside, was unacceptable. For one thing, there was no assurance the water wouldn't rise even higher. For another, Noppadol wasn't Jud's idea of an interesting overnight companion. Jud shrugged. He nodded, and pointed toward the opposite bank.

Noppadol engaged the four-wheel drive and eased out the clutch, They nosed into the swirling water.

They proceeded almost half way without mishap. Suddenly the vehicle lurched and canted sharply to the left as a front wheel dropped into a depression in the stream-bed. The motor coughed, then stalled.

'Shit,' said Jud disgustedly. He turned toward the driver, and froze in momentary astonishment.

Noppadol was slumped over the steering wheel, his face toward Jud. The driver's mouth hung open foolishly. Where his right eye had been, a raw wound oozed blood and a viscous fluid. In the windshield glass, a star of cracks splayed outward from a neat hole.

Jud's reactions were instinctive. He slid forward in the seat to bring his head below the level of the windscreen. His feet and legs were immersed in water which had seeped under the door on his side of the vehicle. He was oblivious to the discomfort. His mind raced. 'Christ, Jesus Christ,' he thought. 'Ambushed.'

The Land Rover jerked, and settled deeper into the hole. The motion dislodged Nappadol's body. It sagged sideways to sprawl against Jud. Impatiently, Jud pushed the corpse beneath the steering column. Inwardly cursing himself for not having stowed the Winchester in the overhead clips, he groped cautiously over the backrest. His fingers touched the cold metal of the barrel, then it slid from his grasp to clatter against the side of the cab.

Feeling to his left, beneath the water, Jud located the door catch. He pulled up, and with his foot he slowly forced the door open against the outside water pressure. Once opened, the current held it in that position. Jud eased himself in the hip-deep swirling water. He touched bottom and shifted his boots on the slippery rocks until satisfied with his footing. With the open car door shielding him from the view of the marksman on the bank, he worked his way toward the rear of the Land Rover.

When he judged he was positioned close to the rifle, he rose quickly from his crouch. As he reached into the back, the Land Rover lurched. Jud was momentarily off balance. The screening door swung partially closed. Something slammed into Jud's leg. The force broke his grip on the side of the vehicle and he stumbled sideways into the rushing water. He tried to regain his footing, and cursed as his leg collapsed under him. He had heard the crack of a rifle shot, and realized dimly that he'd been hit.

With his clutching fingers clawing at the rocks of the creek bottom, and using his good right leg, Jud attempted to regain the shelter of the stranded Land Rover. With a sinking feeling, he recognized that he made an excellent target. Glancing toward the bank, he noted two black-clad figures emerge from the heavy undergrowth. Both men carried rifles. They started to wade into the stream in the direction of the Land Rover.

Taking a quick gulp of air, Jud ducked beneath the surface of the rushing water. He pushed hard with his good leg. His outstretched hand encountered nothing. Fighting to get a purchase on the slippery stones of the creek-bed, he lunged forward again. This time, his fingers brushed against something solid. His lungs were bursting and the blood pounding in his ears. With an effort born of desperation, he struggled ahead another few inches. He was touching the left rear wheel. His fingers found a grip on the underside of the mud-guard. He pulled himself ahead and to the right.

His head broke surface and he gasped for air. He was at the rear of the vehicle, hidden from the view of his advancing assailants. This sanctuary could last but a few minutes. His one chance was to retrieve the Winchester.

Heaving himself up, he peered cautiously over the tail-gate. The two men had separated and were approaching from both up and downstream angles. They were not as close as he had expected, their advances slowed by the precarious footing and the current.

It was now or never. Pulling his head down out of sight, Jud reached his left arm into the back of the car. His searching fingers found the butt of the rifle. Bracing himself with his right arm, he worked his left hand forward until he had a grip on the small of the butt. In one swift motion, he lifted the rifle to swing it over the tailgate.

Jud heard a shout. A bullet clanged against the metal framework and sang as it ricocheted. The crack of the rifle followed almost simultaneously. Closely on the first, came the bark of a second shot. Jud had the impression that the second report had come from behind him.

Jud flipped off the safety catch of the Winchester and slammed a round into the chamber. Handicapped as he was with his wounded leg, it was going to be one hell of a job to get away a snap shot. The man approaching from up-stream was the closer and would have to be his target. Bracing his shoulder against the rear of the Land Rover he dug his right foot firmly into the rocky creek-bed. 'Here goes nothing,' he muttered as he brought the rifle up and pivoted to the right around the end of the vehicle.

A startling spectacle greeted him. The would-be assassin was floundering in the rushing stream . . . but not approaching. Instead, the man was making for the far bank with frantic haste. 'What the hell!' Jud exclaimed in amazement. As he watched the fleeing figure, the man suddenly flung his arms wide, staggered, and pitched forward into the water. The sharp report of a shot rang out. Unmistakably, the sound came from behind Jud.

Raising his head above the side of the cab, he risked a quick glance to locate his other assailant. He saw the black-clad form sprawled against a rock in mid-stream, some thirty yards away.

Jud turned slowly to scrutinize the bank of the stream to his rear. Nothing stirred, but a thin wisp of blue smoke drifted up from a tangle of bushes close to the water's edge. With his shoulders against the tailgate, he waited warily. Nothing happened. For close to a minute, there was no sign of movement in the shrubbery.

In the adrenalin-pumping moments of the action, he had had no time to dwell on his wound. The wounded leg wasn't paining him yet. It felt numbly wooden. He glanced down and noted that the silted water swirling past his left leg was pink-tinged with blood. He wondered how much blood he'd lost, and how much more he could afford to lose. One thing was sure, the wound would have to have attention without delay.

A movement on the stream's bank attracted Jud's attention. Two men stepped from the bushes. They wore black jackets, loose trousers to just below their knees, and on their heads black doughnut-shaped turbans. From their garb, Jud recognized them as Lahu tribesmen. Both men carried long-barrelled muzzle-loading hunting rifles. Three more figures joined the first two. These latter carried no firearms. Two had cross-bows while the third was armed only with a short sword at his waist. It was rare to find these hunters of the high country at elevations below 3,000 feet. Jud concluded that they must be on one of their infrequent expeditions to trade for salt with the plainspeople.

As unlikely a troop of cavalry as I've ever seen, Jud thought wryly. But you sure as hell arrived in the proverbial nick. Don't think I'm not happy to see you boys. You look just beautiful.

Cradling the Winchester across his chest, Jud managed a broad smile.

One of the riflemen squatted down on his haunches, the

long-barrelled weapon across his knees. The other Lahu stacked their weapons on the bank before stepping into the stream to wade toward Jud and the stranded Land Rover. As they neared, they grinned, displaying teeth stained a gleaming ebony by betel nut.

When they reached Jud, the stocky Lahu broke into excited conversation. He tried responding in Thai, but with no success. All he gleaned from the animated chatter was that his attackers had been Meo. This fact probably explained why the Lahu had intervened on Jud's behalf. While the Lahu distrust and avoid all foreign contact, they harbour a special dislike for the Chinese and Meo. Had the ambushers been Yao or Akha, the Lahu would undoubtedly have left Jud to his fate.

Resorting to pantomime, Jud managed to convey the fact that with his wound he would appreciate some assistance to reach the stream bank. The Lahu beamed and bobbed their heads in understanding and assent.

Two of the tribesmen helped Jud toward the bank. A third pulled the metal box, Jud's knapsack, and a plastic bundle of Noppadol's possessions from the cab of the vehicle and followed a short distance behind. The fourth Lahu floundered off in the opposite direction to examine the Meo corpses and retrieve the ambusher's rifles from the creek bottom.

When Jud reached the bank, he hobbled over to a low rock. Seated, with the metal box by his side, he cut away his bush trouser leg to expose his thigh. The leg was covered in blood. Three bloated leeches clung to the flesh of his upper thigh. Carefully, he examined the wound.

It was in an awkward position. The bullet had passed through the fleshy part of the back of his thigh some four inches below the buttock. The edges of the wound were white and puffy from immersion in the cold water of the creek. This had retarded the bleeding to some extent, but now dark venous blood welled from both the entry and exit openings. He probed gently with his fingers. He couldn't be sure, but he didn't think that the ploughing slug had hit the bones.

With the clasp knife he'd used to remove the trouser leg, Jud cut a strip of cloth which he tied around his thigh above the wound. Inserting the clasp knife in the knot, he tightened the tourniquet to arrest the flow of blood. From the first-aid kit in the metal box, he took sulfa powder and liberally dusted the wound. Forming a thick pad of sterile dressing, he held it tightly against the wound before easing off on the tourniquet. Wrapping bandage around his leg, he bound the pad in place. It was makeshift, but the best he could do. He extracted a phial from the medical kit and gave himself a shot of penicillin above the wound. Satisfied he'd done all he could, he pulled off the leeches and threw them into the water of the creek.

Jud glanced out toward the Land Rover. The Lahu who had gone to search for the submerged rifles had evidently been successful. He was standing waist-deep in the stream, the firearms over his shoulder, beside the canted vehicle. The Lahu reached into the front of the Land Rover and tugged at something in the interior. For a moment, the tribesman's actions puzzled Jud. Then the body of Noppadol was dragged partially clear of the front seat. Shifting his grip from ankle to belt, the Lahu heaved the limp corpse clear and dumped it unceremoniously into the stream. The cadaver turned slowly in the eddy beside the car, then was caught by the current and went bobbing downstream. Ignoring the corpse completely, the tribesman reached again into the front seat and pulled out Jud's plastic raincoat. It was obvious, that to the Lahu the raincoat had considerably more value than a dead Thai.

Jud heard the sound of someone chopping in the bushes. He swung his head in the direction, and suddenly felt dizzy and lightheaded. He was aware that the dull throbbing which had commenced in his leg was becoming increasingly insistent. He started to rise. A wave of nausea and giddiness assailed him and he abruptly resumed his sitting position on the rock. He was weaker from loss of blood than he had thought.

Jud watched idly as the Lahu tied liana vines across two bamboo poles. He recognized the work in progress as the construction of a crude litter intended for his transportation. If he was minimizing the effects of loss of blood. it was obvious that the Lahu hunters were labouring under no such delusion.

CHAPTER THIRTEEN

During his field trips, Jud was often temporarily cut off from direct communication with his office in Chiang Mai. As a precautionary measure against the event of encountering trouble which might detain him, Jud had established a simple emergency procedure. His secretary, Mayuree, was apprised of the date of his intended return from each trip. If a period of forty-eight hours elapsed between that date, with no word from Jud amending his intended time of return, she would automatically advise Santa Rosa Lumber's Manila office.

At 4:00 pm on the second Thursday in June, having gone almost a full working day over the imposed time limit, Mayuree reluctantly initiated the emergency procedure. A chain reaction was set in motion.

Sam Harper's immediate response to the news of Jud's disappearance was one of annoyance. His secondary reaction was apprehension. Not knowing what had happened to Winters, he considered the worst possible consequences. Jud's cover identity could have been exposed. He could have been eliminated or, what was even more to be feared, captured and interrogated. At this juncture, there was little Sam could do apart from taking the necessary remedial action. He would have to await further developments before he could make any valid appreciation and recommendations.

In his official capacity with Santa Rosa, Harper dispatched a telex instructing Mayuree to keep Manila advised and telling her that in the event of Winters' continued absence Rudolfo would be flown up the following Monday to take temporary charge of the Chiang Mai operation.

In his covert role, Harper's problem was more complicated. He originated a number of high priority messages. LeFarge was instructed to hold other than urgent reports until further notice. Chris Perkins was advised to route accumulated raw intelligence to Bangkok, and to keep a close watching brief on developments. If, in Perkins' opinion, the network had been jeopardized in any way, codes and files were to be destroyed and Manila advised accordingly. CIA headquarters in Langley, Virginia was informed simply that 'Pitt' was temporarily out of action.

Additional news was not long in reaching an anxious Harper. By Saturday, the Thai district police had discovered both the abandoned bullet scarred Land Rover and the body of the murdered driver. Winters appeared to have vanished completely.

Sam Harper was in an agony of suspense. Without positive knowledge he had to assume the worst possible conditions. While overreaction was a danger, he could not delay further actions. He decided that unless he received more concrete concerning Winters' fate within the next two days the intelligence infrastructure would have to be dismantled.

The coded message Harper received Sunday evening removed the necessity for drastic action. A tribesman from a remote Lahu village had trekked down from the mountains and informed the police post at Mae Taeng that Winters was safe in the village recovering from a leg wound and should be in condition to travel within a few days.

Harper's reaction was oddly mixed. On the one hand, he was profoundly relieved that he was no longer faced with the acute problem of a blown network. Yet Harper also experienced a momentary surge of anger. He was honest enough with himself to admit that secretly he had harboured the hope that Winters had been eliminated miraculously and permanently from the picture. Over the past months, Winters' intransigence, and largely negative situation reports had become a galling thorn in Harper's flesh. He could not escape the growing conviction that sooner or later Winters would have to be removed from the scene.

Winters had legislated for three emergency conditions: that it was discovered his cover was blown, that he be killed by accident or design or that he should simply disappear. All three possibilities called for prompt and specific action on Perkins' part, but it was the latter which would pose the greatest dilemma. Jud had stressed that if missing he must be assumed to have been abducted until there was positive proof to the contrary. If subjected to interrogation by his captors, there was no guarantee that, under the persuasive inducement of torture or drugs, he would not divulge damaging information. The safest course for Perkins to pursue was to conclude that the network had been compromised. Acting on this assumption, Perkins was to initiate security procedures without question or delay.

Initially, Perkins must be satisfied that an appropriate message had been sent to Santa Rosa. Following this, he was to insure that all codes, documents, and filmed reports were safeguarded. Next, he must arrest the flow of incoming intelligence. Then came the most difficult task of all. With no assurance that he himself had not been marked as a target, Perkins must behave totally unconcerned. Nothing in his actions should attract attention to the fact that his relationship with Winters was other than casual.

Aware that Jud was overdue, Chris went to Winters' villa shortly after 3:00 pm on Thursday. As his excuse for the visit, Chris took along a number of photo-studies to be returned to Jud.

Having determined that there had been no word from Jud, Chris suggested that Mayuree follow Jud's instructions and advise the Santa Rosa head office.

In the photo lab, Chris checked the wall safe. The lock plate and combination dial were in the correct position. Chris saw no immediate reason for destruction of the safe's contents. He selected a number of portrait studies from a stack by the wall, satisfied himself that none were microfilm coded, and left the lab.

As he recorded the serial numbers of the studies he'd returned, and noted the numbers of those he was taking on a pad in the office, Chris satisfied himself that Mayuree had indeed sent the required telex to Manila.

He arrived back at his office shortly before five o'clock. There was one important detail remaining. He put through a call to USIS in Bangkok and spoke to Ed Shipley. Chris advised that he would be coming down to Bangkok on Thursday instead of Wednesday as planned. Then, he called the Windjammer and asked for Skidalski, the proprietor. Chris apolgized, and cancelled a dinner reservation for the following Wednesday.

That took care of cutting off the flow of intelligence from the Southern contact, 'Emily'. 'Garth', the Reverend Cox, presented no problem. The pick-up was effected during Perkins' weekly trips to the Karen Mission School in Mae Sariang. The next visit was scheduled for Tuesday, which would be soon enough to advise Cox of the situation.

Now all Chris had to do was to play it cool and await further developments. In the months he'd been associated with Jud, Chris had developed not only a genuine affection for his immediate superior, but a healthy respect bordering on awe for Jud's keen insight and attention to detail. Chris was concerned over the disappearance, but not unduly worried. He had the utmost faith in Jud's ability to handle any situation that might arise.

Within less than forty-eight hours, Perkins' confidence would be badly shaken.

Through his numerous contacts, Hank Keppler followed the events arising from Jud's disappearance. Keppler was aware of the steps taken to advise the Manila head office of Santa Rosa and the response concerning Rudolfo. Early Saturday afternoon, when the report of the location of Jud's abandoned Land Rover and dead driver was circulated, Keppler feigned shocked surprise. By then, Hank was well ahead of the police, having been informed already of the Lahu intervention and the fact that Jud was recovering from a minor leg wound in the hill tribe village. Keppler watched the unfolding events and local reaction with anxious interest.

From Keppler's point of view, the developments were disappointing. If Jud Winters was an imposter; if he was, as Hank suspected, a key figure in the CIA intelligence network, there should have been some indication of alarm on the local scene. This didn't appear to be the case.

A measure of excitement was generated in the U.S. Consulate, but seemingly no more than would have been caused by news of an ambush of any American citizen, not enough to disrupt the weekend plans of the consul or vice-consuls.

The foreign community buzzed with speculation, but this quickly subsided when it was reported on Sunday that Jud was safe in a Lahu Na village. Perhaps, Keppler concluded, this conformation had come too rapidly to permit a build-up of tension and response.

In the year since Winters had taken up residency in Chiang

134

Mai, he hadn't been exactly a recluse, but he'd formed few friendships which could be termed intimate or even close. Of this fact, Keppler was well aware since he was himself one of the select group by virtue of the weekly chess games. Apart from young Perkins, Keppler could think of no other who enjoyed Jud's hospitality on anything like a regular basis. This limited exposure of Winters to *farang* circles restricted gossip to a point where it was virtually useless to Keppler.

To Hank, Jud's connections with the Thai community were equally unrewarding. Winters' contacts were confined largely to those officials who could assist him in business. On the recreational level, some of the more attractive club and bar hostesses were not infrequent overnight guests at Jud's villa. Keppler relied on many of these quasi-prostitutes as prime sources of intimate details concerning their clientele. Jud played the field, and treated the young ladies with almost clinical detachment. While the girls could vouch for Jud's virility, they provided little else of background value.

To all outward appearances, Jud's friendship with Perkins was based on a common interest in books, photography and, to a lesser degree, chess. Keppler did not discount the possibility of some clandestine connection, but had uncovered nothing to lend any credence to his suspicions. But, to be on the safe side, he had taps placed on Perkins' telephones at both home and office.

For want of any more immediate frame of reference, Keppler watched Perkin's reaction to Jud's disappearance with close attention.

Chris was one of the first to know of Jud's failure to return on schedule. From Jud's cook, Hank learned that Chris had visited the villa on Thursday afternoon. The Thursday call had been to exchange a number of photographic blow-ups. Later that same afternoon, Chris had placed two long distance calls to Bangkok. The one to USIS had advised that Perkins was postponing an intended visit in the coming week from Wednesday to Thursday. The second call had been to the proprietor of a restaurant called The Windjammer cancelling a dinner reservation for Wednesday.

In playing back the taped recordings of the telephone conversations, Keppler could find nothing in either tone or content to indicate alarm or concern. No mention had been made of Winters. Keppler dismissed the calls as innocent and trivial.

Saturday noon, Keppler waited at the bar of Pat's Terrace Grill. By this time, the news concerning the location of Jud's Land Rover and dead driver was common knowledge. It was Perkins' practice to stop by Pat's for a couple of drinks, if not lunch, on Saturdays and Hank was anxious to observe Chris' reaction to the latest development.

At 12 : 15 Perkins entered the restaurant and seated himself at the bar alongside Keppler. Nodding glumly at Hank, Chris ordered an Amarit.

Hank ordered a refill of his vodka and tonic. 'What do you make of the news about Jud?' he asked Chris casually.

'Christ,' Chris replied, 'I just don't understand it. Jud's well known in that region. Can't think of any reason for insurgents to attack him. Could have bumped into a party of opium buyers by accident, I suppose, but it isn't the season. It doesn't make any sense.'

'No,' Hank agreed readily, 'it doesn't. But maybe we're all jumping to conclusions. They didn't find Jud . . . just the car and driver.'

Perkins brightened. 'True, and Jud's always struck me as a guy who could look after himself in any situation. Hope you're right.' Chris topped up his glass of beer and continued reflectively, 'Makes me think though. Have to drive to the Karen Mission School in Mae Sariang every week. Been making the trip there and back the same day, which often gets me back here quite late. If insurgents are starting to hot up the action, I'd better exercise a little more caution. Sure have no desire to spend any more time than I have to in a dump like Mae Sariang, but suppose staying overnight is wiser than travelling the road after dark.'

Hank scrutinized Perkins' face thoughtfully. The shift to a personal focus was either skilful dissimulation or an ingenuous expression of self-interest. Keppler could hardly credit the young man with such guile, but it was always a posibility. Hank tacked back onto the original course. 'From the location where they found the Land Rover, I don't imagine Jud was travelling at night.'

'No, suppose you're right. Still, it sure makes you think.'

Discouraged, but not willing to give up, Hank persisted. 'They say they didn't find any trace of Jud and none of his gear was in the car. Do you think there is a chance he wasn't present when the Land Rover was ambushed?'

Chris sipped his beer and appeared to mull the possibility before answering. 'Not likely,' he said gloomily. 'Where could he have been in that region, but in the car? They didn't find any of the driver's effects either. The more logical explanation would be that the insurgents stole everything moveable. No, if Jud got away I suppose he's wandering around somewhere in the jungle.'

'If so,' Hank observed drily, 'I hope he's armed.' He tried one last probing question. 'What makes you so sure he was ambushed by insurgents?'

The directness of the question startled Chris. The astonishment betrayed by his answering tone was genuine. 'Who else? ... He might have surprised some Chinese opium buyers, but at this time of the year that's highly unlikely.' Chris frowned, and allowed a trace of sarcasm to edge his voice. 'Surely you aren't suggesting that his competitors would try and knock him out of the box?'

Hank chuckled in simulated amusement. 'Jud's professional success has created a good deal of envy, even animosity, but that *would* be a pretty extreme measure. Still, he could have other enemies.'

'I doubt it,' Chris said curtly.

Keppler drained his glass and glanced at his watch. He motioned to the bartender for his check and murmured an apology to Chris with reference to a luncheon engagement.

As he scrawled his signature on the check, Keppler chided himself for his heavy-handed approach. True, he had sparked a reaction from Perkins, but it had proved nothing. To his surprise, and faint amusement, Hank found that he had resented Perkins' instinctive self-interest. Still, he admitted ruefully, the allocation of priorities with a preference for self-preservation was a natural reaction, especially in the young. Nonetheless, he felt that Chris might have displayed a little more sympathy for Jud's plight.

Although he was inwardly pleased with the manner in which he'd handled the exchange, Chris maintained an attitude of mild annoyance as he nodded farewell to Keppler and watched his departure reflected in the bar mirror.

Jean-Paul LeFarge was not immediately aware of Jud's

disappearance. By the time he learned of the event, Winters was already back in Chiang Mai.

An emergency meeting of the *capos* of the *Union Corse* engaged in the regional narcotics traffic, with representatives from Ajaccio and Marseilles, had been hastily convened in Saigon.

The crisis which precipitated this conference first manifested itself in the region under Jean-Paul's jurisdiction. His reporting of a growing threat to the suzerainty of the Corsican brotherhood had generated sufficient alarm amongst the hierarchy to necessitate a meeting to determine countermeasures and future policy. Discussions of the aspects and implications of the crisis and suggested remedial action absorbed the better part of a week. The meetings took place in secluded back rooms and private dining rooms of a number of the Corsican-owned Saigon cafes and bar restaurants. In an atmosphere of serious attention as befitted a business enterprise involving millions, in rooms redolent of tobacco smoke, Algerian wine, *pastis*, *café filtre*, and cognac, the matter was debated to conclusion. The measures adopted, as they applied to the Asian operations, were those advanced by Jean-Paul LeFarge.

When Jean-Paul enplaned for Vientiane, it was with the confidence that he'd gained added stature amongst his colleagues. He had secured a position which, if not exactly unassailable, at least placed him in the ranks of the contenders for eventual admission into a more elevated echelon. Jean-Paul was well pleased.

Directly upon his return to Vientiane, Jean-Paul embarked on a series of visits to the outlying districts of his narcotic fiefdom. At Long Chen, he became *au courant* with the developments concerning his clandestine intelligence function. The message suspending operations was there, together with a message from Winters instructing resumption of normal communications.

There were a number of matters, directly and indirectly connected with the Saigon meetings, which must be brought to Winters' attention without delay. The nature of the information suggested that it would be better conveyed by personal contact rather than microfilmed report.

From Vientiane, Jean-Paul sent Jud a telegram advising his intention to visit Chiang Mai the following week.

CHAPTER FOURTEEN

Jud lay with his eyes closed, trying to sort out the medley of sounds and smells which assaulted him.

The discordant noise divided itself into component parts of the cackling of poultry, grunting of hogs, the sharp barking of dogs and a soft rustling sound which defied description. In the olfactory department he mentally classified wood smoke, the acrid odors of dung, urine and stale sweat, and a sweetish smell he finally recognized as opium smoke.

Memory returned. He was, he deduced without visual confirmation, in a Lahu village dwelling.

Something cool and damp brushed his forehead. He opened his eyes. It took a moment for his vision to adjust to the smoky semi-gloom. Turned slightly to one side, rinsing a cloth in a gourd of water, a girl knelt beside him. She was unaware of Jud's scrutiny.

She wore the traditional Lahu garb of cloth leggings, sarong-like shirt and loose tunic decorated with white quilted piping. The top of this garment was tied loosely at the neck but the silver disc which secured the front was unfastened, affording Jud a tantalizing view of her slim waist and the curve of firm young breasts.

She turned to resume her task of bathing Jud's face and became aware that he was awake and staring at her. A shy smile trembled on her lips.

The girl was unlike any Lahu he'd ever seen. Her oval face, framed in loosely-combed long hair, possessed a cameo-like quality. Her eyes were large and wide-set; her nose delicately bridged. Parted in a tremulous smile, her full lips revealed white even teeth. Only a slight prominence of cheek bones hinted at Oriental ancestry. She was, Jud thought, one of the most startlingly beautiful creatures he'd ever seen. He judged her to be young, no more than eighteen at the outside. But what in hell was she doing here in a remote Lahu village?

He tried to speak, but his voice was a dry croak. Grinning apologetically, Jud cleared his throat and tried again. 'Who are you?' he questioned.

'*Na Hti*',' she answered simply.

'Naughty,' he repeated, his expression betraying confusion.

The girl laughed. '*Na . . . Hti*,' she repeated, stressing the division, then added, 'In English, mean 'Dawn'.'

'Naw Tee,' Jud repeated. Then it struck him that this limited conversation was being conducted in English. 'You speak English?'

Her face wore a frown of concentration as she framed her response. It was obvious that there had been little recent exchange in the unfamiliar tongue. 'I learn Chiang Rai . . . mission school. My father teach.' She concluded with a smile of triumph.

Her reply posed more question than it answered. There were a number of mission schools in and around Chiang Rai . . . German, Finnish and American. By implication, her father was a missionary, unless she was using the term in its Catholic sense. From her features and fair complexion, Jud assumed that her father must be Caucasian. Her presence in the village led him to assume her mother must be Lahu. But from where he'd been ambushed to Chiang Rai was a long, long trek. He wondered if her missionary father was spreading his brand of faith in this remote region.

Jud might have probed further had not more pressing problems commanded his immediate attention. For one thing, he was conusumed by a raging thirst. For another, he needed to urinate.

'Water?' Jud queried.

Her face registered concern. 'Water . . . yes,' she answered,

Rising gracefully, she moved across the hut to where a number of bamboo-joint storage containers stood by the door. She filled a gourd dipper.

As she was returning, Jud started to sit up. He became aware of two things which had escaped his attention until this moment. Pain stabbed at his left thigh. Glancing down, he discovered that, discounting a rough bandage encasing his left thigh, he was mother naked.

In order to bathe him, the girl had pushed a cotton blanket down to his feet. Jud snatched at it, drawing it up to his waist. He took the proffered dipper from her, grinning in embarrassment. She appeared to notice nothing unusual.

The water had a smoky flavour, but was cool and refreshing. He drained the gourd.

'Eat?' she asked with anxious concern.

Now that she mentioned it, he was aware he was hungry, but the pressure on his bladder could no longer be ignored. This was no time for false modesty. Besides, by this time she was thoroughly conversant with his anatomy in her capacity of nurse. 'Pee,' he said, struggling to stand on his good leg and, at the same time, tuck the blanket around his waist. He steadied himself with one hand against the slope of the low roof. As he started to hop toward the hut doorway, Na Hti was at his side instantly, lending support on his left side. He was weaker than he'd thought. He wondered how long he'd been unconscious.

'How long . . . how many days have I been here?' he asked.

'You here two day.'

Two days, he thought. He'd have to get some sort of message to the outside world without delay.

Through the doorway, Jud viewed shifting curtains of rain. That accounted for the sound he'd been unable to identify. It had been the whisper of rain on the roof thatch above his head.

They navigated through the door onto a wide porch formed by an extension of the bamboo-pole flooring of the hut. A thatched overhang provided protection from the rain. A single notched log formed a crude stairway leading down to the ground some six feet below the porch level. Even with Na Hti's assistance, the descent was out of the question. He hobbled along to one side of the porch.

Jud sighed with profound relief as his urine arced downward. From beneath the hut a dog ran out, its teeth bared. Curious children watched Jud from the doorway of an adjoining hut. The dog barked furiously.

Nothing like an appreciative audience, mused Jud, directing his stream onto the dog. Snarling, the cur backed off. Na Hti giggled.

Na Hti assisted Jud back into the dwelling and to the pallet of dried grass which served as his bed.

While Na Hti busied herself at the fire-pit preparing Jud something to eat, he took stock of the dim interior.

The fire-pit was an earth-filled, slabsided box which dominated the centre and front half of the one-room dwelling. Smoke drifted up past drying racks laden with peppers and strips of meat. The ridgepole of the thatched roof was obscured by the smoke.

Beside the fire, exchanging an occasional word with Na Hti, a young woman sat contentedly puffing a pipe while she breast-fed a baby. A second child played unconcernedly in the spilled ashes of the fire-pit.

At the rear of the hut, beside a crude altar used to propitiate the 'Father God' and an assortment of good and evil spirits, an elderly woman sat hunched over some needlework. At her side, reclining on a straw sleeping-mat, was an old man, emaciated to almost skeletal dimensions. As Jud watched, the woman put aside her work long enough to form a blob of opium over the flame of a tiny lamp. Satisfied she transferred the bubbling substance to the bowl of a long-stemmed pipe. The man stirred himself enough to drag the bitter-sweet smoke deep into his lungs, then subsided back onto his headrest.

The absence of any other male members of the family, Jud concluded, must mean a hunting party was absent from the village.

At Jud's side, where the roof thatch met the flooring, were stacked his and Noppadol's effects and a neat pile of Jud's laundered clothing.

Jud examined his wounded leg. Gingerly lifting one edge of the coarse cotton bandage, he beheld a sort of poultice which appeared to consist of a mixture of mud, crushed leaves and cobwebs. He was confident of its healing powers. The Lahu were no strangers to wounds and, down the course of centuries, had perfected effective remedies.

Jud ate a satisfying meal of boiled rice liberally fortified with chunks of meat and hot peppers. He wanted to remain awake until the family menfolk returned. The two men, one young and one of middle years, both of whom had been members of the party that rescued Jud from the Meo ambush, returned well after dark. By that time, Jud was sound asleep.

The next morning, with Na Hti acting as interpreter, Jud managed to convey his desire to have Chiang Mai notified of his safety and presence in the Lahu village. After a good deal of debate, the necessity for which Jud could not fathom, it was agreed that a messenger would be dispatched to the police post in the valley.

CHAPTER FIFTEEN

Life in the remote mountain village was simple. The villagers rose at cock's crow. After a frugal meal, those who were not assigned specific chores and housekeeping duties in the village, or were not included with hunting parties, set off for the communal fields situated some kilometers away. In this season, Jud learned, labour was devoted to tending the newly planted corn and dry rice.

At dusk, the villagers returned to partake of an evening meal and retire early. The exceptions to this pattern were the hunting parties which often were absent for several days on end.

For the first few days, Jud ventured no further than the porch. He would sit warming himself in the morning sun unless driven back into the hut's smoky interior by rain squalls. He watched the morning mists swirl up from deep valleys, the clouds forming in convoluted masses over the peaks, and the approaching veils of rain.

He could hear the ringing of axes from the distant clearings. Closer at hand, against an intermittent strident symphony of cicadas, was the laughter of children playing on the hard packed earth around the huts. In fascinated amusement, he watched the boys play a game where they spun hardwood tops from long whipcords; the idea being to strike, and if possible break, the top of one's opponent.

When she was not taking washing to a distant stream and returning laden with water-filled bamboo joints, Na Hti was Jud's constant companion and mentor in the ways of village life.

By the fourth day, the bandage was removed from his injured leg. The wounds were an angry red, but free from infection and healing satisfactorily. The pain had subsided. but the leg was stiff and sore. One of the village men fashioned a crude crutch, which, once he had managed the descent of the notched log, enable Jud to hobble, followed by an interested retinue of pigs and dogs, to the edge of the clearing to relieve himself in the relative privacy of screening shrubbery.

The explanation of Na Hti's presence in the village was the substance of several conversations between herself and Jud. She discovered that her mother was Lahu; her father a Lutheran missionary named Carl Grundlich. The exact status of her mother in the Grundlich household, whether wife, mistress, or servant, was not clearly defined.

Na Hti had little memory of her mother who had died after the birth of her daughter and only child. Until the age of fourteen, Na Hti had been raised by her father and the Thai servants. Then, four years ago, Grundlich had been transferred from Chiang Rai. Na Hti did not know the reason for his sudden move and was vague concerning his whereabouts. The paternal exodus had been with little advance warning and he had been unable to take her with him. Hurried arrangements had been concluded for her to come and live with her mother's people. She had been here ever since.

Her relationship within the household was clarified. The opium addicted oldster was her maternal grandfather. The senior functioning male was her uncle. He was also the *paw khu*, the spiritual leader of the community and, as such, a figure of considerable authority. The young mother was Na Hti's cousin, and the younger man her cousin's husband.

It required little perceptive power on Jud's part to recognize that Na Hti's position in the household and village community was anomalous. It would have been a minor miracle had it been otherwise. Aside from her distinctly Caucasian features and light colouring, there were other marked differences which set her apart from her Lahu kinfolk. The most noticeable of these was her height. At five foot six inches, she towered above the stocky Lahu women and was taller than most of the tribesmen. Her hair, which had appeared black in the gloom of the hut's interior, had a coppery sheen when viewed in sunlight. Disdaining the traditional bun and turban of the tribeswomen, she wore her hair long and loosely brushed. And she exhibited another trait, decidely uncharacteristic in the Lahu.

144

Jud concluded that 'Cleanliness is akin to Godliness' was a tenet that varied widely with theistic persuasion. That the 'Father God' of the Lahu supported no such precept was amply attested by Jud's eyes and nostrils. In truth, such a dictum espoused by a hill tribe deity would have been unduly harsh. Water was a precious commodity, too valued to be put to such frivolous usage as bathing. Built as they were on mountain ridges, the villages were often situated a considerable distance from a source of fresh water. The requirements for cooking and drinking had to be transported daily, in gourds and bamboo joints, from a distant stream. It was unrealistic to presume that the liquid would be wasted in washing. Jud found the powerful effluvia of the hut's interior offensive. It smelled like a combination of a railroad station lavatory and a busy squash court. He doubted if he would ever become accustomed to the smell, which bothered the Lahu not at all.

Na Hti, however, was an exception. Her body gave off only the faintest of musk odours, which he found not only inoffensive, but appealing. Jud decided that she must find time to bathe during her daily treks to wash clothing and fetch water. In this, she must be unique and considered odd indeed by the other women.

Jud itched, and stank to his own nostrils. He had also accumulated a growing population of ticks and lice. A four day growth of beard was an annoyance as well. Jud wished fervently to accompany Na Hti to the source of the village water supply. On his fifth day, he voiced such a request.

They started out early in the morning with a party of women and youths. Before long, Jud and Na Hti were lagging well behind since, even with Na Hti's assistance, he had difficulty negotiating the narrow trail.

They were nearing the stream. Jud could hear the babble of voices and the splatting of wet clothing as it was slapped against smooth rocks. Na Hti stopped suddenly. She parted a screen of bushes to reveal a second track and beckoned Jud to follow. They made slow progress, his crutch more a hindrance than a help as it kept getting caught in a tangle of vines and clutching shrubbery. The track continued to descend steeply. He could hear, but not see the gurgling creek and concluded they were paralleling its course. The voices behind them quickly faded, the jungle silence broken now only by the sound of the nearby rushing water and the occasional raucous call of a bird. High above them, the meshing canopy of jungle foliage filtered most of the sunlight. It was cool in the forest's gloom, but Jud was sweating profusely from his efforts.

After about ten minutes, they emerged at the side of the stream. Jud was confronted with a scene of sylvan beauty.

A dark basalt face formed a small escarpment. To the right, the rushing stream cascaded down over glistening spray-slicked rocks in coruscating splendour. The tumultuous energy of the falls was absorbed by the placid surface of a wide pool. The far side of the natural basin, at the base of the cliff, was in deep shadow from the overhang. At the point where they had broken from the jungle, the foliage thinned and a grassy verge sloped gently to the water and a small crescent of sun-drenched sand.

Jud was enchanted, his pleasure reflected in a smile. Na Hti had been watching his face anxiously to ascertain his reaction to this, her secret glade. Reassured, she laughed softly in response.

She had brought his towel, soap, and shaving articles wrapped in the bundle of soiled clothing she carried. Jud took them from her, and spread them at the edge of the pool. While he worked soap into his growth of beard, Na Hti took the soiled clothing to a point where smooth rocks formed the confining bank. While he laboriously scraped off the accumulated growth of five days, he listened to Na Hti singing softly to herself as she scrubbed the clothes and spread them to dry on the warm rocks.

He had stripped off his clothing, rubbed himself vigorously with the fine sand, soaped himself, and waded chest deep into the cold water. He stood now, his shoulders warmed by the morning sun and his lower extremities tingling in the refreshingly chill water. He listened to the splashing of the falls, breathed deeply of the clear clean air, and for the first time in many months felt completely at peace with himself and the world.

Jud was startled from his idle contemplation as something beneath the surface grabbed hard at his calf. He yelled, thrashed the water and flung himself awkwardly to one side. In front of him Na Hti's laughing face broke surface. Absorbed in his reverie, he hadn't noticed her singing stop as she quietly disrobed and slipped silently into the water behind him.

Scowling ferociously, Jud lunged towards her. With a squeal of mock terror, she twisted from his grasp gracefully and, disappeared beneath the surface. Jud followed in a shallow dive. With powerful strokes, he overtook the flashing slender legs. Catching her by one ankle, he pulled her sharply backwards. As her slim body passed beneath him, he pushed her down into the depths.

Jud surfaced close to the falls and waited until she rose gasping and sputtering at his side. He grinned, and reached to push her under once more. Grasping his wrists, she fought back. Laughing, and slipping on the submerged rocks, they struggled back and forth in the spray and tumbling torrent.

At one point, Na Hti lost her footing and fell against Jud. She clung to him, her firm breasts flattened against his chest. Without conscious direction, his arms encircled her protectively. She looked up into his face, the laughter dying on her lips. Fine droplets of spray splashed her upturned face. Her eyes grew wide, and her lips parted. His own laughter subsided as he gazed down on her. As he gently brushed wet hair from her cheek, he felt a sudden constriction in his chest.

She pulled away from him and took his hand. Wordlessly, she tugged until he followed. Together, with slow strokes, they swam towards the grassy bank.

He lay naked on the sun-dappled grass, his face partially protected from the mid-morning sun by the shade from overhead foliage. A pleasant lassitude engulfed him. His errant thoughts touched lightly on the pleasurable experience of a few moments earlier.

That Na Hti had been a virgin was something he could scarcely credit, but was undeniable fact. The Lahu attitude towards pre-marital sexual relations was notably permissive. It would be preternatural to expect any Lahu maiden to have gone much beyond puberty without defloweration. That Na Hti had attained the age of eighteen and remained untouched was remarkable. But was it? When he pondered the phenomenon, it wasn't really that surprising. To his eyes, Na Hti was a sylph-like creature of exquisite beauty, but to the stocky Lahu she was grotesquely alien. He had remarked in the village that the children tended to avoid her and the youth shunned her. Now that he thought about it, even the adults seemed uncomfortable in her presence. Her virginal status was more likely due to lack of opportunity than any desire for chastity. Certainly, beyond the point of hymenal rupture, there had been no lack of response on her part. He supposed that he should feel a twinge of guilt, but he didn't. Their love making had seemed as natural as breathing.

His train of thought was interrupted by her voice.

'You go away soon.' It was more a statement than a question.

Jud turned onto his side. She sat cross-legged beside him, unabashedly naked, her hair fanned out across her shoulders. Her eyes were downcast.

'Yes,' he answered. 'In a day or two, when my leg is a little less stiff.'

Restively, she plucked idly at a tuft of grass. Her soft voice was barely audible. 'You take me?'

It was a moment before her hesitant request registered on Jud. She was asking him to take her with him when he left the village to return to Chiang Mai. In what capacity? He hadn't discussed Chiang Mai, or his life there, with her. For all Na Hti knew, he could have a wife and many children. God knows, he was old enough to be Na Hti's father. How did she propose to accompany him; as wife, mistress, servant, or adopted daughter? She was, after all, just a child.

Na Hti raised her eyes to Jud's frowning countenance. In his expression, she read refusal. Her face betrayed no emotion, but her voice faltered when she spoke. 'I cook . . . wash . . .' Her voice trailed off into an embarrassed silence.

Jesus Christ, he thought. At least it partially clarified her position. She didn't expect to parley her lost maidenhead into some sort of quasi-marital status. And he amended his earlier appraisal. She was no child. By her age, the other girls of the village were already wives and mothers. He had not thought of her as a child a few minutes earlier, why should he do so now?

The growing silence was broken only by the twittering

148

of birds. Na Hti's face did not register her inner turmoil, but she seemed unable to extend this emotional mastery to her voice. She dropped her eyes, as she advanced her final plea. 'I no trouble.'

Holy Mother of God. No trouble. The last thing he needed was something to add to his problems, such as the responsibility for a teenager, even a damned attractive and mature teenager like Na Hti. But one thing he now recognized. Her request had not stemmed from any spur of the moment whim. It had probably been forming in her mind for days, or she wouldn't be pressing it now against what must be obvious displeasure. Jud tried to place himself in her position. Her life with her mother's people must be desperately unhappy. It was only natural that she should seek an avenue of escape. Then, by purest chance, a wounded stranger was thrust upon the hill tribe. Moreover, the stranger was from that world which Na Hti associated by fond recollection with her childhood. To the lonely girl, this must have seemed like some sign sent from the Lutheran concept of Heaven. Jud could think of no conceivable reason why she should not look upon himself as a means of deliverance.

When he looked back on it later, he couldn't explain just why he had been seized with a compassion wholly foreign to his nature. It could have been a combination of the warm morning sun, the soft splashing of the nearby falls, the seductive twittering of birds, the clear mountain air and the tranquillity of the secluded glade, but was more likely the enchanting supplicant, vulnerable in her nudity. who sat at his side. But defy retrospective interpretation though it might, the fact was that he leaned towards her and placed a reassuring hand on hers.

'You will come with me,' he said simply.

CHAPTER SIXTEEN

They started out after an early breakfast. Their stated intention was to drive to Lampang to inspect teak log stockpiles at the rail yards. Jud had informed the staff that they would be back in time for a late lunch prior to

Jean-Paul's afternoon flight to Bangkok. The 260 kilometre return trip would give them privacy and ample time to discuss the purpose of Jean-Paul's visit.

When they turned onto the beltway which circled to the north of the town, Jean-Paul opened the conversation without preamble. 'The opium business is important, *n'est-ce pas?'*

'It has a marked bearing on the economy and politics of the region. Yes, I would say it's a vital consideration,' Jud replied.

'You must have a pretty good idea how the trade operates.'

'It features rather largely in most of the agent's reports. I would say I have a fair working knowledge, but I'm sure you could enlighten me concerning the more intimate details,' Jud answered drily.

'I could, but first I think you should have some background which I doubt was included in the Brig's briefing. Started to tell you some of it on our first meeting in Vientiane.'

Glimpsing the direction of Jean-Paul's disclosures, Jud interrupted. 'If you're about to confess that your loyalty to the *Union Corse* takes precedence over that to the Agency, it isn't necessary. I'd be pretty naïve to imagine that you could have become a *capo* without a little more than two years affiliation with the organization. From what I know of your feudal brotherhood, I would assume your connections go back some distance in time. My only hope is that this divided allegiance doesn't destroy your effectiveness as an agent.'

Jean-Paul was thrown off stride momentarily. It had been his intention to sketch in his life from early boyhood, explaining that while his mother may have changed the surname to LeFarge, he was still a Ciavaldini, bonded by blood to the powerful Bonaventuri family. He had been brought up to understand the meaning of blood ties and family honour.

'My affiliation, as you put it, with the *Union Corse* goes back to the day I was born. By the time the war was over in France, I was employed full time by the brotherhood,' said Jean-Paul, disposing of his first eighteen years in two sentences. 'In 1948, I was guilty of the small indiscretion

I mentioned once in Vientiane. Acting on orders, I killed a man, but at the wrong time in the wrong place. It could have proved an embarrassment to the brotherhood. They got me to Algeria and arranged for me to join the Foreign Legion as a Belgian by the name of Charles Dubois.

'The Legion didn't suit me. The discipline was harsh, and there were far too many Boche for my liking. I would have deserted, but one day I was called to the office of the commandant. A civilian was there. He told me that I was to be advanced to non-commissioned rank and transferred to *Indochine*. I was given the name and address of a man in Haiphong I was to contact for further instructions.

'In February, 1949, I arrived in Haiphong. For the next four years I saw little combat. I worked with the *montagnards* in the *Haute Terre* and Northeastern Laos organizing guerrilla forces to harass the Viet Minh. What I was actually doing was setting up an organization for the purchase and transport of raw opium.

'I should explain. While the *Union Corse* was a powerful organization in France, North Africa, and Lebanon, we were not at that time too strong in Southeast Asia. From its early beginnings of river piracy, the *Binh-Xuyen* sect had grown to an even stronger position than the *Union Corse* enjoyed in Marseilles. In addition to a stranglehold on gambling, prostitution and the opium traffic, the *Binh-Xuyen* controlled the Saigon-Cholon police force. To crack that monopoly in Saigon was next to impossible, although we were having some success in Hanoi and Haiphong. But since the war was making it difficult to obtain opium, it was in this vulnerable area we were making our bid. With troops and military aircraft at my disposal, and with the cooperation of the *montagnards* who hated all Vietnamese, my job was not too difficult. At least not at first.

'The war caught up with me. By 1953, things were getting pretty hot in the northern highlands and Laos. You may recall that Giap's 316th Division overran Lai Chau in December and then went racing for Luang Prabang, chewing up the small defending garrisons in its path. The 2nd Laotian Battalion, and the 2nd Battalion of the Legion 3rd Regiment covered the retreat towards the new defence perimeter at Luang Prabang. In a small capacity, I was part of that defending force. We got mauled badly in the process and I picked up a leg wound. That wasn't exactly unlucky, since it saved me from being dropped into the stinking trap of Dien Bien Phu in February.

The rest is history – the fall of Dien Bien Phu, and the cease-fire. Most of that time, I was hospitalized in Cap St Jacques and not exactly anxious to leave that seaside resort. My unit was being pulled out to be sent to Algeria. Then, when it looked as though I couldn't stretch my convalescence much further, the *Union Corse* came to my rescue.

'Somehow, the brotherhood had arranged for me to be discharged in *Indochine*. I was to be employed by a French-owned transportation company in Saigon. Using that legitimate business as a front, I was to coordinate light aircraft opium shipments from Laos, explore alternate supply routes from Burma and Thailand, and organize the smuggling of raw opium and morphine base from Saigon to Marseilles. Then, I stupidly went and blew it.

'A week before my discharge, I got into a fight in l'Hotelerie night club at the Cap. Slugged a naval officer and broke his jaw. The owner of the joint, Monsieur Dac Duc, tried to cover for me, but there were too many witnesses. I drew two years hard labour at the Legion detention barracks on Isle de Tigne.

'I'd been there almost a year and had visions of rotting in that hole for the full term before being shipped off to Algeria. Figured that the brotherhood had written me off. I was bitter about that, though I could hardly blame them. But I was wrong.

'One day my cell door opened and a dumpy American colonel was ushered in. Imagine my surprise when this dude pulls out a pocket watch from which is dangling the Moor's-head medallion fob of the *Union Corse*. He puts a proposition to me. I could be released if I agreed to join the U.S. Special Forces. Thought it was some kind of a trick, but the colonel finally convinced me that it wasn't and had the approval of the brotherhood. Anyway, what in hell did I have to lose. I accepted.'

Jean-Paul paused to light a cigarette. He inhaled deeply and blew out a thin cloud of smoke. 'Might interest you to know,' he said idly, 'that the colonel was Lew Cantrell.'

'Of the Brig, I'd believe almost anything, but he hardly strikes me as a typical Corsican.'

'No, he isn't. Seems he worked closely with some of the top men in the brotherhood in France and Italy during the war. Later, in his OSS operations in *Indochine*, they were able to assist him. I gather that it was a mutual lend-lease arrangement. They made him a sort of honorary Corsican. In bailing me out of the Legion Bastille, I thought he was returning past favours. I was wrong, but I didn't find that out until much later.

'Before being sent to English language school in New York, I spent January '56 in Saigon. Things had changed. Ngo Dinh Diem had knocked the *Binh-Xuyen* out of the box. Gambling, prostitution and opium smoking were illegal. The brotherhood was busy consolidating its local position, buying into bars and restaurants not already Corsican owned and operated. Working with Cholon Chinese and some elements of the *Binh-Xuyen* who had gone under-ground, they were setting up a flourishing gold and currency black market operation. The opium traffic had slowed, but showed signs of improving. Most of my friends were optimistic. I could hardly share their feelings. I was struck with my Special Forces bargain and figured myself out of the picture – permanently.

'After six months of language school, becoming more or less fluent in Brooklynese, I was posted to Bad Tölz in Germany. Two years there, and back to Fort Bragg for more training and jump school. Then in '59 I was back in Viet-Nam as demo sergeant on an 'A' Team out in the boonies. Didn't have much of a chance to get together with my old buddies in Saigon.'

Jean-Paul butted his cigarette and slouched back in the seat. 'To be honest,' he said reflectively, 'it wasn't a bad deal. I was a sergeant first, an American citizen, and starting to think in terms of eventual Stateside retirement. Had a gal in Fayetteville and had even got around to thinking about marriage ... but not very seriously. It was just as well I hadn't.

'I was due to rotate back to Bragg at the end of that tour. I didn't ... then, or ever. Was ordered to report to a villa in Saigon, where I met my old friend Colonel Cantrell. Only he was a civilian. It wasn't until later that I found out he held the rank of brigadier general.

'Then came the big fat hook. Seems my former connections with the Laotian army and *montagnards* were valuable assets. The bargain the Brig had made to spring me from the jug on Isle de Tigne was suddenly made clear to me. For four-and-a-half years I'd kidded myself into thinking I was a valued addition to the ranks of the Special Forces. Now I was informed that it had all been nothing but a period of preparation for my real function. I was to be placed on detached duty and sent to Laos as a civilian adviser. My job; to assist in the organization of a secret Meo mercenary force. Cantrell also suggested that I'd better check with a Monsieur Clayard.

'Clayard had taken over the operations of the brotherhood in Saigon. He filled in any gaps the Brig left. Financing of the Meo mercenaries was to be from CIA funds. To gain the confidence – and dependency – of the tribesman, their opium cash crop was to be purchased with Agency funds. Arms and logistic support would be provided from Agency funding delivered by Air America. The opium was suposed to be bought and transported to Vientiane where it would be destroyed. I was to divert most of the crop to Bangkok and Saigon. In addition, I was to take charge of the flow of raw and processed opium coming from Yunnan and Burma into Laos for transshipment to Thailand. It was a pretty good working arrangement for all concerned.'

'Not bad,' Jud observed, 'Not bad at all. A tried and trusted member of your brotherhood who just happens to be an American Special Forces sergeant on detached duty with the CIA. One might say it was an unbeatable combination.'

'Yeah, Anyway it worked out to everybody's satisfaction. Or almost everybody. I arrived in Vientiane in August '60, just in time for Kong Le's little *coup d'etat*. Stayed in Laos for the next six years getting things organized and running smoothly. Was there right up until I was sent to your unit in Nam.'

'Why?' querried Jud. 'If things were going so well in Laos, why the hell did you get your ass shifted to a combat unit?'

Jean-Paul grinned. 'There were a few minor hitches I think they overlooked. Everything went with the smoothness of a well-greased palm up until the end of '62, then things got a bit tough. Technically, all the advisers in Laos were civilians, but most of them were ranking military officers. I was a Special Forces non-com. My initial job of helping to set up Vang Pao's Meo army was accomplished and my main task for the Brig was quietly putting together an intelligence network. I had a good deal of freedom of action and movement. There was a good deal of resentment on the part of many Americans. I played it cool, but it got worse instead of better. It didn't help that most of my friends and associates were in the French community.

'Finally, both the Brig and Clayard concluded that I'd outlived my usefulness in my detached duty capacity and would be better employed as a civilian. The Brig pulled me in to Nhatrang and advised me of the decision for me to be separated from Special Forces. But first, for the record, I required a tour of active duty. Why the hell that couldn't have been in a cushy desk job in Nhatrang, I'll never know, but the Brig insisted it should be combat duty. That's how I got elected to your suicidal band of cutthroats. Weren't you happy?'

'Considering your background, you made one helluva good troop. I might not have been quite so pleased if I'd known all this at the time,' Jud said smiling. 'But interesting as it's been, you didn't come all this way just to fill me in on the rather unique military career of Charles Dubois. I presume you've been leading up to something pertinent to the present operation.'

'Sure have, but figured you'd better know the set-up first. Now, I've gotta give you a few more facts concerning the narcotics business.

'As you probably know, most of the opium for the world market has come from Turkey and is processed in Marseilles. We act more as manufacturers and wholesalers, with our Sicilian associates of the Mafia looking after the distribution and retail end, especially in the North American market.

'That's the way it's been, but the picture's changing. Pressure is being brought to bear on Turkey to cut back on the growing. It's getting hot for the Marseilles factories. So the shift in raw material supply is going to be to this region – the Golden Triangle. We figure we can get production of raw opium from Burma, Thailand and Laos up to 1,000 tons annually in a couple of years – mostly from the Kachin and Shan regions of Burma. That affects your region of responsibility, it's only part of the story.

'Since it's getting tougher for the Marseilles refining plants to operate, more of the processing will have to be done here. You must know of the plants at Tachilek on the Burmese border. They are already sharply increasing production of grade 4 heroin, the pure stuff. Kitchens are now operating in Laos and a new plant, an old sawmill near Pakse is going into full scale production. As things get too rough in Europe and Latin America, more and more of the supply will have to come from Asia.

'That isn't anything new, and shouldn't come as a surprise to you. But I think what I have to tell you now will affect you more directly.

'As I indicated earlier, our control through Laos is pretty strong – but by no means unchallenged. For one thing, the opium trade isn't illegal in Laos, but that may change in the not too distant future. So a good many highly placed officials get into the act. General Ouan Ratikoune has been selling to the highest bidder since '62. He's by no means alone. But since we've been the highest if not the only, bidder, it didn't much matter until recently.'

Jean-Paul favored Jud with a quizzical glance, before continuing. 'For a long time, we've operated on an unwritten agreement with our Mafia associates. We stay out of their end of the business, and they steer clear of ours. It avoids friction. Lately, though, the greedy bastards have been trying to muscle in on our action. It started back in '65 when some of the *Mafiosi* appeared in Hong Kong and Saigon talking direct deals on heroin. It wasn't a very serious effort, and we thought we'd discouraged them. Then, just recently, they've started to show up again. They've been in Saigon, and here in Bangkok. Did you know that an approach had been made to your Burmese revolutionary group?'

Jud frowned. There had been vague mentions of such meetings in Skidalski's reports, but the exact nature of the negotiations had not been clarified. Gambling concessions had been suggested and had sounded reasonable. The exiled Burmese had entered into negotiations for other concessions against the nebulous day of their takeover. To date, they had not had spectacular success with timber and mining rights, but it looked as though they had sparked some interest with a Canadian group representing American oil interests. Jud had already asked 'Emily' to provide more precise details. 'There has been mention of such meetings,' Jud replied, 'but I was led to understand they concerned gambling concessions.'

Jean-Paul laughed. 'That too, but the big bite was for payment against delivery of grade 4 heroin. A large chunk of bread changed hands. I don't know how much, but I'll know within a week and pass along the info. That's your worry. There was a deal for spring delivery from the Karen, and a separate agreement with the Shan. That's going to be my problem; blocking the delivery.

'But that's only part of what I came to tell you. There's another angle you know nothing about. Marijuana has been peddled to the GIs in Nam for a long time, but the grass retailing machinery is now being expanded to include smack – 96 per cent pure No. 4 heroin. Those GI mothers won't know what hit 'em.

'This we don't like. If we could see any way of stopping it, we would. The stuff will move by Royal Lao and South Vietnamese Air Force planes directly to Cholon Chinese over whom we have little or no control. They've got protection, and I mean right up to the top. Clout like that is hard to fight.'

'Why should you want to?' Jud asked drily. 'I'd think that GIs returning Stateside as addicts would be good for overall business.'

'Yeah. It beats pushing the junk in grade schools. But that's not the point. The GIs are running into the pure stuff at a dirt cheap price. They're going to get hooked but good. It's going to be one great big pain in the ass for the military and the folks back home. When Johnny comes marching home a junkie, there are gonna be screams that won't quit. And that is going to generate heat in these parts like you've never seen. And that heat we need like a nun needs a diaphragm.'

'So what do you intend to do about it?'

'Not me, baby, you,' Jean-Paul answered with a grin.

'Me!'

'Yeah, you. When those soldier-boy main-liners start

157

hitting the streets of the ol' home town, you're going to start getting plenty of static. Washington is going to want answers, fast. And you just happen to be the boy on the spot. You and the Long Cheng contingent, but mostly you. The Golden Triangle is your beat, isn't it?'

'Mmm. Your point's well taken.'

'Don't worry. Before questions start to fly, you'll have answers. Long Cheng will have some information supplied by me, but you'll have much more. On my return to Vientiane, I'll start sending a series of up-dated reports which will give names, dates, locations and related facts and figures. You could come out of this smelling like jasmine.'

Jud drove for several minutes in silence. 'If I read you correctly,' Jud finally observed, 'you intend to feed me information designed to put the competition out of business. I take it that your facts and figures will exclude anything of substance relating to your own operation.'

'You read me loud and clear.'

'Has it occurred to you and your associates that when the shit hits the fan you might catch some of the fallout?'

That had been the chief objection voiced by his colleagues at the Saigon meetings, and one which Jean-Paul had countered with some difficulty. 'Yeah,' he said solemnly, 'that we can't avoid. At least for a while, life will get rough for everybody. But look at it this way: the tougher it gets, the higher goes the price. In the long run, it's the junkie who suffers.'

Amen to that, thought Jud, as he swerved to give wide berth to a water buffalo which had ambled unconcernedly onto the highway.

CHAPTER SEVENTEEN

LeFarge's first report dealing with the narcotics trade and traffickers arrived in Chiang Mai ten days after his departure. The interval allowed Jud ample time to dwell on the implications of Jean-Paul's verbal disclosures.

Several things emerged from Jean-Paul's revelations. Not the least of these was a fuller picture of the man himself.

Jud found himself wondering if LeFarge recognized that from his youth he'd been used as nothing but a pawn by his beloved brotherhood. At this point, Jean-Paul displayed a confidence which could only stem from an assurance that his position in the *Union Corse* hierarchy was relatively secure, and that as an American, under the cloak of his CIA activities, he could operate with impunity. Nothing in the record assured the former and Jud harboured grave doubt concerning the latter.

With the exception of periods of army training and combat, and a stint in military prison, LeFarge's entire adult life had been devoted to the traffic of narcotics. He saw nothing reprehensible in his vocation. He was not so much oblivious to the human wreckage strewn in the wake of addiction as he was contemptuous of the jettisoned debris. Several times, in previous conversations with Jud, Jean-Paul had expressed the philosophy that neither he nor his Corsican confreres had invented drugs or addiction, but as long as it existed it would be exploited for profit and that this gain might as well accrue to himself as less deserving citizens. Questioned concerning the introduction of mere children to drug abuses, Jean-Paul had contended righteously that no Corsican kid would ever be allowed to develop such degrading habits.

Jud had little inclination to dispute Jean-Paul's views or debate the moral issues. His own trade, if it could be so dignified, contributed its quota of human suffering with debatable justification. The populations of several hamlets and villages in Viet-Nam had been decimated by retributive justice dispensed under his direction. And his present assignment involved equally disturbing aspects. In arming and supporting a squabbling group of political opportunists, it could be anticipated that death and destruction would be visited on innocent peasants in the path of these ambitions. Long since, Jud had concluded that the reasoning supporting this stirring of a simmering ethnic pot was at best specious, if not altogether invalid. He felt he was in no position to moralize.

Emerging from Jean-Paul's narrative, was another consideration. This was the part the ubiquitous Lewis Cantrell had played in the scenario. To Jud, this was not only illuminating, but had direct bearing on his own position. When, as Captain Joe Stanford, he'd left Indo-China in 1952, Cantrell, then a lieutenant colonel, had not. Cantrell had not only stayed on through the declining days and departure of the French, but had been actively engaged in suport of Ngo Dihn Diem's fledgling Republic of Viet-Nam. He had devoted his considerable talents to emasculating, through bribery and betrayal, the militant sects which threatened the infant regime. For his contributions, Cantrell had been rewarded with a full colonelcy. Later, as a civilian known affectionately as 'the Brig', Cantrell was to apply the same diligence and capacity for intrigue in helping to engineer the overthrow of Diem.

Now he had been permitted a glimpse of another facet of Cantrell's complex character. As far back as 1955, Cantrell had conspired with Corsican cronies for the release of an obscure legionnaire from a military prison; the purpose, to exploit to advantage the experience and contacts the man had acquired in Laos. It had not been intended to utilize the Legionaire's talents until some time in the future. But just how in hell had Cantrell known that those attributes would be required or even desirable at some unspecified future date? The answer was probably that Cantrell had undertaken these painstaking preparations on nothing more than speculation. Perhaps, in Cantrell's position, it didn't take any degree of genius to foresee that when the North Vietnamese realized their plans for re-unification of Viet-Nam through the elections stipulated in the Geneva Agreement would not see fruition, they would be forced into a subversive role. Such an undertaking would inevitably entail utilization of the Ho Chi Minh Trail to build up and supply insurgents in the South. And that in turn, would mean protecting the route through the mountainous terrain of Eastern Laos by sustaining the Communist Pathet Lao in a *de facto* division of the country. And against that condition it would behove the CIA to have reliable agents on the ground.

The Brig could not have foretold the sequence of events, but was astute enough to percieve the broad outline well in advance. When a harried right-wing Laotion government requested military technicians from the United States in 1959, events played neatly into the Brig's hands. Sergeant Charles DuBois was ready and waiting in the wings.

Two salient features stood out like beacons in Jud's assessment of the Brig's manoeuvrings.

The first of these was that it was highly unlikely that Cantrell had sought approval from higher authority in 1955 when he sprang LeFarge from prison. Jud was willing to bet that the record would show only that Dubois had been recommended for Special Forces transfer on the basis of his Legion duty and expertise with northern hill tribes, with no mention of *Union Corse* affiliation. Washington would be aware of LeFarge's activities in narcotics traffic solely as a cover identity masking his intelligence function. Jud would have given sizeable odds that Washington had no knowledge that the cover was in fact LeFarge's primary concern. Perhaps that wasn't entirely true. A very small segment of the Washington machinery knew the truth – at least one man – Lew Cantrell. Since January of this year, Cantrell had taken over as the CIA's Deputy Director of Plans, in Langley, Virginia.

If Jud's assumptions were correct, it meant that Jean-Paul was living in a fool's paradise. If, through the narcotics traffic, or for any other reason, Jean-Paul became an embarrassment, Cantrell would disclaim all knowledge of LeFarge's Corsican connections. Jean-Paul would be thrown to the wolves.

The second point was even more significant. On the military side, there was no valid reason why LeFarge needed combat duty as a prelude to service release. There *was* a reason, of course, but it was purest Cantrell. Jean-Paul had been planted in the counter-terrorist unit for the express purpose of establishing a relationship between himself and his commanding officer. Knowing both men as he did, the Brig had been confident that a rapport would develop. But if it hadn't; if a clash of personalities had been the result, the Brig had nothing to lose. He would simply reshape his plans for his intended working arrangements of the forthcoming intelligence network.

In the light of these deductions, Jud revised his earlier thinking. It resolved down to the fact that his assignment to Chiang Mai had been in the planning stage earlier, much earlier, as much as a whole year earlier, than he'd originally thought. Just how this related to the late Judson Quentin Winters, he wasn't sure, but it was a pretty safe bet that Winters had lived a good many months on borrowed time.

Jud's mental image of Cantrell underwent a subtle alteration. He generally visualized the rotund unkempt figure with the horn-rimmed spectacles and the ever-present cigar, the benignly beaming countenance topped with an unruly shock of gray hair, as seated behind a cluttered desk. In this new version, the desk was replaced by a chess board. Grudgingly, Jud could not help but admire the Machiavellian guile with which the Brig addressed himself to the game. The cunning devious sonuvabitch, he thought; if Jean-Paul is a mere pawn, what piece do I represent to the Brig?

In some respects, LeFarge's initial written report was an astonishing document. He had promised names, dates, places, and related data. He was as good as his word. At first glance, the report looked like a blueprint for the entire set-up. Processing plants and stock-piling locations were noted. Caravan routes from Burma through the mountains to Fang and Tak in Thailand, and points in Northern Laos were designated. The methods employed for the border crossing at Mae Sai and onward routing to Chiang Rai and Lampang were outlined in detail. Sea and air routing and transport facilities to Viet-Nam and Hong Kong were described. Corrupt government, police, customs and investigating body officials were named, as were high ranking officers in the military forces of the countryside concerned. Their positions in the organization, and an estimation of their illicit take were described.

Jud was astounded by the scope and complexity of the operation. But what struck him most forcefully was that this represented only the competition – the people Jean-Paul considered expendable. He noted that little mention had been made of figures in the French communities of Laos, Cambodia, Thailand, or Viet-Nam. If the competition is this extensive, thought Jud, just what in hell must the *Union Corse* organization look like?

On the strength of the report, and Jean-Paul's verbal information, Jud initiated a fourfold course of action.

He had already instructed Skidalski to obtain more details concerning the concession negotiations of the Burmese insurgents, individually and collectively. He amplified these instructions with particular reference to narcotics. In addition, he told Skidalski to make sure that a reliable man accompanied U Thong and his party on the forthcoming round-the-world promotional junket. The man was to report without delay the substance of any negotiations with commercial interests or overtures from the Mafioso.

In relaying his newly acquired intelligence to Harper, Jud exercised caution. Initially, he confined himself to sounding a strong warning that an upsurge in sales of heroin to the troops in Viet-Nam could be anticipated. He reasoned that until the Administration became sufficiently alarmed concerning the sharp rise in addiction, no tough countermeasures would be forthcoming. Premature disclosures could well produce uncoordinated actions which would alert the traffickers to impending danger and allow them time to effect protective measures. And there was another factor to weigh and consider.

LeFarge could not have imparted such detailed information without the approval of his superiors in the brotherhood. Jud was convinced that through his Corsican connections Cantrell was already in possession of the same information. It stood to reason that Cantrell would be watching developments closely.

That he was virtually sitting on a time bomb, was fully appreciated by Jud. His vulnerability had been brought sharply home to him by the Meo ambush. If he did not deem it the proper time to disclose the narcotics traffic intelligence, it was equally inadvisable that he be the only one privy to the information. With this thought in mind, he consolidated the intelligence into a series of microdot reports. This done he took Perkins into his confidence.

CHAPTER EIGHTEEN

That agreeing to take Na Hti with him when he departed from the village had been a rash act, Jud was well aware. Nor could he fully explain the impulse which had prompted his decision. In many an idle moment in the months which followed, he was to speculate on this.

At the time, from the moment of his assent to her entreaty, he'd had misgivings. That same evening, his doubts had intensified.

There was a family conference in the hut. Jud sat apart,

while the group hunkered around the fire-pit in earnest conversation. That he featured largely in the discussion, was attested by the frequent glances and wide grins cast in his direction.

Na Hti and her uncle detached themselves from the circle and came over to Jud. The *paw khu* was beaming as Na Hti relayed the family decision. 'Mother's brother say we can make wedding tomorrow.'

Christ, Jud thought glumly. There had been no mention of marriage. At this point, he came close to backing out, but the unalloyed happiness radiating from Na Hti, and the obvious pleasure of the *paw khu*, stopped him from protest. What the hell, in agreeing to take her he'd accepted full responsibility anyway. A tribal marriage ceremony would have no legal weight in Chiang Mai. If compliance with Lahu custom demanded the ceremony, he might as well accept with good grace. There is a saying amongst the hill tribes: 'Every time a pig squeals, a Lahu is married.' As Jud knew, the proceedings were more festive than solemn ritual. Smiling into Na Hti's eyes, he nodded his assent.

The next day there was a good deal of bustle and excitement in the household, and indeed in the entire village. Two pigs and a number of chickens were butchered and dressed. The women of the household, including the bride, were busy over the cooking fires. Finally, the villagers attired themselves in their best garments; the women resplendent in spangled silver adornments. The musicians dusted off the *naw*, the gourd-and-reed pipes, and lutes twanged in tuning. All was in readiness for the villagers to gather at the house of the bride to enjoy the feast and festivities.

There was one part of the pre-marital arrangements which caused Jud slight embarrassment. It is the custom with the Lahu that the new son-in-law moves in with the family of the bride, donating his services to the household for a period of three years. In lieu of this practice, the groom may pay a 'bride price', commonly 1,000 baht — the equivalent of 50 dollars. Jud found this remarkably reasonable. He could recall having paid more than double that sum for the pleasure of the company of a Parisienne model for a single evening. The hitch was that since he had been on the final leg of his journey, he had less than 500 baht in currency with him. The delicate negotiations were concluded to everyone's satisfaction by Jud's presenting his Winchester to the *paw khu*. Jud got the impression that the *paw khu* was more than delighted. The rifle was something of exceptional value, and Na Hti, a spinster at 18, was probably considered a burden by the family. It was more than a fair trade. Since Jud had intended to donate the .375 Magnum and remaining ammunition to the tribesmen as a gesture of appreciation, its additional service as bride barter was an unexpected bonus.

Jud and Na Hti joined in the feasting and for a while watched the dancing, with the women swaying in a close circle around the men and boys who pounded their feet and stomped vigorously to the keening rhythm of pipe and lute. Then, their union suitably sanctified, they slipped away quietly to the small hut set aside as their nuptial bower.

The following morning, a small party set off down the mountain. Jud was astride a mountain pony, his feet brushing the ground. Four armed Lahu hunters formed a flanking guard. A teenage boy carried the bundle of the dead driver's possessions and Jud's metal box. Na Hti trotted happily along at Jud's side. On her back, in addition to Jud's knapsack, was a woven basket containing her few belongings, and a quiver of quarrels. Across her shoulder, she carried a crossbow.

Without incident, they reached Mae Taeng late in the afternoon.

To the driver and their fellow passengers on the bus which bore them smoothly along the highway towards Chiang Mai, the fair haired *farang* in the faded khaki bush clothing and the beautiful girl in Lahu garb who sat demurely at his side must have appeared an incongruous couple.

Jud had had no very clear ideas concerning Na Hti's future once they had reached Chiang Mai. He had considered schooling would be an essential feature, following which he would try and find an American family in Bangkok, preferably with daughters close to Na Hti's age, who would be willing to accept the girl as a boarder while she continued her education at the International School. Beyond that, he had visualized making some arrangement whereby she would become an American citizen and go to live in the States. But initially she would become part of his bachelor household, although he had dimly perceived this might present problems.

It didn't occur to Jud that the girl might have definite ideas of her own on the subject of her future. It didn't work out quite as Jud had pictured.

Jud enjoyed Na Hti's reaction, her astonishment and delight, on her introduction to the modern conveniences of the villa. Jud noted that she quickly came to accept these outward trappings of a technological age as an integral part of her new life.

In the matter of schooling, she did not adapt as readily. Jud enrolled her in a local school. She lasted all of three days, then steadfastly refused to return to endure the curious stares and ostracism of both the teaching staff and her Thai fellow students. It could hardly have been otherwise, and Jud chided himself mentally for having thought that it might be. Resignedly, he undertook the furtherance of her education. To his astonishment, he found he came to look forward to the daily sessions with keen pleasure. Na Hti proved to be an excellent pupil. She was intelligent, quick to grasp the essentials, and eager to learn.

The matter of her position in the household was resolved quite simply by Na Hti. From the day of her arrival, she installed herself naturally in his room. She assumed the role of wife and mistress of his home with effortless aplomb. It both startled and amused Jud that the household staff accepted her self-appointed position without question.

Jud's acceptance of their relationship was ambivalent. While he ceded her position as chatelaine, and even admitted that the ménage ran more smoothly for her presence and attention, he could not bring himself to accord her the status of a wife. In his thoughts, she occupied a station somewhere between that of an adopted daughter and an enchanting mistress. He did not think of the arrangement in terms of permanency. But, as the weeks stretched into months, he found himself settling comfortably into the relationship. Through Na Hti, he discovered his life was taking on an added depth and meaning.

But if Na Hti had fitted naturally into the household, the same could not be said for the community. To the Thai, she was foreign with the added stigma of a hill tribe heritage. With few exceptions, the *farang* expatriates, especially the distaff side, treated her with condescension, if not thinly-veiled opprobrium. Although he was sure that Na Hti was not oblivious to this hostility, it seemed neither to unduly offend nor annoy her. Nonetheless, it angered Jud. He adopted the practice of rejecting invitations and entertained sparingly at home. This did not appear to distress Na Hti in the least.

The exceptions to this Chiang Mai rejection of Na Hti were the Kepplers, and Chris Perkins and his fiancée Susan Blaine. Susan had arrived in Chiang Mai in late August. She and Chris were to be married in October. It may have been that she was too new to the community and its undercurrents of social mores, or it may have been that as a vivacious and lovely young brunette, secure in her own position of pending marriage, but Susan did not look upon Na Hti as a competitor. From the moment the two girls met at an intimate dinner party hosted by Jud to welcome Susan to Chiang Mai, they were attracted to each other. It pleased Jud that Na Hti had found this friendship and that the two young women were much in each other's company. He was not so pleased that the Kepplers had taken an interest in Na Hti, or that she spent a number of afternoons with Hank, Sasima and the children, but he could think of no logical objection to the association.

The consequence of Na Hti's limited activities in the town was that she and Jud spent a good deal of time at home. Time did not hang heavy on their hands. For one thing, the daily lessons absorbed a good many hours of the day. For another, Na Hti developed an interest in photography and often assisted Jud in the lab. When he was taking care of the limited paper work arising during this slack season in the timber business, when his work in lab or study demanded seclusion, or when Keppler or Perkins dropped in for an evening of chess, Na Hti either busied herself with household chores, or read – laboriously but voraciously – from some of the many books in the study. They were both content with each other's company and the routine which had evolved. If Na Hti missed the open spaces of the mountain terrain, she never mentioned it. For Jud, he was thankful that this rainy season precluded the frequent trips he would be called upon to make in a few month's time.

On a gray afternoon, early in October, Jud stood just within the archway leading from the study to the sitting room. Unobserved, he watched Na Hti. She was seated cross-legged on the sofa, an opened book in her lap. Light from the reading lamp glinted off her hair and illuminated her face. She was frowning in concentration, and her lips silently formed words as she slowly read the page before her.

He smiled affectionately at the picture of domesticity. He must, he thought, instruct her that young ladies of good breeding did not sit in that position – or if they did, they at least wore undergarments.

CHAPTER NINETEEN

If the rainy season slowed the tempo of life in Chiang Mai, it did little to stem the flow of regional intelligence. Jud was kept busy painstakingly piecing together the seemingly unrelated shards of information to form a composite picture of the unfolding events. His approach to this work was ambivalent. On the one hand, he found a certain fascination and challenge in fitting the pieces into some semblance of cohesion and formulating his appraisals of the emerging display. On the other hand, for a man who had devoted the better part of two and a half decades to swift and often violent action, this new task proved tedious. And to add to his frustration was the fact that he had no knowledge of how much his assessment reached Washington, or what weight was placed upon his reports. In at least one area, the progress of the Burmese insurrection, he had reason to believe his appreciations were being discounted.

An element had begun to intrude in a number of the reports emanating from South China. It was little more than vague rumour, but the fact that it cropped up from several widely dispersed sources lent it a measure of substance. Several agents made reference to hints that there had been clandestine overtures which might lead to an American-Chinese dialogue at quasi-official levels. Without speculation or conclusion, and taking care to stress the unsupported nature of the rumours, Jud reported the substance to Harper.

What was causing Jud growing concern was the Burmese insurgency movement. The mosaic developing from the reports channelled through Skidalski was disturbing. What was even more disquieting was Jud's awareness of the existence of conflicting appraisals of the situation.

On Jud's instruction, Skidalski had recruited a reliable source of information within the U.S. Army's Defence Intelligence Agency. Jud learned that, on U Thong's invitation, a number of DIA experts had visited some of the insurgents' clandestine training camps. From the reports to the Pentagon, the so-called experts had been obviously impressed with the training methods and discipline, the military division of forces into Northern, Central and Southern Commands operating under the direction of a unified Headquarters Command, and the glowing reports of successful operations across the border into Burma. When copies of these reports reached Jud, he was astonished.

From his own intelligence sources, Jud realized that the DIA representatives had viewed a carefully staged Potemkin production – and swallowed it as irrefutable evidence. The facts, as Jud knew them, didn't jibe with the DIA assessments. The insurgents' troop strengths were heavily padded and bore little relationship to the actual figures. The training *was* good, and there were a number of first rate unit commanders, but the sporadic harassing raids across the border were little more than nuisance value. To date, the raids had been conducted on a hit-and-run basis with the units expressly prohibited from any penetration in depth. The victories reported to the DIA were largely fabrications. The semblance of unity presented as a divided command structure under coordinated headquarters was purest fiction. The ethnic elements which comprised the insurgency were as disunited as they'd ever been and rapidly disintegrating into a Byzantine shambles of intrigue.

As the months progressed, when it became patently obvious that U Thong was incapable of welding the various self-interest groups together, Jud bluntly chronicled the facts.

The other facets of the operation stirred Jud to rising anger. He had foreseen and feared the possible development of one. While he had not anticipated the second, he had not been wholly surprised by its emergence although he would not have credited the rapidity with which it grew to alarming proportions.

The only checks placed upon the insurgents' procurement of arms and equipment were in the clandestine funding and the cupidity of the Thai general through which they were both obtaining the weapons. What Jud had feared was that the insurgents could become overstocked and discover they could engage in a lucrative side-line of selling arms to guerrilla forces in Malaysia and Indonesia. In August, the the news filtered through to Jud that an illicit trade had started. He was furious, and immediately advocated to Harper that the funding be sharply reduced.

Even before Jean-Paul's disclosures concerning the opium traffic, Jud had been aware of negotiations for the sale of concessions. He had not, however, considered that the insurgents could generate any substantial sums in this manner. He was wrong. During September and October, as U Thong and his group of travelling companions progressed in leisurely fashion on their around-the-world promotional junket, reports of their commercial activities trickled back through Skidalski. To Jud's astonishment, the sums involved were staggering, running into the hundreds of millions.

During this period, Jud's situation reports on the insurgency operation became increasingly dyslogistic. He expected to be summoned by Harper for an emergency policy discussion. He was not prepared for Harper's response when it finally came. The message was terse, suggesting that Jud was overreacting to the situation and counselling a less negative attitude.

The effect of Harper's message on Jud was as sobering as a bucketful of icy water. He reflected on the context and implications, and reached some unwelcome conclusions. If his assessments of the operation were not being diluted at Harper's level, then the DIA reports were being considered more reliable and his reports were considered alarmist. It could only mean that in the broad sense of global operations the Burmese insurgency didn't enjoy much of a priority.

What puzzled him was Harper's attitude. With the sources information at Harper's disposal, it was unlikely that he was deluded by military intelligence reports, no matter how appealing they might appear. Why then was Harper not displaying concern? Was he responding to pressure from a higher level? That the entire project was deteriorating into an expensive farce must be obvious to Harper, if not to Washington.

Jud's options were limited. He could accept the situation and ride along with it. He could short circuit Harper by sending a confidential report directly to Cantrell in Langley. Or, he could precipitate some form of reaction and a possible investigation of the entire operation by the simple expedient of cutting off the cash flow.

He knew himself well enough to know that he wouldn't sit still in the face of the Burmese abuses much longer. The second course of action was unacceptable since in any contest of authority Cantrell would have no choice but to support Harper. That left only the third choice. The question was, when?

The itinerary of U Thong and his party was drawing to a close. The following Monday they were due to arrive in Hong Kong, the last scheduled stop before their return to Bangkok. On Tuesday, U Thong was to address a luncheon meeting at the Hong Kong Foreign Correspondents' Club. That afternoon and evening, Jud understood some of U Thong's diligent fund raisers had set up meetings with some prospective jade and gemstone buyers. The group should arrive back in Bangkok Wednesday or, at the latest, Thursday.

Jud decided to postpone his intended action until a few days after the group's return. If by then there was no message from Harper modifying his last directive, Jud would close the sluice gate on the cash flow.

He was under no illusions concerning Harper's reaction. Even if Jud didn't advise the suspension of funding, the Burmese would scream like wounded eagles and the word would reach Harper from one source or another. Harper would remove fiscal control from Jud's jurisdiction and order an immediate resumption of funding. But no matter how rapidly he reacted, Harper would not be able to prevent word of the interrupted flow of cash from reaching Washington. Jud was counting on that to stir some official response and an examination of the operation.

Harper, Jud was sure, would also consider it imperative that Jud be divested of operational authority. Considering the time and effort expended in fabricating the deep cover, and the fact that Jud had built up a smoothly functioning and efficient regional intelligence network, Langley might thwart Harper in Jud's dismissal. Direction of the Burmese insurgency support would be removed pending an investigation, but Jud might be retained with his activities confined to administering the intelligence network. He was not deluding himself. Unpleasant repercussions were bound to follow his action. Just how unpleasant would depend on the degree of autonomy enjoyed by Harper as Sector Chief.

Jud took a number of contingency precautions. He arranged with Chris and Susan that Na Hti would be taken as a guest until other arrangements could be made should Jud have to leave unexpectedly. He wrote a letter to his Swiss banker and placed it in the safe against a day when he might have to give it to Na Hti for mailing.

In many matters of the network and the insurgency operations, Jud had taken Perkins into his confidence. Strictly speaking, this was contrary to established policy. Under certain circumstances such knowledge could pose problems, if not constitute actual danger, for Perkins. In Jud's estimation, such conditions might soon present themselves.

Without divulging his intended course of action, Jud disclosed that he was contemplating an unorthodox approach to the Burmese insurgency question. This could lead to his removal as Area Coordinator. Should that occur, it might be preceded or followed by an investigation. He cautioned Perkins that, in the event of any investigation, Chris was to pretend ignorance to anything other than the knowledge he would normally have as a mere cog in the intelligence machinery. He would, for example, know only the identities of his two assigned contacts, 'Garth' and 'Emily'.

Under Jud's tutelage, much of Perkins' initial naiveté had disappeared. He now appreciated that the various arms of America's intelligence-gathering bodies often worked at cross purposes. He recognized that there were dangers from within as well as outside the Agency. He was troubled by Jud's guarded disclosure but did not press for a fuller explanation and promised to exercise due caution should the need arise.

Chris did not accept the next admonition readily. Jud indicated that, as a prior act to his dismissal, an attempt might be made to discredit him. Should that happen, under no circumstances was Chris to come to Jud's defence. Chris only agreed reluctantly to this condition when finally convinced that in supporting Jud he could well do him a disservice.

Jud made a final point. He stated that Chris might be approached by an investigator or team of investigators from the Agency who would be discreetly checking Jud's conduct of affairs. It would be unlikely that the investigator or investigators would disclose their identity. Chris could be called on by someone claiming to be a journalist, an insurance adjuster or a sales representative. Whatever the guise, Chris was to freely give any information requested concerning Jud's habits, personal life and employment as a hardwoods buyer but to disclose absolutely nothing concerning the Agency activities even if presented with what appeared to be bona fide Agency credentials. And, if inquiries were launched through Chris, Jud wanted to be advised as soon as possible.

Anyone making discreet inquiries concerning Jud's whereabouts, habits and movements, would not be an investigator. He would be a skilled professional on an entirely different mission. It was the type of assignment with which Stanford was all too familiar and Jud found his old instincts and caution coming to the fore. If past performance was any criterion, it was the form of employment termination Harper would favour.

The hit, if it came, would probably be made to look like an accident. If Jud had advance warning of inquiries concerning his whereabouts and pattern of daily activities, he would be alerted to the danger and may be able to arrange a nasty surprise for his would be scorpio or scorpios. He was confident that he had lost none of Stanford's skills.

On November 4th Jud issued instructions to stop all further disbursement of funding to the insurgents. Four days later he advised Harper of this action by coded message.

PART THREE

THE MENDICANT

CHAPTER ONE

There had been no further communication from Harper in the week that had passed since his terse message advising that funding control was switched to Bangkok. Jud was not altogether surprised, therefore, when Chris Perkins advised him that a freelance journalist was in town making inquiries concerning the teak business and that Winters' name had cropped up.

From Chris, Jud learned that the journalist was young, affable, sandy-haired, carried a letter from the Los Angeles Times assigning him to do a story on the teak trade, and was staying at the Surawongse Hotel. The journalist went by the name of O'Neill.

Jud was thankful that Harper's boy appeared to be going the accidental death route. On the other hand, O'Neill was being so open in his inquiries that it probably meant he wasn't working alone. It was not unlikely that Jud's residence was under surveillance.

He had let it be known around town that he was planning a trip north to Chiang Dao and Fang. The Land Rover was gassed and contained what he would need for the journey – plus a few additional items.

Early tomorrow, he would drop Na Hti off at Chris and Susan's, then drive leisurely north. Since the death of Noppadol, Jud drove alone. It would present his executioner, or executioners, an excellent opportunity to make their play. When and if the assassination attempt took place, Jud had several surprises in store for his assailants. If no attempt was made, the Land Rover would eventually be found at the bottom of a gully, and Judson Q. Winters would be a very difficult man to locate.

Na Hti was over at the Keppler villa visiting Sasima and the children. Hank was coming for dinner and a few games of chess. He would bring Na Hti back when he came. They weren't due for another hour, which gave Jud time to take care of a few last minute details.

He went down to the office and let himself into the photo lab in the rear. When he locked the door, he went directly to the concealed wall safe. From the interior he took his passport, the envelope containing the American dollars, the bank passbooks in Quentin's name, two stacks of baht banknotes and the letter to his Swiss bankers. He surveyed the remaining contents; the narcotics reports, code books and microfilm. He felt a twinge of guilt concerning the narcotics reports. What the hell, he owed the Agency nothing. He shrugged.

Closing the safe door, he turned the key in the safety lock to the upright position then eased the door open a crack. When he heard a faint hissing he slammed the door shut and spun the knob. Thin wisps of smoke seeped around the edges of the door. Jud smiled grimly. So much, he thought, for my career as a master spy.

Before leaving, he made a last inspection of the lab. A stack of blow-up photo studies rested against the wall. None of them included microfilmed reports, but on an impulse he took a beaker of acid and poured it over the stack. It was a gesture of petty defiance, but it gave him satisfaction.

He paused on the front porch before entering the villa. He surveyed the grounds, now dimming in the gathering dusk. Nothing stirred. The only sound was the croaking of bullfrogs at the far end of the garden. Jud shivered. The mid-November evening was unseasonably chilly. If someone *was* watching the villa, Jud didn't envy him the task.

A fire crackled cheerily in the study grate. Jud and Hank were engrossed in the final stages of a chess game.

It was Jud's move. In the middle game he'd established a strong position. He was now pressing the attack. Confidently, he moved his queen diagonally. Unless there was something he'd overlooked, he should checkmate Keppler in five more moves.

Frowning, Hank studied the board for several minutes. He reached the same conclusion as Jud had concerning the outcome. 'Resign,' he said as he reached forward and toppled his king.

Setting up the board, Jud said mildly, 'Seem off your game tonight Hank. What prompted you to exchange knights?'

Hank sighed. 'I don't really know. Afraid I played badly. Quite a few things on my mind.' His chair scraped as he pushed back from the chess table. 'I've come to look forward to our weekly jousts. I shall miss them.'

Intent on placing the pieces in their starting ranks, Jud didn't look up. 'Another business trip?' he questioned.

'No. I'm not going anywhere. I'm afraid you are.'

Jud glanced up sharply. He found himself staring into the muzzle of a 9 mm Luger.

'What the hell! Is this some sort of joke?' Jud's voice betrayed genuine astonishment.

'I wish it was. I truly do wish it was. But it's no joke. Jud ... or whatever your real name might be.' Without shifting his point of aim, Keppler edged his chair further away from the table. 'Please keep your hands on the table. Don't attempt anything foolish. It has been some time since I used one of these, but I assure you I'm quite a good marksman.'

At this range, Jud thought wryly, Keppler didn't need to be a marksman, good or otherwise. His mind raced furiously. He was struck by the irony of the situation. He had been preparing to meet a threat from one quarter, yet here he was facing death from a totally unexpected source. Could it be that Keppler was a double agent? Was it possible that Keppler was the assigned executioner?

Stalling for time, Jud adopted a tone of righteous indignation. 'If it isn't a joke, what in hell are you playing at?'

'Convincing,' Keppler said flatly, 'but of no avail. May I suggest we stop sparring.'

'Have you flipped your lid?'

Keppler sighed. 'Very well. Perhaps I can persuade you to change your mind. It seems to be fairly common knowledge that I am the regional representative of the *Komitat Gosudarstvennoi Bezopasnosti* – the KGB. You have had me at a disadvantage. I have long suspected that you are not the man you represent yourself to be. That suspicion has now been confirmed, although I still don't know your true identity. I have also suspected you to be employed by our counterpart organization, the CIA, although I have no proof of that assumption just yet.'

Jud experienced a faint surge of relief. At least Keppler wasn't Harper's hit man. Jud said nothing. His features wore a puzzled frown of disbelief.

A suggestion of a smile eased the tenseness of Keppler's

set features. 'I must admit,' he continued, 'that my suspicions were based originally on intuition rather than any convincing evidence. I will also confess that from time to time my conviction has wavered, which is a sincere tribute to your competence and acting ability.'

'Hank.' Jud interjected, 'you're talking sheer nonsense.'

Keppler waved his free hand in a gesture of annoyance. 'You had me fooled. I don't know if I would have discovered your deception under normal circumstances. Probably not. But your timing was bad. You arrived at a time when I was smarting from a rebuke from my superiors, a time when an old-fashioned and creaky CIA intelligence network was obviously being replaced by a more efficient organization and a time when some most unwelcome initiatives were beginning to manifest themselves. For you, that was an unfortunate combination.

'As Winters, you were subjected to far more than the normal checks. I must say that, on the face of it, there should have been no doubt that you *were* Winters yet I could not escape a nagging suspicion that you were not. Call it sixth sense, if you will.

'I cultivated your friendship, watched you closely, surrounded you with informants and had this villa fitted with listening devices. With the exception of this particular room, those devices have been most effective. No matter. None of this is news to you.

'To your credit, all this effort netted me exactly nothing. I suppose I should have abandoned my close surveillance. But the better I got to know you, the less you added up to the Winters of my growing dossier. No point in going into the difference point by point, but you displayed too much competence in areas where Winters had shown little aptitude, ability or interest. I concluded that, unless Winters had undergone a truly remarkable transformation, you and he were not the same man. But who were you? You could be the very man I was searching for – the prime mover in a revitalized intelligence organization.'

It had an unreal quality which Jud found bordering on the absurd. Here he was marked for death by his own people and no longer of much value to Keppler. Had Keppler acted a few weeks earlier, Harper would have been saved a good deal of anxiety. Had Hank delayed a day, it would have been to find his quarry dead or departed from the scene. Whichever way you looked at it, Keppler's painstaking research wasn't going to show much profit.

At this point it may be of purely academic interest, but Jud was intrigued. Where had been the blunder which confirmed Keppler's suspicions concerning an identity switch?

Keppler shifted his weight in the chair. He transferred the Luger to his left hand. Flexing the fingers of his right hand, he glanced briefly at his watch.

'I hope I'm not boring you,' Keppler said mildly.

'Not at all,' Jud answered truthfully.

'I hadn't intended to indulge in a monologue,' Keppler said apologetically.

'Why don't you come to the point?'

'I shall, but we have about another half-hour before my ... ah ... associates are due here. I'm afraid our game took much less time than I anticipated.'

A warning bell sounded in Jud's mind. He discerned a more alarming scenario in the making. Cautiously, he inched his foot forward to make contact with the base of the chess table.

'To continue then,' Keppler said, clearing his throat. 'The informants with which I'd surounded you weren't very intelligent. I needed a more reliable source of information and devised a rather complicated scheme to serve that purpose. Then something happened to throw me almost completely off the track.

'That event was the coincidence of your meeting with Jud's childhood sweetheart. You have no idea how often I have replayed the tapes recording that tender reunion. I reasoned that if you were an imposter the fact was sure to reveal itself. The reverse was the case.

'I revised my thinking. You must be Jud Winters. The only acceptable explanation was that your present capabilities were due to a late-blooming maturity coupled with employment which had developed hitherto unsuspected talents. I held that view until quite recently.'

'Something caused you to reverse that opinion? Jud prompted as he moved his free foot slowly to gain a position of purchase.

181

'Not at the time. The Burmese revolutionary movement, which we had taken as something of a joke, suddenly assumed significance. With British connivance, U Thong appeared on the scene to provide leadership. Financial support and arms were being discreetly supplied. The operation was being handled with such a degree of professional skill that we could hardly credit it as being CIA inspired.

'These events caused agitation in certain circles. I, and my colleagues, came under extreme pressure to uncover the scope and intent of the operation at any cost.

'I concluded that the Burmese insurgents were being directed from a location at, or near, Chiang Mai. I reviewed all those I considered could have any possible connection. Ultimately, this brought me back to you, or rather Winters, as the prime suspect.

'It struck me that Winters' performance record in the Philippines could have been an elaborate fabrication to mask a high degree of professional competence. Far from being the small cog and casual informer as portrayed, Winters was a skilled agent. Certainly the Winters I knew here gave every evidence of being such a man.

'At that point, I put into action the plan I had been about to initiate when Christina changed my thinking. I had no guarantee the scheme would bear fruit, but all the elements were present which should lead to some interesting developments.'

In spite of himself, Jud's interest quickened. He had a cold presentiment that he knew what was coming next. 'I don't recall,' he said, 'having experienced anything as dramatic as you imply.'

'You did,' Keppler said with a touch of smugness. 'It started with an ambush.'

'I came damned close to killing your Meo playmates.'

'It wouldn't have mattered,' Keppler stated blandly. 'The Meo were instructed to kill your driver but only wound you. They had no idea that their own executioners were in hiding nearby. The driver had served his purpose and might have been an embarrassment if questioned later by the police. The plot called for a wounded Winters – and a timely rescue.'

Jud took over the story, his voice edged with bitterness, 'The next act was to have the wounded hero nursed back to health by a beautiful half-caste, in gratitude for which he would blurt out the family secrets.'

'Something along those lines. Na Hti is an uncommonly attractive young woman. She was desperately unhappy in the Lahu village. Her uncle, the headman, would have been more than happy to get her off his hands. He is, moreover, under obligation to me and was instructed to do everything possible to encourage a relationship between you and the girl. I was confident that some degree of intimacy would develop which could prove useful, then or later. I must confess that I was delighted when you returned to Chiang Mai with the girl. I may have hoped for something of that nature, but didn't expect it to happen. I could hardly believe my good fortune.'

Keppler had been watching Jud intently as he unfolded the story. Jud could not hide his feelings. His face betrayed his hurt and sense of betrayal. Keppler was pleased. He dwelt a brief pause, then continued in a reflective tone.

'Na Hti, of course, was not a party to the deception. She was, and is, my unwitting ally. She is deeply in love with you. You are a fortunate man.

'It isn't necessary, but I feel I owe you a bit more of an explanation. Grundlich, the girl's father, went by another name during the Second World War. After the war, a number of people would have liked to get their hands on him. Your Military Intelligence were intensely interested in his whereabouts. So was Reinhard Gehlen. Our own military intelligence, the GRU, were equally anxious to locate him. It was my good fortune to recognize him masquerading as a Lutheran missionary in Chiang Rai. I should have turned him over to the GRU. I didn't.

'In return for my silence, Grundlich was extremely helpful. Through him I was able to recruit the services of some of the hill tribes. Then I arranged for him to undertake a delicate mission in South America.

'It is difficult to command the loyalty of a man like Grundlich. The only person he valued in this life was his daughter by a Lahu mistress. As insurance, I made Grunlich leave the girl with her mother's people, under my sponsorship. Na Hti knows nothing of her father's true background, nor is she aware that he was killed a few years ago . . . in line of duty, shall we say.

'Since her arrival here, I have gone out of my way to make her welcome. It has been no hardship. Sasima and the children have grown very fond of her, as I have myself. She hasn't the slightest idea I have been pumping her for information. It requires little effort on my part. She loves nothing better than to talk about you and will discuss the most intimate details of your life together without prompting.

'To be honest, I was beginning to despair of ever gleaning anything of value. She knows nothing of your clandestine activities. I commend you on your discretion. Then, quite recently, she mentioned a scar on your back. It rang a bell.

'There had been mention of the scar in your conversation with Christina. A wound from the Korean war was your explanation. I rechecked the photostats of Winters' service medical records. Nowhere is any such wound recorded.'

Jud thought quickly. With an apologetic grin, he said, 'You couldn't expect me to tell Tina that the wound is a souvenir of a back alley brawl in Manila.'

'Just so,' was Keppler's mild response. 'Some such explanation occurred to me. It would be more in keeping with Winters' character. There is, however, another small matter. And again it relates to medical documents.

'As an ex-naval reservist, Winters availed himself of the services of the Subic Bay Naval Hospital in 1967 for an emergency apendectomy. Na Hti, who has taken a thorough inventory of your blemishes, heatedly denies that there is any scar in that region of your anatomy.'

Jud experienced a sinking feeling. What incredible folly for the Agency to have gone to such lengths to create an imposture and then overlook something as basic as the alteration of medical records to substantiate the masquerade.

As though reading Jud's mind, Keppler favored him with a look of sympathy. 'No, my friend, you are not Judson Winters. Who you are, and your exact function, I don't yet know. But we soon will. The gentlemen who are due shortly are members of our *Mokryye Dela*. Perhaps you are familiar with that department.'

The Department of Wet Affairs, the KGB's infamous department for terror and assassination. He had encountered

184

them in the past and had no illusions concerning their expertise in persuasive interrogation. For the first time in the confrontation, Jud felt a chill of real fear. Short of cheating them through death, he could not recall a single case that had withstood a *Mokryye Dela* interrogation. Jud hadn't any qualms about blowing the Burmese insurgency operation. Without compunction he would implicate Harper, but, if he didn't succumb first, a lot of his network's agents would be identified and subsequently eliminated. 'Do you think you can bring some thugs here to murder me without Na Hti and the servants raising an objection?' Jud said coldly.

'The interrogation won't be conducted here, and I've been assured you won't be killed ... if you cooperate. Na Hti believes we are going to a party after the chess game and, on my instructions, gave the servants the evening off after dinner. She should join us in a few minutes. After all, we are going to a party, of sorts.'

'You bastard!'

'I imagine such invective is not uncalled for. For you, the game is over. You have nothing to gain by heroics. But it occurred to me you might prove obstinate. Let's say that Na Hti is my insurance for your cooperation.'

The muscles in Jud's legs tensed as he prepared to kick the table toward Keppler. His chances of making it to the study archway were slim, but better than he'd originally calculated. Keppler would shoot to wound, not kill. The last thing Hank would want would be to present a corpse to the interrogation team.

An unexpected movement by Keppler arrested Jud's attention. Keppler's gaze shifted to the archway and a disarming smile lit his countenance.

'Come in my dear,' Keppler said pleasantly. 'We were just talking about you and ...' His sentence broke off abruptly. His smile congealed as he swung the Luger toward the doorway.

The bark of a revolver shot echoed in the study. Keppler was slammed backwards in the chair. His lips worked to form some word of protest.

A second shot cracked closely on the heels of the first. The bullet caught Keppler above the right eye and jerked his head sideways as flesh and splinters of bone splayed against the upholstered back of the chair. Keppler's body convulsed then sagged into the angle formed by the chair's backrest and wing. The Luger dropped from nerveless fingers to clatter on the floor.

CHAPTER TWO

She stood in the archway. Her face was expressionless; her eyes wide and staring fixedly at the crumpled corpse. Her right hand was extended, still gripping tightly the .38 revolver. A thin feather of smoke curled upwards from the barrel.

Na Hti must have been about to enter the room earlier when something she had overheard caused her to hesitate. Her command of English was not sufficiently good that she could have followed too much of Keppler's dialogue, but somehow she must have grasped the menace of his tone and words. She must have peered into the study and observed the threatening Luger. With the directness of thought of the Lahu hunter faced with danger, she had seen only one possible course of action. She had known of the revolver in the bedside table She had not hesitated. From the moment she had seen the Luger in Keppler's hand, he had been virtually a dead man.

Stepping in front of her, Jud blocked her line of vision. Gently, he took the revolver from her hand. Her eyes raised to meet his gaze. Slipping the .38 into the pocket of his jacket, Jud reached out and lightly stroked Na Hti's hair in a gesture of affection and understanding. Touching her shoulder, he turned her and eased her from the room.

It would be fifteen minutes at the most before the interrogators arrived. That didn't give Jud much time. He weighed his chances of defending the villa. He had no idea how many of the *Mokryye Dela* he would be facing. Against ordinary assailants it might work, but against the Russian experts the odds were too heavily stacked, against him. He discarded that tactic.

Na Hti wouldn't be safe with Perkins, or any other haven Chiang Mai. Whatever he did, Na Hti would have to remain with him. He accepted that.

Fleeing by car was out of the question. He might get past the Russians. Assuming his house was being watched by an Agency assassin, he might evade that trap as well. But within a few short hours the alarm would be sounded and he and Na Hti would be caught at a highway check point or by a police patrol.

He could think of no place they could go to ground in or close to Chiang Mai. That left only flight on foot, and damned quickly at that.

Leading a still dazed Na Hti by the hand, he steered her into the bedroom. From his closet he pulled out a spare knapsack. Handing it to Na Hti, he spoke urgently, 'We must go into the hills. You'll need warm clothing. We'll need food. Get what you need from the kitchen, but we must be quick. When you're ready, go out the back bedroom window and wait for me behind the house. Do you understand?'

Na Hti noded. As she left the room, she was already rummaging in a dresser drawer and stuffing articles into the knapsack.

His sleeping bag and most of the items he would need were already packed and stowed in the Land Rover.

He left the porch light unlit. Two at a time, he raced down the front steps. In the darkened carport, he located the items he wanted in the back of the Land Rover. Then his hand encountered one of the jerry cans of spare gasoline and he was struck by an inspiration. When he ascended the front steps, he was carrying a jerry can in addition to his camping equipment.

He stood for a moment on the porch. The grounds were still. The night was silent.

Entering the villa, he bolted the front door. He left the can of gasoline near the door. Glancing at his watch, he noted that less than five minutes had passed.

From the gun rack he selected the Sprinfield .30/06 and took two boxes of 220 grain soft-nosed shells from the shelf. Laden with the rifle, knapsack and sleeping bag, the shells stuffed into the pocket of his sports jacket, he proceeded to the bedroom. Na Hti must have completed her packing since the room was empty.

He undressed quickly and changed into bush clothing. He transferred the shells, his passport, Quentin's passbook and the currency he'd taken from the safe earlier to the pockets

187

of his bush jacket. As an afterthought, he scooped his and Na Hti's personal identification documents from the bedside table and crammed them in a breast pocket. On his feet, he left the moccasins he'd been wearing. He knotted the laces of his jungle boots together and stood up. He was almost ready.

With the letter to his Swiss bankers in his hand, Jud returned to the front hall and retrieved the jerry can. In the study, Jud scarcely glanced at Keppler's corpse as he poured gasoline over the body, the rug, the chairs and splashed some on the drapes. The remaining gasoline he splashed around the sitting room. With his lighter, he set flame to the letter and tossed it onto the rug. Flames raced along the floor.

Back in the master bedroom, he pulled on the knapsack, hung his boots around his neck, tucked the sleeping bag under one arm and slung the rifle over his shoulder. As he headed for the back bedroom, smoke clouded the hallway.

He poised for a moment on the windowsill, scrutinizing the sharply rising ground to the rear of the villa. Moonlight bathed the thin scrub jungle. It wasn't to his liking, but couldn't be helped. He dropped the two metres to the soft earth of the flowerbed.

He didn't see Na Hti until she detached herself from the deep shadow behind the house. He smiled. She was wearing the same Lahu garb in which she'd arrived in Chiang Mai six months earlier. Along with the knapsack, she had strapped to her back a woven basket and the quiver of arrows for the hunting crossbow she carried over her shoulder. Jud wondered where she had kept these articles stored. He hadn't seen them since the day he'd brought her to the villa. He had told her they were to go into the hills. She hadn't questioned. She was prepared for a return to the mountains.

He heard a car engine, then the trees to his left were briefly etched by arcing headlights as the vehicle climbed the incline and swung through the driveway gates. Jud grinned. 'Punctual,' he said. 'A few minutes earlier might have posed us a problem.' He reached out and took Na Hti's hand. 'Come on, honey, let's get the hell out of here.'

They climbed into the thin screen of trees and started to circle to the right. Jud guided Na Hti towards the line of trees which marked the boundary between his grounds and the university property.

Once within the protective shelter of the trees, Jud paused to look back at the villa. The study and sitting room windows facing his direction glowed with flickering red from the flames within. Heavy smoke billowed from beneath the roof overhang.

He could make out the vehicle parked in the driveway and several figures on the porch. A single form was moving up the sloping ground towards the rear of the villa. He was no longer curious concerning the identities of these adversaries. There was little point. With few exceptions, every man's hand was turned against him.

Na Hti watched the burning villa with morbid fascination. She gasped as a tongue of flame shot from the study windows to curl around the eaves and lick at the roof. She turned questioning eyes to Jud. He shrugged. 'It is best,' he said laconically. Turning away from the spectacle, he headed deeper into the trees. On the other side of the tree line a large drainage ditch ran from the base of the mountain to the outskirts of the city. Beyond this gully, most of the foliage and scrub jungle had been cleared. To cross these grassy slopes would be to invite almost certain detection.

Jud guided Na Hti into the knee deep water coursing down the ditch. Instinctively, she turned towards the looming mountain. Jud stopped her with a restraining hand. He pointed in the direction of the town. Half crouching, they started to wade down the gentle decline.

Jud's aim was to put as much distance as possible between himself and the pursuit which must inevitably follow. His initial objective was the high-canopy jungle which mantled the slopes of the mountains beyond Doi Suthep. The trackless rain forest should provide sanctuary and give him time to devise some workable strategy.

Already, his would-be interrogators must be scouring the villa grounds. The conflagration would attract firemen and police from town and generate confusion which might hamper the searchers temporarily. By dawn, however, it would not be difficult to follow the tracks of the fleeing couple to the drainage ditch. In the muddy defile, the evidence of their flight eastward, in the direction of Chiang Mai, would be readily discernible. It was a ruse Jud hoped would provide a false scent and mask his true intent. It was at best a crude delaying tactic.

They followed the ditch to where it emptied into the concrete-sided irrigation canal which circled the city's western limits. In hip-deep water, they waded northward against the sluggish current.

Jud fully appreciated that this was the most perilous part of their escape route. If trapped in the conduit, they had little or no chance. At one point, they waited several minutes in the deep shadow of an overhead foot bridge while a number of vehicles passed on the dirt road skirting the eastern bank of the canal. Nature favoured them. For the better part of the journey the moon remained mercifully obscured by clouds.

It seemed an eternity, but could not have been much more than a quarter of an hour, before they reached the point where a culvert discharged the tumbling water of a large stream into the canal. He lifted Na Hti up into the descending stream and scrambled after her.

Moments later, seated on a rock in mid-stream, Jud slipped of his sodden moccasins and laced on his boots. He threw the moccasins into the stream and watched as they arced into the canal and went bobbing southward in the slow current.

To the south he could see a rising pall of red-tinged smoke. It was, Jud thought, a fitting funeral pyre in honor of Keppler, a worthy antagonist, and symbolized the ending of a chapter in the life of Joe Stanford. God alone knew what lay ahead.

Moonlight, an unwelcome curse earlier, now became a boon as they scrambled up boulder-strewn stream beds. Jud calculated that they had about seven hours of darkness remaining. They must make every minute count. At several points, accepting the risk in favour of time gained, he took to the paved road which would wound up the mountain to Wat Prathat and the King's Bhu Phing Summer Palace beyond.

When they descended from the pine forest onto the ridges along the southwestern folds of Suthep, Jud set a killing pace. He was out of shape from months of relative inactivity but could not afford the luxury of even a moment's rest.

Na Hti trotted along behind Jud happily. The months of city living had taken their toll and she was tiring, but as they moved ever deeper into the mountains her heart lifted. This was her element. Here she was not prey to uncertainties and bewilderment which assailed her in the urban environment. Here, her knowledge could serve her man to best advantage. That she had killed in his defence was a source of pride. She gave no thought to the dead Keppler for, after all, survival was the first law.

She appreciated that they were fleeing from some dire threat. When Jud had directed their initial course toward the city intead of up the slope, she had been puzzled. Then, when they had been in the canal and had ascended by the stream, she had perceived his strategy. When he had changed to the boots and had directed their course through streams and over hard or rocky ground she had eyed him with growing respect. At one point they had heard the sawing cough of a hunting leopard and Jud had veered unhesitatingly to keep them downwind of the predator. She had not suspected that her man possessed such skills. As the night advanced toward dawn Na Hti's respect grew to admiration. She followed Jud with perfect confidence.

Na Hti was blissfully ignorant of the fact that the object of her confidence did not share her abiding faith in his abilities. He was jungle-wise and had tracked and been tracked. He was confident that if they could penetrate far enough into the rain forest he could elude their pursuers. Beyond that, he had formed no clear picture. Nor could he dwell on it at the moment when his every faculty must be directed toward the immediate problems.

Dawn came up on them as they entered heavier jungle foliage. The course he set was southwesterly in the general direction of Doi Inthanon and a region of dense hardwood forests, jungle-choked gorges, forbidding peaks and virtually uninhabited.

It was an arduous day. They trudged through the semi-gloom of triple-canopy rain forest, scrambled in and out of gullies and waded along the courses of rushing mountain streams. He allowed several rest breaks, but of short duration since he feared that if the halts were prolonged they would be unable to continue. The only food they had throughout the day was some cold meat and cheese from Na Hti's knapsack.

During the day, they had twice heard the unmistakable thumping of helicopters high above their forest cover. They encountered no signs of human intrusion nor did they see much in the way of wildlife. Their slow progress was accompanied by a tocsin symphony warning game of their approach – the screeching of birds, the mournful hooting of gibbons and the chatter of agitated monkeys.

Jud called a halt shortly before dusk. The place he selected was beside a small stream in a heavily wooded defile.

They were both bone-weary, but there were still tasks to perform. Jud helped Na Hti gather dry branches and light a small fire. When the blaze was kindled they stripped off and removed the day's accumulation of ticks and leeches from each other.

While Na Hti busied herself preparing a simple meal, Jud sat on the projecting root of a banyan tree which towered above them. For the first time, he allowed himself to ponder the full extent of their predicament.

Keppler's death would set in motion a chain reaction. His body should be well incinerated, but not beyond identification and the cause of death would certainly be determined. Keppler was popular, and Sasima had powerful connections. The search for the murderer would be vigorously pursued by the regular police, the Border Patrol Police and the Thai military. The helicopters they'd heard probably meant the search was already in progress.

What of the others that were anxious to lay their hands on him? If the KGB had wanted him for interrogation and disposal before, they should now be doubly anxious to capture him now that he'd eliminated their man in Chiang Mai. Of them all, however, Jud was more concerned about the CIA assassin. That eliminated the only avenue which could have afforded protection from the Thai authorities and the KGB. The Agency, having already decided to remove him forcibly, would now pursue that objective relentlessly. The killing of Keppler would be interpreted as evidence that Winters' cover was blown. A live Winters was a threat to security. A Winters effectively muted by death was infinitely preferable.

Just yesterday, Jud thought ruefully, I had one bloodhound baying at my heels and figured I knew how to cope with it. Now, the whole pack is snapping at my ass and I haven't a clue where to turn. He would devise some solution, but at that moment he was too tired to think straight. Besides, somewhere along the route he'd twisted his ankle and the damned thing was swollen and throbbing.

He turned out the pockets of his bush jacket. The local currency and the envelope of dollars, he transferred to his knapsack. They were of no value at the moment but would undoubtedly come in handy at some future date. After a moment's hesitation, he slipped Quentin's bank book into the bush jacket pocket. He was left with a passport, Certificate of Residence and Alien Registration book in the name of Judson Q, Winters and the Thai Identification Card he'd procured for Na Hti. They were useless documents. Worse, they could identify himself and Na Hti as wanted criminals. He tossed the identity card into the fire, tore the pages from the other documents and fed them into the flames, then threw the empty covers in last. He watched the covers char and curl with a touch of sadness.

Stirring the ashes of the destroyed documents, Jud thought, so much for Jud Winters, hardwoods buyer and super spy. Winters was now dead once and for all and could rest in peace. As for himself, he couldn't even revert to his true identity. He was officially dead. He would have to dream up an entirely new identity.

The lyrics of a remembered song came to him. 'Pore Jud is daid,' he murmured softly.

Na Hti glanced up at the sound of his voice. He grinned at her reassuringly.

After their simple but satisfying meal, Jud bathed his swollen ankle in the icy water of the stream. While he sat again on the tree root, Na Hti, with tender and loving care, bound the ankle in strips of cloth cut from one of his shirts.

Jud looked down on her head. She would have been better off, a thousand times better off, if she'd never met him. His gaze strayed to the swelling flesh of his midriff. Those signs of soft living would melt away in the days ahead but the resilience of youth as displayed by Na Hti was forever lost to him. She could have chosen a better protector, he thought glumly.

They crawled naked into the sleeping bag. Within minutes, they dropped into the sleep of exhaustion.

CHAPTER THREE

Of the four men assembled in the living room of the house in Makati, three had recently returned from Chiang Mai. They had gone and returned singly, although their missions had resolved around a common purpose. The last to arrive back in Manila had been Sam Harper, who had returned only that morning.

In his capacity as an official of Santa Rosa Lumber & Plywood Company, Harper had flown to Chiang Mai to ascertain the extent of damage sustained by the company-owned villa from the devastating blaze and to investigate the serious charges that their Chiang Mai representative was wanted for murder and possible arson. Two men had accompanied Harper. One was Rudolfo, who would take over as buyer on a temporary basis. The second was an insurance claims adjuster named Cranston, who would also remain in Chiang Mai for an indefinite period. Cranston was a CIA agent. His primary function was to take charge of the on-the-ground search for Jud Winters.

Harper was conducting the meeting informally, yet there was an air of tension in the pleasant sun-filled room. The discussions had been underway for a half an hour and had covered a good deal of ground. Harper completed an account of his various meetings and discussions with the Thai police. He turned to face the youngest member of the group, and picked up questioning where he'd left off.

'Then it's your impression that Perkins did not believe you were a freelance journalist?'

'I have no way of proving it,' the young man answered, 'but there was something about his manner ... he was cautious and on guard. I would say he was definitely suspicious. Yet, at the same time, I wouldn't say he had the slightest inkling of the true purpose of my visit.'

'Yet you say he was cooperative in giving you information concerning Winters' normal schedule?'

'To a point. When I set up my appointment with Perkins, it was to seek his assistance in gleaning background material for a new feature story on the dwindling teak industry.

During the initial discussion, he was affable and relaxed. It was only when I said I'd been advised that there was an American named Judson Winters involved in the business, and requested any help Perkins could give me in contacting Winters, that the attitude underwent a subtle change. He readily admitted knowing Winters personally, and indicated that he could probably set up an appointment, but suggested I should telephone myself during normal working hours and check with Mr Winters' secretary. I pressed a bit. Wanted to know what Winters' considered normal working hours, and if he was in the habit of making frequent out of town business trips. Perkins stated that Winters did make frequent trips during the dry season, which is now, but that to the best of his knowledge Winters was in town at the moment. Don't misunderstand me. Perkins wasn't evasive. He just seemed to be feeling his way with a degree of caution. I had the feeling that he'd been briefed to expect inquiries concerning Winters.'

'He probably had been.' Harper interjected drily.

One of the men, Bill Abbott, spoke up, 'The police confirmed that Winters and the girl were headed for town. We have no way of knowing whether or not the KGB picked them up somewhere along the way. They've simply vanished without a trace.'

Of only two men in Southeast Asia who knew the true identity and resources of the man known as Winters, Harper was one. 'We must assume,' Harper stated flatly, 'that they eluded capture by the KGB. What O'Neill here told us concerning events at the villa tends to confirm that.' Turning to the young man, he said, 'Would you go over that part again.'

'Hendricks was watching the villa from a vantage point up the hill. During the late afternoon I learned from a forestry official that Winters was planning a trip up-country probably the following day. We would both be required and need two cars to follow Winters if he left town. About eight o'clock I went up and checked with Hendricks. Winters had a guest answering the description of Keppler. It looked as though he wouldn't be going anywhere that evening so I pulled Hendricks off watch so we could get a good night's sleep and resume surveillance before dawn.

'Shortly after ten, I was about to go up to my room when I

learned that Winters' villa was on fire. I phoned Hendricks to stand by, then drove directly to the villa.

'I arrived at ten-twenty to find the house burning furiously. There were some firemen and policemen on the scene and four men who claimed to be friends of Keppler; said they'd come to pick him up after a chess game. It appears they'd arrived just after the fire broke out. They had smashed down the locked front door and somehow managed to drag a charred body from one of the rooms. I understand the body was later identified as that of Keppler, who had not died in the fire but as a result of gunshot wounds.

'That's about it. Bill arrived on the scene the next afternoon and I sent Hendricks back to Hong Kong. Hung around for another couple of days making like a newshound. The town was in an uproar over the missing Winters so there didn't seem much point in sticking around longer. Came back here for further instructions.

'We have just learned that the four men O'Neill saw at the fire were KGB special interrogators. They billed themselves as a Russian Cultural Mission.' Harper paused, then went on, 'They stayed in town two days and their movements are a matter of record. If they had known where Winters was they would not have still been at the scene of the fire. If they'd apprehended Winters and the girl we would have known about it.'

Harper paused to let what he'd said sink in, then turned to Abbott. 'Bill, we've had your report. To recap, when you accompanied Perkins to the villa, or rather the ashes thereof, you met me already on the scene as the deeply disturbed employer. When I cleared everybody from the area, you returned with Perkins. The photographic lab on the lower level had been cut into the earth and rock foundation beneath the house and had been only partially destroyed by the fire. The rear wall was intact, and Perkins was able to open the document safe. Frankly, the fact that Perkins was in possession of the combination and a destruction device key, I find most disturbing. For the moment, I'll let that ride. What you discovered was that Winters had thoughtfully destroyed the entire contents ... unless he took something with him. Can you add anything to that?'

'No. Except perhaps that Perkins seems to have a very high regard for Winters.'

'Very well, I'll review the situation as I see it, and as it stands at the moment.

'Perkins has been shifted to Schrieber's control in Bangkok. LeFarge, will report through Bailey in Long Cheng until other arrangements can be made. Cranston will remain in Chiang Mai to direct any operations we may require, and to maintain close liaison with our advisers with the Thai Border Patrol Police, the local police, and the Thai army. You,' Harper said, nodding towards the fourth man of the group, 'will return to Vientiane and keep us closely advised concerning LeFarge's movements. I can think of no immediate requirement for your services,' he said, directing his gaze to the young man, 'so you might as well return to Los Angeles tomorrow.'

Harper leaned back in his chair. He placed the tips of his fingers together. 'My interpretation is this. Winters, with the girl, has gone deep into the mountains. Don't forget, he's had past experience in tropical jungles, excellent training in Mindanao, and almost two years to become thoroughly familiar with the forests of Northern Thailand. I'm convinced he was somehow warned by Perkins concerning our intentions, otherwise Winters would have appealed to us for assistance by now. He had no choice but flight.

'He knows he will be wanted for Keppler's murder and that the borders and all means of egress from the country will be under surveillance. All highway check points, trains, buses and internal airlines will be subject to close scrutiny. Thailand is pretty much a military police state, which severely limits his movements. He is well aware of this. Therefore, for the moment, he can only hide in the jungles of the mountainous regions. There, I feel, he will stay until he thinks the hue and cry has died down sufficiently that his movements will not be unduly hampered. Eventually, therefore, he will emerge from hiding. We must be prepared when he does.

'He knows that he can never be safe as long as he remains in Thailand. When he does surface, it will be in an attempt to flee the country. What are his actions likely to be?

'He has formed close attachments with his two immediate contacts, Perkins and LeFarge. I think he will seek the assistance of one or the other. My guess would be LeFarge, but we cannot rule out Perkins. Accordingly, both those agents must remain under the closest of surveillance, without their knowledge or suspicion. I hope I'm making myself abundantly clear on this point.

'We can assume that Winters will have adopted some form of false identity. But I don't think he will abandon the girl. So we are looking for two people, not one. Both are rather distinctive and should stand out against a background of Thais.

'Granting that Winters must leave the country, we are faced with a bewildering array of possibilities. Which way will he go? Which border will he cross? While I can't eliminate any border, logic restricts the choice to acceptable limits.'

Harper used a count-down of his fingers to explain his reasoning. 'Burma, while the closest, should be his least likely choice. He has no connections to assist him and Burma is even more of a police state than Thailand. Also, our Russian colleagues operate there with a degree of freedom which would invite almost certain apprehension by the KGB.

'Malaysia is too distant from his present location. In addition, as the isthmus narrows, his freedom of movement becomes more and more restricted.

'Cambodia, while ideally suited to his purpose in many ways, again presents him with considerable distance. Every kilometer he travels over open country, reduces his chances of success.

'For these reasons, I favor Laos, and suggest we devote major attention to that border region. His most likely course is to circle to the north of Chiang Mai, cut to the east until he reaches the Mekong and then select a loosely patrolled section for a crossing into Laos. There is another reason why Laos is appealing. As I stated, he will probably seek help from either Perkins or LeFarge. He knows that we will be watching both men. Of the two, LeFarge, through his peculiar cover activities, is by far the hardest to keep under surveillance. In addition, and again due to his cover activities, LeFarge is in a better position to assist in smuggling Winters and the girl out of the country. Ultimately, of course, Winters must try and remove himself from Southeast Asia entirely, if he wishes to enjoy any sort of freedom.' Harper left a significant pause. 'Any questions?'

Abbot rubbed his jaw. 'Burma proper may be a poor choice for Winters but what about the Shan region?'

'Bear in mind I'm not excluding *any* possibility. The Shan States would offer Winters a temporary haven from which he could cross over into Laos at his leisure. However, he'd be crossing into Pathet Lao-controlled country. To reach the Shan States, he must traverse the region of the opium routes; territory jealously guarded by Ling Po's Koumintang mercenaries. I think those are risks Winters is highly unlikely to take.'

'Couldn't he hole up with the girl's Lahu tribespeople? Surely her people would grant sanctuary to the fugitive couple,' Abbot said.

'They would. But Winters knows that the police will be watching the tribe and its movements closely. Too dangerous.'

Harper waited. There were no further questions. 'Let me recap,' he said flatly. 'Winters will be relying on an eventual relaxation of police vigilance. We must not allow the authorities that luxury. If the pair are caught in Thailand, it will most likely be the police who effect the capture. We must be prepared to move without delay. We must reach Winters before he is interrogated by the Thai police, the KGB, or *anyone*. What happens to the girl is unimportant, but I want to stress one vital point.' Harper leaned forward, and said with grim emphasis, '*Winters must be liquidated.*'

Following the departure of the others, Harper sat in the living room, sunk in deep thought.

He'd struck a note of confidence concerning the capture of Winters, but was not nearly as sanguine as he'd appeared. As the others did not, Harper knew Winters as Stanford. While he had developed an abiding hatred for Stanford, he had not allowed this to cloud his reason. He retained a healthy respect for Stanford's capabilities.

LeFarge was another issue. Harper had only learned from a coded message awaiting his return to Manila that LeFarge, under another identity, had once served under Stanford in the Special Forces and that a durable bond existed between the two men. Harper bitterly resented the fact that he had not been advised of this at a much earlier date. True, it now gave him a probable slant on Stanford's action, but he could conceive of no valid reason why the information should have been withheld for two years.

Stanford, Harper appreciated, had the expertise to live out his remaining years in the jungles of Thailand with impunity. That he would not choose to do so, Harper was confident. He would emerge from hiding, and would probably elude capture in Thailand. What then? Harper would direct every means at his disposal to the ultimate destruction of Stanford, but if the man broke through the tightening net in Thailand, what would the next moves be? Harper was not at all sure that Stanford would leave the general area. It could well be that Stanford, with the instincts of the killer that he was, would attempt to remove the body which threatened him. In that case, he, Harper, would be the target. The hunter would become the hunted. To be relentlessly stalked by Stanford was a possibility Harper did not relish.

For the first time in his life, Harper was experiencing an emotion closely akin to fear.

CHAPTER FOUR

Na Hti's love for Jud was deep. It combined the adulation she had accorded her missionary father, the passions of awakened and wondrously satiated sexual appetites, and a profound gratitude for her release from the bondage of the Lahu village. She knew that Jud did not consider the Lahu ceremony as a binding contract of marriage, even if she did. While this disturbed her, it was of small consequence. She was content to serve him in any capacity within her power. For him, she had killed without qualm and would not hesitate to do so again. If necessary, she would gladly give her own life to shield and protect him.

Early in November, she discovered to her intense joy that she was pregnant. While she wanted to communicate the happy tidings, for some reason she could not define, she held back. Some instinct warned her that he might not receive this news with the same ecstatic pleasure it brought her. She would tell him, of course, when she felt the moment was right. So far, such opportunity had eluded her.

She had no false modesty and was not at all self-conscious in being unclad in Jud's presence. She derived satisfaction from the fact that her lithe body pleased him. Her only misgivings concerning pregnancy were that her body would become gross and unappealing in his eyes.

The unseasonal cold snap which had caused discomfort during the first day of their journey passed, giving way to normal November weather. While the nights at that altitude were crisp and chilly, the days were sun-warmed to a comfortable temperature. True, Jud avoided the grassy ridges and sloping alpine meadows, confining their passage, where possible, to the concealment afforded by high-canopy jungle. There little sunlight penetrated the vine-festooned leafy cathedral, yet it was still warm enough for them to perspire freely during the day. In the late afternoon of the third day, Jud called a halt where a cascading rivulet widened into a hushed and shaded pool.

While Jud sat in his underwear in a patch of slanting sunlight on the bank, Na Hti, unabashedly nude, was rinsing their sweat-soaked garments in the pool. She turned to wade back to the bank, and surprised a look of puzzlement on Jud's face.

'I hadn't noticed it before,' he said, 'but your breasts seem to be getting a little bigger.'

Na Hti blushed in confusion. In imagining how she would divulge her secret, she hadn't pictured a setting such as this. She dropped her burden of wet clothing to the grass, and patted her flat belly in an eloquent gesture. 'Baby,' she said lamely.

Jud's eyes widened in astonishment. 'You mean you're pregnant? When? How long?'

'Almost seven weeks,' she answered simply.

'Jes – sus! Why in hell didn't you tell me?'

Her eyes dropped in embarrassment. It was as she'd feared; he was not happy with the news. 'I think maybe you not want baby,' she replied in a barely audible voice.

Suddenly, Jud was laughing. 'Of course I want my wife to have my child. But I think our timing's screwed up.'

She looked up into Jud's face. He was *not* angry. His

words had accorded her the status of his mate. Her heart swelled with a burst of happiness. With a choked sob, she flung herself into his arms and clutched herself fiercely to his chest.

Jud stroked her hair, and held her trembling body close. Her head was buried in his chest. He kissed the tip of her ear. 'You poor kid,' he said softly. 'Did you think I didn't love you enough to want our baby? I've been a blind idiot.'

To Na Hti it was the fulfillment of a cherished dream. To Jud his own words came with the force of sudden revelation. He *did* love this woman with passionate possessiveness. He'd been a damned fool not to recognize the fact until this moment.

Jud cupped her firm young breast in the palm of his hand. As he caressed it gently, he felt the nipple harden in response.

It was a good deal later, and the sun had almost set, before they gave thought to an evening meal.

Jud awoke to find himself alone in the sleeping bag. He sat up, expecting to see Na Hti preparing an early meal. She was nowhere in evidence.

Alarmed, Jud scrambled from the bag and snatched for his bush clothing. He was struggling into his boots, when Na Hti appeared at his side. She was fully clothed and carrying her crossbow. He was about to greet her, when she held up a warning hand. Her face serious, she pointed in the downstream direction; the way they'd come the previous afternoon.

Picking up the Springfield, Jud followed as she led him up a sharp rise to a rocky promontory. Dropping to her stomach, she wormed her way forward to the grassy lip and cautiously parted a thin screen of foliage. Jud moved to her side without a sound.

From this point of vantage, he could see a considerable distance downstream. The defile was heavily shadowed in the early light, but he could make out movement along the stream banks. Two black clad figures were working their way slowly along the edges of the stream. The closer of the two was about two hundred meters distant, on the same side of the rivulet as the promontory. The second was on the opposite bank, about fifty metres further down stream. The approach was slow and cautious as the figures scanned the grass, rocks and foliage flanking the stream bed.

Jud's eyes narrowed. Yesterday afternoon, he'd heard, but not seen, a helicopter pass low over the heavy jungle. He hadn't been concerned, since they were safe from detection. This, however, was a very different matter.

Silently, Jud and Na Hti worked their way back to a point part way down the slope. They held a whispered conference.

'Who?' Jud questioned laconically.

'Lisu hunters.'

Jud was thoughtful while he debated the action to be taken. There was no doubt in his mind that the hunters were tracking Na Hti and himself. They had left scant trail. but the Lisu, distant cousins of the Lahu, were skilled trackers. There could be more in the party. He looked dubiously at his rifle. He couldn't risk a shot. He looked at Na Hti's crossbow.

'Can you stop a man with that?'

Na Hti nodded vigorous assent.

'Good.' In terse phrases, he outlined his plan. He would cross upstream and work his way back down to a rock outcropping some sixty meters downstream on the far bank. She would wait on the promontory. From there, she would be able to see Jud, although the trackers would not. On his signal, she would take out the Lisu on her side of the stream. Jud would look after the other man. Again, Na Hti nodded her agreement.

He leaned the Springfield against a tree, eased the knife in its sheath, and slipped silently down the slope.

He reached his position of ambush well before the Lisu came abreast of the rocks. From here, he could see the lip of the promontory clearly. He slipped the knife from its scabbard and waited.

On the opposite bank, the leading tracker came into view and moved slowly upstream, his attention fixed on the water's edge. Then, Jud could hear the faint splashing as the second man approached the rocks. Jud tensed. He held up his hand. When he judged his quarry to be but a few feet away, he dropped his hand.

As Jud catapulted from his place of concealment, he heard from upstream the twang of the crossbow and a strangled grunt. Intent on his own target, he didn't see the upstream Lisu struggling in the shallow water, clutching at a crossbow quarrel which had pierced his throat. At the startling spectacle of his companion's predicament, Jud's quarry was momentarily off balance.

The distraction was what Jud had counted on. He was upon his man before the Lisu could recover. With a throttling forearm around the stocky hunter's neck, Jud swung him sideways and viciously stabbed upwards into the man's kidneys. The struggling man went limp and sagged without a sound.

Jud glanced upstream, just in time to see a second arrow catch the floundering Lisu in the chest. Seconds later, the still morning air carried the sound of the snapping of the bowstring and the singing of the shaft as it sped to its work.

Jud was impressed with Na Hti's marksmanship, but even more by her quick grasp of the essentials of the situation. He had feared that her target would be able to sound a shout of warning. To forestall this, she had placed her first arrow unerringly in the throat, and dispatched him with the second.

Jud hauled the corpse of the Lisu he'd killed across the stream, onto the rocky bank, and into the screening bushes. He went upstream and brought the second body to the same place.

When he joined Na Hti on the vantage point, it was to find her cradling the Springfield to cover the downstream approach, Jud grinned at her, and patted her arm approvingly. They settled down to wait for any others who might be in the tracking party.

They waited two hours. When no more Lisu hunters appeared, they waded down stream to the spot where Jud had concealed the bodies.

One at a time, Jud carried the bodies deeper into the forest. With Na Hti's help, he scooped a shallow grave in the soft earth and buried the cadavers. Tramping down the soil, they covered the grave with a thick carpet of dead leaves. As they retreated back to the stream, they obliterated as best they could all signs of their presence and activities.

The only witnesses to these strange proceedings were a number of bright-plumaged birds and a troupe of inquisitive monkeys.

CHAPTER FIVE

While Jud had been cautious before the event of the trackers, he now employed every jungle skill at his command to obscure and conceal signs of his and Na Hti's southerly passage. In the evenings, and again in the pre-dawn, he and Na Hti back-tracked in search of evidence of continuing pursuit. But after the incident with the Lisu, there were no further indications of trackers.

Jud had come to many of the same conclusions as had Harper concerning the options available and his severely restricted chances of getting himself and Na Hti safely out of Thailand. Like Harper, Jud had considered, and discarded, the thought of flight to Burma. Again, he appreciated that road, rail and domestic air travel were out of the question – at least until he could devise some means of blending into the background. Then too, there was the problem that neither he nor Na Hti could produce identification which would pass muster at the numerous police check points. There was, however, one means of transport available which Harper had overlooked, or had not given the serious consideration it warranted. In Harper's appreciation of Jud's probable destination, such an error was understandable.

Jud *had* considered seeking assistance from Jean-Paul. Knowing that the Frenchman would be closely watched did not concern him. Jean-Paul could be contacted without too much difficulty and without alerting the trailing blood-hounds. What did trouble Jud was that once contacted Jean-Paul might not be able or willing to lend support. If, in any way, assisting the fugitives entailed risking his position in the sensitive structure of the *Union Corse*, Jean-Paul would reject the appeal. It was this factor which dissuaded Jud from an attempt to contact the Frenchman.

Since Harper was unaware of the fact that LeFarge's cover in the narcotics traffic was his primary concern and his CIA affiliation of secondary importance, Harper could be forgiven for having attached too much importance to the past association between LeFarge and Stanford.

And in another area, there was a radical departure between Harper's thinking and that of Jud. Harper might have been easier in his mind had he known this. While Jud considered Harper's action in dispatching an assassin a stupid overreaction, it had been done and could not be altered without appeal to a level of authority considerably higher than Harper. To reach that authority, was Jud's ultimate aim. To do so, he would have to travel half way around the world to Langley, Virginia, a hunted man every step of the way. He had formulated a rough plan of how this objective could be achieved. It did not include a delay for senseless retaliation against Harper.

Jud's immediate consideration was how to reach Bangkok undetected. Once there, he would require all the assistance he could muster for the next stage of their journey.

From his experience in the timber industry, Jud was familiar with its past history. Before the railhead reached Chiang Mai in 1921, it had been the practice to float logs down river during the flood seasons. Out of respect to the valuable hardwoods, this means of transportation had fallen into disuse, but the rivers continued to be used for transporting large rafts of high-forest bamboo. With the completion of the Bhumiphol Dam in the mid-sixties, the Ping River could no longer be utilized in this manner. Below the dam, however, at the confluence of the Ping and Wang rivers above Tak, bamboo was still rafted in the high-water season, until the river levels dropped to expose the permanent fish weirs which obstructed further passage. It was this water-borne route which Jud intended to follow.

From the second day, he had shaped a more southerly course to take them well to the west of Mae Klang Falls, then to the southeast, to negotiate the Chaem River crossing through the Ob Luang Gorge, to bring them to the upper end of the 100-kilometer long man-made lake in the vicinity of the town of Hot. It was his hope that Na Hti could purchase some kind of boat by which they could proceed south to the dam. Below the dam, he hoped to be able to buy or bribe their passage on the rafted bamboo.

He had yet to resolve the problem of how he and Na Hti could travel the waterways without attracting curiosity and decidedly unwanted attention. Just how do you disguise a blond blue-eyed *farang* and a Caucasion-featured half-caste girl so that they pass unnoticed in an Asian crowd? A helluva good question, thought Jud. He didn't have the answer. He hadn't discussed it with Na Hti, since he didn't want to worry her unnecessarily. It would take them ten days or more to reach Hot. In that time, he hoped he could come up with some satisfactory answer.

Helicopters had thumped overhead a number of times during the first week of their flight, but Jud had heard none since. That did not mean that an air search had been abandoned. He was chary of exposed ground and reluctant to move from the protective cover of overhead leaves and branches. Still, it could not always be avoided as they traversed grassy slopes to reach fingers of forest which clutched the depressions.

They were moving cautiously along a bluff, in waist high grass. Suddenly, a furious squealing and grunting, intermingled with a coughing roar came from the hollow on their left. Dropping flat in the grass, they worked over to the edge of the bluff to investigate. A dramatic spectacle unfolded before their gaze.

At the base of the bluff, some ten meters below, was a grassy meadow bounded on one side by a rattan and bamboo thicket, and on the other by a willow brake edging a marshy swamp. A herd of wild pigs had been rooting in the soft ground at the edge of the swamp. But now, all was confusion. With frantic squeals, the young pigs and gray long-snouted sows, were milling in all directions. That is, all but one. A large tiger was making off into the broomgrass hauling a freshly killed young sow. Hoarsely grunting in largely futile rage, two young boars were harassing the retreating cat.

There was a stirring in the willow brake. A noise like stones cracking together was followed by a blasting cough. A magnificent russet-gray boar burst from the willows in full charge, his sabrelike tusks glistening in the morning sunlight as he streaked for the tiger. In a blur of black and tawny yellow, the tiger dropped its kill and spun to meet the charge. With a spitting snarl, the great cat lashed out with one slashing swipe of its forepaw. Caught off stride, the boar stumbled and rolled sideways, his shoulder ripped by the raking claws.

Retrieving its kill, the tiger started to tug it once more into the thick grass. But the fight was far from over. With astonishing speed, the enraged boar recovered and whirled to the attack. The tiger released its kill and gave vent to an ear-shattering roar. The charging boar was beneath the swiping forepaw and slashing savagely upwards with his tusks. This time, it was the tiger's turn to be off balance. It crashed backwards into the grass. The din was terrific, with the screams of the cat, the hoarse blasts of the wounded boar, and the piercing squealing of the frightened herd.

The action was obscured as the boar and tiger thrashed in the dense broomgrass.

Na Hti, some three meters along the bluff from Jud, stood up and moved to the edge of the bluff to get a better view of the fierce battle. The overhang gave way, and with a startled scream, she disappeared. Then, even above the din of battle still raging below, Jud heard her trembling wail of terror.

He was on his feet and racing for the ragged lip where she had fallen. Even as he crashed downwards through ripping thorns, he had the presence of mind to snap off the safety catch on the Sprinfield.

He landed with a bone-jarring thud on a rocky ledge less than four meters down from the crest of the bluff. He froze in horror at the sight which met his gaze.

Na Hti stood with her back against the shale bank. No sound came from her lips as she gazed as though hypnotized at the king cobra which swayed in front of her, looming, in fact, well above her. If the snake had been about to strike, the sudden arrival of Jud momentarily distracted it. Swaying slightly, it turned to view this new menace. Jud gasped. A chill of fear gripped him. He was actually looking *up* at the flaring throat and wicked looking head.

Jud acted from sheer instinct. With the rifle barrel extended, he swiped in a slashing arc at the snake's head. The blow caught the snake at the flaring neck and flattened

208

the sinuous column against the rocky cliff face. The body, thick as Jud's forearm, convulsed and the head slid around and over the barrel. Inching the muzzle back, Jud fired into the neck. Mouth open, the snake thrashed. Jud fired again, this time with better aim, directly into the head. Behind the frayed head, chips of rock and dirt sprayed from the cliff. Again and again, Jud struck at the mangled head of the dead but still writhing monster.

He stopped abruptly and turned anxiously to Na Hti. In an instant, she was in his arms, holding him tightly. She gave a long convulsive shudder, then grew calm. Her grip relaxed and she looked in fascination at the grayish-black loops and coils of the still-quivering cobra. 'Vui na,' she said wonderingly.

'Yes,' Jud answered. He had heard of the black king cobra which inhabited the mountains of the region, but this was the first time he'd encountered one. He hoped it would be the last such meeting. Raised one third of its length to strike, it had reared two metres or better. Its fully extended length must be in excess of six metres. Jud had rarely seen pythons of that length. He wondered why the snake had not struck at either Na Hti or himself, and thanked God for whatever distraction or peculiar reptilian process of thought that had made the snake hesitate. Had it not, the odyssey would be over for at least one of them, terminated by the lethal neuro-toxic cobra venom.

Something struck him as being odd about this scene, then he realized it was the silence. A few moments earlier, it had resounded to a furious din, but now it was eerily hushed. It was as though his struggle with the cobra had been the curtain-dropper in this feral dramatic perform-ance.

With his arm around Na Hti, he moved to the lip of the ledge. The herd of pigs had vanished as if by the stroke of a sorcerer's wand. The grassy meadow, willows and broom-grass were tranquil in the soft morning sunlight. Had it not been for smears of blood on the trampled grass, and the abandoned corpse of the sow, like a discarded prop, as mute testimony to the life and death struggle so recently enacted, it would be hard to credit that the drama had ever been presented in such a peaceful setting. He wondered idly which beast had triumphed. The odds were heavily in favour

209

of the big cat, yet he found himself hoping that the boar had vanquished the predator. Never had Jud seen such a magnificent boar; awe inspiring in the ferocity of its wrath. Even if the tiger had killed its adversary, it was obvious that it had, at least temporarily, lost its appetite and was somewhere in the thicket licking its wounds.

Jud turned his attention to their own predicament. They were both scratched and bleeding from their precipitous descent through the thorn bushes, but attention to the lacerations could wait. The immediate problem was how to get back to the top of the bluff and retrieve their possessions still lying where they had left them in the grass.

The crumbled edge of the overhang was about twelve feet above him. It looked to be an impossible ascent. From the tangle of thorn bushes, the rocky face sloped outwards and offered no foothold. On his right, the ledge narrowed, then ceased altogether. In the other direction, blocked by the coils of the dead cobra, the ledge sloped gently upwards and curved out of sight beyond an outcropping.

Using the stock of the Springfield like a shovel, Jud scooped the coils and loops of the snake over the ledge. Warily, he and Na Hti started around the curve. It had been Jud's experience with cobras, that where you found one, you were likely to encounter the mate not far away.

Beyond the outcropping, the ledge continued and sloped more steeply towards the lip of the bluff. The ledge widened a few meters past the curve. Here, Jud stopped and scrutinized the dust. The pug marks of the tiger were clearly imprinted in the soil. It was here the cat had waited patiently, to launch itself upon the unwary sow.

Had he not paused to examine the tracks of the tiger, Jud might easily have missed the grotto. His attention was attracted to what appeared to be a fissure in the cliff face, partially hidden behind a screen of foliage. When he parted the bushes, he was confronted by a wider opening. Cautiously, he peered within.

When his eyes became accustomed to the semi-gloom, he found himself looking into a shallow cave. In a far recess, a splash of colour caught his gaze. Jud stepped into the grotto for a closer scrutiny.

It was a strange and moving spectacle. What had caught his eye was a faded saffron robe draped loosely around a time-whitened human skeleton propped disjointedly in a crevice of the rock. On a crude alter, sat a foot-high Buddha image. A natural shelf of rock at the level of Jud's chest held several folded robes, a pair of worn sandals, and a number of other articles. Over the entire interior, lay a fine patina of dust, attesting to the fact that the small shrine and final resting place of its sole inhabitant had remained unmolested for a considerable period of time.

Jud gazed thoughtfully at the skeletal remains. He was looking, he realized, at all that was left of a Buddhist *Dhutanga* monk. These mystics, at some stage in their spiritual pursuits, feel compelled to shun the companionship of the wat, and seek remote spots where they live the life of a recluse, devoting themselves to solitary meditation. What had brought about the monk's death? There were no signs of violence. The hermit had more than likely simply expired from illness or old age, alone and unattended in his last moments.

Jud shook off these reflections. Death is for the dead; life for the living. Then a strange thought struck him. It was almost as though the idea had been fully formed already and just waiting for this moment to express itself. Vividly, he recalled Jean-Paul's account concerning the post-war subterfuge of Colonel Masanobu Tsuji. Jud pictured the fugitive Japanese, clad in the saffron *Pha-trai* of a mendicant bonze, wandering in safety for a full three years throughout Thailand and Indochina, while he waited for the war crime heat to cool.

Jud regarded the folded yellow robes upon the shelf. There, he thought, lie our passports to Bangkok.

Na Hti joined him in the cave. As he reached for the folded robes, she placed a restraining hand on his arm. 'No,' she said, in hushed tones. 'Do not touch. I feel evil spirits of death here.'

Jud looked down fondly into her upturned face. What a strange mixture of beliefs must haunt her thoughts. To the stern Lutheran concept of the Almighty, had been added the gentle doctrine of the Theravada Buddhism of her childhood playmates and the Father God and myriad spirits of the animistic Lahu. 'You are wrong,' he said gently. 'The spirits who have led us to this place are good, not evil. They have shown me the path we must follow.'

It struck him, even as he spoke, that there was a mystifying element of truth in what he'd said. He was no believer in the super-natural, yet it was more than passing strange how they had found themselves in this particular hidden grotto. Had they not been attracted by the savage drama, and stopped to investigate, Na Hti would not have fallen onto the ledge. The fearsome sentinal *naga* had not struck. He had been arrested by the pug marks of the giant cat, or would have passed the cave entrance without noticing it. Truly, he mused, our destinies could well be guided by forces beyond our comprehension.

He gathered together the contents of the shelf. Along with the robes, he took a *yam*, the cloth shoulder bag of the monks, a battered aluminum tea kettle, the ubiquitous *batr* or covered food bowl with which the monks received their gifts of daily sustenance, the furled umbrella known as a *grod*, and the pair of worn sandals.

When he removed the folded clothing, a group of small Buddha images were revealed at the back of the rocky shelf. Jud hesitated, then took one for closer examination. It was only a few inches in height and Jud was astonished by the heaviness of the object. When he rubbed off an accumulation of grime and dust, the image shone with a dull sheen. Gold, solid gold, he concluded. The other five images proved to be the same. He wondered where they'd come from. Gold images were not a common find. Perhaps the recluse had unearthed these images in some long-forgotten mountain shrine. Jud placed them at the bottom of the shoulder bag. They could well be items for barter or bribery much more effective than currency.

They emerged from the cave, squinting against the strong sunlight. Jud took Na Hti's hand in his, and they continued their ascent of the fateful ledge.

CHAPTER SIX

It is one thing to conceive of a masquerade and yet another to put it into action. Where a Japanese, such as Colonel Tsuji, would have little difficulty blending into a Buddhist background, the same could hardly be said for Jud.

In his years in Viet-Nam, Joe Stanford had met and dealt often with bonzes of the militant Mahayana Buddhist sects. As Winters, he had been exposed on every hand to wats and monks of the various Theravada sects. He had been sufficiently interested in the Buddhist philosophy to give the doctrine more than cursory study. But his knowledge was scarcely adequate to meet his present needs.

It would be virtually impossible to avoid casual encounters with other monks somewhere along their way. The local inhabitants would wish to gain merit by offerings of food, and diversion by discussions or seeking advice on weighty or trivial matters. True, there were foreigners who had become ordained monks, but they were so scarce that they attracted attention and curiosity even in a cosmopolitan city such as Bangkok. In the countryside, a *farang* monk would cause a minor sensation and be a source of gossip. And while Jud's command of Thai was fluent enough for normal conversational exchange, he had no idea what formalities of speech might be used between brother monks, or between monks and the laity. At all costs, he must avoid contacts where possible and limit the risk of exposure where such contacts could not be avoided.

During the 12 days it took them to reach the near vicinity of Hot, Jud pondered the many obstacles which would have to be overcome. One by one, he resolved the problems; if not to his satisfaction, at least to the point where he thought there was a better than even chance of success.

The first concession he made to the role he was to adopt was to shave all the hair from his head and chest. Na Hti, who assisted this defoliation, could not restrain her giggles at the spectacle he presented. Jud found nothing amusing in the procedure. Later, when he had a chance to view his reflection in a mountain pool, he grinned wryly in acknowledgement that the transformation did have its ludicrous aspects. It was, nonetheless, an essential prerequisite.

His face, hands and forearms were tanned a deep mahogany, but the rest of his body, protected by the bush clothing, was of much lighter hue. It was essential that he acquire an even darker tan of uniform consistency. And, since he would have to be shaven-headed, his scalp would require time and exposure to the sun in order to match his tanned features. To this end, Jud changed the pattern of their travel to include gradually increasing breaks devoted to sunbathing where and when a suitably secluded spot could be located. He also took to travelling barefooted, with his bush trousers rolled up to his knees. Not only must his legs be tanned, but his feet needed to look tough and weathered. The fine blond hair on his arms and legs would also have to be removed, but that could wait until he was due to assume the actual role.

His part was to be that of a *Dhutanga* monk who was temporarily abandoning his reclusive meditation in order to journey to a holy shrine in Bangkok. It was to be no mean task of faith, since he was to be no ordinary hermit monk. In his long years of seclusion, he had been afflicted with the loss of his faculties of sight and speech. Dark glasses to protect his sightless eyes would also disguise the coloration of their pupils. To any attempt at a conversational exchange, he would remain an unfortunate mute. To guide and assist him on this perilous pilgrimage, he would be accompanied by an acolyte; a youth of Thai and hill tribe parentage, the son of devotees who had attended the recluse monk in his affliction. This was the part in the one act play reserved for Na Hti.

To transform Na Hti into a credible facsimile of a boy would take a minor miracle. With his knife, Jud cut her hair short. It was his turn to be amused at her consternation when the shorn tresses tumbled to the grass. From the remnants of his spare shirt, they fashioned a wide bandage which would tightly bind and conceal the swelling of her breasts. Surveying his handiwork, Jud remained sceptically dubious. Despite her slim boyish hips and flattened breasts, she managed to retain an aura of unmistakable femininity. It was a fortunate thing, thought Jud, that many youthful

Thais were decidedly effeminate in appearance. More than any other artifice, Jud was relying heavily on centuries-old tradition to support the deception. She would be a travelling companion to a monk, who was forbidden by the disciplines of his order to associate, or have bodily contact, with the opposite sex. It would be assumed, appearances notwithstanding, that she could be no other than a boy.

As they journeyed toward the head of the lake, Jud coached Na Hti carefully in the role she was to portray. In large measure, the burden of their imposture would depend on her guile and skill. She would have to fend off the curious and inquisitive with plausible answers. She would have to make any purchases and conduct any negotiations without arousing suspicion. If they were stopped by a river patrol, she would have to explain their lack of identification, for even Buddhist monks are required to carry identity cards. The fact that her blind mute companion had remained for many years in isolated seclusion, and that she was from a remote mountain village, should provide acceptable explanation.

Na Hti was an apt pupil. She grasped the essentials quickly and fully appreciated the importance of her supporting role. She delighted Jud with her swaggering imitation of boyish gait and the hours of practice she devoted to coax her voice into a lower register.

Jud detoured to bring them as close as he dared to the highway and village of Ban Sai. In the early hours of morning darkness, Na Hti stealthily approached the outskirts of the hamlet and stole some boy's clothing. The garments were ill-fitting, but would serve their purpose.

They negotiated the rugged Ob Luang Gorge. In the hours of darkness, they slipped across the Mae Sariang highway and into the scrub jungled hills beyond. Jud circled wide of the town of Hot, to bring them onto the shore of the lake at a point south of the town where the forest-clad hills sloped steeply to the water.

Na Hti set off well before dawn to journey into the town. She had a number of tasks to perform, which would take her the better part of two days.

Jud waited for her return with growing anxiety. He filled the long hours with practising the seated position he would have to adopt as a monk. His muscles ached from the awkward and unfamiliar positioning of his crossed legs. He persevered, and gradually his stiff and protesting muscles accepted the self-imposed torture. It helped to fill in the time and take his mind off his worry concerning Na Hti.

Just before dusk on the second day, Jud heard the sputtering of an ancient outboard. From his position of hiding, Jud watched a young boy steer a weathered craft to the bank and secure the boat to the tree-lined shore. As the boy looked up to scan the slopes, Jud's heart surged in relief. Despite the newly-acquired attire, he recognized Na Hti.

She joined him and proudly displayed her purchases, chattering away the while recounting her experiences. She didn't believe that her presence had aroused any undue curiosity. The boat she had managed to purchase was admittedly old and in poor condition, and she ruefully conceded she had paid far in excess of its value, but as he had instructed her she had played the role of a stupid boy from the mountains and easy prey for the cunning townspeople. It was much better to be cheated than to arouse suspicion. The fisherman who had parted with the craft might brag about his duplicity to his fellows, but would not be likely to advise the authorities of such a transaction.

Jud examined the articles, nodding approval. There were several bottles of black hair dye, some candles, a new pair of sandals, a cheap cotton shirt, and dark glasses. She had been unable to obtain the wrap-around glasses he'd stipulated, but the ones she'd purchased had heavy plastic rims and wide plastic side pieces which would be equally effective. The sandals had been a necessity since the pair he'd taken from the grotto had proved much too small.

The following morning, Jud completed his transformation into a monk. His stubbled hair and eyebrows were dyed black. He carefully shaved the hair from his arms and legs. Soft wax from the candles was inserted in his nostrils to distend and alter the contour of his nose. Then, with Na Hti giving detailed instructions, he donned the saffron robes.

Of all the times Jud had observed monks as they strolled through the streets of towns and villages, or watched them in the pagodas and wats he'd visited, it had never occurred to him to pay attention to the manner in which they went about draping themselves in their simple raiment. To determine this procedure had been one of the duties he'd imposed on Na Hti, and was the reason her stay in town had been prolonged. She had visited several wats. The presence of a youth in and around these informal sanctuaries was natural. Unobtrusively, but attentively, she had watched as the monks donned their habits. Now, she was able to direct Jud in the not uncomplicated process.

He had often worn the comfortable lower garment of the tropics, the *sampot*, or sarong. The monk's *sabong* under-robe was essentially a sarong and presented no problem. He drew the sheath to his waist, tied the gathered cloth in a simple knot, then drew the excess material into accordian folds which tucked into his waist over the knot. The *angsa*, the upper undergarment was nothing more than a T shirt. Apart from the fact that the dead monk's *angsa* was a snug fit, there was no difficulty. It was the *jivara*, the overall outer robe which required a mastery he lacked. As Na Hti instructed, he placed the wide sheath over his head and held it extended at shoulder level with his left hand. Then, raising his left arm, he furled the cloth slowly from the inside until it was tightly wrapped about his left arm. When it was snugly furled, he tossed the remaining loose fold over his left shoulder and dropped his raised arm to hold the furled robe in place. It sounded relatively easy, yet it took Jud several tries to master the simple art. Even then, he felt that at any moment the robe would come unfurled and drop in loose folds to his feet.

As he strode around the small clearing, learning to keep his left arm close to his side, Jud's confidence mounted. But his instruction was not yet complete. In the wat, and in the confines of quarters such as covered water transport, the robe was worn in a different manner. Na Hti showed him how to don the sheath to leave the right arm and shoulder exposed. Extended diagonally from the right armpit, the garment was held in the left hand and furled this time from the outside. As before, the loose folds were thrown over the left shoulder.

Fully clad in the garb of a travelling monk, Jud stood before her. His carrying bag was slung from his left shoulder. Draped over the same shoulder was the folded spare robe, called a *sanghati*. The bowl for food offerings was slung across his chest by means of a braided sling. In his right

217

hand, protruding from the loose folds of the *jivara*, he held the battered tea kettle and the furled umbrella. His tanned calves and ankles and sandal-shod feet extended beneath the robes. Na Hti viewed him critically, then solemnly brought her finger tips together and bowed her head in a *wai*, the gesture of greeting and supplication.

Jud grinned broadly. She was acknowledging that, at least in outward appearance, he would pass muster as a wandering medicant.

They were not yet ready to leave. There were still a number of matters to be attended to. Na Hti had bought needle and thread in the town. With strips cut from his bush jacket, she sewed a belt complete with pockets and tie strings. This, Jud would wear beneath the *sabong*, tied securely at his waist. In the pockets, he would keep the Thai and American currency, and Quentin's passbook. while she worked, Jud busied himself disrobing and donning the robes a number of times to acquire an ease and facility in the deceptively simple process.

The money belt completed, they dug a hole and buried the articles they would no longer require; the Springfield rifle and ammunition, Jud's belt, knife, tattered jungle boots, what was left of his bush jacket, and his spare clothing. To this, they added the now redundant knapsacks, Na Hti's Lahu garments and crossbow with its quiver of arrows, foodstuff they would no longer need, and the small evidence of her seamstress activities and their frugal morning repast. The last item was placed with reverence on top of the rest. This was the sleeping bag which had shielded them from the chill of the mountain nights and warmed their ardent love making.

Na Hti carried only the woven basket upon her back. It contained a supply of rice, salt and dried meat, Jud's bush trousers and cheap shirt she'd purchased for him, the needle and thread, the hair dye and candle stubs, and, tucked well down beneath the clothing, the golden Buddha images. In his shoulder bag, Jud had stowed the aluminum kettle, a bar of soap, his razor, and a couple of rags. The *grod* was tucked under his left arm. In his right hand was a rough staff such as a blind man would use to guide his faltering steps.

They were ready to take their departure. It was well into the afternoon.

Slowly, the boy guided the blind monk down the steep incline to the lake.

Na Hti tugged and tugged at the starting lanyard as the fisherman had demonstrated. The balky outboard refused to acknowledge her efforts with other than a few fitful coughs. Exasperated, she turned to Jud, requesting his assistance.

Jud laughed softly. 'As you saw fit to remind me when I wanted a mouthful of food before our departure, a monk cannot eat after the sun has reached its zenith. Now its my turn. A blind monk can hardly be expected to wrestle with an outboard motor.'

With a muttered oath which sounded suspiciously like, 'Shit', Na Hti addressed herself to the motor. At her first angry yank, the engine obligingly roared to life.

As though the gods were smiling upon them, their waterborne odyssey proved ridiculously easy and passed almost without incident.

Their rugged journey through the forest-mantled mountains had taken almost a month. The moon had waned and waxed again almost to the full. Steering the frail craft through the night, while Na Hti slept curled in the bow, Jud had no difficulty navigating on the placid moonlit lake.

They encountered several fishing boats the following day, but in each case, seeing the yellow-robed passenger seated hunched beneath an umbrella, the fishermen shied away. To kill any living thing is against the Buddhist faith, and the superstitious fishermen did not wish to invite censure or a miraculously depleted catch. With only two stops to replenish their fuel, at the lakeside hamlets of Ban Ko Tha, and Sala Phak Ka, they reached the southern extremity of the lake the following night. Here, they stove in the bottom of the leaky craft, and proceeded on foot to the point where the Ping and Wang rivers joined.

To Jud's relief, even though it was mid-December, the rains in the northern mountains had continued late into the season and the water levels of the rivers were still high. In the morning, while Jud sat in meditative posture on the grassy bank, Na Hti went off to bargain for their passage on one of a number of large rafts of bamboo which rode at the rivers edge making preparations for downstream departure.

She returned, muttering dark imprecations against the thieving rivermen. None had displayed sympathy for the plight of her blind and priestly charge. All had rejected her offered 500 baht, claiming it was bad luck to take a monk on a river journey. Besides, it would be too much trouble to construct the separate sleeping shelter which would be mandatory to accommodate the holy man. Finally, she had produced one of the small Buddha images as an inducement. The man with whom she was haggling underwent a sudden change of heart. Ah yes, though this image was but a paltry token, it was perhaps much blessed. Perhaps he had been too hasty and harsh in his judgement. Yes, he thought in taking the poor monk, he an even poorer merchant and river navigator, might make much merit. He had reconsidered. He would accept the 500 baht – and the trifling image. He would instruct his crew to build a snug shelter for the monk without delay. They would be ready to proceed down river well before noon. The holy man and his young companion could share their meagre fare.

Drifting with the lazy current by day, and tying along the river bank at night, the two bamboo rafts took the better part of four days to make the downstream passage. The rafts travelled in tandem; one providing the sleeping quarters, and the other cooking facilities. Jud's 'snug shelter' was a hastily thrown together structure of bamboo and banana leaves.

There were but two things to mar the tranquil passage. One was that Jud found his meditative posture induced an agony of muscle cramps which he could only ease with the greatest of difficulty by surreptitious squirming by day and longing for the night time repose which would bring relief to his cramped limbs.

The second occurrence to add a jarring note was something he hadn't foreseen. It happened on the first night of the journey. One of the river youths had displayed considerable interest in the monk's young companion. When the crew had settled down for the night, the youth crept over to where Na Hti lay curled in front of Jud's so-called shelter. Between Thai youths, affectionate displays and the fondling of each other's genitals is by no means uncommon. Na Hti pretended

220

sleep as the youth snuggled close. Then she gasped in horror as she felt the exploring fingers groping towards her crotch.

His tired muscles aching dully, Jud was unable to sleep. He watched with growing apprehension as the young raft crewman took a position alongside Na Hti. Jud gripped his stave tightly. He must take some action, but what? He heard Na Hti's startled gasp. He rapped his stave imperiously against the bamboo uprights of his shelter.

On the raft deck, several people stirred and there was a low muttering of voices. Na Hti scurried to Jud's side, leaving the baffled youth.

'Did he . . .?' Jud whispered. She cut him off with her fingers pressed against his lips.

'No,' she whispered. Then, in more normal tones, she said, 'Lie down, Master, and I will massage your tired back.'

There was no repetition of the incident. The amorously inclined boy was convinced that while the holy man may have lost his sight and powers of speech, his hearing was acute beyond belief. The monk may even have been granted some other form of divine perception. Of one thing, the youth was certain: the monk was jealous of any attention shown his young companion. There was no point in inviting divine wrath.

When he thought back on it, Jud realized that in his moment of rage he had come perilously close to exposing the imposture. His next blow, had Na Hti not been so quick, would have been aimed at the youth's skull.

A small river craft nudged the raft to the bank at a point where a klong emptied into the Chao Phya River. Downstream, in the late afternoon haze which hung like a pall over the city, Jud could make out the span of Krung Dhon Bridge. Their journey was far from over; had, in fact, scarcely begun. But the 600 kilometres they had now completed were likely to be the most hazardous they would encounter. If their luck held . . .? Jud breathed a silent prayer.

Jud adjusted his *jivara* for street wear, throwing the loose end over his shoulder and snugging it securely under his left arm. A plank had been run from the river bank to the deck of the craft. Tapping and groping along the edge of the board, and with Na Hti guiding his faltering steps, Jud crossed the swaying plank.

The blind monk, escorted by a handsome youth, attracted but passing interest from the busy city dwellers. Only once, as they proceeded slowly along Patipat Road, were they accosted. An elderly monk stopped them to inquire if he could be of any assistance. With head bowed as though in deep contemplation, Jud waited patiently while Na Hti pantomined that he could neither see nor speak, thanked the monk for his solitude, and assured him that they had but a short distance to go. The old monk nodded and continued on his way.

Darkness descended on the city. They slipped into a quiet alley. With Na Hti standing guard, Jud divested himself of the saffron robes, donning in their place his frayed bush trousers and the cotton shirt. With some difficulty, he removed the wax from his nostrils. The umbrella, he pushed beneath a hibiscus hedge. The kettle and food bowl disappeared down a convenient manhole into a sewer. He folded the robes and shoulder bag, stowing them in Na Hti's basket. He left the staff where it lay.

At the corner, they hailed a taxi. It dropped them at the Suriwongse Hotel.

As Jud registered under an assumed name, the clerk looked with mild curiosity at Jud's shaven head. He had learned to expect almost anything from *farangs*. At least this was a change from the long and matted hair of the hippies who found their way to this hostelry. As for Na Hti, the clerk gave her scarcely a glance. It could be a transvestite *katoy*, a masculine *puying*, or an effeminate *puchai*. To the clerk, it made little difference.

CHAPTER SEVEN

Chris Perkins received the long-distance call from Shipley in Bangkok shortly before noon on December 18th.

'Reason I'm calling,' said Shipley, 'concerns a Señora Aurora Palma. Name mean anything to you?'

'No, can't say that it does.' Good God, thought Chris – Aurora – Dawn – Na Hti.

'She telephoned earlier this morning. Claims she bought one of Winters' photographic studies back in May. You

222

wanted it for some display, or something. Promised to send it to her. She thinks you must have forgotten and wants to know when you plan to be in Bangkok. Told her I'd telephone you and let her know.'

'Jesus,' Chris lied easily and convincingly. 'I remember now. It was when we were shifting the library from Patpong over to the AUA building. I asked her to lend me the photograph for a display we were setting up for the official opening. Holy Christ, I forgot about it completely.'

'Hope you haven't unloaded it on another photo lover.'

'No. Still have it here. Did she leave a number in Bangkok where I can reach her?'

'No. Said she'd call back this afternoon. What can I tell her?'

'Apologize all over the block for me. Tell her I'll be down tomorrow afternoon. I'll be staying at the Rama. She can reach me there.'

Shipley chuckled. 'Sure. By the way, who is she? Her English was lousy, but she sure had a cute accent.'

'Think her husband has something to do with the Philipine Embassy.'

Na Hti had made the first phone call to Ed Shipley at USIS from the hotel room. Jud had coached her carefully beforehand and was satisfied she had carried it off without a hitch. Although he considered the precaution unnecessary, he had her place the second call from a nearby shop. She returned to advise Jud that Chris would arrive the following afternoon and would be staying at the Rama Hotel.

That evening, Jud wrote a short note. Na Hti delivered it to the hotel the following morning.

Jud was in Lumpini Park well before the hour he'd indicated in his note to Perkins. Jud had donned the monk's habit in the privacy of the hotel room. He'd slipped out through the alley and had no difficulty melting into the crowd of passing pedestrians. Now, in the park, he strolled leisurely along the path which skirted one of the ornamental lakes.

Chris was prompt. At 10:30 a.m. on the dot, he arrived at the concrete bench at the edge of the lake. He glanced about him casually, then unfolded a morning paper, as the note had directed.

Jud idled along the path. Behind his dark glasses, his eyes swept the vicinity. An American sailor, with a young Thai girl, had been not too far behind Chris as he arrived, but they had continued on and were now seated in the shade of a small tree some fifty meters from Perkins. The sailor could well be tailing Perkins, Jud thought, but he seemed a reasonable enough distance away for Jud's purpose. Satisfied that there were no other idlers in the vicinity, Jud lengthened his stride. When he came within a couple of metres of the seated Perkins, Jud dropped to the grass and sat cross-legged at the waters edge. His back was to Perkins.

'Play it cool, Chris,' Jud said softly.

'Jesus Christ!' exclaimed Chris.

'Not exactly,'' Jud said, with a low chuckle. 'If anyone looks like they're aproaching us, cough and fold your paper. I'll keep it brief. Can you think of an excuse to drive to Songkhla?'

'Yes, The American Consul there's a friend of mine. I could always pay him a visit.'

'Good. Can you get a car?'

'Can always borrow Ed Shipley's car and driver for a couple of days.'

'No driver. You'll have to drive yourself. Tomorrow morning at six, drive slowly around the traffic circle at Victory Monument then turn down Rajvithi Road. There will be a couple of hitch-hikers on the corner. Pick them up. Got that?'

'Okay. Anything else?'

'Yes. Go to an optical shop and get a set of clear contact lenses with brown or hazel pupils. Your own eye shade will do. And go to a gun shop and buy a small .38 calibre revolver and a supply of ammunition. Did you bring enough money to handle all that?'

'If not, I can cash a cheque.'

'Good. I'll pay you back tomorrow. Did you bring one of my blow-ups for poor Señora Palma?'

'Had to, if only to satisfy Ed Shipley's curiosity.'

'Bring it along tomorrow. You can give it to your consul friend as a Christmas present.'

Perkins was seized by a fit of coughing. Jud heard the newspaper rustle. He sat with head bowed contemplatively.

224

After a few minutes, Perkins said softly, 'Okay, they're well out of earshot.'

'Who?' Jud questioned.

'Just a sailor and a Thai chick.'

'We'd better break it up. But first, what sort of a car will you be driving tomorrow?'

'Mercedes 220. Dark green. Don't know the licence number.'

'Doesn't matter. Shouldn't be too much traffic at that hour.' Jud paused for a moment. 'All right Chris. Leave the same way you came. I'll stay here for a few minutes.'

Jud heard the newspaper rustle, then Perkins' footsteps crunching on the path as he departed. Jud remained motionless. After a moment he made a slight adjustment to his *jivara*. This action allowed him to turn his head slightly. From the corner of his eye, he could just see the retreating figure of Perkins nearing the park gates. Well behind Perkins, the sailor and his girl friend were strolling in the same direction. It was as Jud had suspected. The sailor was keeping Chris under observation. There were probably others assigned to the task. But there had been no point in alerting Chris, which might have made him act suspiciously.

Jud remained at the lake's edge for another fifteen minutes.

He was wearing hip-hugging blue jeans with a wide elephant hide belt adorned with a massive buckle. His shirt was a loose collarless sheath of coarse black hill tribe cotton, ornamented front, and back and at cuffs and neck-slit with a garish pattern of red and yellow. A chain around his neck, from which was suspended at stomach level a heavy metal 'ban-the-bomb' medallion. On his feet, he wore the well-scuffed sandals which had served him since Hot.

Jud adjusted a wig of tangled dark brown hair and grinned at his image in the mottled hotel mirror. Quite a change, he thought. Monk to drop-out. Skin-head to mop-top. But though his garb may have undergone a startling change, he was still, if in different sense, very much the mendicant. It was a sobering thought.

He stepped into the bedroom. Na Hti was packing the few articles they would take in a cheap suitcase. Her outfit was similar to Jud's with a few minor departures. On her feet she wore zori sandals. Suspended from her neck, several strands of beads and a thick-linked chain looped to her waist. A colourfully-beaded band encircled her short hair and forehead. She wore no confining bra, and her breasts peeped tantalizingly from behind the beads as she moved.

She glanced up at Jud's entrance and smiled at his long-haired appearance. With an answering smile, Jud said, 'Like wow, man, we're the most.'

A few days earlier, Na Hti had assembled their attire by purchases at a number of shops. With the aid of several bottles of bleach, numerous washings in the bathtub, and rubbing the clothing on the floor and outside window ledge, the outfits had acquired a suitably soiled and faded appearance.

Jud had settled their bill the evening before. They took a last look around the room, then slinging shoulder bags, and with Jud carrying the suitcase, they left through the hallway to the back alley.

There were few people stirring in the streets at the early hour. Two hippies walking along the sidewalks in the pre-dawn hours attracted no special interest. The city had grown used to the strange behaviour of this breed of wanderer and paid scant heed to their comings and goings.

They arrived at the Victory Monument traffic circle well before six, and idled near the corner where Rajvothi Road branched off from the wide expanse of pavement. They didn't have long to wait.

A minute or so after six, a green Mercedes nosed into the circle and circumnavigated the monument at slow speed. Jud watched closely. No vehicle seemed to be following the Mercedes. In fact, apart from a gasoline tank truck, no other traffic was in evidence at that moment. The tank truck continued on up Phaholyothin Road. Perkins completed the circuit and steered for the Rajvithi Road intersection. Jud stepped to the curb, his thumb extended.

Chris pulled into the curb. Jud got into the front seat next to Chris, while Na Hti scrambled into the back. Jud was silent, watching through the rear window. After several blocks satisfied that they were not being followed, Jud relaxed and sank back into the seat.

Wordlessly, Perkins handed Jud a parcel. It contained a

226

snub-nosed revolver, a box of shells, and a small plastic case. Jud placed the .38 and ammunition in the bottom of his shoulder bag. Opening the plastic box, he examined the miniscule contact lenses.

'Thanks Chris, what do I owe you?'

'Forget it,' Chris said gruffly. 'Consider them as Christmas presents from Susy and me.'

'As you wish.' Jud smiled. 'Na Hti has a small present for you two in the suitcase. Just a little Buddha image, but you might find it interesting.'

As they drove west, then south, the conversation covered a wide range of subjects. Jud learned that even though Sasima had spread the story that Jud owed her husband a large sum of money, which had obviously led to a violent quarrel and the shooting of her husband, most of the townsfolk favoured a version involving a fight over Na Hti since she was also missing, it was claimed that Na Hti had been killed by Winters or was an unwilling hostage somewhere in the mountains. Witnesses claimed to have seen Winters in almost every town in North Thailand and as far away as Burma, the Shan States and Laos. The police were running in circles chasing down false leads. There were even rumours that Winters was dead. But while some of the initial steam had gone out of the investigation, the police and the Thai military were under pressure and the matter was far from being a dead issue.

In response to Perkin's questions, Jud explained that through a stupid mistake Keppler had concluded that Winters was not who he claimed to be. With a warning glance to silence Na Hti's protest, Jud described how he was being held at gun point by Keppler awaiting the arrival of some KGB interrogators. Chris agreed that Jud had had no option but to kill Keppler and did not press for further details.

Chris was curious concerning the freelance journalist, who had left town a few days after the disappearance of Jud and Na Hti. Perkins wanted to know if Jud still considered him to have been an Agency investigator. Jud replied that he still thought it a strong possibility.

When Chris started to tell him what changes had taken place in the network structure, Jud cautioned the young man against disclosing information to unauthorized people, pointing out that, at the moment, Jud Winters was the least authorized citizen he knew of.

Chris wanted to know how they had managed to reach Bangkok undetected. Jud let Na Hti tell the story. He filled in the gaps only when in her excitement she lapsed into Lahu or Thai. As the story unfolded, Chris gazed on them with something akin to awe.

Jud brought things back to the present by pointing out that neither he nor Na Hti had any identification. If stopped, Chris was to say nothing other than that he'd picked them up on the highway and leave Jud to sort it out.

It didn't look as though they were being followed. Already they had been waved casually through several check points. It was as Jud suspected. Chiang Mai was a long way from their present location and strict vigilance, if it had ever existed, was now relaxed. But there was no guarantee things would stay that way. Once the group or groups keeping Perkins under surveillance realized they'd lost him, highway check points might be alerted.

If they reached Songkhla without incident, sooner or later it would be disclosed that Perkins had been accompanied by companions on at least part of his southern journey. To cover himself, Chris was to make no secret of the fact that he'd picked up two kookie flower children who had first wanted to go to Phuket and then changed their minds and went on to Hat Yai. On his return to Bangkok Chris was to repeat the story to Shipley, embellished with suitable anecdotes concerning his weird passengers. It might be suspected that Chris had assisted the fugitives, but unless Jud or Na Hti were apprehended it would be impossible to prove.

That they were not being tailed Jud attributed to some stratagem on Perkins part. He questioned Chris on that score.

Chris grinned boyishly. 'Simple,' he said. 'Told Ed I was going to Pattaya and had his driver deliver the car to the hotel parking lot last night. Left a call at the hotel for eight this morning advising them that I was going to Pattaya for a couple of days but to hold my room. Then I just got up a few hours early.'

Jud smiled thinly. The human bloodhounds were fallible. They hadn't mounted an around-the-clock check on their quarry.

Although it was a long drive, normally calling for an overnight stop, Jud felt they'd better keep rolling while their luck held. Na Hti slept comfortably in the back seat while Chris and Jud took turns to drive through the night.

CHAPTER EIGHT

The car was not detained at any of the check points along the way. They reached Hat Yai early in the morning.

On Jud's instructions, Chris drove on through the town. On the far side, Jud directed Chris to pull to the shoulder of the highway at a point where a windbreak of feathery bamboo extended almost to the road. From the shelter of the bamboo, Jud and Na Hti watched as the Mercedes pulled away.

The gaudy shirts, Na Hti's headband, beads and chain and Jud's medallion and wig went into the valise. Before placing his shoulder bag along with Na Hti's in the suitcase, Jud loaded the revolver and stuffed it into his right hand pant's pocket. They donned plain cotton shirts, tucking the shirt-tails into the tops of their jeans. Jud put his dark glasses into the pocket of his shirt and in their place fitted the contact lenses into his eyes. Blinking in discomfort Jud nodded and picked up the suitcase.

As they trudged along at the side of the road, flagging the passing cars, they still looked like a couple of hippies, but of the less flamboyant variety.

The battered pick-up truck dropped them in Songkhla. He supposed he should feel pretty good about the fact that they'd made it this far. They were now better than 2,000 kilometres from their point of hurried departure. Yet they were still in Thailand. He wouldn't be able to breathe easy until they had covered a good deal more ground – or water.

As they walked down the road leading along the spit, Jud glanced longingly at the Samila Hotel. It had been a long, tiring day and night of driving. He would have liked nothing better than to check into the hotel for a good sleep. He didn't dare chance it. Whereas in Bangkok there had been little likelihood that their hotel registration would be reported to the police, he felt sure the same would not hold true here in Songkhla.

While Na Hti dangled her legs over the edge of the jetty, Jud squatted on the gunwhale capping of a small craft engaging a fisherman in earnest conversation. She was not close enough to overhear their words, but from the frowns, gestures and shaking of the fisherman's head, she gathered that Jud was not meeting with much success. Finally, however, the man smiled and nodded. Some money changed hands.

They spent the remainder of the day at a secluded section of the long beach. Na Hti was delighted by this new experience of sea bathing. She splashed happily in the waves while Jud grabbed a few hours sleep in the partial shade of a casuarina tree.

They lunched at a small beach kiosk. In the evening, they returned to the fishing craft, shared a simple repast with the fishermen and his family, then settled down on straw mats on the afterdeck to get a night's rest.

He was awakened by someone roughly shaking him by the shoulder.

Jud looked up into a weathered pock-marked and evil looking Oriental countenance. The man grinned, displaying three gold-capped teeth. He motioned for Jud to rise.

Dawn was graying the eastern sky. In the dim light, Jud crouched down with the man beside the deck housing. In lacerated English, and without preamble, the man launched into the business at hand. 'My fliend say you want go Tioman Island.'

'Singapore,' Jud corrected.

'Yes, yes,' the man said impatiently. 'Go Tioman. Catch boat Singapore side.'

'Yes.'

The man looked back to where Na Hti lay curled on the deck, still sleeping. He noded slowly. 'Maybe police want catchee you?'

'Maybe.'

'Why I not turn you over police? Catch big reward.'

The man was bluffing. At least Jud hoped he was. One of the reasons he'd placed such confidence in these fishermen was the knowledge that they were chiefly Chinese.

Most, if not all them, supplemented their incomes by smuggling contraband from Singapore to Thailand. For a good many, smuggling was their prime occupation. Their natural enemies were the marine patrols, customs officials, and the police. It should be contrary to their code to turn fugitives in to the police. Yet, cupidity was the governing factor and if the reward was large enough . . . ?

'Because,' Jud said simply, 'I pay much more than reward.'

The man gave a throaty chuckle. 'How much you pay?'

'Three hundred dollars . . . American.'

'Eight hundred American.' came the sharp counter-demand.

Jud hesitated. 'I can pay no more than four hundred.'

The man shrugged eloquently, and started to rise.

'Wait.' Jud went back along the deck. From the suitcase, he took one of the three remaining Buddha images and returned to the squatting man. 'Four hundred . . . and this,' he said, extending the small replica.

The man took the image. He examined it closely, rubbing it with his thumb and hefting it into his palm. He looked up, and again the gold teeth flashed in a grin. 'Okay.' He pointed out a delapidated trawler tied alongside a nearby wharf. 'That my boat.' He glanced at the lightening sky, now gray-green and tinged with bronze. 'Get missee. Come now. We sail few minutes.'

They were ushered into the wheelhouse and conducted down a short ladder into a small saloon which stank of stale food, paint and diesel fumes. They sat on a narrow settee, while above them they heard the sounds of feet on the wood decking, and the clatter of casting off. The diesel coughed and roared to life.

They chugged slowly out of the sheltered harbour. Soon, the cabin swayed as the trawler rolled to the swells of the open sea. Na Hti looked apprehensive and decidedly uncomfortable.

The gold-toothed skipper looked down into the cabin. 'Okay,' he said, grinning, 'You come up now.'

They emerged on deck. A red-gold sun was above the horizon. The shoreline was receding into a thin blur. The sea was glassy calm, but with a long running swell to which the trawler rode with an easy roll.

Suddenly, Jud lurched and almost lost his balance. Be-

231

neath his feet, there was a strong vibration as powerful twin-diesels roared to life. Astern, the wake boiled as the craft surged forward. They were, he recognized with a wide grin of appreciation, on board a fast smuggling vessel.

Taking the suitcase with them, Jud guided Na Hti aft past centre hatch. They settled themselves in the stern sheets. The clean salt air acted as a tonic and Na Hti became more cheerful as the morning progressed.

About noon, the wind freshened to send cats-paws skittering across the smooth surface of the sea. Soon, the waters became choppy and commenced to build into a short running sea. The trawler had altered to a more southerly course, and the following sea was quartering. Jud appreciated that it was neither a rough sea nor a fresh breeze, still the trawler added pitch to roll and, as the larger seas rolled beneath the stern, the craft yawned with a peculiar corkscrew motion. Na Hti became violently seasick. There was little Jud could do to comfort her. To escape the occasional curtains of spray which swept across the exposed stern, Jud moved their position to the comparative shelter afforded by the hatch coaming. There they were to remain for the duration of that voyage.

Jud too felt queasy, but with each turn of the churning screw his spirits lifted despite the recurring nausea. For some time now, they'd been well into Malaysian waters. While they would still have to contend with the police and immigration authorities of a number of countries, the Thai police were no longer a threat. By tomorrow, or the following day at the latest, they should be more than 3,000 kilometres from Chiang Mai, with two international boundaries between themselves and the Thai authorities. Now, he could devote most of his energies to evading his other pursuers; the KGB and CIA trackers who knew no boundaries and would not abandon their relentless hunt.

Tioman Island lies off the Malaysian coast some 300 nautical miles south-southeast from Songkhla. By Jud's estimation, the trawler was making 15 knots or better through the water. Assisted by the stern-quartering seas, a following wind and favourable coastal currents, Jud figured they should be secured in the island's harbour a couple of hours after midnight. He sympathized with Na Hti as dry heaves of seasickness continued to convulse her. Stroking her spray-dampened hair, he prayed the time would pass quickly.

In the late afternoon, the winds started to abate. By dusk, the seas moderated. The motion of the pulsing trawler dampened down to a slow roll as she rode comfortably to the swells. Na Hti began to feel a bit better, but when one of the crew brought them a platter of fried chicken, her hand flew to her mouth as nausea returned at the mere thought of food.

Jud's estimation was on the low side. The trawler had averaged close to 18 knots. Midnight found them nosing into the small harbour.

The skipper asked Jud to remain on board while one of the crew was sent ashore to locate a captain whose Singapore-based craft would take Jud and Na Hti on the remaining leg of their voyage.

Jud watched the bustle of activity with interest. The trawler's hatch covering was removed. To the accompaniment of shouted commands and the rattle of the winch, case after case of cigarettes and liquor descended into the yawning maw of the hold. It was an efficient operation. He was so absorbed that he did not hear the two men approach. The voice startled him.

'Captain Harold Lee at your service, Sir.'

Jud swung around to behold an amazing sight. Beside the trawler's grinning skipper, stood an excessively fat Chinese clad in nothing but khaki shorts and sandals. The man looked like an almost exact replica of the 'laughing Buddha' statues. From this beaming caricature, the voice issued in flawless British-accented English. 'My friends call me Harry Lee, but I assure you I am no relation to any other who might bear the illustrious name. My Thai colleague, here, informs me that I am to have the pleasure of welcoming you and your good lady on board. I have already instructed one of my lads to tidy up the spare cabin. You and your charming companion may repair on board at your pleasure, so you have ample time to take your rest.'

They had finished dressing, when there was a knock on the cabin door. Opening it, Jud found Captain Lee on the threshold.

233

'We sail within the hour. Trust you had a pleasant night's sleep,' Lee said affably.

'It seems a rather inappropriate time to mention it,' Lee said blandly, 'but there remains the little matter of your fare.

'What fare? You were to get that from the Thai captain.'

Lee looked concerned. 'My colleague made no mention of prior payment. Unfortunately, we cannot discuss it with him since he sailed this morning quite early. He left me with the impression that you would find four hundred American dollars a not unreasonable figure.'

Jud emptied his pockets, spreading bills on the unmade bunk. 'There,' he said, 'is all I have left until we reach Singapore. It's a little less than three hundred. We'll need *some* money when we disembark.

'Indeed you will. Travel is expensive nowadays.' Adroitly, Lee's pudgy fingers separated the two American hundred dollar bills from the baht notes. Pocketing the American money, Lee said, with a beatific smile, 'Considering the relative shortness of the voyage, four hundred might have been a trifle excessive.'

They followed the waddling figure of the Chinaman forward toward the small saloon. It occurred to Jud that the jovial smuggler had accepted a fifty percent reduction in the asking price with remarkable alacrity. There was no doubt in Jud's mind that the obese Captain Lee had already received payment from the Thai mariner.

The coastal passage to Singapore was uneventful and pleasant. Captain Lee's trim craft was shipshape and freshly painted. Like her master, the vessel was comfortably wide of beam. She handled the swells with a slow and dignified roll, dipping her bow but rarely into the unruffled and gently undulating expanse of the South China Sea.

Na Hti had not complained, yet her expression betrayed her trepidation as they had boarded the vessel. As the day progressed, however, and the lenient motion proved more soothing than distressing, her spirits improved. She ate a small lunch, but by the evening meal she had recovered her normal healthy appetite and did full justice to the heaped plates of rice with fish, meat and fowl courses. Captain Lee acted as a witty and genial host. The captain, Jud decided, came by his ample girth honestly.

As they idled in the outer harbour, a sampan slid alongside. Jud and Na Hti disembarked. As they were skulled silently into the darkness towards the lights of the city, the sleek craft of Captain Lee passed astern, heading for harbour.

During the evening before their arrival, Jud had obtained some useful information from Captain Lee.

CHAPTER NINE

Sam Harper was furious. He stabbed his cigarette viciously into the ashtray. In the resulting shower of sparks, a glowing fragment settled on his finger. Cursing, Harper jerked his hand back.

Five days, he thought, five goddammed days.

The report he'd just decoded dealt with Perkins' activities from the 19th to the 24th of December. It had not been dispatched until the 29th.

From the day following Keppler's death, Perkins had remained under tight surveillance. His telephones, already bugged by the KGB, had been tapped also by the Agency. His incoming and outgoing mail had been intercepted and scrutinized. His every movement had been closely watched. Then, by an incredible series of blunders, Perkins had gone for a period of almost three days totally unobserved. A reconstruction of Perkins' activities during this lapse was the body of the report Harper had just now received. Perkins' movements had been significant, yet it had taken another five days to forward the report.

In response to a telephone call from Shipley of the Information Service office in Bangkok, Perkins, had flown to Bangkok on the afternoon of the 19th. He had been routinely picked up at the airport and followed by an operator to the Rama Hotel. Perkins had received a message at the hotel desk on his arrival. but a subsequent search of his room had failed to produce any trace of the note.

On the evening of the 19th, Perkins had dined with Mr. and Mrs. Shipley at the hotel. He had made no other contacts and had retired early.

On the 20th Perkins had gone for a stroll in the park then had returned to the hotel for lunch. In the afternoon, Perkins had gone shopping. He had bought a saphire and garnet dinner ring, an expensive flask of perfume, several ties, a belt, a revolver and a pair of contact lenses. Returning to the hotel, Perkins had called Shipley and had requested the loan of Shipley's car for a couple of days, stating that he intended to drive to Pattaya Beach. He had also stated that a Señora Palma, who was to have picked up a photographic reproduction Perkins had brought to Bangkok, had not put in an appearance at the hotel. Perkins had seemed mystified by Señora Palma's lack of interest, since the trip to Bangkok had been primarily to deliver the photograph. He had asked Shipley, that should Senora Palma contact him, to relay the message that Perkins would be at the Nipa Lodge and returning in two days. Perkins had dined at the Oriental Hotel's Normandie Grill. On his return from dinner, Shipley's driver had delivered the vehicle and had been waiting to turn over the keys to Perkins. At the hotel desk, Perkins had not checked out but had advised that he would be absent for a couple of days and could be reached at the Nipa Lodge in Pattaya. He had arranged for a wake-up call at 8:00 a.m. Following a nightcap in the hotel's Tropicana Room, he had retired at a reasonable hour. None of the agents assigned to the surveillance had reported any contacts for that day.

It had been the following morning that everything had collapsed. The agent assigned had arrived at the hotel at 7:00 a.m. He had been advised that Perkins had left the hotel more than an hour earlier.

The agent had not been unduly concerned. He had driven down to Pattaya. Perkins had not checked into the Nipa Lodge, nor could any trace of Perkins or the Mercedes be found at any other resort hotel. The agent had wasted valuable time checking out Sattahip and Bang Saen. He had concluded that Perkins must be staying with friends, but would surely check with the Nipa Lodge for any messages which might be relayed from Bangkok. The agent had not returned to Bangkok until the following day to report failure.

A routine highway check had then been established in an attempt, a sadly belated attempt, to locate Perkins and the Mercedes. By late evening of the 22nd, it had been reported that the car had passed south through a number of check points along Highway 5. The reports had indicated that there had been a driver and two passengers. Follow-up reports had been requested. When they had started to accumulate, the Mercedes had been checked as now driving north along the Highway 5 route, this time with only a driver. It had then been the morning of the 24th.

Why, thought Harper, why in hell did they have to wait five days to file a report? The excuse was that the report had been delayed in order to check details. The bald facts should have been relayed without delay; the fill-in could have followed.

On his return, Perkins had called Shipley to apologize for having made a switch of plans. Perkins had explained that he had awakened early on the 21st, and on the spur of the moment decided to drive to Songkhla and visit an old friend, the American Consul. Had he realized it was so damned far, Perkins had stated, he wouldn't have attempted the journey. He hoped that Señora Palma had not contacted Shipley, since Perkins had given the photograph to his friend in Songkhla, although he had cautioned the consul that it might be necessary to take it back and have a reproduction made. Perkins had said that the journey south hadn't been too bad since he'd picked up a couple of hitchhiking hippies who had proved bewildering but diverting, but the long drive back had been an exhausting drag.

Perkins' story had checked out. Discreet inquiries through the Songkhla consul had confirmed that Perkins had mentioned the nomadic hitchhikers, whom he'd dropped off at Hat Yai.

Perkins story could be correct in every detail. The trip to Songkhla could have been nothing but a sudden impulse and entirely innocent. The hitchhiking hippies could be anyone; and by now, anywhere. Yet Harper was convinced in his own mind that Perkins had made contact, directed by the note at the Rama, and that the two passengers on the southern journey had been Jud and the girl.

He could verify this. Perkins could be sweated. But what good would it do? Assuming that the hippies were in fact Jud and the girl, Perkins would know nothing of their plans beyond Hat Yai.

Harper regarded the wall map long and thoughtfully. Hat Yai was less than a hundred kilometres from the Thailand-Malaysia border. With the ingenuity Winters – or rather Stanford – had displayed, the border crossing should present little difficulty. Given a full week, the pair could be anywhere in Malaysia, if not already in Singapore.

On the off chance that Perkins was telling the truth, Harper could not afford to relax vigilance or ease his pressure on the Thai authorities in any sector. But now, with his conviction that the fugitive pair were headed south, Harper could concentrate his efforts in that direction. Had he had up-to-date intelligence, it might have been possible to place a tighter seal on the border crossings. As far as Singapore was concerned, it might not yet be too late.

He wondered how in hell Jud and the girl had managed to make it as far as Bangkok, through what Harper had considered as a well-nigh inpenetrable net?

For Harper, the burning question was: How close were the Russians to the fleeing pair?

Harper might have been somewhat relieved to learn that the KGB was no more efficient than his own organization.

The telephone call from Shipley to Perkins had been monitored. The interpretation had been that Perkins' visit to Bangkok concerned Winters. In Bangkok, Perkins' movements had been watched. However, lacking the manpower resources at Harper's disposal, they had not even considered tailing Perkins to Pattaya. Even before the Agency, however, the KGB operators had discovered that Perkins had driven to the southern extremity of the isthmus. Like Harper, they had deduced that the young hippy couple were Winters and Na Hti.

With more agents at their disposal in Singapore, the KGB were concentrating their efforts on that region. But, unlike Harper, they were not so concerned that their quarry had temporarily slipped through their fingers. They wanted Winters, but the time factor no longer seemed of such importance. Sooner or later, somewhere in the world, Winters must surface. When he did, there would be no escape. The outstanding account would be settled; marked: 'Paid in Full'.

CHAPTER TEN

Jud located an unobtrusive hotel situated off North Road.

Most of the required shopping was delegated to Na Hti. Jud ventured from the hotel as little as possible, yet there were certain errands and negotiations which could only be undertaken by himself.

His hair was growing back slowly. He had the sides trimmed so that it resembled a very short brush-cut. He switched to a lightish-brown hair dye. At an optometrist's shop, he was fitted with new contact lenses with hazel pupils. These concessions made to his new role as a tourist, Jud embarked on more serious business.

Identification for himself and Na Hti was of paramount importance. Acting on instructions provided by Captain Harry Lee, Jud located the dusty antique shop in an alley off Kelantan Lane. Satisfied of Jud's bona fides by a cryptic verbal exchange, an important feature of Lee's instructions, the Chinese proprietor undertook the provision of the forged documents. There were to be two American passports, two Social Security cards, and a driver's licence from the State of California. The passports were in the names of Joel and Caroline Burgess. Exercising a prerogative vouchsafed him as creator, Jud narrowed the age differences. Caroline Burgess was to be 22, while her husband Joel was a mere 36. The Social Security cards were to be in the same fictitious names, while the driver's licence would have been issued a few years earlier to Joel Burgess of Santa Barbara, California. The Chinese craftsman indicated that it would take a week to prepare the documents, and required a number of passport size photographs. He recommended a photographer on Sungei Road who would, by skilful retouching, give Caroline and Joel becomingly vacuous expressions and, in Joel's case, more hair.

Jud made discreet inquiries around the waterfront. A Chinese shipping company agreed, for an outrageous fare, to take two American tourists as passengers to Hong Kong.

The coastal freighter was due to sail from Singapore in ten days.

The Hong Kong weather in January is generally cool to downright chilly. At Robinson's, Jud and Na Hti bought two suitcases and some ready-made clothing. Jud's purchases consisted of a medium weight suit, a pair of sturdy brogues, a raincoat and necessary accessories. Na Hti bought a wool jersey dress, coat, blouses, two woollen skirts and undergarments. She also bought a small engagement ring and a plain wedding band. These latter acquisitions delighted her, inexpensive though they were.

Jud would have liked nothing better than to take Na Hti to some of the excellent restaurants boasted by Singapore. It would have been a foolhardy risk. Na Hti's classic Eurasian beauty attracted attention wherever she went. They could ill-afford to be seen together. Instead, they ate in obscure food stalls or had food brought to their sleazy hotel room. This troubled Na Hti not at all. Since leaving Bangkok, during their flight to the south, their love-making had been curtailed by exhaustion and lack of opportunity. She was more than happy to spend long hours in their room, making up for lost time. Jud had bought a number of books and during the days continued her instruction in English. The nights, when they made love tenderly and passionately, or when they lay curled in each other's arms in peaceful slumber, she liked best of all. The close intimacy which had developed in the mountains of Northern Thailand, had grown even stronger in their continuing adversity. For neither of them, did the hours drag.

They were to join the Hong Kong registered coastal freighter on Monday afternoon. It would sail at midnight, carrying a motley cargo and two unmanifested passengers.

Friday afternoon, Jud went to pick up the forged documents.

On examining the passports, Jud was amused to note that Mr. and Mrs. Burgess had done a good deal of travelling to far-flung destinations, but not together. While the covers and opening pages of identification were spurious, the remaining pages were from valid passports. Jud wondered idly from which unsuspecting American tourists the passports had been stolen. The only dates and location common to both passports were cleverly-forged visas to Indonesia with entry and exit stamps at Djakarta. There were no visas or entry stamps for Singapore. Jud had reasoned that if picked up by the local authorities such a falsification could be checked out too easily. In the unlikely event that they were discovered, his story would be that they had embarked on a private yacht at Djakarta. After touching at Pangkalpinang and a number of small islands, the yacht had arrived in Singapore. Taking unauthorized shore leave, Joel and Caroline had returned to find their host's yacht nowhere in evidence. The stranded couple had tried to locate the yacht, or news of its destination, but to no avail. The same story, with a few added embellishments, would serve them in Hong Kong, where again the passports would contain no records of entry.

As he returned to the hotel in the gathering dusk, Jud thought ruefully of the high cost of fugitive travel. He had considered the funds he'd brought with him from Chiang Mai as more than ample to cover any contingency. They were now alarmingly depleted. In Hong Kong, he would require even more forged documents. It was also his intention to establish Na Hti in safe anonymity in the colony before proceeding on alone to complete his mission. He was cheered by the thought that once in Hong Kong he could arrange for a transfer of funds from his Swiss account, but for the moment, his financial situation was getting uncomfortably tight. He hoped that nothing would delay the freighter's sailing.

No light showed beneath the door. Jud rapped softly. When there was no response, he concluded that Na Hti must have stepped out to get some food. He fitted his key in the lock, swung open the door, and entered the darkened room. He was reaching for the light switch when a grating voice froze him in his tracks.

'Stay right where you are, Jud. Don't move a muscle.'

There was a click as the bedside lamp was switched on. Harper sat stiffly in a straight-backed chair close to the bed. In his hand, he held a revolver fitted with a silencer. It was pointed unwaveringly at Jud.

When the initial numbing shock subsided, it was replaced by an emptiness born of despair. Jud said nothing.

'Does it matter?'

'No. I just thought you might be curious. But for gross stupidity, you wouldn't have got this far. You should have been picked up when you made contact with young Perkins.'

Alarm had been growing within Jud. He tried not to betray his anxiety, as he asked, 'Where's Na Hti?'

'I take it you mean the young lady. She stepped out on some errand. I took advantage of her absence to let myself in. But to return to the matter of how we found you, it will interest you to know that Harry Lee is in the habit of passing along useful information for a modest fee. We were gratified to learn that a couple had joined him on a clandestine voyage from Tioman Island. He further indicated that these people had sought advice concerning the availability of forged documents. As you are aware, it calls for skills which somewhat limits the profession. We kept a close watch on the few gentlemen engaged in this illicit trade. You were recognized and followed to this hotel. I flew down from Manila to look after the formalities personally.'

The fact that Na Hti was not as yet involved was some consolation. 'My wife's pregnant, Sam. She knows nothing of my Agency activities. Keep her out of this.' Jud said coldly.

Harper's eyebrows raised. 'Wife? We considered her to be your mistress. Not too smart of you to undertake this futile adventure burdened by a pregnant woman. You should have thought of that before you took her along. We have no particular interest in her, but I guarantee nothing.'

'Spare me your advice, Sam. Cut the crap and get it over with.'

'I have no intention of killing you, if that's what you're thinking. I merely want your cooperation. I have a few questions I want answered, then we'll leave here. You will accompany me. Willingly, I trust. Should the young lady return before our departure, I suggest you make some logical excuse.'

That Harper intended to kill him, Jud knew with cold certainty. That he might not want to do it here in the hotel, which might prove inconvenient, Jud grasped. He felt, for the first time, a thin glimmer of hope. And he sensed a bargaining position he'd not counted on. 'If I cooperate, I want certain guarantees for my wife. I want you to see to it that she gets some money which I will arrange through my overseas account. And I want you to get her safely to Hong Kong. Is it a deal?'

Harper frowned. He hesitated for a moment. 'All right, if I consider I have your full cooperation, it's a bargain.'

'Okey. What are your questions?'

'How was your cover blown, and what exactly did you tell Keppler or his friends concerning the Burmese operation and your part in it?'

'The answer to the first part is simple. As you put it a moment ago, gross stupidity . . . yours.'

Harper regarded Jud, with no change of expression. 'I don't quite follow you.'

'Keppler didn't know who I was, but he knew I wasn't Winters. It shouldn't have been too difficult for you to ensure that Winter's medical documents made no reference to an apendectomy and did show an old machete wound scar of mine. How Keppler discovered those discrepancies doesn't matter. He did, and for the want of a little foresight on your part, my cover was blown.'

Harper's eyes had narrowed. 'Very well, I'll admit the error. Now what about Keppler or his friends?'

Jud was stalling now. He evaded the question. 'You knew that his friends were *Mokryye Dela*?'

'Yes. Which has been causing us some concern.'

'Causing *you* concern.'

'Get to the point,' Harper said with a trace of impatience.

Jud looked thoughtful. 'I'll try to give you the discussion verbatim, as closely as I can recall the details.' He reached absently towards his pocket.

'Stop!' Harper snapped.

'Stop what?' Jud queried innocently. 'I thought you wanted to know what transpired?'

'Keep your hands away from your pockets.'

'Oh,' Jud smiled. 'Wanted a cigarette.'

With a frown of annoyance, Harper reached into the pocket of his shirt and tossed a pack of cigarettes to Jud. Jud caught the pack adroitly, took a cigarette, and threw the pack back – a bit wide of the mark. Harper ignored the package, which fell on the scrap of rug beside his chair.

'Light?' added Jud. Harper lobbed his lighter. Jud fumbled the catch. Retrieving the lighter from the rug, Jud said, 'Sorry.' As he stood up, his left foot was resting on the rug.

There is a fascination about an open flame. Eyes, like moths, are attracted to the flickering luminescence. Jud counted on this phenomenon to gain him the fraction of a second's distraction he would need.

He flickered the lighter. The flame danced and as it did he dropped the lighter and launched himself at Harper.

The push of Jud's foot against the rug was transmitted as a sharp tug where the front legs of Harper's chair were resting on the fringe. At the instant he fired at the hurtling figure, Harper's aim deflected slightly to the left. Before he could snap off a second shot, Winters was upon him.

Jud heard the flat cough of the silencer and felt a sharp stinging sensation in his shoulder. Then, he had Harper's wrist firmly gripped. Jud's forward momentum smashed his right shoulder into Harper's chest. The flimsy chair collapsed under their combined weight and both men toppled with a crash to the floor. Harper's head cracked against the bedside table edge, stunning him momentarily.

With his full weight behind it, Jud brought his left knee down on Harper's right biceps. The revolver flew from Harper's numbed fingers and slithered beneath the bed. Dazed and in pain, Harper struggled to pull himself from beneath Jud's weight. Then Jud's palm edge knifed into Harper's throat. Harper gagged in agony.

Jud found the purchase he needed for his feet and swung Harper around into a head-lock. Working his left arm into position, Jud partially lifted Harper then applied full leverage in a downward wrenching twist. He heard the cracking sound as Harper's spinal column parted at the cervical vertebra.

He let Harper's limp body sag to the floor. Jud rose slowly, gasping for breath from the exertion. He gazed down on the inert form which sprawled on top of the broken rungs of the chair. There was blood smearing the back of Harper's shirt.

Looking at his chest, Jud realized that his own shirt was soaked in blood. He probed at his shoulder and winced as his fingers encountered a ragged furrow where the bullet had creased the base of his neck.

He would have to think of some means of disposing of the body, but first, he'd better attend to the flesh wound and staunch the bleeding. Jud strode the few paces to the closed door leading to the bathroom.

He opened the door, took a half-pace into the room, and stopped in stunned horror.

Na Hti had not left the hotel room on any errand. Her face ashen; her eyes staring unseeingly at Jud, she lay naked in the bathtub. One arm hung limply over the edge of the ancient porcelain tub. From a small hole between her breasts, a thin trickle of viscous blood trailed into the crimson water of her bath.

CHAPTER ELEVEN

It could have been but a few minutes. It could have been as much as a half an hour. He didn't know how much time had elapsed.

He sat on the toilet, his forehead resting against the rim of the washbowl. His fragmented thoughts churned sluggishly.

He straightened slowly. Gripping the bowl, he pulled himself to his feet and turned to face the mirror. He beheld a haggard countenance he scarcely recognized as his own. A livid welt ran diagonally across his forehead where it had rested on the basin rim. His shirt was caked in dried blood. His neck an shoulder ached dully. He turned from the mirror in disgust.

He walked woodenly into the bedroom. As he eased out of his shirt and knotted a kerchief around his throat, he stared at the crumpled body of Harper. He had had no compunction in killing Harper. He was only glad that he'd killed the murderous sonuvabitch with his bare hands. He pulled on a fresh shirt and let himself out of the room, carefully locking the door behind himself.

It was several hours before he returned to the hotel. It had taken him that long to find what he'd wanted. He came back in a taxi which he asked to wait in the alley at the back of the hotel.

245

He packed all that he would need in one of the suitcases, adding the passport and Social Security card made out in the name of Mrs. Caroline Burgess. He went through Harper's pockets and transferred the contents to the valise without examining them. Next, he unscrewed the silencer from Harper's revolver. Along with his own snub-nosed .38, he stowed the cylindrical object in a side pocket of his bag.

Harper's revolver in his had, he walked into the bathroom. Na Hti lay in the same position in the tub. He gazed down on her corpse and closed his eyes briefly as pain flooded over him. Taking the revolver by the barrel, he wiped it clean of fingerprints with his handkerchief. He pressed Na Hti's stiff fingers onto the butt, then let the gun drop to the floor beneath her hand.

The service in the hotel was desultory. Today being Saturday, there was small chance that the cleaning staff would attempt to enter the locked room until sometime Monday afternoon. They would then discover Na Hti's rigid corpse immersed to the breasts in a bath of murky brownish water. The thought repelled him even though he knew he was being a fool. Na Hti was beyond embarrassment, hurt or pain forever.

It was unlikely the police would consider her death as suicide, but at least they would have to consider the possibility. It might cause some delay in the search for himself. He hoped that the case would eventually end up in the dusty archives of the Singapore police as another unsolved crime. They would want to locate a man with a short brush cut on suspicion of murder. That man would be hard to find.

In a last gesture, he leaned down and tenderly brushed a stray lock of hair from her cold forehead.

Softly shutting the bathroom door behind him, he stepped back into the bedroom. A partly filled bottle of bourbon sat on the dresser. He took a healthy slug, then sprinkled the liquor liberally over Harper's sprawling corpse.

The back stairs served as a fire escape for the hotel. At the bottom, a door with a push bar gave one-way access to the alley. He took his bag and descended to the door. Opening it, he placed the suitcase to prevent the door closing. The taxi was still waiting.

Getting Harper's body down the short flight of stairs was more difficult. Awkwardly, he manoeuvred the dead man onto his left shoulder in a fireman's lift. With grim satisfaction, he noted that the head flopped drunkenly. Leaving the room, he locked the door, dropped the key to the hallway floor, and kicked it under the door back into the room.

With some effort, he managed to deposit Harper's body in the back seat of the taxi. He returned for his suitcase and then got into the rear seat alongside Harper's body. He gave directions to the driver, adding, 'Gotta get him back to the ship.'

As they drove off, he noticed that his collar was sticky with a mixture of blood and perspiration. The wound had reopened and blood was seeping through the neckerchief. It couldn't be helped.

The taxi turned down a side street short of the bridge. He paid the fare, adding a generous tip. The cab drove off, leaving him with Harper's body propped disjointedly against a building fronting on the narrow sidewalk.

It was only a short distance to the river embankment, but it was a struggle getting the body to that point. With the left arm of the corpse around his shoulder and his right hand gripping the dead man's belt, he half dragged and half carried his inert burden. Staggering under the dead weight, he hoped they looked like a couple of drunks; they certainly smelled the part.

With relief, he observed that the skiff he'd stolen up-river bobbed gently between two empty barges, just as he'd left it. He let Harper's body slide down the sloping rock facing of the embankment, scrambling after it. He fished the dripping corpse from the greasy water and draped it into the stern of the skiff. Then, he once more negotiated the stone embankment, returning with the suitcase he'd left in a doorway close to the spot where the taxi had dropped them.

In the deep shadow between the barges, he sat in the boat for some time. Even at this late hour, the Singapore River bustled with launch, barge and sampan traffic. The skiff rose and fell in cadence to the lapping wakes. He wasn't expecting the commercial going and comings to lessen. He was waiting for the tide to reach close to the high water mark.

On their arrival off the harbour, Captain Lee had explained to him that the tidal currents were strong, even in the inner roads. He would have more than a half mile to row, and the last thing he wished was to stem a strong current.

Finally, at close to 2 : 30 am, he judged the tide to be approaching high water slack. He untied the painter and pushed out from between the barges.

Rounding the stone sea wall at the mouth of the river, he struck out for the outer harbor. It was moonless, yet the glow of the city, the neon emblazoned shoreline, and the riding lights of small craft provided far more illumination than he desired.

A light onshore breeze stirred the harbour. He threaded a course through anchored small craft towards the merchant ships which swung to their cables in the roadstead. His one fear was that he'd be accosted by a harbour police launch. His story, that they were a couple of merchant seamen returning to their vessel after a rewarding night sampling the delights of Bugis Street, would hardly withstand very close scrutiny.

In the offshore shadow of a darkened launch, he stopped rowing. In the bottom of the rowboat, he'd stowed other purloined items; a length of heavy chain, and some stout cordage. He wound the chain around the corpse's ankles, securing it in place with the cord. As he toppled the body over the gunwale, he came perilously close to swamping the fragile craft. Dispassionately, he watched as Harper's silver-gray hair floated for a moment close to the surface then swayed downwards through a rising stream of phosphorescent bubbles.

It was some fifteen minutes later that he pulled under the stern of the Hong Kong freighter and came alongside the accommodation ladder. He heaved his suitcase onto the grating and stepped onto the platform. He pushed the rowboat off with his foot and watched it drift slowly astern to disappear beneath the counter.

A sleepy gangway watchman conducted him to the cabin reserved for himself and Na Hti for two days hence.

He was sore, stiff and unutterably weary, yet sleep eluded him. He paced the small cabin, then lay fully clothed on the bunk, staring at the deckhead.

He gave conscious direction to his drifting thoughts only when the image of Na Hti flashed onto his mental screen. He tried to blot out these pictures, but with scant success.

Slowly, one salient feature emerged from his chaotic reflections. His dichotomy of personal identification was becoming less indistinct. For two years, he had accepted his identity as Jud Winters to a point where identification as Joe Stanford had often been blurred. This should have changed when he burned Winters' passport. But even that act of severance had made little difference. To Na Hti, he was Jud Winters and any explanations of another identity would have been too difficult and confusing. At the time, he had pushed the thought of such an attempt from his mind. To Chris Perkins, he was Jud. Even Harper, who was fully aware of his true identity, had called him Jud but a few hours back. But when he had watched Harper's body sink into the depths of the harbor, he had been struck with the macabre thought that he was witnessing Winters being swallowed by the shark infested waters off Cebu. It had come to him then that Winters was at long last irrevocably dead.

And, he thought bitterly, with Winters had died all the compassion, tenderness and love which the role had vicariously bequeathed to Stanford. Perhaps such emotions had never been meant for Joseph Asquith Stanford. So be it. Let them die unmourned.

As the faint light of dawn seeped through the porthole, he dropped into fitful and dream tormented sleep.

He awoke a few hours later. He had a raging thirst and his neck and shoulder throbbed painfully.

Seeking out the Portuguese captain of the Hong Kong Chinese freighter, Joe asked if there were any provisions for first aid on board the vessel. The captain examined the neck wound and turned Joe over to the second mate who cleaned and dressed the wound.

That Joe was on board two days ahead of the appointed time, and alone, didn't seem to disturb the captain. He questioned Joe as to the whereabouts of the woman passenger and only shrugged when Joe advised that there had been a change of plans and his wife would come on a later sailing. It was agreed between himself and the captain that should customs and immigration officials board the ship prior to sailing, their sole passenger, Mr. Joel Burgess, had joined the vessel at her last port of call, Djakarta. Due to illness, Mr. Burgess had not gone ashore in Singapore. The passenger manifest, if requested, would substantiate the fiction. There was no mention on the captain's part of any

249

rebate of fare with respect to Mrs. Burgess. Joe didn't bring up the subject.

The voyage to Hong Kong took a week. The sturdy little ship averaged barely ten knots, bucking into head winds and short breaking seas for three full days of the 3,000 kilometre journey.

Joe kept to himself, spending most of his time in the small cabin. He joined the officers for meals in the grubby little saloon, but discouraged any further contact with either officers or crew. He made only one exception. He joined the second mate on the bridge during the afternoon of the last day out and engaged the Chinese officer in earnest conversation.

It was a clear night, with a cold northerly wind sighing across the deck, as they sailed up West Lamma Channel in the approach to Hong Kong harbour. They were rounding Green Island when the incident occurred.

A high-pooped junk stood close in to the island, her lug sails slatting in a windless dead patch. As the freighter nosed around the island, the junk flattened sails, caught a puff of breeze, heeled to port and on a starboard tack bore down on the freighter. The Portuguese captain, already proceeding at slow speed, rang for dead slow. He ordered one short blast on the whistle to indicate his turn to starboard to come under the junk's stern. The junk had nearly crossed the freighter's bow when, seemingly oblivious to the merchant ship's presence, she paid off on her batten-spread sails. Bearing off the wind, she headed directly for the merchantman.

A marine police launch, idling in mid-channel, speeded up to close the scene of the impending collision. On board the freighter, then on the junk, a shrill babble of Cantonese cursing and hoarsely shouted commands shredded the stillness of the night. The big junk scraped down the port side of the freighter, slowing almost to a standstill despite her filled sails. Then the junk's crew managed to fend off. The junk bore away, then paid off under the freighter's stern.

The police launch slowed and turned back towards mid-channel. On the freighter, the wheelhouse telegraph jangled as the order for slow ahead was rung down to the engine room. The merchant ship proceeded into harbour, with no need for a passenger manifest.

250

Suitcase in hand and screened by the square mainsail, Joe had jumped lightly to the cluttered deck of the junk. He mentally congratulated the two skippers on a skilful piece of seamanship and wondered idly how long the junk had lain off Green Island waiting to collect her lone passenger.

He stayed at the Wonner Hotel on Lockhart Road in Wanchai. It is the section of the city which abounds with small shops, restaurants, dance halls, girlie bars and hourly-rate hotels. For Stanford, Wanchai's attractions were of a different nature. In the teeming port city of Hong Kong, Wanchai affords the 'foreign devil' a degree of transient anonymity. But even more persuasive was that, on the recommendation of the freighter's second mate, Joe was to contact a Chinese who frequented the Crazy Horse Bar, next door to the Wonner Hotel.

There were a number of things Joe required, the pursuit of which took him from the sanctuary of his hotel room.

He contacted the Chinese in the Crazy Horse Bar, and was directed to the upstairs back room of a printing establishment in Causeway Bay.

The skilled craftsmen at the printing shop agreed, for a not inconsiderable sum, to prepare forged documents. These were to be the U.S. Merchant Mariner's Document, known familiarly as a 'Z Card', in the name of John Quentin, and a British Columbia driver's licence and Canadian passport in the name of Donald Francis Corey. As in Singapore, a number of passport photographs were required.

For his Canadian passport, Joe had his photograph taken with his brown-dyed hair and hazel-tinted contact lenses. For the Z Card, he had his hair trimmed to a more respectable brush out and dyed back to its original blond coloring. He had the second photograph taken without the contact lenses. Joe reasoned that in assuming the identity of Quentin, Winters had not bothered to disguise his appearance.

Knowing he would need money on his arrival in Hong Kong, Joe had written his Swiss bank to transfer 5,000 dollars to a Mr. Joel Burgess in care of the Hong Kong American Express office. Although he was reluctant to use the Burgess passport, he now had no alternative. The bank draft was waiting at the American Express Office on Connaught Road Central. Identifying himself as Burgess, Joe had no difficulty cashing the draft. He took a devious routing back to Wanchai, but as far as he could determine he was not being followed.

Five days after his arrival in Hong Kong, Joe collected the spurious documents, which also included forged shot records in the names of both Corey and Quentin. As he walked back along Lockhart Road, he examined the plastic-encased Z Card. A photographic likeness of a blond-headed man of indeterminate age stared up at him vacantly. Turning the card over, he observed the smudged thumb print, the vital statistics vague enough to apply to almost anyone, the place and date of issue as Seattle, Washington, 6/19/68, and a trade designation of 'Messman, Steward's Department'. He would have preferred slightly more exalted qualifications, but he couldn't think of any other function he perform on board a merchant ship. The plastic casing was yellowed and cracked as though from much usage. The forger was an expert at his trade.

A week later, John Quentin signed on the *M/V Deneb*, a tramp cargo vessel of Panamanian registry, as a 'pier-head jump' replacement for a Puerto Rican messman who had jumped ship in the colony. The Deneb sailed the next morning.

The voyage was long. The ship stopped to off-load and take on cargo at Keelung, Osaka, Yokohama, Hakodate, Prince Rupert and Vancouver. The ship was to go on to Seattle and Tacoma, but it was in the British Columbia port of Vancouver that John Quentin was missing when the ship sailed.

During the voyage, Quentin kept pretty much to himself. He performed his duties as messman with quiet efficiency. He mingled little with the crew. There was something about the lean hard taciturn messman with the cold blue eyes which invited neither confidence nor familiarity. His fellow crew members left him strictly to his own devices.

In Vancouver, Quentin drew an off-duty weekend. Indicating his intention to spend Saturday and Sunday ashore in a hotel, he packed his suitcase and took a taxi from La-Pointe Pier to downtown Vanvouver. He checked into the Devonshire Hotel.

At 10:25 Saturday morning, Quentin walked into the Homer and Hastings Street Branch of the Bank of Montreal.

He produced a pass book and asked to be advised of the remaining balance in his savings account. In a few moments, the girl returned to inform him that the balance was 3,000 dollars.

The information startled him. He frowned. 'Are you sure, Miss? I thought several, large cheques were sent to this account quite recently. Would you mind checking again.'

'Certainly, sir.'

The girl returned with a young man bearing an account record form. 'Ah, Mr. Quentin,' the man said. 'You're quite a stranger. Must be well over two years. You certainly look fit. Well, sir, we have no record of any recent deposits. The account has been inactive for some time. I assume you've been getting your statements. As you can see,' he placed the record form on the marble-topped counter and turned it to face Stanford, 'there have been nothing but interest payments recorded since your large transfer of funds to Hong Kong.'

Joe's glance scanned the columns rapidly. There was the entry of a transfer of 45,000 dollars. With accumulated interest, the balance in the account stood at 3,086 dollars. His voice betrayed no surprise as he said mildly, 'Seems to be in order. I'd instructed that some money owed me be forwarded to this account. I'll have to check on it.'

'Would you like to draw against the account now?' the man asked.

'Yes,' Joe said absently. 'Might as well draw 3,000 in American currency.'

The man hesitated, then said apologetically, 'It's been quite a while since we had the pleasure of serving you Mr. Quentin. You've lost so much weight I scarcely recognize you. I, ah . . . I hope you won't be offended if I ask for some identification.'

'Certainly.' Joe pulled out his wallet and extracted Quentin's Z Card. 'This do?'

The man looked at the card intently. 'We had no idea you'd taken up a career in the merchant marine. It certainly accounts for why we haven't seen you for a few years. Yes, this will do. I'll make out the foreign exchange form. Won't be a minute.'

Joe counted the bills, mostly hundreds, and put them carefully in his wallet. His mind grappled with the irrefutable evidence presented by the account record. Apart from himself, someone else had known of Winters' fictitious account in the name of Quentin. The transfer had been effected, or at any rate recorded, on August 28th, 1968 – 11 months *after* Winters' death at Cebu.

John Quentin checked out of the Devonshire Hotel at noon.

Twenty minutes later, Donald F. Corey completed arrangements for the rental of a Hertz U-Drive.

At the Blaine, Washington customs and immigration, Corey was checked through with no more formality than a few perfunctory questions and a cursory glance at his suitcase in the back seat.

He reached Seattle shortly after 3:30 pm and drove straight on through to Seatac International Airport. He turned in the U-Drive at the Hertz check-in counter at the airport, receiving the balance owing him from the deposit he'd paid in Vancouver.

At 7:00 pm., Don Corey was airborne on a United Airlines jetliner bound for New York.

CHAPTER THIRTEEN

Joe had intended to spend only a day or two in New York, but it was four days before he completed his business. For one thing, the barber botched the dye job and it had to be done a second time. As Donald Corey, he was dark-haired again. But what took the most time was locating a gunsmith who would fit the silencer to his .38 revolver.

On Thursday afternoon, he caught an Allegheny Airways shuttle flight from La Guardia to Washington.

After dinner at a downtown hotel, he made a phone call from the lobby. There was no answer.

On M Street, Stanford hailed a taxi which took him over Chain Bridge and into McLean, Virginia. He found the street he wanted and had the cabbie drop him at the corner.

The address turned out to be a large corner lot two blocks further down the street. The house was a substantial brick colonial residence, its outline softened by a mantle of ivy. The house was set well back from the street. From wrought-iron gates at the street entrance, a gravel driveway curved to an expansive portico. The gates were locked.

He followed the brick wall along to the street corner and then down the intersecting street. There was no one in evidence. He scaled the wall and approached the house from the rear across a lawn studded with bare shrubs and leafless oaks. He studied the house carefully.

To the back of the house, the grounds sloped gently downwards. The foundation level was extended into an extensive flagged terrace. Tall windows and French doors opened onto this terrace.

The street light cast a tracery of branch shadows against windows and doors and gave ample illumination for his task. Employing a lock pick, he opened the French doors and let himself quietly into the house.

He drew aside the drapes to allow some light into the room. It was a comfortable combination den-study with book-lined walls and a fireplace in which glowing embers attested to the room's usage at an earlier point in the evening. Next to the fireplace was a leather reclining chair, a low table and a small mobile bar. Dominating the room, was a huge blackwood desk.

He shrugged out of his topcoat and draped it over a chair behind the desk. He didn't remove his gloves.

At the bar, he poured himself a generous bourbon. Glass in hand, he drew the drapes closed and stood by the French doors until his eyes became accustomed to the darkness which was relieved by only a little of the street light's glow through the drapery and the faint red of the embers. He found his way back to the reclining chair and sank into it. From his jacket pocket, he took the revolver and silencer. He fitted them together. Placing the revolver on the low table beside the chair, he settled down to wait.

He must have dozed. The crunch of car wheels in the front drive alerted him to Cantrell's return. Stanford listened as a door opened and closed somewhere towards the front of the house. In a few moments, a light was switched on and approaching footsteps echoed in the hall. Good, thought Stanford. He'd counted on Cantrell wanting a night-cap before retiring.

From the height and general outline of the figure in the doorway, Stanford judged it to be Cantrell. He allowed the man to come into the room and walk to within a few feet of the desk. With quiet authority, Joe spoke from the depths of the reclining chair. 'Freeze, Lew.'

The figure stopped in mid-stride and stiffened. A low chuckle then the deeply resonant voice Joe remembered. 'Well, well. Joseph, my boy. I've been expecting you, but not quite at this hour.'

Joe snapped on the table lamp. Cantrell turned, his eyes narrowing as he saw the silencer-fitted gun in Joe's hand.

'Why don't you sit down, Lew.'

As Cantrell started around the desk, Joe motioned to a chair in front of the desk. 'No, sit where I can see you.'

Stanford was shocked by the change two years had wrought in Cantrell's appearance. The cherubic counten-ance was gone, replaced by sunken eyes, hollow cheeks and sagging flesh. His face had a gray unhealthy pallor. His clothes hung awkwardly on his frame, as though tailored for a bigger, more portly figure. Indeed, they had been. About the only feature that remained unchanged was the untidy shock of gray hair.

When Cantrell was seated, facing him, Joe said, 'Lew, you look like hell.'

Again, the rumbling chuckle. 'They tell me at Bathesda that I'm afflicted with a not uncommon wasting ailment. Good thing you came when you did, since I'm supposed to go in for a check-up and possible surgery at the end of next week. But you didn't come here to talk about my health. I gather we are here to discuss yours.'

'Correct,' Joe agreed.

'And what name would you prefer; Joseph, Judson, Joel or John? Must say you seem partial to the letter 'J'.'

He was not too surprised that Cantrell knew of the Bur-gess alias, but the reference to John Quentin surprised him. 'Joe will do,' Stanford said tersely.

'As I said, I've been expecting you. I've followed your progress with interest. No doubt, if I knew the lurid details, it would be a fascinating story. But some other time, eh Joseph.

'Did my use of the name John startle you? It did me, when I learned that a merchant seaman by the name of John Quentin had jumped ship in Vancouver. A further check revealed that you'd closed out a savings account in that name. Ah, cupidity, cupidity. It's been the undoing of many a good man. But we had no idea you knew of that spurious identity.'

Joe didn't answer. Cantrell continued, 'The last official word I had on you was Harper's report from Manila. You and a young lady who was accompanying you had been located in Singapore. Harper stated he was going to Singapore to give his personal attention to the matter. He hasn't been heard from since. Am I correct in my belief that you eliminated him?'

'You are.'

'Just as I thought. But you must admit it somewhat complicates your predicament. You have, I take it, come here to request that I call off the dogs. Under the circumstances, an audacious petition. Or don't you think so?'

'I do not,' Joe said evenly. 'Unless my reports were being cut to ribbons in transition, you must know that I carried out the job assigned as affectively as it could have been undertaken by anyone. There was no justification for Harper's arbitrary decision to have me liquidated. If he died in the process, it was because he gave me no choice in the matter. I do not regret my action. And I *do* expect you to take the heat off.'

'Where is the girl, Joseph?'

He could not repress a spasm of pain and knew it must have shown on his face. 'Dead,' he said flatly.

'Harper?'

'Yes.'

'That was foolish of him. Foolish and unnecessary.'

'He gave her no more chance than he did Winters. He may have been an administrative genius, but the sonuvabitch was a sadistic killer.'

'So you believe Harper killed Winters. What motive do you suggest?'

'To prepare the way for my cover identity.'

257

Cantrell sighed 'I don't know what led you to those conclusions, but I was afraid it might be your interpretation. Its tardy. Long overdue. But I feel you deserve an explanation.

'In the first place, I did *not* recommend you for the assignment in Chiang Mai. It may surprise you to know that I strongly opposed it. Had I had then the position I now hold, you would never have been sent to Chiang Mai. It was out of my hands. You were selected by a goddammed computer.

'I have been quite intimately connected with your career. I believe I know you better than anyone in the Agency. Certainly one helluva lot better than any computer. I should. In a sense, I created you. And there were times when I watched your progress in a somewhat esoteric field that I feared I had created a Frankenstein monster.

'You became a cold, deliberate killer – who grew to enjoy assassination. You derived a sort of exhilaration from the act. I doubt if you ever recognized it in yourself, but maybe you did. You looked upon yourself not as a paid assassin, but as a godlike figure dispensing celestial justice.

'Then, in Viet-Nam, something happened to cause you to question your ethics and motivation. I could see doubts and cynicism creeping into your actions. It didn't destroy your effectiveness, but you started to question your fitness as a member of the human race.

'But all that's in the past. Why did I feel you not suited for Chiang Mai?

'One attitude to develop as a natural consequence of your peculiar profession was distrust of human emotions and associations. You epitomized the lone wolf concept. As a team worker, you could lead but never follow. You were resentful of all authority, even the thin leash I imposed on you.'

Joe considered the things Cantrell had just told him. Two years ago, he would have agreed with Cantrell's appraisal of Joe Stanford. They were conclusions he'd reached by himself. Not that he enjoyed killing, perhaps, but there could be an element of truth in that as well. He had sickened of death and killing in Viet-Nam. He had certainly become cynical and started to question the reasons, if any, behind policy. And he had come to think of himself as an outcast from human society, totally devoid of sensibility and incapable of emotions.

That was two years ago. Now, he would question the assessment. On the long eastward sea voyage he had had plenty of time to think. Attributing his emotions to the dead Winters was ridiculous. They had been his emotions, his, Joe Stanford's. And Stanford had known compassion, tenderness and love. He could no longer consider himself a pariah.

He was aware that Cantrell was watching him closely through a haze of cigar smoke. 'All right, Lew,' Joe said, 'Assuming for the sake of argument you had me tagged correctly, what then?'

'You would be assuming the duties of Area Coordinator. It would require a high degree of cooperation both upwards and downwards in the chain of command. I had no qualms about your abilities to command the respect of your subordinates, but serious reservations concerning your loyalties to your superiors. If thwarted, I considered you capable of disastrous unilateral action.

'There was something else I feared, not without justification. In many ways, Harper was similar to yourself. I felt conflict was inevitable.

'So I was against your selection. I was overruled.

'At that point, I strongly advised that you be fully briefed. Again, I was overridden. By the time I took over here, I considered rectifying the earlier error, But by then, Joseph, you'd managed to paint yourself into a corner and it was too late.'

Joe was confused. He had always considered his Manila briefings as, if anything, too elaborate. He had no idea what possible omission there could have been. 'What wasn't I told?'

'Quite a few things. That no great weight or hopes for success were being placed on the Burmese insurgency, for one. Oh, we hoped it might prove nettlesome to our Russian friends, but not enough to provoke violent reaction. You changed that. Toward the end, you began to suspect the operation had low priority, but you'd never been told why. The other small matter was that Jud Winters was far, very far, from being a dead man.'

259

At the look of disbelief that spread across Stanford's face, Cantrell gave a short humourless laugh. 'I'll have to go back a bit on that one. I don't think you believe me.'

'You're losing me, Lew. You're sure as hell losing me. If Winters isn't dead, why this moronic farce?'

'Farce, maybe, but not exactly moronic. It ...' A paroxysm of coughing seized Cantrell. Pulling a handkershief from his breast pocket, he covered his mouth as he fought to gain control. The racking coughs finally subsided. Cantrell tucked the handkerchief back into his pocket, as he wheezed, 'Now where were we?'

'Winters,' Joe snapped.

'Ah yes. Well, every once in a while in this exacting business of ours, we get a break. Winters was one of those happy accidents.

'He was employed by us in a small way in the fifties. By chance we discovered something of interest.

'When he separated from the navy after the Korean War, he lived it up for a while in Japan. Set up housekeeping with a cute little dancer. But it turned out she had another protector on the string. He was a wealthy Hong Kong Chinese industrialist, who came to Tokyo but rarely, but when he did Akiko invented some excuse to leave the Winters *menage* for a day or two. Jud found out about the rival. There was an angry confrontation between the two men.

'As sometimes happens in these cases, the men found they had something in common ... in this instance, Akiko. An unlikely friendship grew out of the initial heated encounter. Our Chinese friend was a mainland Communist with connections in high places.

'It suited our purpose to exploit this friendship. We encouraged Winters to visit Hong Kong to renew the acquaintanceship. It proved rewarding. Just how rewarding, we couldn't have guessed at the time.

'There was a small problem. While the Chinese hadn't minded an association with a young American in Tokyo, it was an entirely different matter in Hong Kong. So, on his first visit to the colony, Winters adopted the identity of a Canadian businessman named John Quentin. Not very imaginative, but we found ourselves stuck with it.

'Quentin's chum was no minor cog, and no fool. He, and

his mainland friends, knew who Quentin was and who he worked for, but they were confident that neither British, Russian, nor any other intelligence body were aware of the imposture. They trusted us to keep it that way. We did. Over the decade which followed, we slowly built a plausible background which gave Quentin an impeccable set of Canadian credentials. It proved to be well worth the effort.

'As trust grew in Quentin, and us, his value as a communications link increased in direct proportion. As Winters, his extended drunks and unscheduled vacations became more and more frequent. Too frequent. It became necessary, for a while, to plant him in Viet-Nam where visa requirements necessitated periodic visits to Hong Kong.

'In the fall of '66, and again in the spring of '67, Quentin attended the Canton Trade Fair. Overtures made in '66 were amplified in '67. It was suggested that a dialogue at the highest levels could be arranged, which could ultimately go a long way towards breaking the deadlock of diplomatic isolation which had existed for almost twenty years. There were a good many details to work out, such as some innocent exchange on a trade, cultural or sports level, to break the ice, and the Chinese were in no great rush, but the suggestion looked both feasible and infinitely appealing.

'We would have liked to introduce a more qualified man. The Chinese wouldn't hear of it. I think they were right. Quentin had been handled with uncharacteristic discretion on our side. Only a mere handful knew of his existence. And, Winters had gained a good deal of maturity and had the complete confidence of the Chinese. So Quentin it was.

'But now we were faced with a dilemma. Quentin would have to be employed full time in Hong Kong, and free to travel to China if and when required. The negotiations were reaching a sensitive stage, and looked as though they would be protracted. That meant disposing of Winters without arousing any suspicions which might eventually lead to the exposure of Quentin. It was by no means as easy as it looked at first glance.

'Winters couldn't simply disappear. His connections with the CIA, no matter how minor, were known. Disappearance would have given rise to unwanted speculation. The next best thing was a substitution. But the man who would take Winters place must not know of the existence of Quentin. Also, to reduce the possibilities of Winters' surrogate being exposed as an imposter, a suitably safe slot would have to be found for the new Winters, far enough from his Philippine haunts to minimize chance encounters with old cronies. By unhappy coincidence, there was an opening for a bright young man in Chiang Mai. And no matter what you were told at your briefings, Joseph, that should have remained a safe and quiet assignment.'

Stanford had followed the account intently and with growing presentiment. Dimly, at first, but with increasing clarity, he perceived a highly undesirable conclusion. 'So a phony Winters was the name of the game ... but why me?'

'Machine record cards were fed into the gizmo. Six likely candidates popped out. Some prior association with Southeast Asian affairs was desirable, since we did have an intelligence network to administer in the region, but the prime consideration was a resemblance, a striking resemblance, to Winters. In that department, you weren't the first choice. One man, in fact, was almost an exact duplicate and would have required little or no cosmetic surgery. But you had a big edge. Major Joseph Stanford had no ties and was in a situation where he could be written-off without question, fuss or bother. In short, Joseph, nobody gave a damn about Major Stanford. And on that basis, you won the contest hands down.

'But I've had a bit more experience in this area than most. I was far from convinced that the region was, or would remain, a quiet backwater. For a number of years, I'd been grooming a candidate to get well into the narcotics traffic which I suspected would become a very large pain in the ass at some future date. I strongly felt that your introduction to the scene could be disastrous for all concerned. So, I opposed your selection. You should have gone to Manila in October. I seconded you to the Song Lon Valley operation. When that was postponed until December, I thought I'd won. The hell I had. Harper was mad. He'd set up a little death scene in September, purely for the benefit of the incoming agent who was to believe he was stepping into a dead man's shoes. Harper was having increasing trouble explaining Winters' disappearance. I couldn't stall

262

any longer. In January, you went, with or without my blessing.

'For about a year, nothing much happened and I thought I must be getting senile. But then you blew it. The trouble is you were just too damned good. To the fouled-up Burmese insurrection, you started to introduce a few professional touches which made it look as though it might have a chance of succeeding. Your handling of the arms shipments, and the abduction and introduction of U Thong were strokes of brilliant direction.

'Harper opposed your suggestions. Rightly so. Incidentally, your reports were never altered by Harper. They went, together with his recommendations, directly to this office. My predecessor should have accepted Harper's recommendations, but he was due for retirement and was more swayed by your arguments. If I'd been sitting in the seat at that time, I'd have applied the brakes. Or tried to.

'You accomplished what we'd most feared. Attention was focused on the operation. By now, I was in the saddle and watching closely for reaction. I can assure you that there was more than a little agitation in certain circles in Moscow, but confusion in pin-pointing the focal point of the operation's direction. In my estimation, sooner or later, the signs would point to you. Disclosure of your true identity was relatively unimportant, but exposing a fake Jud Winters could have been disastrous. Quentin's delicate negotiations were bearing fruit. If even a hint of CIA connections leaked to the Russians, or for that matter, the British, the Chinese would back off. That could not be allowed to happen.'

Cantrell paused to eye Stanford closely. 'Are you reading me, Joseph?' Cantrell questioned softly.

Stanford's face was hard: his eyes slitted. 'You're telling me that I had become a liability . . . and expendable.'

'Exactly.'

'Was the decision to eliminate me taken before or after my cutting off the funding?'

'Before. Your rash action in the fiscal realm would have earned you remedial visitation, but the decision to cut you off at the pass was prompted by something else. From Moscow we learned that a team of specialists were being sent to Chiang Mai. To me, it meant one of two things. A little

263

local housecleaning, or, without your knowledge, your cover was blown. I couldn't afford to take any chances on the latter being the case.'

Cantrell was seized with another fit of coughing. When it subsided, he didn't return his handkerchief to his breast pocket. Instead, he took off his glasses and polished them absently. Replacing the spectacles, he left the hanky in his lap. Sighing heavily, he sank back in his chair.

'Joseph,' he said wearily, 'I'm really sorry you got caught up in this tangled skein. It seems a crying shame that you have made such a long and perilous journey to come here and appeal to me for help. I'm the one person who can help you least.' His voice hardened. It had the quality of a nail rasped against cement. 'I'm the one who ordered your execution . . . *and that order stands.*'

CHAPTER FOURTEEN

During most of Cantrell's discourse, Stanford had held a loose grip on the revolver, allowing it to rest in his lap. But on Cantrell's closing statement, Joe raised the gun to point directly at Cantrell's forehead. The two men remained in this position for some minutes, as though the projector had broken down and they were frozen in a single frame of a motion picture. The ominous silence lengthened.

Cantrell's lips twitched in a semblance of a smile. 'In your place, I believe I'd have pulled the trigger.'

The angle of the gun muzzle remained fixed. 'What makes you so damned sure I won't? You've just given me the best reason a man ever had for killing another.'

'Yes, I suppose I have. But you're a gambler. You hope to minimize the risks, but in the end you'll accept the long odds. You know that when you walk out those doors, all I have to do is pick up the phone and the chase commences. Killing me would gain you valuable time; time you will need desperately. But what's stopping you is the thought that one day Quentin's mission will be completed and you will no longer pose any threat. At that time, I might pull the baying hounds back into their kennels. I might. I just might. But if you zap me, my successor isn't likely to adopt such a charitable attitude. So, if I give you any choice, you'll let me live. Is that how you've been debating the issue?'

'Something along those lines.'

'I won't bargain with you, Joseph. I won't guarantee you a damned thing. But I think you're making a wise choice. A good deal wiser than you imagine.'

Cantrell chuckled. 'From the moment I walked through the door, every word spoken in this room, and every one of our actions, has been taped by multiple recorders and video cameras. Kill me, and rip the room apart if you want. You might find some of the recording devices, but you won't find them all. So my murder would be a matter of record with no doubts concerning its perpetrator.'

Joe knew with chilling certitude that Cantrell was not lying. 'So, kill you or not, there's a photographic record of my present appearance?'

'Yes. But I don't think that worries you too much. After all, if you could travel 15,000 odd miles undetected, you are probably confident you can slip away from here without much difficulty.

'I will say, Joseph, that your exploits as a fugitive have filled me with grudging admiration. I honestly believed Sam Harper would nail you. You've displayed more enterprise than I credited. The only thing which puzzled me was why you should go to the trouble of taking the identity of Quentin for a paltry 3,000 dollars. That mystery was cleared up when I contacted Quentin and learned that he had misplaced a bank book which he thinks might have been left in his trunk in Cebu. Incredibly stupid of him. It seems he had been putting money in that Vancouver account for some time. When he established himself in Hong Kong, he withdrew the bulk of those undisclosed savings to make some investments in the colony. He mentioned a sum of 45,000 dollars. For that amount of loot, your actions made a bit more sense.

'The impersonation did us no great harm. We had to advise the Canadian immigration authorities to drop any investigation into the illegal entry of an American merchant seaman named Quentin. All the use of the name did was to alert me to your impending arrival.'

Cantrell started to slowly tuck his handkerchief into his

265

breast pocket. 'Well, Joseph, mustn't detain you. You'll forgive me if I don't see you to the door. I trust you can find your own way out. So, we'll just have to say our good-byes here. I'd advise you not to dawdle. Might have some difficulty finding a cab at this hour.'

A prickling sensation of warning crawled over Stanford's scalp. He tensed, and eyed Cantrell narrowly. Cantrell's hand was coming out of the breast pocket. Joe detected a metallic glint between the fingers.

'Lew,' Joe snapped, his voice almost a shout, 'don't be a damned fool.'

There was a sardonic smile on Cantrell's lips as he brought his clenched fist across his chest towards Stanford. An object protruded from between the third and fourth fingers. Joe fired.

The splat of the silencer sounded loud to Joe's ears. A neat hole, slightly off-center, appeared between Cantrell's eyes. He jerked backwards in the chair, then slumped downwards, The smile was frozen on his features. A small palm gun thudded onto the carpet.

Stanford rose slowly and stood looking down in wonder at Cantrell. 'Why, Lew, why?' Joe said softly. 'You knew I'd shoot. And you knew damned well I'd shoot to kill.'

He reached down and retrieved the palm gun from the floor. Both the cylinder and the short firing chamber were empty. The weapon had not been loaded.

As he placed the palm gun on the desk, comprehension came to him. Cantrell had known he was coming, and for what purpose. Knowing that his answer would be unsatisfactory to Joe; knowing that he would not lift the sentence of death, Cantrell could have guarded himself and this house against intrusion. He hadn't done so. In fact, it was almost as though he'd invited the intrusion. Yes, Joe thought, that's exactly what he did do. Why? He thought back on Cantrell's words. . . . 'if I give you any choice, you'll let me live.'

Cantrell had given him no choice, none at all. Joe turned and looked at the body with its wasted vacant features. More of Cantrell's conversation came back to him: . . . 'a not uncommon wasting ailment,' Cancer. It had to be the answer.

He looked at the corpse with a mixture of pity and anger.

'You bastard, Lew. You didn't want to put a gun to your temple. You had to play the puppet master to the end and rig your own suicide to look like murder. You knew what this would do to me. And you enjoyed it. You sonuvabitch, you enjoyed every goddammed minute of your deathbed scene.

His gaze swept the room slowly. He didn't doubt for a moment that the events had been recorded on sound tape and film. To search for the recording devices would only be a waste of time. With a sinking feeling, he appreciated just how incriminating that evidence would be. By no later than tomorrow, it would be known that he was now in possession of knowledge of the identity, scene of activity and mission of John Quentin. Early in the conversational exchange, he'd admitted killing Harper. And, as a grand finale, it would look as though he'd murdered kindly old Lewis Cantrell in cold blood. If Stanford had been under sentence of death before this night's performance, the warrant was now doubly and triply sealed.

In the last few hours, it had grown colder. A breeze had sprung up from the direction of the river. A few large flakes of wet snow swirled around him as he poised atop the wall before dropping to the sidewalk.

His hands jammed deep in the pockets of his coat, head down and shoulders sagging, he trudged towards the street light on the corner.

A tangled skein, Lewis Cantrell had termed it. When had it started? Chiang Mai, or years earlier? He had scarcely noticed the nearly-invisible gossamer threads slowly enveloping him. The threads were no longer weightless and filmy. He was enmeshed in a cobweb of steel cables.

In the pool of light beneath the lamp standard, he paused to turn up his coat collar against the chilling wind. He walked slowly towards the fading edges of the street light's glow into the darkness of the cold night.